D1038552

MAR 2 (			
APR 3 01			
APR 30 '01			
MAY 29 2001			
DEC 1 9 2008			
MAY 2 9 2008			

F   G716

Gottschalk, E. P.

Double malfunction.

DOUBLE MALFUNCTION

DOUBLE
MALFUNCTION

E.P. Gottschalk

DAEDALUS PRESS

DAEDALUS PRESS
P.O. Box 375, Chambersburg, PA 17201

ISBN: 0-9628633-0-0
Library of Congress Catalog Card Number: 91-70202

Manufactured in the United States of America.

Dedicated to the spirit of
JOE SMITH
*a spirit that, on a clear day,
can be found soaring above the mountains
of central Pennsylvania.*

Author's Note

This is a work of fiction. The author does not promote any activity discussed in this book that is inconsistent with federal regulations or accepted practice with regard to air safety, including the unauthorized alteration of parachute equipment. All names are used fictitiously, and none of the characters or airplanes are based on any real person or airplane, living or dead, flying or wrecked. Any resemblance to actual names, persons or airplanes is purely coincidental. And with the notable exception of Davis Field in Muskogee, Oklahoma, none of the skydiving drop zones are based on any real drop zone.

During the years 1981-1990, the United States National Skydiving Championships were held annually at Davis Field. Although the championships in this book take place at that airport, they should not be confused with any real event. These Nationals are entirely fictional.

All of the incidents that make up the plot of *Double Malfunction* are solely a product of the author's imagination. The legal climate in which the story takes place, however, is not.

Part One

FINDLAY

1

The midwestern sky began the day wearing brilliant blue; it finished the night cloaked in somber black. But the sun had nothing to do with it.

It was the Saturday of Memorial Day weekend, about six in the evening. I'd been sitting in the saddle of my '83 Honda GoldWing since about ten, gliding first north and then west toward the outskirts of Findlay, Indiana, a small farming community twenty-five miles west of the Indianapolis Speedway. My thigh, back, and arm muscles were all twitching spasmodically, and something close to rigor mortis had settled in the back of my neck. Holding the same position for eight hours straight may be no challenge for the young and resilient, but it's sincere hard labor for those of us past thirty.

I signaled to the car behind me, then turned right onto Airport Road.

Despite my aching body, I was in an upbeat mood. I was coming off a spring season in aviation paradise, and now the weather service was predicting a holiday weekend of mild winds, comfortable temperatures, and no clouds—perfect conditions for skydiving. And as if that weren't enough, I was expecting to spend my weekend in the company of a very select member of the opposite sex. I gripped the handlebars a little tighter. I was almost there.

I spotted the orange windsock about three hundred yards in front of me. Then the hangar and the loft. As I got closer, Airport Road's smooth blacktop turned into dusty gravel—good for twenty miles an hour, not more. I slowed down. When I reached the Findlay Airport

3

parking lot I stopped my bike and scanned the vehicles for a particular red van with Illinois plates.

"That you, Chance?" someone yelled.

My helmet garbled the sound, but I recognized the voice. I turned my head and saw Twig Buckwater, drop zone owner and friend, striding toward me. We hadn't seen each other in almost exactly a year.

I smiled and waved.

Good ole Twig Buckwater. Even from a distance you could sense his imposing presence. He was about six feet tall with strong, blue-collar arms. He had deep-set eyes, prominent cheekbones, and a firm square jawline—all of which combined to give his face a sharp, masculine look.

Twig didn't smile back, but there was nothing unusual about that. He was a serious, no-nonsense man committed to his parachute business. If he wasn't teaching a student how to skydive, repairing a plane, directing his weekend staff, rigging a parachute, maintaining the airport grounds, talking with the FAA, putting together a new rig, settling disputes between his customers, scrounging up good pilots, reading the newest regulation, emptying the trash, fixing the plumbing, repairing student jumpsuits—if he wasn't busy doing all the things necessary to run his drop zone, then he was busy making detailed plans for the next day or weekend or season. Twig was a high-principled man who really believed all good things came to those who put in an honest day's work, and he'd be the first to admit that without work he'd die.

Actually, he hadn't been involved in sport skydiving all that long. He'd spent the first twenty years of his adult life serving God, country, and Army paratroopers. When he retired in the early eighties, he moved back to his hometown of Findlay and sank his entire savings into thirty-five military surplus parachutes and a Cessna 182. Two months later he opened up his skydiving business here at this unused airport. He once told me he'd conceived of the idea for his own drop zone the day he made his first military jump. Then he'd spent the next nineteen years of his life planning his future business while serving out his time.

All those years of preparation and patience seemed to have paid off early on. I first jumped here his second summer of operation, and by then he'd cleared several hundred acres of weeds, stoned in a parking lot, and completed construction on a large parachute loft of his own design. In it were an office, a lounge with video, a student packing area, a rigging room, two bathrooms, an unheard-of *four* showers, and a student training area complete with two airplane mock-ups scaled to the nearest half-centimeter—all built with his own knuckles and guts. To his fleet of one he'd added two more Cessnas. The following year there was a hangar, the next year a Twin Beech and several state-of-the-art student rigs.

Over the din of the Honda he shouted, "How's the forehead?"

I flashed an insider's grin. "How's the wrist?"

It had been our standard greeting for the last seven years, since my first visit here. I don't think either one of us expected a lasting relationship to come out of the brief but intense event that initially threw us together. It seemed rather to be a matter of chance.

A skydiver flying high on PCP had cornered me in one of Twig's new shower stalls with a martial arts weapon of some kind. The skydiver was demanding his car keys, which I had confiscated for the safety of the entire world, and I was refusing on principle. I had quickness but he had size, not to mention a weapon in his clutch and a distorted mind intent on using it. The odds were hardly in my favor.

Fortunately for me, Twig was passing by on his way to the john. Ten minutes later Twig had a broken wrist and my forehead had a deep gash, but we'd won. While the other guy slept off his injuries, Twig made an inquiry into his background. Then in the morning, after I gave the man back his keys, Twig booted him off the drop zone for good. You see, hard-working and high-principled Twig Buckwater had no tolerance at all for people who earned their living dealing illegal drugs.

After a trip to the local hospital following the fight, Twig and I had stopped for coffee at an all-night restaurant and ended up talking till four in the morning. We talked about the fight and about drugs. We talked about Communism and about terrorists. We talked about acid rain, about abortion, about the historical slaughter of people in the name of religion and the continuation of that same sort of slaughter today.

At the time I was a student of law with too much schooling for my own good. Twig was not well read, and his old-fashioned work ethic molded most of his thoughts. But I was humbled to realize that a former career military man, so adept at taking orders, could discuss these issues quite intelligently, thank you. I was grateful to Twig for

5

the insight, and since then had made it a point of biking up here each year for his Memorial Day boogie, no matter how far my journey. Twig, for his part, seemed never to forget what I'd done about those keys.

He was standing beside the Honda. Up close, he looked much older than he had last year.

I turned off the bike and we shook hands. "Expected you the middle of the week," he said. "Was beginning to wonder if you were even gonna show this year."

"Twig, I wouldn't miss your boogie if they were forecasting a hurricane." I unbuckled my helmet and massaged my stiff neck. "But I was finishing a job. Couldn't get away till the last minute."

"Doing anything interesting?"

I grinned wide at the memory. "There's an eccentric barnstormer in South Carolina. I spent the last two and a half months building him a hangar for his collection of biplanes. And I got to fly them as part of my paycheck."

Twig's eyes lightened, and he almost smiled.

I pointed upward. "Looks like the weather intends to cooperate this weekend."

He squinted up at the sky and nodded. "Been dry and crystal clear like this all spring. Good for us, but the farmers are worrying. They don't get rain soon, their crop'll be lost."

I'd already guessed as much. Throughout Indiana the fields were all still brown and barren, unusual for the last week of May. I gazed out beyond the airport boundary at the fields of dry dirt. Neither Twig nor I wished the farmers any bad luck, but we both hoped any rain would hold off till Tuesday.

In front of the fields stretched Findlay Airport's thirty-five-hundred-foot grass runway. In front of the runway and out from the hangar Twig's white Beech sat closed up with its wheels chocked. Next to it an unfamiliar silver Beech E-18 glistened in the early evening sun. Twelve skydivers stood by, waiting to cram into its fuselage.

"Contracting it for the boogie?" I asked.

Twig followed my gaze and shook his head. "Bought it a few months ago. I could have gone for something newer, but I always wanted to own an E-18."

I nodded approvingly. Actually, I'd been wondering if he'd bought the plane, but hadn't had the nerve to ask him straight out. Although

Twig had never discussed his financial situation with me, it was common knowledge that he'd been strapped for money the last few years.

Not that business over the years had been bad for Twig; business in fact had been quite good. He'd pulled together and trained a responsible weekend staff, had excellent physical facilities and safe gear, had never had a fatality or a major injury, and—despite his stubborn refusal to advertise—had a customer base that continued to expand each summer.

If that's all there were to running a sport drop zone, Twig Buckwater would have had it made. Unfortunately, in all his planning while in the military, Twig did not foresee and therefore did not take into account the draining effects of a single factor outside his control. One which subsequently intruded into his life and dined gluttonously on his earnings.

That factor was tort law. The American legal philosophy with regard to torts had undergone a radical change between the planning and implementation of Twig's retirement dream. As a result, the concept of personal responsibility had been turned inside out. By the mid-eighties the skydiving industry became a frequent—though by no means lonely—victim of this. Lawsuits by students injured while skydiving began to bleed drop zone operators and parachute manufacturers of substantial financial resources. Twig had to fight a number of them, but one in particular, pressed by a man with no case but plenty of power and wealth, was especially rough.

The man's twenty-year-old son, after signing a liability waiver and successfully completing Twig's first-jump course, had turned his parachute right on landing when he'd been instructed to turn it left. A broken ankle was the result. The father, peeved that his son had disobeyed his command not to skydive, sicced his company attorneys on Twig and tried to have him shut down. Twig had to pay God knows how many thousands of dollars defending himself from all their legal maneuvering.

In January, while I was wintering in Florida, it had trickled down through the skydiving grapevine that Twig had finally won. If you could call it that.

From my seat on the Honda I admired his new airplane. It's not an expensive turboprop, I thought, but if Twig can afford another Beech, he must be rebounding from all that oppressive litigation.

"How's business so far today?" I asked more boldly.

7

"Can't complain," he said in a neutral tone of voice. "I'm over-hauling an engine on my old Beech, so that leaves the drop zone with just the new E-18 and the Cessnas. At the last minute I wrestled Satin Cruise away from the Sullivan drop zone for the weekend. It just took off on its fourth."

I couldn't help grinning. Satin Cruise, based in Fort Crystal, Flori-da, each winter, itinerant during the warm-weather months, was the quickest and best-maintained DC-3 jump plane in the country. Taking a ride to altitude in that airplane with owner/pilot/mechan-ic Dominic Salvino in the cockpit sparked in me visions of golden chariots gliding effortlessly over the Elysian Fields. It had just the right balance and tuning, he had just the right touch. Of all the air-craft that serviced the sport of skydiving, bar none, Satin Cruise was my favorite. A fact Twig knew well.

"Thought you'd like to hear that," he said. "Want me to put you down for the next load? It'll be the last of the day, and I'm still a man short for a six-way."

"Just tell me where to sign in."

Twig pointed to a booth in the packing area in front of the loft, then strolled over there himself to put my name down on the manifest.

The booth, which Twig said was for registration, manifesting, and gear inspection, was new and looked hastily built. It was approxi-mately eight feet wide, eight feet high, and four feet deep; but only the bottom half had been enclosed. The top half consisted of six ver-tical two-by-fours connected at the top by six horizontal two-by-fours, two of which had been nailed on slightly crooked. A rough con-struction, I thought, for Twig Buckwater.

I shrugged to myself and restarted the Honda. The parking lot was overflowing with cars and a disproportionate number of vans— maybe a hundred fifty jumpers in all. I found the red van with Illi-nois plates I'd been looking for earlier. I squeezed the Honda in be-tween it and a turquoise TransAm that must have been airlifted to the drop zone from a Pontiac showroom—immaculate, with not a speck of road dust. I made sure not to touch it.

I slipped off my bike and accidentally brushed my shoulder against the red van. A sensation of giddiness came over me. I couldn't help it. An entire weekend skydiving with a certain lady *and* a certain airplane . . .

I shuddered, pulled off my helmet, and unlatched the trunk of the

Honda. I scooped out my rig, stashed my helmet inside, and got down to some important business.

Gear inspection is a safety requirement at any skydiving boogie, and I knew that in its current state my rig would not pass. Its reserve parachute was several weeks out-of-date. To remedy that situation I decided to do something naughty.

The FAA says only certified riggers are allowed to pack reserve parachutes. So far so good. But the FAA also says it is illegal to jump a rig unless its reserve has been opened, aired, inspected, and repacked within the last hundred and twenty days, with the pertinent facts about who did what where all meticulously recorded on the reserve's packing card.

This regulation is necessary to provide for a measure of control. But a reserve doesn't turn into a pumpkin on the one-hundred-twenty-first day, and a rigger can ethically tinker with the rules so long as the gear is his own.

After spying around the parking lot for any busybodies, I turned up the top flap to my rig's reserve container and slid the folded three-by-six-inch packing card from its pouch. I opened the card, dug up a pen, and quickly pencil packed my reserve. Below the last entry I wrote in yesterday's date, my rigger's license number, and a fictitious location. Then I signed my name. I folded the card and slid it back into its pouch.

My rig was now ready for inspection, simple as that. Out-of-date reserves cost most jumpers thirty dollars a repack. But for the few of us with a rigger's license, all it costs is the price of a ballpoint pen.

I'd been a rigger for seven years, the last four a master rigger. But not even master riggers can certify their own gear at a boogie, so I hurried over to Twig's manifest booth. Ten minutes later Ken Popadowski, a member of Twig's staff, had inspected my rig and declared it safe and in-date.

I'd known Ken casually for several years. Like most of Twig's help, he was a white-collar professional during the week, a skydiver on weekends. We exchanged how-ya-doings, and he handed me a boogie registration form and a liability waiver to fill out. When I was done he took my paperwork and my ten-dollar registration fee. "Twig's waiting on you," he said, pointing in the direction of the hangar. I thanked him, grabbed my rig, and hustled over.

Twig was standing in front of his white Beech with two other jumpers. "This is Chance, the guy taking the last slot," he said to them. "Chance, this is Macintosh." He pointed. "And Danny Death Grimes, who you may already know. Eleanor's on the dive too. She just went to the ladies' room."

He paused, scanned the packing area, then motioned toward a middle-aged man busy packing his rig. "That's Cheeks," he said. "With me and you, that gives us six."

Eleanor I knew, of course. Danny Death I recognized from previous boogies here, but couldn't recall ever jumping with him. Macintosh and Cheeks were from California, Twig said. "Came here for tomorrow's Indy Five-hundred out at the Speedway."

What an odd pair, I thought. Macintosh was in his early twenties and prep school clean. His eyes were covered with vivid blue contact lenses and his hair, parted just to the side of a small cowlick, looked sprayed in place. He was wearing a multi-colored polo shirt and a pair of neon blue athletic shorts. On his feet were expensive running shoes that had never been used for running. When Twig had introduced us, Macintosh had given me an uncertain smile, like maybe he was a newcomer to the sport.

Cheeks, on the other hand, was at least forty and had been around awhile. He moved with smooth confidence as he packed his rig, manipulating its black-and-white canopy and solid black container with the deftness of experience. A secure man, I thought. Not like his companion.

I looked over at young Macintosh and wondered about his name. "Computer programmer," I guessed out loud.

Macintosh positively beamed with recognition. "Actually," he said, "I sell them. My family calls me Jim." He smiled broadly. He was enjoying the unexpected attention.

"As for Cheeks"—he said the name with an abundance of awe—"I don't know his real name. He was Cheeks already when I started jumping two years ago. They call him that from the loose skin on his face that flaps around in freefall."

Macintosh and Cheeks weren't the only ones in our group with nicknames. Twig got his in the military ages ago. On a routine training dive his main malfunctioned, and because the military jumps out so low a reserve was useless. He was all ready to bite the dust when a single healthy branch of a dying American elm snagged his streamering parachute fifty feet above the ground. He'd been known as Twig Buckwater ever since.

10

And Danny Death? I didn't know the history behind that one, but I didn't need to. Any jumper given a name like that could be figured out with little imagination: It was a title of foreboding.

My ears picked up a hum in the eastern sky. I cocked my head upward and listened closely. It was a DC-3. Satin Cruise. Then I saw the piercing reflection of sunlight off its fuselage.

Over at the manifest booth Ken Popadowski yelled, "Jump run!" and almost everyone in sight looked up. At most boogies that have reached this size, skydivers on the ground rarely take an active interest in the jumps of others. Maybe it was because this was the North and the season was still young that today, here at Findlay Airport, a skydive was still an event.

Satin Cruise came by on a low jump run at approximately six thousand feet. The pilot, Dominic Salvino, throttled back the engines. A few seconds later a ten-way speed star team popped out.

"They came down from Wisconsin," Twig said. "Practicing for Nationals."

On this practice jump there was a miscue on exit—the whole dive for a speed star. Two jumpers ended up way out. They could have been salmon trying to make it upstream for all the effort it took them to arrive, and the time for their star was a poor eighteen seconds. Three minutes from now, after landing, the jumpers might disperse and pack in total silence. Alternatively, they might punch each other upside the head.

With my eyes I followed them in freefall. They released grips at the normal break-off altitude of thirty-five hundred feet, tracked away from each other in a star burst, and pulled at about twenty-five hundred feet. All canopies opened uneventfully.

Dominic Salvino had already given power to Satin Cruise. He'd continue climbing to twelve thousand feet, where he'd drop the remaining twenty-five or so jumpers still huddled inside his plane.

The Californian named Cheeks finished packing his rig. He stood up, pocketed a box of expensive foreign cigarettes, then joined the rest of us.

Now all we needed was Eleanor and we'd be ready to dirt dive our jump. And I'd be all set for the weekend. In fact, at the moment I had such high expectations for the next few days that not even Danny Death Grimes could dampen my spirits.

"Lookit all the fuckin' whuffos out there geekin' us," he griped. "They got nothin' better to do than sit there on their fuckin' cars geekin'. Probably waitin' for a freakin' broken leg or some such shit to make their day."

I turned to where he was looking and saw several cars pulled off along the shoulder of Airport Road. A group of teenagers, two whole families, one pair of binoculars, four cameras, and a lot of pointing.

"Parents wouldn't bring their kids along if they expected that," I said good-naturedly. "Before you started jumping, skydivers must have fascinated you, too. Otherwise, you wouldn't be here."

Danny Death scrunched up his nose. "Well, ya know what I mean," he persisted. "Their own lives are so fuckin' booooorin', but they're too damn scared to do anythin' about it. Yellow, they are. So they geek anybody who's got the guts to do a little livin'."

His slovenly speech made me think of my high school English teacher, Miss Bidwell, a dictatorial schoolmistress right out of the nineteenth century. I could just hear her now: "That's *fucking*, Mr. Grimes, not *fuckin'*."

The very idea of Miss Bidwell and that particular word on the same continent amused me and I smiled. Danny Death thought I was making fun of him. He mumbled something inaudible and huffed over toward the parking lot. He seemed to have a chip on his shoulder that even Atlas couldn't shrug. I wondered if that was simply his mood for the day, or if it reflected a permanent state of mind.

"Been like that as long as I've known him," Twig said, reading my thoughts. "Since he moved to Indianapolis a couple years back."

"All the time?"

"Mostly. He's an artist. Guess they're allowed." There was a hint of sarcasm in Twig's voice.

"How did he come by that name of his?"

"Oh, not any one thing. Just the way he lives—always on the edge. At a party once, he downed a fifth, then strutted around the parapet of a six-story building with a twenty-five-knot wind pushing at his sides and nothing but concrete below. That kind of thing. He's usually high, spaced out on something. Been told he's taken a jump or two down to eight hundred feet before pulling." And as an afterthought, "Not at my drop zone, of course."

Not that you know about, I thought.

He shook his head. "Danny sure is a hell of a skydiver, though. As relaxed in the air as he is uptight on the ground. He's got your awareness and flying ability, but his drawback is, he's not consistent. Has a tendency to brain lock. More than most." He paused, then sighed. "Probably the drugs."

I knew that issue was a source of considerable irritation for Twig. While he could throw a drug dealer off his drop zone and get away with it, banning drug users would be financial suicide for him. His customers, users or not, would rebel and take their business someplace else.

The prevailing opinion among skydivers is that people have a right to ruin themselves if they choose; and anyone who tried to challenge that notion would be compared unfavorably with the Gestapo. So Twig was forced to compromise his values in the face of reality—something I didn't think he'd ever really get used to.

Not that Twig was a rigid conformist. He had his own set of rules, and they didn't necessarily follow those of the FAA. He'd had no second thoughts, for instance, when approached at last year's boogie by a herd of horny jumpers clamoring to punch through a cloud cover at nine thousand feet, contrary to federal regulations. That no-jumping-through-clouds rule was designed to keep skydivers from jumping blindly into dangerous places like cities and lakes, Twig had rationalized. And there aren't any of those within twenty miles of Findlay. Unless you count the Eel River. But anybody stupid enough to land in that little creek deserves to drown.

"How does an artist with a drug habit pay for his jumps?" I wondered out loud.

"Lives in downtown Indianapolis in his studio," Twig said. "Or with some girl off and on. Does odd jobs around." There was a note of disapproval in his voice that he quickly tried to mask. "Nothing wrong with a man doing odd jobs, you understand . . ."

He looked over, concerned that he'd offended me. I smiled back to assure him he hadn't. He nodded uneasily, then turned his attention to four jumpers dirt diving in front of us.

Danny Death was now in intense conversation with a young woman near the parking lot. I studied him, trying to imagine what type of artwork he might produce. Nothing representational, I decided. Abstract or surreal would be more his style. And nothing too commercial. His scraggly, unkempt appearance suggested a creature interested in scraping together only the minimum necessary for food, art supplies, and a weekly fix of drugs and skydives.

He was probably in his mid-thirties, though his face made him look older than that. The lines fanning out from the corners of his eyes were as thick as the lines that no doubt passed through his nose, and betrayed years of mind- and body-altering experiences. He was small, maybe five feet six and a hundred thirty pounds, and had sandy-blonde hair that hung straight to his shoulders. His clothes were typical for a drop zone—jeans and a T-shirt—only his were tattered.

In the seventies, Danny Death would have been right at home on most drop zones in the country. But the typical drug-using skydiver had long since changed in appearance. The long-haired hippies who could be seen thumbing to airports as recently as a decade ago had given way to yuppies driving expensive sports cars and vans, and donning designer gear. No different from the rest of America. Today, people like Danny Death are fossils, things to examine and discuss with academic interest, but not emulate.

Satin Cruise approached the airport on another jump run. I forgot about Danny Death and looked up. At a spot directly above the runway Dominic Salvino throttled back. Six seconds later a blob emerged from the plane with quite a few specks trailing behind. Someone said it was a sixteen-way, first formation a quadri-diamond.

All but three of the specks merged with the base. Two got close, but the other was way out. He must be a cameraman, I thought.

The jumpers with grips broke apart and began to re-configure themselves. A speck shot out from the group and flew toward the cameraman—geeking the lens, no doubt, for mom. As they got closer, I could see the cameraman wobbling. At thirty-five hundred feet the group split up, tracked, and pulled. One parachute had a slight snivel, but inflated at about eighteen hundred feet. The cameraman was taking it a bit low.

Another, smaller, group of canopies mushroomed farther west—maybe eight or nine. They would have exited immediately after the sixteen-way, but I hadn't followed their dive.

My attention was brought back to the cameraman. He grew larger with each passing second. I became edgy as he approached a thousand feet.

"Come on, man, pull!" someone hollered.

Anyone not watching now stared up.

"Pull something! Just pull, you idiot, pull!" Twig pleaded, a clot of sudden desperation apparent in his voice.

14

But he and I and the rest of the experienced skydivers knew from the way the cameraman was falling that it wasn't going to happen. His arms were out in front. He wasn't struggling with a main pilot chute or a reserve ripcord, wasn't even attempting to pull. He was unconscious.

A moan went through the crowd as he fell below five hundred feet. No hope for survival now. Even a reserve chute takes several seconds to deploy, and he didn't have several seconds.

I turned my head away and closed my eyes.

"Shit!" muttered Twig as the body bounced.

2

There is nothing more natural than death. Except maybe birth. And sex, of course, without which there would be no birth.

At one time natural meant in accordance with or determined by nature. But that was before advertisers and marketing executives latched onto it as a buzzword to sell their products. Now, not only do we have natural cereal—the first naturally natural product—but we also have natural vitamins, natural shampoo, even natural prophylactics. In the mass media lexicon, natural has become a synonym for healthy, hearty, and wholesome.

But there's nothing healthy or hearty or wholesome about watching someone die. Most jumpers go a lifetime without seeing anyone bounce. I hadn't been that lucky; I'd seen it twice before. I didn't literally watch the second one go in. The first was more than enough.

It happened in Florida, the spring of '84. The cloud base was nine grand, the winds were twelve knots, the temperature was hot. He was a novice with sixty-two jumps. Early twenties, masculine, always accompanied by a bosomy lady friend. On jump sixty-three he was trying to impress a new one—platinum blonde, bikini bound—with a low pull at a thousand feet. He misjudged his distance and bounced. The lady was not impressed.

I watched that novice all the way to the ground that day. Then I calmly stepped over to a nearby weed field and threw up.

The second time around I didn't get physically sick, and today's was my third. All the same, I could feel my stomach begin to knot and my fingertips go numb. When I cut over to the parking lot, my knees wobbled.

I have no idea how I would have reacted had I suspected that this fatality was no accident.

I leaned against Eleanor's van for support and counted seconds— one thousand one, one thousand two, one thousand three—until my knees stabilized. One thousand fourteen in all.

I stashed my rig back in the Honda's trunk. At very large boogies, airplanes continue to fly after a fatality. But at smaller boogies like this one, jumping stops while the authorities are notified. Because it was already early evening, I knew Twig would close up shop for the night. My appetite for skydiving had been thoroughly squelched anyway.

I gazed out at the whuffos parked along Airport Road. The open-mouthed grown-ups were motioning upward to their wide-eyed kids at the jumpers hanging in midair under a rainbow of colors. They stared through binoculars, snapped pictures, and waited anxiously for their heroes to alight. It was obvious they had missed the one that had already landed.

Twig asked for a volunteer to go out and investigate. Revolting or not, it was necessary to be certain that the man or woman was, in fact, dead. In this case, a formality only. There had been no partially deployed parachute to create drag or snatch a branch à la Twig. So there was no chance of survival for a human body that had impacted the earth at a hundred twenty miles an hour. Macabre. Something only the most sadistic among us would have wanted to inspect.

After a momentary impasse, during which no one so much as blinked, two jumpers reluctantly agreed to go out there together. They crossed the runway toward the field whose brown barrenness now spoke openly of death.

Twig was over at the manifest booth looking at the manifest. He glanced up into the sky, then down at the manifest. He consulted with staffer Ken Popadowski. He pointed up to a jumper, then studied the manifest. He picked up a pen. Methodically he checked off the skydivers under canopy who could be identified by the color patterns of their gear.

An invisible cloud of nervousness hung over the airport as jumpers waited to learn the name, quietly hoping it wouldn't be one they'd recognize.

One by one the fifteen remaining jumpers from that group and the eight or nine from the group that had trailed them out approached the packing area. They faced into the sinking sun to harness energy from the western breeze. It would help burn off some of the forward speed built into their canopies. Like sea gulls alighting on sandy beaches, most met the earth gently, or with a modicum of force. But some with a history of not getting it right—the grass-stained evidence on their jumpsuits—duly crashed and burned.

The young Californian named Macintosh padded through the parking lot toward a black Ford van sitting catty-cornered from my bike. The van had two bright bands—one aqua blue, the other hot yellow—winding around the chassis. Five would get you ten those identical colors could be found in his main canopy. Maybe even in his reserve.

He slid open the side door. Inside, he lifted the lid to a blue cooler wedged behind the driver's seat. He removed two bottles of Yukon Cream Ale, flipped off their tops, walked over, and offered me one. I nodded my thanks and took it.

He was biting down on his lower lip. In a quavering voice he said, "I overheard the drop zone owner, Twig Buckwater, say he's accounted for all the jumpers on that load except one guy. Name's Lonny Carmichael. Know him?"

I swallowed some ale. A small lump the consistency of marble formed in my throat.

"I think I made a couple with him at the Z-Hills Turkey Meet last Thanksgiving," I replied. "But we didn't really jump together. If I'm remembering the right man, Carmichael liked big, static formations, no less than twelve jumpers. I prefer small groups and sequential."

Macintosh inhaled nearly half his beer, then gouged his lower lip again with his teeth.

"It was my impression," I added, "that Carmichael came from this general area—the Midwest, that is—though I can't say for certain."

My throat began to relax and I swallowed my beer more regularly as I realized the man was less familiar than the name. No less important, just less familiar.

Signs of stress were beginning to manifest themselves at the corners of Macintosh's eyes, but he insisted on talking detail. "The guy sure didn't seem to be moving, not to me he didn't. As if he was out cold . . . or something." A question, really.

19

I nodded. "Could have been a medical problem. Epilepsy perhaps. A brain aneurysm. But it was probably a bump on the head during exit. He never even made it to the first formation."

Macintosh said, "I guess the coroner will tell us for sure."

I stared over at him. "How long did you say you've been in the sport?"

"Nearly two years," he said with misplaced confidence.

"And I take it you've never seen a bounced body before."

"No," he admitted, his confidence evaporating.

"Well, Macintosh, let me explain. The first thing and the last thing you need to know is that nothing much useful is left for the coroner to work with. Oh, the contents are there all right, but in a bizarre jumble. A blob of flesh and bones, pieces in the wrong place, everything mashed up. The coroner might be able to figure it out, but the chances are better that he won't. It's often impossible to say this bruise happened on exit and that one on impact. Sometimes they never know for sure."

Macintosh was looking pallid now and slightly faint, sorry to have asked. And I was sorry to have answered so crudely.

A police car with its red light flashing hustled along Airport Road too fast for conditions. It kicked up dry dust, and the whuffos had to shield their faces.

The car screeched to a halt near the hangar. I stared at it. It was ivory white and had an inch-thick red racing stripe painted along its side. An official symbol emblazoned the door. The left front tire looked like it could use some air, and if I stared at it long enough I could probably identify the brand.

Concentrating on insignificant details, I once discovered, helps the mind divert itself from the ugliness of an unforeseen, unwelcome event.

Two uniformed men climbed out of the police car. I turned to Macintosh.

He was swaying next to me. He gave me a weak half-nod, steadied his unfinished ale on the front fender of the turquoise TransAm, and rushed off toward a patch of weeds south of the parking lot. He didn't quite make it.

I tossed both bottles of ale into a garbage can beside the manifest booth and looked through the packing area for Eleanor. She still hadn't come out of the loft.

We've got the whole weekend, I told myself. I'll see her later tonight.

I went back to the parking lot, slipped on my helmet, mounted the bike, and drove out past the whuffos. They were squinting at the policemen, and a few were getting suspicious.

In town, I headed for a place to eat and drink. I wasn't particularly hungry, but I couldn't think of anything else to do while the authorities out at the airport took care of business. At least I'd be occupied.

Findlay was just large enough to require three full-fledged traffic lights and another one that blinked only amber. Downtown proper included a hardware store, a small supermarket, a mom and pop grocery, a police station, a post office, a bowling alley, two restaurants, a half-dozen boutiques, three gas stations, four bars, and forty-two parking meters—I had counted them once.

Except for the fresh coat of brown paint on the door jambs and window molding, Jake's was as I'd left it a year ago. The main door swung out instead of in, and would be an illegal pedestrian hazard in most large cities. But this was just a small-town good-ole-boy bar and grill. The majority of the jumpers wouldn't come here. They'd head down the road to Greenville, a town three times the size of Findlay with at least that many more bars.

It was too early yet for the evening crowd and the place was all but deserted. I sat at a rear corner table veiled in red-and-white Wal-Mart checks. When the waitress came I ordered a corned-beef sandwich on rye and asked what kind of imported beer they had. She said only Beck's and Heineken. I said I'd like a Heineken.

Two hours later Jake's was crowded with townspeople gossiping about the death out at the airport. I listened because even if I tried not to listen I could still hear what was being said.

In the most popular version, a parachutist pulled his ripcord but the parachute stuck, so he frantically yanked at his backup ripcord but that jammed too, so he fell, flailing and screaming, all the way to the ground, and Mary Biggs and her two kids seen it all, and that's a fact.

I clenched my teeth and fought to keep my blood pressure down. Any other day stories invented by whuffos about skydiving might have amused me, but coming after a fatality they sounded callous, even malicious. I wondered which of those whuffos out on Airport Road had been Mary Biggs, or if Mary Biggs had even been out on Airport Road today.

I knew what these people didn't—that it takes a trained eye to follow freefall action. When a man exits at twelve thousand feet he is little more than a speck of dust to those on the ground, even through binoculars. Unless you carefully spot the plane and know precisely when exit will occur, you're going to miss him. And once he's out the door and in freefall, he blends with the birds and atmospheric spots in the great expanse of sky. If you haven't been following him from the start, you'll never find him. Even if you have, you may lose him. And it helps to know about wind direction and velocity, since a body seldom falls straight down.

I burped up some tension, plunked my chin into the palms of my hands, and rubbed my eyes. I was all set to get up and leave when someone tapped my left shoulder.

"Been a while, Chance."

I pulled my hands away from my face. Standing next to my table was Newt Becker, unofficial photographer and part-time mechanic with the Satin Cruise DC-3.

The average sport skydiver is male, early to mid-thirties, medium-small. In that respect, I was just a stereotype. So was Newt Becker.

But physical statistics on paper don't tell all. Newt had a body that was unique and readily recognizable. There was a gangly feel about him. He had long double-jointed limbs, a thin neck, and a mild stoop like you find on a self-conscious kid who shoots up too tall too early, except that Newt had long ago stopped growing. His feet were long and narrow, and he had a unique bounce to his gait that triggered a subtle bobbling movement in his shoulders. His build and his movements always reminded me of a shadow box puppet named Jeepers whom I'd watched breathlessly at the county fair many summers during my youth.

"More than two months," I replied, and pointed to an empty chair. "Unfortunate circumstances."

"That's for sure." He was holding a bottle of Beck's, which he set down on the table. He twirled the chair so that it faced the wrong direction, straddled its seat, and leaned both his elbows on its back.

Newt lived outside Fort Crystal, Florida, his home drop zone. Only a few professional photographers could earn a comfortable living through skydiving, and Newt didn't quite make the grade. I'd never heard anyone criticize the quality of his pictures, but the general consensus seemed to be that he was no businessman. He was outgoing and likable enough, but if you wanted your pictures on time, you went to someone else.

We'd first met three years ago at a Florida boogie. A seam on his container needed emergency stitching, and I was the one rigger available. Though I'd gotten the job by default, Newt liked my work enough to make me his exclusive rigger.

Since then I'd packed his reserve every four months, repaired his main, and modified his rig to accommodate the special needs of a freefall photographer. He appreciated my work, I appreciated his business.

"You know," I said, "at first I thought it might have been you that bounced. He was outside the formation the whole dive, and I took him for a cameraman."

Newt threw his head back as though he'd just heard the most ridiculous joke in his life. "Not *me!*" he said in a cocksure tone of voice. "*I'll* never die jumping."

He drank some of his Beck's. When he spoke again, he was more matter-of-fact.

"Actually, I *was* in the air at the time, but I was taping Octagon, the eight-way that followed the sixteen-way out. Didn't see the guy bounce, though. Didn't even know someone went in till I got to the ground."

That was understandable enough. If Newt had been close to the unconscious jumper, he *might* have realized something was wrong. But he'd been in the second group, hundreds of yards away. And he'd had his video equipment, an additional burden most jumpers never have to deal with. So it would have been odd if he had seen what happened.

"The name I got was Lonny Carmichael," I said. "Has that been confirmed?"

"Yeah, that's him," Newt replied with an air of finality.

I shook my head. "Do they know what happened?"

"He hit his head on exit, that's what Alex Laird says, the guy that followed him out." Then he added, "Carmichael had *over* two thousand jumps."

For some reason that irritated me. "Come on, Newt. You know the number of jumps in a guy's logbook doesn't necessarily mean anything."

"True," he said, retreating.

I tapped my empty Heineken bottle against the table. "Sorry," I said. "I've been listening to some absurd whuffo stories the last half-hour. Didn't mean to take it out on you."

"Already forgotten."

I put the bottle down on the table and leaned on my elbows. "So if this Alan Laird saw Carmichael hit, why didn't he stay with him and try to pull his reserve?"

"*Alex* Laird," he corrected. "Says he didn't *see* it really, and didn't think there was anything to it, not at first. Says he heard a bump on exit, but assumed it was Carmichael's arm hitting the door frame. Says he got suspicious when Carmichael didn't show at the formation, and that's when he scanned the sky and saw him unconscious, but couldn't get to him in time."

"Yeah," I said, "I saw that part."

"You did?"

I nodded. "Only at the time I thought it was a jumper geeking the camera for a close up. Like I said, I thought the guy was a camera-man—maybe you."

Newt raised his eyebrows and became unusually pensive. Perhaps it bothers him that I imagined him as the dead man, I thought.

At a table off to my left three jumpers had been drinking steadily for more than an hour. Now two of them began to sob. Friends, I guessed. They'd spend the night telling each other jump stories about Carmichael. Some exaggerated, all made more spectacular with the passing of time. And Carmichael.

I was already depressed. I didn't need more negative emotion heaped on top. I paid my bill, said good night to Newt, and left.

One and a half beers in three hours was safe enough for me. And legal, if anyone bothered to check. I got on my bike and went seventy-five yards to the mom and pop grocery. I made it inside minutes before the cashier flipped the sign in the window from YES, WE'RE OPEN to SORRY, WE'RE CLOSED.

I stocked up on bananas, apples, and surprisingly fresh whole-wheat pita bread. The Americanization of gyros the last few years is making pita available in all but the most remote outback of Appalachia. Freshly baked bagels are beginning to catch on, too. I looked forward to the day when they'd be so commonplace I'd have no need to cross a city limit ever again.

It was dark by the time I got back to the airport. There were six cars filled with curious townspeople parked near the entrance. I swerved around them and pulled into the parking lot. Only a few jumpers had stuck around. Most, including Eleanor, had driven off in search of food, drink, and—especially—escape.

Twig had an old pickup that he used for hauling and a car that he used for everything else. Both, I noticed, were still parked behind the hangar.

In front of the hangar his white Beech sat like a sentry on never-ending duty. Beyond it I could see one wing of the silver Beech E-18. I walked around behind the white Beech. Twig was leaning over and chocking the wheels on the E-18.

That's when it hit me. How could I have been so selfish?

I'd spent the evening at Jake's brooding over my bad luck that a near stranger had died in my presence. But here was Twig, a man very intimately affected by the fatality. It had occurred at *his* drop zone out of a plane which *he* had contracted on a jump that *he* had profited from.

There is a myth that drop zone operators become hardened to death, like seasoned soldiers after years and years of bloody battle. I doubted it was true for soldiers, I knew it wasn't for drop zone operators. In all my years of jumping I'd only come across two of that ilk. The rest might erect a concrete facade to shield their vulnerabilities from the world outside, but if you take a sledge hammer to that facade you discover behind it real human beings with their innards all ripped up.

"Anything I can do to help?" I offered.

He didn't even turn around. "No," he mumbled. "Have to secure the door yet. Then I'll be done."

"Twig—"

"I can finish up myself, Chance."

And that was as far as he'd let me take it. He knew what I was trying to do, and I knew enough about him to realize he wanted no part of it. He had twenty years of military training in the art of masking pain. He was going to suffer his own licks and reject any sympathy, even from a friend. I respected his right. I withdrew to the parking lot.

I rode the Honda about forty yards beyond the southwest corner of the loft. The more sociable skydivers had grouped their tents and vans along the margins of the parking lot, but I preferred this spot. It was remote and private and always available.

I parked next to the trunk of a forty-foot American elm. Twig had had the tree transplanted here in memory of the one that had saved his life and given him his name. If the original elm had not already died, he'd have done whatever he could to nurse that one back to health. Twig, who followed the do-unto-others philosophy, considered this memorial an appropriate way to repay his debt.

I hung my helmet on the Honda's mirror. In addition to my trunk, I had two large saddlebags strapped to either side of the bike and a tank bag in front. The four of them were strained to capacity with essential gear for skydiving and subsistence living. With the exception of the sleeping bag and extra helmet strapped to my passenger's seat, they contained everything I owned.

I took my ground cloth, tent, and air mattress out of my right saddlebag and chose a flat area devoid of pebbles, roots, or clumps of unreasonably hard earth. I spread out the ground cloth. Then I stretched my tent, made of faded green ripstop, over the ground cloth and plunged eight stakes diagonally into the dirt to secure the eight tent lines. The ends I propped up with two four-foot poles.

I had it set up in less than ten minutes.

The tent was an older model and heavily worn. The seams had begun to fray visibly along the bottom edge, and whenever it rained hard I woke up wet. I'd restitched them several times and globbed on tent sealer, but the fabric no longer held well. The whole tent needed replacing, but a tent was a major expense. I hoped this one would last till winter.

It had been my home for five years, since I'd said no thanks to an offer of steady employment in a high-profile law firm just off Wall Street and a long way from home. I'd grown up in New Hope, Ohio, a village an hour south of Columbus where high school Homecoming and the Senior Prom are the main events in people's lives. Graduation day there is the beginning of the end, after which come a factory or farm job, engagement, marriage, and baby-making—not always in that order. And after that, divorce and remarriage for some; divorce, remarriage, and divorce for others.

I hadn't been able to find a lot of hope in a life like that, and had decided early on that my future would be different, and someplace else. I was an idealist back in those years, determined to make the world a better place for humanity, conquer injustice, end inequality, and all that. And get out of New Hope while I was at it.

My parents had been too consumed with their own problems to raise me, so I'd done the bulk of that myself. Not easy, but I'd survived, working sometimes two jobs at once. I got myself through New Hope High, Ohio State, and Columbia Law School in New York City. Then the dam burst.

It wasn't the pressure of law school, because I'd already finished. And it wasn't my distaste for urban living, because I could have practiced anywhere. My idealism had long been shattered, so it wasn't that either. It was the complete mental and emotional commitment to a demanding career, in exchange for which I'd receive my alloted share of middle-class money and upper-middle-class prestige, neither of which, I decided, I had ever really wanted.

There were other rewards of living, though, that I did want. The ones that cannot be measured with a yardstick or a diploma or a dollar sign or a public opinion poll. There is no way to quantify them. They can only be experienced and felt in the abstract, not touched, not seen, not planned, and not described. Time just to be, I decided, was what I really wanted.

So I left.

Since then I'd been living in my tent, usually on drop zones, often in Florida. Though rent was usually free, money was still something I had little of. There were the monthly payments on my school loans, which had another six years to run. And then there were skydives. At fifteen dollars a crack for a trip to twelve grand, with more than two hundred jumps a year—that left precious little for anything else.

My income came from freelancing: rigging, parachute instructing, flying, maintenance, or whatever odd jobs I could scrounge up. It was a financially insecure existence, but I enjoyed the work, so there were no regrets. I wouldn't ever go back.

But even paradise has its bad days, and today was turning out to be one of them.

I put my air mattress inside the tent and inflated it. Next I dug into my left saddlebag and pulled out a clean T-shirt and my only other pair of jeans. In the right saddlebag I found my small terrycloth towel. I bundled them together and slipped into one of Twig's showers.

Back at my tent, I hung my towel over the Honda's handlebars and jammed my dirty clothes in my laundry bag. I took my sleeping bag from the passenger's seat. Its zipper had broken for good two months ago, and the fill was hopelessly matted. Like the tent, it would soon need replacing.

I spread it over the air mattress and went back to the Honda. I got out my rig and a battered copy of Richard Bach's *Illusions*. There was a powerful spotlight at the northwest corner of Twig's loft that gave off enough light for me to read. I placed my rig at the head of my sleeping bag just inside the door, then tied up the tent flaps, climbed in, and zipped up the mosquito mesh. That done, I lay back against my rig and opened the book to the page I'd dog-eared last night.

My mind wandered. I was trying to imagine what wisdom Bach's hero Donald Shimoda might have imparted had he seen Lonny Carmichael go in, here in his own stomping grounds of Indiana. He probably would have said it was an illusion, that if I closed my eyes and wished hard enough, the blob of decaying flesh and crumbled bone would resuscitate and return to make another jump tomorrow.

I was being unfairly cynical, I decided. I forced myself to stop thinking, and just read.

I read the book through to the back cover. I put it aside and did some waiting. Literally twiddled my thumbs. Now and then I scratched a line across the whorls of one thumb with my other nail.

I got up and squeezed out through the mesh.

The moon was nearly full. It was resting comfortably above the trees in a clear, dark sky. I walked over to the parking lot. Many of the cars and vans had returned, but to different spots. I looked at every single vehicle, but none of them was Eleanor's red van.

I went back to the Honda and pulled two long pieces of suspension line from my tank bag. Inside my tent, I methodically disembowelled them, core from sheath, then cut them into eighteen-inch pull-up cords. Skydivers are always losing pull-up cords, and someone might be scavenging extras in the morning.

Sometime later, with the moon high overhead and no sign of company for the night, I released my tent flaps, and begrudgingly fell asleep.

3

The roar of an engine jolted me awake.

Satin Cruise, I realized. Dominic Salvino's annoying but effective wake-up call.

I gave myself five minutes, then crawled out of my tent and checked the sun. A little before seven.

Except for the sun, the sky was completely blue. Not a single cloud. Farmers would have another day of worry.

I glanced down at the windsock. It was hanging limp. No wind an hour after sunrise usually means low-to-moderate winds during the day, and all but guarantees lots of activity and empty wallets by sunset.

I walked over and looked through the parking lot, but there was no red van with Illinois plates.

Forty or so jumpers were up and about. One of Dominic Salvino's gimmicks was to offer a half-priced load lifting off before eight, and I guessed that's who these jumpers were. The majority of the campers, however, made it clear they resented his wake-up call. "Fuck" was a very common word this morning, Dominic's mother repeatedly maligned.

I went back to my tent and changed into my running shorts, socks, and New Balance running shoes. I took off and circled the airport five times, consciously avoiding the field where Lonny Carmichael had bounced. That wasn't particularly rational, since his body was no longer there. But computers are the only completely rational beings, especially in the early hours of the day before coffee.

29

After showering, I washed my shorts and socks thoroughly. Then I hung my sleeping bag, towel, shorts, and socks over the Honda for airing or drying, wolfed down half the pita bread, bananas, and apples I had picked up in town last night, went over to the manifest, paid for a cup of coffee, and wondered where Eleanor was.

Satin Cruise tore down the runway, and the day's first load lifted off. I noticed Twig motioning to me through the loft door. I finished my coffee and went inside.

I could tell right away he hadn't slept well last night. His jaw was long, his eyes were red with fatigue. In fact, I seriously doubted he'd even gone home to his wife. He was wearing the same clothes from yesterday, he hadn't showered, and there was a day's growth of beard on his face. It took him more than two minutes to collect his thoughts before he was able to speak.

Police Chief Eugene Smedley, he said, wanted an independent and objective *expert* to examine Carmichael's gear and advise them on its possible role in his death. So last night, while I'd been brooding at Jake's, the police had been busy soliciting out-of-state jumpers for recommendations. My name had popped up frequently, and this morning Smedley had phoned to see if I was still here.

"Just wanted you to know," Twig said. "He'll be out shortly."

I nodded, and we made our way outside to the packing area. Smedley drove up a scant three minutes later. The same man who'd driven out yesterday, only today he came alone. He was short for a cop and quite a bit overweight. I guessed him to be about fifty.

He spoke to Twig. Twig pointed. He spoke to me.

I really didn't want to get involved. For the last five years I'd been minding my own business, and that's how I liked it. Earn a buck, make a skydive, run a mile, live in my tent. I mind my business, you mind yours, and we all live happily ever after. That's all I wanted.

But Smedley seemed insistent, and I realized I'd have to put up a fight to say no. And I did have a rigger's curiosity about the gear.

"It depends," I said.

"On?"

"On whether you want me to come down right now or whether it can wait till Tuesday. I already have plans through Monday."

He didn't want to wait till Tuesday, but I reminded him it was a holiday weekend.

"Oh, all right," he said. "First thing Tuesday."

I nodded. He left. I had a queasy feeling about that nod.

Just then Ken Popadowski came over with the manifest in his hand. "You guys want me to put your six-way down on the next Satin Cruise load?" he asked. "Since you never got to jump yesterday."

"Sure," I said. "I could use a jump."

We both looked over at Twig, but he just shook his head, turned, and walked slowly toward his hangar.

"He's taking it pretty hard," Ken said.

"Yeah," I agreed. "But I don't think he wants our sympathy."

Ken nodded, and I told him to go ahead and announce the rest of our group. Fifteen minutes later we had everybody.

Young Macintosh was wearing neon shorts again, only today they were yellow. Cheeks was smoking one of his foreign cigarettes. Danny Death Grimes, who'd dragged along a friend named Arn, was grumbling about the meaningless of life to no one in particular. And no one in particular was paying him any attention.

Eleanor had driven up just as Ken Popadowski was reciting our names. "Hi," she said to me shyly when she walked over. She offered me a faint smile and an even fainter hug.

She was gorgeous, as usual. Her silky off-black hair was hanging loose around her shoulders. She had on a pair of designer jeans, a cream-colored top, and a flimsy gold necklace that sparkled with reflected sunlight.

I wanted to say something like, "Missed you last night," but I could tell right away that she was in a serious, detached mood, and that something was definitely wrong. With everybody else standing within earshot, though, I really couldn't ask her about anything more personal than the weather.

After the dive, I thought. We'll be able to talk privately then.

When nobody else took the initiative, Cheeks decided to organize our dive. It was basic enough: star, wedge, donut, bi-pod, repeat. We each took slots in the exit and built the dive from there. We walked through the entire sequence of points over and over until the rhythm felt smooth and in sync. I tried to keep my mind on the dirt dive, but it wasn't easy. I kept thinking about Eleanor, and wondering.

Satin Cruise landed from the wake-up load and we hurried to put on our gear. I snatched my rig from my tent and, as always, examined its two pins—one on the reserve, one on the main. I slipped into my jumpsuit and flung my rig onto my back. I adjusted the leg and chest straps for a safe, comfortable fit, and carried my helmet, goggles, and gloves with me to the plane.

Our group was the first to climb up the ladder and through the doorless entry between the left wing and the tail. We organized ourselves in rows on the floor. Two eight-ways, one of them photographer Newt Becker's Octagon, followed us in. The ten-way speed star team from Wisconsin brought up the rear. They would leave first.

Satin Cruise bumped with the crests and gullies that made up Findlay Airport's runway, then lifted into the air.

I listened to the smooth purr of the plane's engines until we reached a thousand feet. I noticed the muscles in my arms loosen up as we crossed over the imaginary safety line. Other jumpers on the load responded as well: their chatter became smoother, their jokes more clean. Still, there was anxiety in the plane. There usually is after a fatality.

Eleanor was in front of me and to my right. I rubbed my foot tentatively against her thigh. She seemed to hesitate. Then she slid her pinky through my shoelace. She didn't turn around, and I wasn't sure what to think.

At six grand, Dominic banked a mild left. Then he straightened Satin Cruise, leveling its wings with the horizon. Jump run for the speed star team.

They stood and checked their gear one last time. One of the team members asked Newt Becker to tape their exit. Newt nodded and positioned his camera out a window over the plane's wing. Ready to capture the first few seconds on video.

The team's spotter stood in the doorway, peering down at the ground. There were electrical switches located behind the door frame to signal the pilot, but they must not have been functioning because the spotter pulled his head back inside and yelled, "Five left!"

"Five left," Cheeks repeated into Dominic's ear above the engine noise. The plane move slightly in that direction.

"Another five left and cut!" the spotter shouted.

Cheeks relayed the message. Dominic corrected the plane another five degrees and throttled the engines back. The spotter took his position among his team, squashed tightly near the entrance. Their stark concentration overwhelmed the fuselage of the plane. None of the rest of us moved or spoke.

They got ready.

They got set.

They went.

A quiet stillness set in as the group exited in perfect harmony. Goose bumps broke out on my arms.

Dominic increased power. He'd be taking the rest of us to twelve grand. A few slept, but most stared blankly toward the tail of the plane, imagining themselves in freefall, mentally flying through each planned maneuver.

At eleven grand the airplane was stirring. Thoughts of Lonny Carmichael swirled around inside. The exit would be tough. After that we'd be fine.

We slipped into gloves, tightened helmets, adjusted goggles, and checked our rigs.

I slid my right hand methodically over each piece of equipment in a well-established order, searching for any irregularities that could turn a routine jump into a tragedy. Beginning at the top in front, I examined the two three-ring releases to my main. Then my chest strap, and my reserve ripcord and main quick-release handles located just below on the left and right respectively. Both leg straps. In back, I checked my main pilot chute and the routing of its bridle. Finally, my main pin. I detected nothing unusual.

At twelve thousand feet Dominic headed Satin Cruise into the northwest wind and initiated jump run. A skydiver from the third eight-way spotted for us all. After yelling corrections and calling for a cut, he, along with his group, awkwardly departed the aircraft. Five jumped, three fell. Perhaps they haven't yet recovered from a late-night party, I thought. Or they could be novices. Or maybe they just aren't any good.

Octagon exited next. Gangly Newt Becker left with them, video rolling.

It was our turn. Eleanor climbed outside the plane as rear-rear floater, Danny Death's friend Arn followed as front floater, then Danny Death and Cheeks as rear and middle floaters. All faced inward across the entrance and grasped the door frame with one hand, the jumpsuit of the person next to them with the other. Macintosh, the least experienced in our group with only three hundred jumps, knelt down inside opposing them. He closed his fists around Danny Death's and Cheeks's chest straps. I stood over Macintosh, half-hunched, and clasped the shoulder of his rig with my left hand, Cheeks's harness with my right.

Cheeks did the count: "Ready. Set. Go!" We pushed off in unison. Or so I thought.

A second later I knew how wrong I'd been. The tension in my grips mounted instantly. My fingers were ripping where they grasped Cheeks's rig, and the joints in my arms screamed in agony. For Eleanor, Arn, Danny Death, Cheeks, and Macintosh it was the same. We all fought to stay afloat on a precarious cushion of air, fought to keep from sliding under or flipping over each other. Our timing had been just a fraction off.

I had a decision to make, and I had to make it quickly. I could continue to hang on, betting that together we could make the necessary adjustments, that the formation would settle out in the relative wind. But that choice had a significant risk attached: if it didn't pan out a funnel would result. We'd be hurled across the sky at distances too great to be overcome quickly, and the dive would be a loss.

If I let go, the other five could more easily recover. But that would leave me above them and in front. It would eat up a chunk of our fifty-five seconds of relative work time while I caught up.

I had half a second in which to decide.

The base began to twist uncontrollably. It propelled me upward in relation to everyone else. I was being catapulted over the top into the vacuum created by the bodies below me. Once there, I'd come crashing down on Cheeks and Danny Death with a terrifying force.

I had only one choice now. I released my grip.

The abrupt change from the dramatic fury of the exit to the peaceful serenity of solitary freefall shot an electrical current through my nervous system that momentarily paralyzed me. The ecstasy of freefall, something that cannot be described with mere adjectives or adverbs, nouns or verbs. Airgasm, it's been called, but even that term fails in the end. That unique quality of freefall that compels jumpers to return ritually to the sky—nothing but space around the physical self, creating nothing but space around the spirit: total and uncompromising freedom—can only be experienced in person. It was my raison d'être. Perhaps my companions' too.

I recovered myself and dove downward—legs extended, arms at my side—toward a solid and stable base. It had mellowed out below and off to my left. I slotted myself between Macintosh and Arn.

We shook grips and transitioned easily to the wedge. That was followed by the donut. Despite perfect positioning, Danny Death had difficulty getting into his slot. His body, rigid and unyielding to the relative wind, bobbled circuitously on its fountain of air. Cheeks, whose face more than lived up to its fleshy reputation, reached up and yanked him into place.

We built the bi-pod, then started the series over. This time Danny Death had a problem with the wedge and almost didn't get in. As he took grips I looked down at the ground. Thirty-five hundred feet. Except for the exit and Danny Death's occasional meanders, six decent points. We shook, tracked, and dumped our mains.

Complete line stretch jerked me upright in my harness. I gazed up and exhaled a routine sigh of relief at the sight of my fully inflated, totally operational, two-hundred-twenty-square-foot main parachute. No reserve ride this trip.

I pushed my goggles up from my eyes and gazed out at the earth's quiet beauty.

When you are in the sky, the world below stands still. It is like a fast running stream that transforms itself into a pond, allowing you to bathe in its sweet water without having to fight the flow. There is a certain spiritual oneness that I'd only ever encountered from this perspective—suspended beneath a delicate seven-pound piece of nylon several thousand feet above the ground. You can not experience it by looking out the window of an airplane, because airplanes are too enclosed. Or by taking a trip in a hot air balloon, because balloons are far too big. A ride in a hang glider comes close, but it was only under the canopy of a parachute that I'd ever felt in true harmony with Mother Nature and at the same time completely removed from her.

I drank in the scenery below me for perhaps fifteen seconds. Then I tugged on my right steering line and held it level at my waist. My chute spiraled downward, and I lost two hundred feet quickly. I eased up the line and leveled out over a wooded patch southwest of the runway. Ten feet above me a lavender-and-gray parachute drifted alone. I released some of my brakes, ascended relative to the other chute, and lightly tapped the middle cell of my canopy on the back of Eleanor's suspended legs.

"Honestly, Chance, you could have at least warned me!" she scolded, all the while descending adroitly down my lines.

"You're up to the task," I replied with a devilish grin.

She hooked her Nikes into my risers two feet above my head, and we were a biplane.

We flew our canopies together like that for about thirty seconds.

It was a calm flight, above the empty fields and the small groves of trees. When we reached a thousand feet, Eleanor detached her feet from my risers and turned off to the right. We both prepared to land.

At two hundred feet, I positioned myself into the wind along the south side of the runway. It was blowing at about five miles an hour on the ground, not enough to bleed off my chute's forward speed. I needed to make a careful and well-timed approach to avoid crashing in on my knees.

The ground began to rush toward me. At about fifty feet, I drew on my brakes, cautiously at first. Then with one swift, final movement I swooped both steering lines down below my waist in a flare. The canopy stalled, my feet six inches from the grass. Lightly, gently, I tiptoed down to earth, as if taking my last step off the stairway from heaven.

In fact, I'm sure I had.

Eleanor flared her canopy between me and the grass runway. She smiled over in a friendly but circumspect way, daisy chained her lines together, and gathered up her chute. She didn't make the first move toward conversation.

"I waited up quite late," I said finally.

She looked back over at me and pondered something distant for a long minute. Then she let out a sigh and heaved the lavender and gray back to the grass.

"I owe you a big apology, Chance. I should have tried to find you before taking off like I did last night."

"No need to apologize," I said. "But I am a little confused."

"Of course," she said. "It's just that Lonny Carmichael and I jumped together for years, and after he bounced . . ." She closed her eyes and paused. "I just needed to be alone, I guess."

She opened her eyes. "I waited in the loft till they knew for certain. When they confirmed it to be Lonny, I felt a sudden urge to collect my gear, toss it in the van, and take off. So I did. No specific destination. I just drove." Then she looked deep into my eyes. "And by the way, *you* disappeared quick enough."

"Point taken," I said. "I guess we all just wanted to get away from the drop zone fast. Besides, I hadn't considered that you and Carmichael might have been friends."

She shook her head. "Not friends really. We were both part of the Midwest mega-load crowd, so we'd run into each other a couple times a year. But that by itself wouldn't have triggered such a reaction in me. It was something else. Something a shade more personal."

"I'm a good listener, if you want to talk."

She nodded. "I know," she said. "And, yes, I think I do."

She plopped down beside her canopy and patted the grass next to her. I took a seat.

"Once, during a casual conversation about birthdays," she said, "Lonny Carmichael and I discovered we were born on the same day. I don't mean the same day of the year, I mean the exact same date. Only three hours apart—eleven in the morning for him, two in the afternoon for me. It's surprising how a minor detail like that can bind you emotionally to the fortunes, or in Lonny's case the misfortunes, of someone who isn't an active part of your life."

"It means you're human, that's all."

"I suppose," she said uneasily. "You know, it's strange, but for the first three hours after Lonny died, I kept waiting for an accident to happen to me—a tree to fall on my van, a drunk driver to hit me head on, something like that. Why I was out on the road when I felt that way . . ."

She was shaking her head, baffled by her own behavior.

"You know," she confessed, "I didn't want to come back to the drop zone at all—I was that upset. But that wouldn't have been fair to you. The very least I owed you was an explanation. And now I feel as though I overreacted to the whole thing."

"Not necessarily," I said. "How long had you known Carmichael?"

She thought. "Six years, I guess. Since I moved back to Chicago. Lonny started jumping here at Twig's drop zone after he moved to Cincinnati three or four years ago, but before that he lived up near Milwaukee. He'd come down to my drop zone once or twice a year, whenever a big plane was there. And I'd see him at any large formation planned anywhere in the Midwest. He got invited on most of the dives, but that was more politics than skill. He didn't have good body control or awareness, and flew stiff as a board. But his small size allowed him to hide a general lack of talent. Of course, drugs may have played a role, both in his inept flying and in the fact he got slots on the big dives. Rumors had him bribing his way onto a couple sixty- and seventy-way formations with grams of coke for the organizers."

My mind started to click. "Was he a regular user when he jumped?"

She shook her head vigorously. "I'm ahead of you there, Chance.

You're wrong if you think that's what killed him. I asked around right after he went in. Everybody says he was clean yesterday. They're positive an autopsy will back them up. A resource deficiency, they say. It was either drugs or skydives this week for Lonny Carmichael, and he chose skydives."

Neither of us wanted to touch that one.

We were silent for a time. Eventually she stood up and brushed some grass off her jumpsuit. I got up, too. "Any ideas about where we should go for dinner tonight?" I asked.

She gave me a half-smile, then reached over and hugged me affectionately. She was wearing only her natural scent and smelled fresh. I held her close, but didn't really enjoy it the way I should have. This, I knew, was Eleanor's "Sorry Babe" hug. We each had one that got used now and then.

"Sorry Babe," she said. "There's nothing I'd like better this evening." She loosened my chin strap, removed my helmet, and combed my hair with her long, willowy fingers. Then she backed off. It's always easier to say no from a distance.

"Work?"

She didn't even bother to nod. "I have to be at the office by seven-thirty tonight, which means leaving here no later than five, preferably earlier."

Actually, she *had* called last week to warn me that her schedule would be tight. She'd committed herself only for last night, but I had let my imagination stretch that into an entire weekend.

"We have a major promotional campaign underway," she explained. "The completed project has to be on the marketing director's desk first thing Tuesday. I'm running behind and still have about twenty hours of work left to do."

"Sounds important."

She nodded. "For two reasons. First, the project is a team effort. There are four of us on it, and I have a commitment to the other three. Second, a job promotion is in the offing to fill the vacancy left by my boss—he's been hired away by one of our vendors. I've been recommended by several managers, but our vice president of sales and marketing belongs to the Neanderthal period. He isn't exactly excited about a woman in that position. There's no one else inside the company who can match my qualifications, so I'm hopeful. But a poor showing on this project would be all the excuse the V.P. needs to overlook me and hire a man from outside, which is what he really wants to do." She compressed her lips. "I have no intention of letting that happen."

"No, Eleanor," I sighed, "that definitely wouldn't be you."

Eleanor Venzetti and I were two very different people. Some university professor somewhere with a Ph.D. in sociology might say it had to do with the colossal disparity in our childhood experiences. Her father was a Chicago millionaire who had made his fortune the easy way—through inheritance. Her beautiful mother, ever the social hostess and charity organizer, had insisted that their only child have everything: a nanny, private schooling, designer clothes, ballet lessons, a horse at ten, France at twelve, a sports car at sixteen.

And love. Eleanor got lots of love. So much, in fact, that by the age of seventeen she was determined to give some of it away. To the dismay of her doting parents, who expected her to become the next prima ballerina of New York, Eleanor quit dance, which she'd decided was narcissistic, and took up child psychology. She was going to make herself useful by helping the poor and deprived children of the world get off to a more positive start.

That was back in the seventies, when things like that were still being done. After college, she spent nearly five years working in a Kentucky mining town before *her* dam burst. Caring and concerned Eleanor Venzetti was too caring and too concerned about her patients, and just couldn't take the emotional grind and the countless failures of the job another day more. She, too, had burned out.

The past six years she'd been employed by a Chicago company that distributed business information systems, a fancy code name for telephones. "There's nothing emotionally draining about phones," she had told me when I asked about the change. The money culture that came with the job bored her as it would anyone already rich, but she enjoyed the work, and her face could tackle a genuine laugh once again.

During Eleanor's stay in Kentucky, a neighbor had introduced her to skydiving. It became her therapy, a source of escape from her neurotic patients and their even more neurotic parents. By the time she made the switch from kids to phones she'd already become hopelessly addicted to freefall.

We'd met two years ago in the sky over her home drop zone in Sullivan, Illinois, a farm town south of Chicago. An eight-way that I'd agreed to do as a favor for a novice organizer ended in a funnel at nine grand, where I learned that the rest of the eight were novices, too. Except for Eleanor. She flew over to me and planted a bold kiss on the entirety of my mouth. The two of us turned eight more points on that dive before break off, and we'd been turning all kinds of different points since.

It wasn't just my flying technique that had caught her attention, she admitted to me later. Anyone who lived in a tent, got around on a motorcycle, and read *Death of a Salesman* had to be worth knowing. I didn't bother to tell her I'd bought the book earlier that day as a gift for a friend.

We got along well all the same. Despite our opposite backgrounds and contrasting lifestyles, we did have something in common: both of us had rejected the world of our youth, burned out on the world of our choice, and now lived in a world that was neither. It was an intimate yet incomplete connection, an elastic string of putty that would not quite harden but would never entirely break. We might have had each other every night of every day, except that she was city and I wasn't—three years in New York had seen to that.

So our trysts were infrequent, scheduled during the gaps in her very full business calendar that left little room for romance. A weekend every few months, maybe nine days in Florida over Thanksgiving, always at drop zones. For the most part, that seemed to suit both of us. But we each had days when we felt it was not quite enough.

And at the moment, standing out along the runway, I was feeling it wasn't quite enough. But I could tell Eleanor wasn't feeling the same way. I sensed she had something on her mind, maybe something besides Lonny Carmichael's birthday and besides her work. She apparently knew I was here yesterday, yet she chose to go into the loft instead of coming over to greet me.

I didn't ask her about it, though. Whatever it was, if it was anything at all, she'd tell me about it in her own time.

She hugged me gently. "We'd better get back. The others will be waiting."

"Yeah," I said, "I guess they will."

4

Back in the packing area we post dived our jump. Arn said he hung on the plane too long and the bad exit was all his fault. I said I held back a little and it was partly mine. Macintosh said he was just relieved to have the first jump over with, and everyone seemed to agree on that. It was taken as a matter of course that we'd make another.

No one criticized Danny Death's poor flying in his presence, but privately Cheeks suggested we find a replacement for him. Macintosh seemed keen on the idea, Eleanor had no opinion, Arn resisted. His friend Danny was a dynamite sequential flyer, and everybody has a bad one now and then. I put in my lot with Arn, and Cheeks diplomatically withdrew his suggestion, at least for the next dive.

In front of the loft Danny Death was kneeling next to a picnic table and sloppily packing his rig. Once or twice a minute he lost his patience, swore, and belted his container with a tightly wadded fist.

I finished packing my rig, stuffed my pull-up cord into my pocket, and walked over. He was really none of my business, but if I could get him calmed down, there would be less dissension in our group. And I was all for that.

"It's not a punching bag," I said.

He replied with a less-than-polite "Fuck off."

I hesitated.

"Wanna talk?"

"What about?"

"Whatever's bothering you."

"Nothin's fuckin' botherin' me!" Punch, swear, punch, swear.

I tried a different approach.

"Arn insists you're a hotshot flyer. But after that last dive—"

"So don't fuckin' jump with me, then!" he blurted, loud enough to turn heads. His arm muscles tensed, resembling strings on a concert violin.

"That's what some of the others want—not to jump with you. Arn and I bought you another shot."

For a fleeting second he appeared emotionally vulnerable. Then he regained a measure of control and turned his attention back to his container. Or that was the appearance he gave. Another three slaps produced several more invectives but no better result. He shoved his rig aside, sat back on his haunches, and stared sullenly at the ground.

"Look, man, I'm sorry about the goddamn dive, okay? I admit it. I screwed up." He was fighting back tears. For the second time in half an hour I sat down and listened.

"It's just that Lon and me were pretty tight, ya know. We started in the same student class eleven years ago. How many fuckin' jumpers from the same class you know who make it *eleven* years together?"

"None," I admitted. "You must have lived in Wisconsin then."

He nodded. "We made our first jump from the same sleazebag Cessna up at Saratoga. Arn started there, too, but that was after Lon left. Then I left. Then the DZ shut down when the old man croaked last winter. Fuckin' heart attack at four grand. Crashed in one of them lakes they got up there. Saved him from burnin', I guess. Then they cremated him anyway. Guess it's all the same when you're dead. The jumpers moved to a place west of Madison. Arn says it's a better DZ. Never been there myself. Plannin' to go later this summer. See what's left of the old guys."

He was rambling. I let him.

"Lon was a good guy, he was. Not much of a flyer, though. Liked those big dives. I kept tellin' him, 'You'll never learn to fly doin' the big ones, fallin' and waitin' for everyone else to dock.' Waste of freefall, I told him. Never listened, though. Then he moved to Cincinnati, started comin' here. Oakland Ridge in Ohio is closer, ya know, but they only got Cessnas and Twig's got the Beech. Now he's got two," he remembered.

He reached down and extracted a clump of healthy grass, roots and all, and threw it aimlessly into freefall.

"But Lon did know about exitin', I'll give him that much. All those fuckin' big dives. He was small like me, so they always put him out near the end. That's why I can't believe him doin' somethin' stupid like hittin' his head on exit. It's not like Lon. Exitin' was the one thing he knew about."

"Remember the guy in Arizona last year," I said. "With nearly three thousand jumps and a national medal, he did the same thing. It only takes a second of lapsed concentration, Danny. Everything in life has risk, you know that. Maybe having or not having a certain skill sets the odds, but you can't totally eliminate the element of chance."

He shook his head. "I still don't buy it. Lon wouldn'ta hit. He wouldn'ta."

"Did you talk with the jumper who tried to save him? Alex Laird, I think his name is."

"No!" Flat and definite. A ring of insolent disdain circled Danny Death's mouth. "Laird and I don't really hit it off. He's a fuckin' redneck, ya know," as if that single fact explained all the world's problems. "That's him over there," he gestured—intentionally, I was sure—with his middle finger to a man clad in a navy blue T-shirt and sweat pants.

I followed his finger with my feet.

The man was standing alone not far from the hangar. He was exceptionally big and brawny for a skydiver—more than six feet tall and about two hundred pounds. Except for a slight beer gut, he appeared to have excellent muscle tone—forearms well developed, biceps bulging. Testosterone. You could smell the brute at twenty yards. Probably ate lots of raw steak.

"Excuse me," I said. "Alex Laird?"

He turned.

The first thing you noticed about his face was his nose. It was bent awkwardly directly below the eyes and then again before the rounded tip. Small crimson capillaries lined the sides. The skin that covered his cheekbones was pockmarked, evidence of once chronic acne. He had a thick bush of brown hair. That and a well-shaped jaw saved him from the category ugly, making him instead irregular, different.

I introduced myself and explained my interest. He said no, he didn't mind repeating what he'd already told the police and half the drop zone.

43

"Went after Carmichael as soon as I saw him unconscious," he said, "but just couldn't get there."

"That's not exactly what I meant," I said. "I'm more interested in how Carmichael hit the door frame."

He shrugged. "Don't know. Heard him bump, but thought it was his arm. I myself nicked my arm, so there was no reason to think it different with him."

"True," I said. "It's just that I've been told Carmichael was an expert on exits." I hadn't meant to insult Laird, but realized too late that I had.

"Wouldn't know about that," he replied woodenly.

There was an awkward pause. Finally I said, "When did you become suspicious?"

"About seven grand, when he still didn't show. That's when I thought about the bump, and I started looking. Wasn't till we turned for the jewel—uh, our second point—that I spotted him. I tried for him, but went low. You know how it is . . . difficult with my weight. And I'm not real current. Only started jumping again after a couple years off."

I nodded. Laird didn't need to explain. I could tell just by looking at him that he would have had a tough time reaching Carmichael. His body was dense relative to the surface area he would expose to the relative wind. So he would naturally fall faster than smaller, lightweight jumpers, and he would have less control over his speed. He was just too big and dense to be effective. And he wasn't current, either.

"If he'da been a fuckin' redneck, you'da saved him!"

Out of the corner of my eye I saw Danny Death approaching.

Laird's face flushed with anger. "Go to hell, Grimes! I did what I could."

"I seen! I heard! Even if what you say is true—and I don't say it is—anytime someone hits on exit you're supposed to make sure they're okay. You didn't fuckin' care 'cause Lon wasn't no fuckin' redneck like you. Look at you, making out like you're some hero. But you're just a mother-fuckin' jackass. All you cared about was beatin' everybody to the formation so you could say what a hot dick you are. Well, you're no hot dick. You tracked off at thirty-five hundred insteada followin' Lon down to a grand like you coulda."

"Take a hike, Jack!" Laird retorted.

I felt caught in the middle. On the one hand, I sympathized with

Danny Death. Every jumper could understand how he felt. When the corpse belongs to a stranger, you can impassively believe the mistake and shake your head at the stupidity behind the fatality. Closer to home, though, and it's not so easy to accept.

On the other hand, I thought he was being unfair to Alex Laird. The sixteen-way had jumped from twelve grand, which gave them about sixty seconds of freefall. Not enough time to think; time only to react.

Laird hadn't started to look for Carmichael till seven thousand feet, about thirty seconds after exit. But there was nothing particularly unusual about that. True, if Carmichael had been a highly skilled flyer, Laird and the others might have missed him sooner. But even Danny Death admitted his buddy wasn't a good flyer, so Laird had no reason to be alarmed right away. Except, perhaps, that he'd heard Carmichael hit on exit. But jumpers *do* hit limbs and gear on exit, so Laird's assumption wasn't out of line.

I really couldn't be blamed, then, for not suspecting Laird's account: it all made perfect skydiving sense. And Danny Death was hardly a convincing advocate for any alternative point of view.

Laird turned and headed for the loft. I started after him, thinking to thank him for his time, when Danny Death suddenly zipped by me and leapt onto his back. He tugged at Laird's thick bush of hair with his right and threw ineffectual blows to the face with his left. Unsophisticated childishness that reminded me of the techniques I'd employed against my older sister more than twenty years ago. It might have been comical had I not known what lay behind it.

"Fuckin' jackass! Mother-fuckin' jackass!"

Laird grunted and attempted to shake him off. He staggered, lost his balance, and fell to the ground with Danny Death squirming on top. He escaped, feinted a left, then landed a solid blow to Danny Death's mid-section with his right. Danny Death responded with profanity and a bite to Laird's left forearm. Laird smashed a fist into Danny Death's face. Danny Death yanked out a handful of Laird's bushy hair, roots and all, and threw it aimlessly into freefall.

The fight was attracting a large audience. I noticed Twig hurrying over from the hangar. He looked as angry as Alex Laird and Danny Death.

"Not on my drop zone you don't!" He wedged himself between the two, then glared at Laird. "I don't need another fatality the same weekend. You guys want to kill each other, leave the damn airport!"

"Wasn't *my* fault. He came up from behind—"

"You're big enough to stop it!" Twig was adamant, and Laird wisely backed off.

Twelve jumpers from a Beech load began to land on the airport. One of them turned right when he should have turned left, and by a fine hair missed pounding in on the hood of the turquoise TransAm. A woman in the packing area shrieked something about her car and ran toward the parking lot.

The near miss had a scattering effect on the drop zone. It diverted the attention of the crowd, and in less than a minute everyone was going about his own business. The fight was ancient history.

Danny Death Grimes, whose appearance now matched his last name, crawled off to the bathroom with the aid of his friend Arn to clean up the blood gushing from his nose and broken lip. It was dripping onto his off-white T-shirt, which now looked tie-dyed with cranberries.

Laird came out of the fight less bloody but more incensed. His crop of hair was highlighted by a small bald spot behind his right ear. It had the aura of a well-groomed lawn with an incongruous bare patch where the neighbor's dog habitually peed.

The fight did have one positive side effect: it released the tempest raging inside Danny Death, and on the next dive he flew like the ace Arn assured us he was. A steady stream of blood continued to leak from his injured, though apparently unbroken, nose. In freefall, the upward flow dared us to lose concentration. At least no one floated above the formation.

Immediately after the dive Macintosh and Cheeks climbed into Macintosh's van and took off for this year's running of the Indy Five-hundred.

"Tomorrow we'll make more jumps together, right?" Macintosh had asked me before leaving. He had the insecurity of a newcomer anxious not to be left out.

"I'll be here," I assured him. "Come find me when you want to make another jump."

I didn't think he altogether believed me, but he said, "Tomorrow, then," and drove on out.

Most of the skydivers at this boogie, as at any other, had been drawn here by the big airplane. With big airplanes it's possible to make large formations, and by late morning the mega-load organizers had effectively taken over Satin Cruise.

Two thirty-six-way attempts were made. The first funneled at only twenty, the second built to thirty-five. Next on the agenda: a forty-eight-way using Satin Cruise and the Beech flying in formation. Eleanor participated. Danny Death and Arn disappeared into the parking lot. Twig went into his hangar. I sat on the ground and watched.

Big loads were definitely not my thing. On most of them, each jumper performs just one maneuver. As Danny Death had said, most of freefall time is spent falling and waiting for your turn to dock. Unless you happen to dock first, in which case you fall and wait for everyone else to dock. I didn't have fifteen dollars a jump just to fall and wait.

Neither did a lot of other jumpers. But big is flashy, big is in. Being offered a slot on a mega-load can have political and social significance within the skydiving community. For some, it is an honor bestowed by the elite skygods, a symbol of acceptance into the "in" crowd. And with the gentrification of the sport, that has become important.

The major mega-load organizer at this boogie was a guy named Bradford Rey. He crept next to me as I enjoyed the mid-afternoon shade of Twig's memorial elm. He was handsome and single, and I didn't like him. He was to arrogance and meanness what Mae West was to sex appeal. His epithet was The Pit Bull—a cliche, but appropriate. Where others wanted to teach, he tried to trample. Where others encouraged, he impeded. Aggressively insecure, he blamed people for things that were not their fault, and he was never wrong. He would never have made it into the skydiving elite without his flying skills, which were unquestionably spectacular. So he survived, even becoming a guru of sorts to those in need of a contemporary god.

"I need a few more absolute guarantees for the last wave on the forty-eight-way," he stated icily. "You'll be there in your assigned slot when you're supposed to be."

Our dislike was mutual. There must be a serious dearth of skilled jumpers, I thought, for him to come begging to me.

I issued a polite no—thanks, and all that, and tossed my sleeping bag, towel, shorts, and socks into the tent. I brought out the rest of my fruit and pita.

"Want some?" I said. No reason we couldn't be civil.

He ignored my offer. "Eleanor's in the next to last wave," he said. "You could dock on her if you like."

For years Eleanor had been—and continued to be—the only person Bradford Rey trusted. The one person who tolerated his abusive tantrums but did not condone them. Nor did she seek any favors in return for her friendship. Even The Pit Bull, it seemed, could distinguish between the genuine concern in her and the sycophantic brown-nosing in all the others.

I wasn't jealous of Brad, exactly. I knew Eleanor's interest in him was only clinical—even after six years out of the business, she still cared. But I was human, too. Eleanor and I saw each other so sporadically that when we did have a weekend together, I felt no obligation to split time with him.

Brad, as far as I could tell, had no romantic interest in Eleanor, but he disliked me nonetheless. Eleanor said it was because I represented everything he wanted to be but wasn't, whatever that meant. In the past he'd made a point of avoiding me at all costs, which made this afternoon's invitation something of a desperation bid.

"No thanks," I repeated. I forced a smile, my teeth firmly clenched. The Pit Bull had been turned down, not something he was used to. He told me I'd be blacklisted. I told him, smile still intact, that I didn't care. I overheard someone give him a faint I-told-you-so as he fumed toward the parking lot in search of another jumper for his dive.

An hour later Satin Cruise and the Beech E-18 were on jump run. I listened as the pilots slowed their planes. Seconds later forty-eight jumpers and two cameramen exited. The bright cloudlessness of the afternoon created a glare, but as the charcoal mega-blob approached earth I could see it building nicely. Jumpers patiently waited to dock in their designated wave. After fifty seconds only five jumpers were still outside the formation—two photographers, three unfortunates. The outermost wave turned and tracked, then the next wave, then the next. Then pop, pop, pop, pop, and fifty main canopies opened up. No malfunctions, no reserves. The jumpers shouted and whistled and kicked their dangling legs.

Eleanor came over from Bradford Rey's lengthy post dive positive and upbeat. I was strapping on my gear.

"From the ground it looked good. Except for the three out."

"It's the best I've been on for nearly a year," she said with a radiant smile. "No tension at all in the grips. And no potato-chipping. It definitely satisfied."

I made a two-way teaching dive from the Beech with a thirty-jump novice still trigger-happy with his pilot chute—four thousand feet and it was out and gone. Another hundred jumps under his helmet and he'd mellow.

That jump also satisfied.

Eleanor was packed and showered by the time I landed. She came over to where I had my canopy stretched out on the grass.

"Will you be going to the Nationals boogie?" I asked.

"Possibly," she said. "Sorry, Babe, but that's the best I can do right now. I have a business trip scheduled that week in Dallas. I'm hoping to finish early and drive up to Oklahoma for the boogie, but I can't commit yet." She shaded her eyes from the late afternoon sun. "What about you?"

"I'll be there."

"Where will you be going from here?"

"Can't say right now. Have no plans after Tuesday. Depends on the work opportunities."

She nodded. "You have my number. Let me know."

I said I would. Our agreement was that I'd always call her first, since she had the luxury of a voice mailbox answering system if she wasn't in, and I had no regular phone. Not perfect, but in two years only one message never got through.

She said, "I'm very sorry about the way the weekend turned out. Disappointed, too. Especially in myself."

I slipped my hands under her hair and hid my own disappointment. "It's not your fault Lonny Carmichael went in."

"But I wish I hadn't taken off like that. I mean, you came all this way—"

"I always come up here for Twig's boogie," I reminded her. "And we'll have other weekends together. Nationals is only five weeks away."

We hugged, but she still seemed a little distracted, and she was the first to let go. She squeezed my hand, then hustled over to her red van, backed out of the parking lot, and headed north toward the Windy City and an office in the Sears Tower. High enough to sky-dive from.

Maybe it *was* just Lonny Carmichael and her job, I thought. Maybe her detached mood has nothing at all to do with me.

Later, after sunset, I was sitting at Twig's picnic table feeling sorry for myself when Ken Popadowski closed up the manifest and came over with an extra Moosehead.

"Got any plans for tonight?" he asked.

"My plans left for Chicago a few hours ago."

He nodded. "That's what I thought. How about coming with me, then."

"No offense, Ken, but you'd make a rotten substitute."

He laughed. "What I was thinking about was a night of food and poker with a couple friends of mine. We only play with quarters, so it won't get expensive even if you're lousy."

Normally, I'd have said no. I preferred to spend my evenings alone. But for the past week I'd expected to share the weekend with Eleanor. When you plan on company, you expand your private space. When the plans fall through, there is a pocket of emptiness that takes a while to be absorbed.

"Sure," I said. "Why not?" I accepted the Moosehead, then decided on a whim it wouldn't be my last.

And it wasn't.

5

BZZZZZZZZZZZZZZZZZZZ . . .

Damn. Turn the damn engine *off*!

. . . ZZZZZZZZZZZZZZZZZZZZ . . .

I groaned and cupped my hands over my ears.

Bits and pieces of last night floated in and out on waves of consciousness that never quite crested. Twig's picnic table trapped a moose head, then a queen and two jacks ate it for dinner. A nearly full moon cried from loneliness, and gallons of quarters rained down from the sky. Ken Popadowski was there, Eleanor wasn't. Someone else drove, I got plastered.

Two beers at the drop zone, three at the restaurant, four or five more over at Ken's tent. I should have taken some aspirin before passing out. Why didn't I think to take any aspirin?

. . . ZZZZZZZZZZZZZZZZZZZZZZZZZZ . . .

I'll go out and tell Dominic Salvino enough already, that's what I'll do.

I supported my weight on one elbow planted in my sleeping bag, and rolled left. I pulled my legs up under me and forced myself upright, with immediate regret. Vertigo struck like August lightning, and I collapsed in a heap. I withdrew into partial consciousness for an interminable period of time. Or at least long enough for the first load to lift off. Afterward, the mellifluous sound of silence.

I did not get drunk often. It would be a long while before I'd do it again.

I tried once more. Elbow down, roll sideways, push upward. This time no dizziness. None I couldn't handle, anyway.

Outside the tent, rays of brilliance made me squint. I trudged over to the loft for a shower. Once inside, though, I stumbled in the wrong direction and ended up in the student packing area. I came across Danny Death sprawled on an old packing table.

He was out cold. His skin was pale and clammy, his features glacial, his limbs brick-like. Had he passed out in a morgue, even the most competent pathologist could have been forgiven for mistaking him for the real thing. In fact, my own heart skipped a beat until I saw his chest move. I checked his pulse. Eighty, normal for the chronically unfit. I asked myself which substances had he pumped through his body last night, then decided I didn't really want to know. I let him sleep another half-hour, then hauled him into a shower, stripped his body naked, and released the valve painted blue.

"You fuckin' sonova bitch!" was all he could think to say, though he managed to repeat it about twenty times. I knew how he felt: I'd just done the same thing to myself.

I gave Danny Death my towel and bought two cups of hot, black coffee. He climbed back into the same grungy clothes he'd been wearing since Saturday, cranberry stains and all.

"You have a change of clothes?" I asked, handing him a coffee. "That shirt is disgustingly foul-smelling."

He moved closer to me and raised his arms to liberate any trapped odor. "Serves you right for puttin' me under the fuckin' cold water."

I blew on my coffee. "You must have laid one on heavy last night."

He stuck his chin out. "Why don't you get the fuck off my back!" He flung the towel at me, knocking my coffee to the floor.

"Whoa, Danny, take it easy. I was going to say that I identify, that's all."

He took a deep breath, sipped his coffee, then examined his sneakers. Each shoe had a hole in the toe and a callused pinky poking through.

"Sorry," he said. "I mean . . . it's just that . . . well . . . ya know, man, I'm still touchy, is all."

"Forget it," I said, and mopped up the mess. Then I remembered the twelve dollars and fifty cents in quarters I'd won at poker last night. "How about breakfast—on me?"

I didn't think he'd take me up on the idea, but after some thought he said, "Make it a place with links and I'll go."

"Links?"

"Yeah, ya know, real sausage. Not them fuckin' patties."

"It's a deal," I said, and we set out in search of some links.

The Indiana House of Pancakes was filled with lethargic and bleary-eyed jumpers. Danny Death and I were sitting in a back alcove, away from the sharp rays of light that stabbed through the front windows. He had on one of my spare T-shirts, which he'd agreed to wear only after I convinced him we'd be turned away if he didn't. I'd given him my red one, in case he got into any more fights.

I had an anxious moment when Alex Laird sauntered into the restaurant while we waited for our order. Fortunately, Danny Death had his back to the door. When he finally did turn his head in that direction, Laird was safely tucked away in the smoking section shooting the bull with Macintosh and Cheeks.

Despite his despondency, his drug hangover, and his slightly mashed face, Danny Death had a voracious appetite: three large blueberry pancakes, six sausage links, three eggs over easy, four pieces of heavily jellied toast, an order of hash browns, two large milks, and nearly a quart of coffee. Only when he was almost finished did he admit he hadn't eaten since Saturday lunch, "before Lon went in."

"I still say it don't make sense," he said. "What happened to Lon, I mean."

I said, "I can understand your feelings for your friend."

"But you think I'm fulla shit, like everybody else."

I cleared my throat. "I think Alex Laird's explanation fits."

"I don't give a fuck what that redneck says. Lon knew how to exit, man. I'm tellin' ya, he *knew*."

I finished my French toast. "Then maybe he had a seizure."

Danny Death shook his head. "Me and Lon were best buddies for eleven years. He didn't have epilepsy."

"There are different kinds of seizures. Some strike adults with no previous history."

"Maybe," he said, but the intonation of his voice said he didn't think so. "Any anyway, even supposin' it was a seizure, if it'd been me followin' him out, I'da pulled his reserve. That damn Laird's the reason he's dead."

I shook my head. "No one forced Lonny to jump out of that plane,

Danny. You can't blame someone else."

"I'll blame who I want," he said defiantly. "Laird never liked Lon. And besides, he's a real jackass. Just started comin' out a couple months ago and already he thinks he owns the place. Other jumpers say he used to jump here years back, before I moved here, and he was a jackass back then too. A truck driver that likes to push people around and pick fights. They say that's why Twig threw him off the DZ back then—for pickin' fights. Shouldn'ta ever let him come back, if you ask me."

"Even if he is a bad egg, that doesn't make him responsible for your friend Lonny."

But Danny Death was shaking his head. "I'm tellin' you, there's somethin' not right about this. I don't know exactly what, but there's somethin' not right. Lon wouldn't hit, he wouldn'ta."

I was too busy trying to mind my own business to listen. The Wisconsin speed star team walked in the front door just then, and I used them as an excuse to change the subject.

"Going to Nationals this year?" I asked.

"Nope," he said. "Don't belong to USPA. Fuckin' establishment."

Membership in the U.S. Parachute Association is a requirement for jumping at Nationals and at most drop zones, primarily for insurance reasons. If a jumper were to land on the windshield of a Piper or the hood of a TransAm, for example, the association would pay the third-party damages. So long as the airplane or car belonged to a non-member. Otherwise, the owner would have to collect from the jumper himself. Good luck and all.

"Oh," was my well-thought-out reply to Danny Death's comment.

Macintosh stopped by our booth on his way back from the john. He slid in alongside Danny Death and propped his elbows on the table. His mouth was turned down at the corners.

"How was the Indy Five-hundred?" I asked.

"Okay," he moped. The event he had traveled two thousand miles to watch was already old news.

"I wish I'd known they were organizing big dives," he said, explaining his mood. "I'd have tried to talk Cheeks out of going to the race. I'd rather have stuck around the drop zone and tried to lurk on one of them. I've never done a big dive before. Now they've already picked the jumpers for today's fifty-four-ways, and I won't have a chance. Cheeks has been invited, though. He's done lots of big loads all over the country and knows the guy they call The Pit Bull."

Danny Death rolled his eyes and reached for his milk.

"Guess you guys are in on them," Macintosh sighed.

"As a matter of fact," I replied, "we're free to jump with you."

Danny Death nodded fractionally with milk-filled cheeks, swallowed, then added that his friend Arn would probably oblige us as a fourth.

Macintosh was thrilled but confused. "But I don't get it," he said. "You're two of the best flyers I've ever jumped with. Better even than the skygods out at my home DZ. How come you're not on the big dives?"

"A waste," Danny Death sneered.

Macintosh nodded and gave him a look of comprehension, but I didn't think he got it. Everybody is supposed to want to jump on the mega-loads.

He went back to his booth in an appreciably better mood. While he finished his breakfast, Danny Death and I biked back to the airport. Danny Death went off to find Arn. I parked the bike next to Twig's memorial elm, hung out my sleeping bag with my towel, and rested in my tent. I had with me a copy of a local newspaper that a machine in the restaurant's vestibule had allowed me to take in exchange for one of last night's quarters.

All of the front page and the back page and most of the inside were devoted to yesterday's car race. The moon could have burned out last night and the people of Indiana would never have known. On page four, the editors did find space for a small snippet on Lonny Carmichael. The police, it said, were investigating.

That reminded me about my commitment to Police Chief Eugene Smedley. I really didn't want to get involved in an official investigation of Lonny Carmichael's death. I wanted to keep to my own world, where I was accountable to no one. Maybe, I thought, I'll just pack up the Honda and skip town tonight. Be a no-show in the morning.

Danny Death poked his head into the tent and said Arn was willing to make it a four-way, so he'd gone ahead and signed us up. "Can't jump outa the big planes, though, 'cause of all the fuckin' big loads. It's either take a Cessna or don't jump."

We made three Cessna dives in all: seven, twelve, and ten points. Despite his lack of experience, Macintosh made an impressive showing, and Arn was competent. But it was Danny Death's finesse and flying agility that I marveled at. His body in the air had nothing in common with the corpse I'd picked up off the packing table this morning.

Late in the afternoon Bradford Rey finally managed a completed forty-eight-way, scaled down when the first and only fifty-four-way crumbled at thirty-three: a well-organized funnel.

The parking lot began to empty out about five o'clock, and by nine the airport lay deserted except for me. Those staying at least one more night had all gone out for food and drink.

I was stretched out on my sleeping bag inside my tent. I briefly considered leaving Indiana tonight, then decided I was too tired. Besides, I *had* promised Police Chief Smedley.

All the drop zone lights were out. I reached over and picked up my skydiving logbook and my flashlight, a small but powerful pen affair. I flicked on the light, then carefully entered a detailed record of my dives into the logbook: where, when, what, with whom, and exactly how the dive turned out. When I finished, I pulled out a paperback thriller. It didn't thrill, and I dozed off somewhere in the middle of Chapter Two.

I dreamed about the Sears Tower and Eleanor. It was a perplexing dream, and at the time I didn't understand its significance. I was scaling the Tower barefoot, no ropes. A truck engine was idling in the background. Then the truck drove off and I continued up toward Eleanor's office, but I couldn't remember which floor. A plane started up and tormented my ears with its cacophony. It made the Tower vibrate and I just barely hung on. Then the plane rushed by me fast and I lost my grip. I fell and fell and fell—no parachute. Before I slammed into the ground I woke up.

Tuesday morning, I thought. Time to go meet with the local police.

I heard a car drive off. I turned around and peered out through the tent's mesh. Except for the moon, the sky was pitch black.

Monday night, late.

I fished around in my sleeping bag for the flashlight and the paperback thriller. I found the flashlight off and the paperback all bent up. I set both aside. Then I sealed up the tent, closed my eyes, and finished my sleep.

6

I should have listened to my instincts and left Indiana last night.

It was late Tuesday morning. I was in Twig's parking lot, slouched against the seat of the Honda. Except for my bike and Macintosh's van, the lot was completely empty. A layer of clouds covered the sky at about ten thousand feet, making it exceptionally calm on the ground, no wind whatsoever.

Inside I was anything but calm.

I tapped the knuckle of my forefinger against my upper lip. I was debating whether to go for a run or eat lunch. I was hungry, but if I ate first I wouldn't be able to run for several hours, and I didn't know if I dared to wait that long. There's nothing like a seven-mile run to relieve stress, and right now I was in need of some relief.

I'd suffered more than three hours this morning with Police Chief Eugene Smedley, Findlay's finest. Man of intelligence and wit, reason and logic. It would be nice, I thought, if I could bury the entire experience in some unobtrusive niche behind my left ear.

"I have a town witness prepared to swear under oath she observed the aforementioned decedent tugging at both ripcords prior to impact."

Police Chief Eugene Smedley actually said it like that.

We were in his small bare office, and I was sitting on a hard metallic chair. Its left front leg came up shorter than the other three, causing it to wobble whenever I shifted my weight.

I explained Lonny Carmichael's last jump to him a second time, exactly as I saw it. But before I could finish, he slammed his hand down on his desk. "Who you trying to shield, anyway?"

That's when I began to realize he honestly believed I was lying.

I knew none of those whuffos had seen Carmichael "tugging at both ripcords." But what could I tell Smedley? That his townsperson had imagined it?

"Your witness was mistaken," I said carefully. "Carmichael was unconscious, and I don't think any of the spectators saw him bounce."

"Bounce?"

"Uh . . . impacted with the earth. It's a skydiving term."

"You skydivers always so disrespectful to the dead?"

I wasn't just a liar; I was a disrespectful liar. My reputation was slipping fast.

The relationship between jumpers and most everybody else can be a precarious thing, a tipsy seesaw that never stays in the same place very long. Like any group, we have our allotment of slimeballs and scalawags to balance out our paragons and angels, with the vast majority falling somewhere in between. But because we leap out of airplanes and call it fun, we're viewed with suspicion by the average joe on the street, whose perception of us can swing from one extreme to the other in response to a single person or event. A renegade jump by a publicity-seeking rogue into a televised sporting event, for example, can quickly obliterate years of public relations work by well-intentioned jumpers. But all we can do is wait it out, till the next person or event comes along and makes us all heroes.

The door knob turned, and the man who'd been with Police Chief Smedley out at the airport on Saturday walked in. He was clutching the middle of a two-by-three-foot cardboard box with his left arm. He latched the door, then turned toward me and held out his hand.

"Officer Davidson," he said.

"Chance." I shook his hand. "Police Chief Smedley here asked me to make a statement regarding the fatality out at the airport."

"Yes, I know."

His strong but noncontentious grip matched his appearance. He was tall, medium built, with an athletic chest that was not overdone. He had smooth, cleanshaven skin and brown eyes. On top, healthy auburn hair combed off to one side. A portrait that dropped hints of belonging to a former high school quarterback, not quite thirty.

He eased the box onto Smedley's desk. Inside was a complete parachute rig, property of the Lonny Carmichael estate, I assumed.

Davidson picked the rig out of the box, cradling it the way a parent might a sleeping child, and deposited it with the same sort of care on an empty table across the room.

Smedley strolled over to the table and lit a cigar. Davidson took his cue and backed off.

"If Carmichael never activated either parachute, as you're claiming, then why were both activated when we found him?"

"That's nylon," I said. "You should never smoke near any parachute equipment."

My remark annoyed him, but he did move his cigar away from the rig.

"You didn't answer my question. You big-time city folk think you can pull one over on a small-town cop, don't you?"

I tried to remember the last time I'd been called city folk. Or big time.

"Don't think I don't know something's going on," he said seriously.

I was lost. "Exactly what are you implying?"

He pointed his cigar at me. "Like maybe you guys got a secret deal going with the manufacturer of this equipment to hush up the real reason Carmichael died, so they don't get sued. You know conspiracy's a crime, don't you?"

"There's been no—"

"You really think I'm stupid, don't you? Well, I've been doing some checking. You riggers and operators have business dealings with parachute manufacturers—distributing their gear, things like that. Am I right?"

"Some do. I don't."

In the fluorescent light of his office Smedley's eyes gleamed green, like perfectly cut emeralds. "Buckwater's staff deals Courier parachutes, the very brand Carmichael died using. The one you say he never activated."

I said I hadn't known that, but anyway it wouldn't change the way Carmichael had died.

Smedley refused to listen. He went on and on about all the research he'd done on the skydiving industry and how conspiracy's a crime and did I want to change my story.

When reason fails, opt for silence. That was the conclusion I'd reached after years of convoluted conversations with a manic but not-at-all depressed aunt.

Smedley strutted over to the other side of the room and spoke to Davidson. "How about this," he said. "Our expert here clammed up on us."

Davidson used the occasion to move back over to the table. He surveyed the rig with his eyes.

"Do you have another explanation for Carmichael's open parachutes?" he said to me without looking up. The words came straight and without insinuation.

I glanced across the room at Smedley. He smiled and invited me to take the floor. He was so sure he was right.

I got up from my chair and went over to the table. Smedley came back and stood beside Davidson. I examined the rig carefully.

The binding tape outlining the container, the harness webbing, and the thick thread that held it all together were cerulean blue, the container fabric flamingo pink. It was, as Smedley indicated, a Courier, manufactured by Parachutes International, one of the most reputable companies in the business. Except for the splattered dark-brown stains that had been blood red when wet, the rig appeared normal. One that I or any other jumper wouldn't hesitate to trust on the next jump.

I used the rig to demonstrate. I started with the main deployment system, because that's where Lonny Carmichael would have begun had he attempted to pull.

"Your witness was wrong about several things," I said. "For starters, modern main parachutes don't have ripcords. That's the old military surplus gear she's thinking of. These days we deploy our mains by tossing a small nylon and mesh pilot chute into the relative wind—the sort of wind you feel when you stick your hand out of a Ferrari doing one twenty down the road. Not real wind, wind only relative to the moving object. This pilot chute is usually stowed outside the container in a pouch on the back right leg strap because it's easy to reach there." I pointed to the pilot chute and pouch on Carmichael's gear.

"A bridle cord connects the pilot chute to the top of the main canopy. It's usually about seven feet long and has about a foot of Velcro stitched along the middle."

I showed them.

"When the main parachute is packed, the pilot chute end of the bridle is tucked into the pilot chute pouch and the middle section is Velcroed to the outside of the rig. The other end leads to the pack opening for the main parachute. The main is packed in its deployment bag, which is packed into the main container, which rests in the small of a jumper's back."

I held up the curved metal pin attached to the canopy end of the bridle. With my other hand I pointed to a broken nickel-sized loop sewn to the bottom closing flap on the container.

"See this pin? It's inserted into this loop after the loop is threaded through the metal grommets in the three other flaps. That's what holds the parachute in place."

Davidson was nodding, but Smedley was impatient. What did all this bull and malarkey have to do with Carmichael. I shot him a rude glower, and, to my surprise, he shut up.

"When a jumper lets go of the pilot chute, it's caught by the relative wind. The jumper continues to fall, and the force of the air speed rips the Velcro apart, stretches the bridle taut, and pulls the pin. The flaps of the container open, and the bag that holds the canopy pops out.

"Suspension lines lead from the canopy toward the jumper. The lines are attached with connector links to risers, which are connected to both sides of the harness at the clavicle area. When the rig is packed, the risers rest back over the shoulders and run down along the sides of the reserve container at the shoulder blades to the main container below. The suspension lines are gathered neatly and stowed from side to side in these rubber bands hooked to the outside of the canopy bag."

I held up Carmichael's bag. It was made of a bright-red material that clashed with his flamingo-pink container.

"Returning to the deployment sequence," I said. "When the bag catches air, the lines unravel stow by stow, the last one in place being the first one released. When the final stow is out, the canopy pulls out of its bag and fills with air. That's when the jumper experiences opening shock. The bag itself is attached to the bridle and rests on top the canopy."

Smedley inhaled on his cigar. "So what's the point? Since when are we taking parachute lessons? So what if the witness was mistaken about the ripcord. You can't ignore the fact the parachute is sitting in front of us activated."

I could see a look of comprehension pass over Davidson's face. He knew what I was about to say.

"Chief Smedley, when you found the container it was open, is that correct?"

"It is."

"And where was the pilot chute?"

"Inside . . ." He stopped.

I finished the sentence. "Inside its pouch. Lonny Carmichael never pulled his main."

He paused and thought for several minutes. Then he said, "Maybe one of you skydivers shoved it back in the pocket before we got there."

I wasn't prepared to respond to a remark like that. Fortunately, I didn't have to.

Davidson said, "If Carmichael never pulled the pilot chute, how do you explain the open container?"

"That sort of thing can happen on impact, especially if the jumper hits at terminal velocity, which Carmichael did. That's a hundred twenty miles an hour. The force generated by that kind of speed is more than capable of popping the container open. If the pin had been pulled while Carmichael was still falling, the line stows would have unraveled—they're only held with rubber bands. You can see that not a single stow came undone."

Smedley said, "That could have been fixed, too, just like that pilot chute."

Davidson said, "What about the second parachute—I believe you called it the reserve? Its deployment design looks different."

"That's right. The reserve pilot chute is spring-loaded and packed inside the reserve container, and the reserve deployment bag detaches on opening. That way, if the reserve pilot chute entangles with the main, the reserve canopy still has a chance of inflating. Also, the reserve *does* have a ripcord. The handle is kept in a pocket on the left-hand side of the harness."

I picked up Carmichael's rig by the left webbing and pointed out the components that made up the ripcord.

"A steel cable is connected to the ripcord handle, with either one or two pins swaged to the other end of it, depending on the container model. Carmichael's has one pin. Like the main pin, it holds the reserve flaps shut. The cable is threaded through this metal housing that runs up over the left shoulder to the reserve container."

Davidson pointed to a button-sized seal hanging by a thread from Carmichael's reserve pin. "What's this?" he asked.

"It's a rigger's seal. Whenever a rigger packs a reserve, he seals it with his three-letter ID. It's just held there by thread. It doesn't inhibit deployment."

"And you're saying the reserve pin was also released with the force of impact?"

I nodded. "It's the only explanation. The bag is still in the container, the suspension lines are still stowed in the rubber bands, and the ripcord is still in its housing."

But Police Chief Eugene Smedley was not convinced. "You people had time alone with this gear before we got there," he said. "You could have rigged it up like this."

"Could have," I admitted, "but didn't. I saw Lonny Carmichael fall. He wasn't tugging at his gear—his arms were out in front. The guy following him out of the plane says he heard a bump when Carmichael exited, so it's reasonable to assume he hit his head."

"I've talked to a skydiver who says different," Smedley said.

"Oh?" I hadn't expected that. "Who?"

"A guy named Daniel Grimes. He says Carmichael couldn't have hit his head."

I sighed. "Danny was a close friend of Carmichael's and obviously upset. He was talking figuratively when he said that. I don't think he'd dispute the fact that Carmichael never pulled."

"That *is* true, Gene," Davidson admitted. "I already asked him."

Smedley's green eyes suddenly turned black, and he glared at Davidson. "Whose side you on?"

So that was it. There were battle lines drawn here. Unfortunately, I had no idea what the war was all about. What I did know was that I had no intention of getting caught in the cross-fire.

It wasn't until an hour later that I was free to leave. Smedley seemed to be taking a personal interest in Lonny Carmichael, and he'd requested another go at each detail. He was fishing for something. Anything. I finally suggested he call the United States Parachute Association in Washington for a recommendation on another *expert*. I made it clear to him I didn't want that distinction anymore. This fatality was none of my business.

I found myself looking over toward the hangar. Twig's pickup was parked behind it, and his Beech sat closed up in front. The Cessnas were tied down along the far side. About seventy-five yards beyond the Beech, Dominic Salvino had parked Satin Cruise. At the moment he was perched on a ladder under the right engine.

"Didn't know you were still here."

I turned my head.

Macintosh had stumbled out of his van. He was carrying a towel and a change of clothes. His knotted hair and half-closed face probably meant he'd just woken up.

"I won't be staying much longer," I said. "What about you and Cheeks?"

"Huh?" he said, still not quite conscious.

"Now that the Indy Five-hundred and the boogie are both over, I suppose you'll be going back to California."

He used his fingers to force his eyelids up. "Yeah," he said. "I'm leaving as soon as I wake up. Cheeks is already gone. I took him to the airport in Indianapolis last night so he could get back to work. He's pretty high up."

"What does he do?" I asked, because the flow of the conversation seemed to warrant it.

"International salesman," Macintosh said, coming quickly to life. "Works in the airplane parts business. They market all over the world, and he travels an awful lot." This obviously impressed Macintosh, a young salesman himself.

"So you made the drive out here to Indiana all by yourself?"

"Yeah. It was my first real trip in the van. I worked a lot of weekends last month, so I had comp time coming, but Cheeks couldn't take much time off. He flew in Friday, sacked out in my van over the weekend, then had to get right back."

Macintosh seemed quite honored that Cheeks had chosen his van to bunk down in.

"Those sure were some good skydives we did this weekend," Macintosh said. "All those points."

"Not bad," I agreed.

"Well," he said a little awkwardly, "if you ever make it out to California, we jump at Ridgeway, north of Los Angeles. Good weather all year."

He seemed to be trying to thank me for jumping with him. "Maybe I'll get out there this fall," I said, and made a mental note of the place.

Macintosh nodded, then his eyes came alive again. "I hear they're going to make some big formations at the Nationals boogie this year."

"They usually do."

"You going?"

"Uh-huh."

"Then I'll see you there," he said. "I'm gonna try to lurk on some of those big loads. Cheeks put in a good word for me with The Pit Bull yesterday. And maybe you and I can make some jumps together too, with people you know. It'll be my first Nationals, and I won't know anybody."

"Sure," I said. "Remind me when the time comes."

He gave me the thumbs up, then slipped into the loft. I went over to my tent and changed into my running shorts and shoes. Pacing myself at eight-minute miles, I circled the airport, ran north along the outer road for half an hour, then retraced my steps. When I returned, the Honda had the entire parking lot to itself.

I was sitting at the picnic table finishing off two turkey sandwiches I'd bought in town when Twig drove up in his car.

He'd held himself aloof from everybody Sunday and yesterday. Except for breaking up the Danny Death-Alex Laird fight, he hadn't spoken a word beyond what was necessary to keep the planes flying.

We made fifteen minutes of small talk before he said, "The autopsy tests came back on Carmichael. They didn't find anything."

"That's what most people seemed to expect."

"I guess." His voice sounded miles away.

"I examined his gear this morning," I said. "As we thought, he never pulled either his main or his reserve."

Twig was the last person I wanted to unburden my morning to, but I thought he should have some idea of what Smedley was thinking. "I suppose you know Carmichael's rig was a Courier."

Twig didn't see the connection. "So?"

"Your Police Chief Smedley is intrigued by the fact that your staff deals for Parachutes International."

Twig closed his eyes. "Smedley's way off base. That's Ken Popadowski he's referring to."

"Well, at least one person from town claims she saw Carmichael struggling with both parachutes. Smedley's trying to put some stock in that."

Twig didn't seem surprised. "Smedley would be inclined to," he said.

"Why do you say that?"

He shrugged. "Last year he went to the farmers around here and tried to get them to file complaints about skydivers landing in their fields. They wouldn't, though. With the students using squares now, they don't land off the airport like they used to. So Smedley started harassing any jumper he'd see in town. We try to keep our distance from him."

"What does he have against skydivers?"

"Don't really know."

"You haven't asked him about it?"

Twig nodded wearily. "Tried to once. He wouldn't go into it. But the way he talked made me think it might have something to do with his son Kyle."

"How's that?"

"Oh, the kid hung out here at the airport a few years back. Kyle had no quarrel with us; he even considered jumping. But he was big and didn't want to risk injury—he had a football scholarship to some college. He was a little boisterous, even got into a scuffle with Alex Laird once, but basically he was an okay kid. I never saw him after that summer. I assume he went off to college, but I don't really know."

Twig had been peering down through the slats between the picnic table boards. He looked up, and I could see he wanted to talk about something else. "You available the week after the Fourth of July?"

I thought ahead. The Nationals boogie would be held over the Fourth, the Nationals relative work competition after that. I had no particular desire to watch the competition. "I don't have anything definite," I said. "Why?"

"I'm expecting a large group of kids that week for a special first-jump course. They're from the university downstate. It'll be too much to schedule them for the weekend, so I'm planning to do half on Thursday, the other half on Friday. All my instructors and jump-masters work their regular jobs during the week, which puts me in a bind."

"Consider me signed on," I said, and not only for the money. Teaching kids I enjoyed. Their fears of the sky haven't yet solidified, and consequently they tend to relax and perform better than more mature adults.

"We'll have to use the old round T-10s," Twig said. "The eight student square chutes I have won't be enough without people here to repack them. You still remember how to teach jumping with rounds?"

"I don't like to, but I can."

"Me neither," he said. "But there's no other way to do it. I'll have a pilot lined up, and Josie, the university club president, will be here. She can work the landings."

Like me, Twig had always liked teaching kids, but today he showed no enthusiasm at all as he talked about the class. His voice was mechanical, as though he'd consider the class a success if he could just get the job done. I tried not to worry about him too much. Without his say-so, I couldn't do anything to help him get back on track after his first fatality. It would be up to him to accomplish that himself.

Out near the runway, Dominic Salvino had descended his ladder and was walking toward us.

Dominic was about five seven, stout but not fleshy. He had black curly hair, a wispy beard, and short stubby fingers stained dark, like those of any self-respecting mechanic.

There wasn't a better pilot/mechanic in skydiving than Dominic Salvino. Some were as good, but none better. He had learned his craft in Vietnam during the last years of the war. He was a remote, stoic person who never bothered anyone and seldom let anyone bother him. Whether he was the same before Vietnam, no one knew. He never mentioned family, and only his native pronunciation of the Mardi Gras city told you where he came from. A loner. Small airports across the country are littered with people like us.

He acknowledged Twig, but had come to speak to me.

"Got any plans?"

It was a question I liked hearing from the owner of Satin Cruise.

"What did you have in mind?"

"I've had a pilot from Illinois flying right seat for me since I came north from Florida, but I'll be going east on Tuesday and he doesn't want to travel that far. Also, Newt's preoccupied with his photography business and hasn't really helped me with maintenance since Easter. I've been trying to get my regular copilot up from Florida to replace the both of them, but he won't be available till just before Nationals." Dominic paused. "You could add to your flying time. As for maintenance work, I pay by the hour, if you're interested."

I was. I'd only ever flown right seat in Satin Cruise twice before, so the opportunity to do it for a whole month was something I couldn't pass up.

"I don't have much mechanical experience on airplanes," I warned.

"Neither did Newt when he first started. What I really need is two extra hands."

"You sure Newt won't mind?"

"It was him who suggested you."

"Then it's settled," I said. "Which drop zones?"

"This week Oakland Ridge, Ohio. Following two weeks Litchfield, Pennsylvania. Then to Farmersville, Ohio, the week before Nationals." Twig wandered over to his hangar, and Dominic and I talked compensation. Besides the flying, there would be under-the-table cash for maintenance work with a guaranteed minimum that both of us could live with.

Dominic had already arranged for a local pilot he knew to fly right seat for the trip to Ohio. The pilot arrived within the hour, and the three of us loaded up all the spare parts for Satin Cruise. Then they and photographer Newt Becker—who surfaced via a hitchhiked ride a scant fifteen minutes before take off—lifted into the sky and headed east.

Dominic had elevated my spirits tenfold. From Police Chief Eugene Smedley to the Satin Cruise DC-3 in little more than twenty-four hours . . . I couldn't have asked for a more radical shift in my fortunes than that.

I was to meet up with the plane tomorrow in Oakland Ridge, Ohio, a place I knew well. I'd made my first jump there nine years ago, one day after graduating from the Poly Sci Department at Ohio State. My home town of New Hope was only ten bird-miles from the drop zone, and after that first jump I'd wondered how this sort of thing could have gone on so near for so long without my knowledge. I went on to make four hundred more jumps over the next fourteen months, before flying east to law school.

I had fond memories of my first year jumping. I'd learned on clunky military equipment, standard student gear back then. There wasn't much in the way of canopy control with those monstrous T-10s, but my instructors and jumpmasters had been enthusiastic and forgiving. I chuckled to myself as I thought about all my cornfield landings. Arriving back at the clubhouse with enough ears in my chute to take care of dinner.

I skipped over to my tent. As of this minute, I thought, I'm starting my future all over again. I'm going to forget my ruined holiday weekend sans Eleanor. I'm going to forget Danny Death, Alex Laird,

Police Chief Eugene Smedley, and the whole damned controversy surrounding Lonny Carmichael's death.

During the next month, I'm going to fly Satin Cruise right seat. I'm going read good books, eat good food, run good miles, make a little money on the side. And then I'm going cap off the month with a Fourth of July weekend at the National Skydiving Championships in Muskogee, Oklahoma. Eleanor will be there, and we'll spend a pleasant weekend together in freefall and in lust. By the time I return here next month to work the class of students, Twig will have bounced back from his temporary depression and I'll be a contented man.

I got ready to leave Indiana with the eagerness of a teen going off to first-year college. I energetically repacked my reserve—for real this time. I called Eleanor's telephone mailbox and left an entertaining message that included details of my itinerary for the next month. Then I zipped into town for some food. What remained of the day I spent maintaining my bike.

By the time I decamped early Wednesday I couldn't have been more optimistic.

Or more wrong.

Part Two

NATIONALS

7

On Wednesday the temperature was in the upper seventies and the sky was once again blue. A few puffy clouds followed me as I headed for Oakland Ridge, Ohio, but none carried rain for the farmers.

I spent most of the four-hour trip staring into the sun and reminiscing about my first year skydiving. The reminiscing made the trip short. Before I knew it the Honda was gliding over a familiar macadam straightaway, uniquely named Airport Road. A quarter-mile from the drop zone clubhouse my nostalgic thoughts were bluntly interrupted by a man lying face down in the middle of the road.

I recognized the gangly arms and the long thin feet. They belonged to a shadow box puppet named Jeepers. They belonged to freefall photographer Newt Becker.

I screeched to a stop. Jolly good, I thought. Well, jeepers, there 'tis.

I wasn't going crazy. That was how Jeepers would end each of his parables on justice and fair play: Jolly good. Well, jeepers, there 'tis. Then, after a histrionic bow to his juvenile fans, the long-limbed creature with the distinctive stoop would hunch his way toward the left wing of the stage. And a forlorn little boy from New Hope, Ohio, would hunch his way from the puppeted world of make-believe to another, less enchanting, booth at the county fair. And wait for next year.

I hadn't thought about that farewell line in centuries. But here I was, back in my childhood haunts in southern Ohio not far from the county fair grounds; and there Newt Becker was, his gangly look-alike arms and his long thin feet clearly visible. It was a coincidence powerful enough to trigger Jeepers's trademark slogan, tearing it from its submerged cubbyhole in my memory and tossing it into the passing breeze.

Newt's arms were folded above his head. I bent down, then carefully rolled him over and found his artery. His pulse was strong. I observed his chest. He was taking the deep, even breaths of a person asleep.

I surveyed his body. Nothing appeared broken, though much was contused. His face was swollen, and his left eye had turned the darker colors of autumn. His left eyebrow and right forearm were lacerated and sticky with blood. I sniffed his breath. Just normal breath.

"Newt?"

No response.

"Newt?" This time I included a gentle shake.

His lashes twitched. Then he was gazing up at me blankly.

"Did I—Did I—bounce?"

"Oh, you bounced all right. And now you're lying in front of the Pearly Gates and must account for all your earthly sins."

He swiveled his head counterclockwise, frightened until it came to him that I was joshing. But he still strained to put himself in context.

"You're in Oakland Ridge, Ohio," I said. "In the middle of Airport Road."

He looked up at me blankly again. "What the hell am I doing in the middle of the road?"

"That's what I was about to ask you."

His eyes latched onto the Honda, standing behind me, and his mouth widened with sudden inspiration. "Did I fall off your bike?"

"Afraid you can't blame the Honda, Newt. I only pulled in from Findlay a few minutes ago. I found you here in a heap and unconscious."

His mouth twisted and his eyes grew small. "What are *you* doing here?"

I squinted at him. "Dominic hired me for the next few weeks to help out with Satin Cruise. He said it was your idea."

Newt seemed confused, but nodded. Just then a red-tailed hawk working the meadow to our left let out a high-pitched scream, startling him.

"It's just a hawk," I said. "Over there in the field."

He nodded again, relieved.

"So back to your question," I said. "What the hell are you doing in the middle of the road?"

By now he was more alert; he was capable of thinking, not merely reacting. His facial muscles tightened in concentration, as though he were rewinding his memory. After a minute he appeared to pause, study a particular frame, then continue on. He did this three times before the muscles in his face loosened perceptibly. It would have been obvious to even the dense of mind that he'd figured it out, but he didn't feel obliged to share it with me.

He got up slowly, carefully. Then he asked if I'd give him a lift. After rearranging my sleeping bag on the Honda, I eased him onto the passenger seat. Against his objections, I slipped my spare helmet over his head before transporting him the quarter-mile to the clubhouse.

The Oakland Ridge Parachute Club, located at the Oakland Ridge Airport, was a nonprofit organization run for the benefit of its members. As such, it was a much smaller operation than Twig's commercial center. A rickety old house trailer, gutted to make room for two forty-foot rigging tables, served as the core of the clubhouse. For zoning reasons, it had no plumbing facilities.

Onto the end nearest the trailer entrance the club had added a tiny bunkhouse. They called it The Suite—someone's idea of humor. The spartan room had in it eight hard wooden slabs stacked four high on either side. Insulation hung down from the ceiling, and when the heavens opened up it wasn't just the pounding on the roof that told you it was raining.

At the steps of the trailer Newt pressed his weight against my back and worked himself off the Honda. He handed me my spare helmet, then practiced his balance while I parked.

The drop zone had no official lot for vehicles, but it was accepted practice to park in a spread of crabgrass fifty yards from the trailer. A dull-red VW bug that the club lent out-of-town visitors was sitting there. At least twenty years old, it lacked an outside mirror and its rear bumper was all but off. I pulled in next to it.

Inside the clubhouse, Newt took four painful steps toward one of the rigging tables. He leaned one of his hands against the table for stability, reached down, and pulled a heavily decaled cooler into the middle of the floor. He flipped up the lid. Inside were two empty beer cans and four inches of water.

"This was here when we flew in yesterday," he said. "Left over from the weekend."

He jettisoned the beer cans into the trash, then used the water to wash and soak his wounds. By the decisive manner in which he turned his back to me, I gathered my assistance was no longer required. Or at least no longer desired.

I wandered through the trailer. Nothing had changed in the three years since I'd been back. Clumps of dust, dead flies, and parts of former dead flies crowded the window indentations that substituted for sills. Old military gear still cluttered the shelves beneath the packing tables. There was no video equipment anywhere in sight. A television set, black and white and small, and a pay telephone were the luxury items here.

I poked my head into The Suite. The top slabs were empty, but on the bottom slabs and the floor were what had to be Newt's belongings—lots of camera equipment—strewn about. Pieces of clothing and rolls of film intermingled freely. There was an empty gray suitcase sitting on one of the bottom bunks. Newt's green skydiving gear took up the other bottom bunk. His sleeping bag was unzipped and lying on the floor. Beside it were two dumbbells.

Newt had never been known for his neatness, but before today I wouldn't have thought to call him a slob.

I left The Suite and slipped down to the other end of the trailer. On the wall was tacked an edge-worn poster that had been in that exact same spot the day I took my first-jump course. It featured a symmetrically perfect skygod tracking on a forty-five degree incline of atmospheric resistance. Seeing it again rekindled in me the performance anxiety of my student days, when I had sought to emulate him.

Newt staggered up next to me, his cuts and bruises wet but clean. After thanking me for the lift to the clubhouse, he moved his eyes away from mine and fixed them on the poster. He said he now remembered what he was doing out on Airport Road. He said he'd taken a walk toward the intersection to get some fresh air, to recover from some heavy drinking. He said two cars—one southbound, the other northbound—passed each other. He said because the road was narrow the southbound car veered off the shoulder to avoid sideswiping the northbound car, and accidentally brushed him. He said that's why he was lying out there unconscious.

I allowed for a spasm of quiet.

"You were in the middle of the road, Newt. A car would have thrown you into the roadside ditch."

"I crawled there afterwards," he said. "I remember that much. I was trying to get up, but—I guess I passed out."

I pointed out that what he'd just described was hit and run, a criminal offense, by the way. He shrugged, and my feeble point crashed dead between his long thin feet.

"No serious harm done," he replied. "Only bruises and the like. The driver doesn't even know about it, I bet. It was the rear fender of the car that nicked me, and not hard or I wouldn't be here."

Just then Dominic Salvino came into the trailer. He made straight for the catch-all tool cabinet near the entrance to The Suite, unlatched the cabinet door, and began rummaging through the shelves. Deep in thought, he failed to notice us until Newt's feet scuffed the floor.

Dominic glanced over his shoulder. His eyes showed definite surprise, but whether it was from my presence or Newt's appearance, I couldn't tell.

"Look who came from Indiana," Newt said a shade too casually.

There followed an awkward moment. Dominic seemed ready to remark on something, only to change his mind after Newt shot a determined stare at him. A "later" type of stare. There was unspoken tension between them.

Dominic gave me a short nod of welcome and turned back to the cabinet. From the bottom shelf he yanked out a wrench. He flipped it over in the palm of his hand a few times and seemed satisfied. Then he left the clubhouse and went back to Satin Cruise, which was basking in the sun a hundred fifty yards away. Newt followed along behind him.

I wondered if this was "later."

I went outside and pitched my tent. My thigh muscles were cramping from the four hours on the road. I changed clothes and shoes, stretched, and ran out to Sinking Spring Road, which intersected Airport Road north of the drop zone. Its shoulders were flat and wide, ideal for cross-country running.

I headed east. I ran and ran and ran and ran—eleven miles in all. The run helped to pound out the annoying leg cramps, but not the uneasiness my first hour in Oakland Ridge had brought.

I washed in the bathroom over at the airport office, then turned my attention to my running clothes. Hand-washing cotton and polypro goes only so far, and no matter how many times I soaped and rinsed my shorts and socks, they continued to give off that slightly rank odor that comes from weeks and weeks of absorbing human sweat. I'd have to think about finding a commercial laundry soon.

After spacing my laundry over the Honda's handlebars to dry, I went into the trailer. Dominic was shutting the door to the tool cabinet. I asked about the Indiana pilot who'd flown right seat in Satin Cruise. Dominic said the guy had a friend pick him up early yesterday.

Newt was resting his battered body on his sleeping bag, now rolled out over one of The Suite's hard wooden slabs. Next to him he had a case of video cassettes. He had organized his belongings, separating camera gear from clothing, clothing from parachute gear. His suitcase was on the bunk below him. On the floor he had pinned his two dumbbells between his shoes.

"Anybody hungry?" Newt piped up.

Forty-five minutes later Dominic, Newt, and I were sharing a booth at a local diner. The waitress brought Newt's soup. A little later bread and salads for Newt and for me. Then my spaghetti, Dominic's double burger and fries, and Newt's T-bone steak.

Newt's left eye was almost totally black and his face was puffed out on that side. His mood was incongruously cheerful. He seemed quite pleased with himself, and he channeled his personal excitement into a lively monologue on next month's competition at Nationals.

"No question the Golden Knights will be repeat champions in both four-way and eight-way," he predicted. "The competition isn't there this year for the gold."

The Golden Knights belonged to the Army. They jumped from airplanes and helicopters and practiced for competition as part of their military duty. As the only enduring professional relative work team in America, they seldom had difficulty outclassing their amateur competitors.

"But Octagon has the best chance for the silver in eight-way," Newt said with certainty. "I've heard the California teams' practice scores, and they don't match Octagon's. Of course, anything can happen in competition, but we got the definite edge for second place."

Octagon was made up of eight jumpers from the Chicago area who were regulars at Eleanor's home drop zone in Sullivan, Illinois. During March and April they had taken off work and practiced at Satin Cruise's winter home in Fort Crystal, Florida. When Dominic ferried the plane north after Easter, the team hopped aboard and returned to Sullivan. Newt had been taping Octagon's practice dives almost from the beginning, hence the "we" business.

In March, I'd passed through Fort Crystal en route to my South Carolina hangar job, and had joined three members of Octagon on several four-way dives. If their flying ability represented the level of the entire team, Newt wasn't exaggerating about their chances at Nationals: they knew what they were doing.

Newt dragged his analysis through a chocolate sundae. My interest in competition was superficial at best. Dominic, who as far as anyone knew had never voluntarily jumped out of a plane (a bailout in Vietnam didn't count), munched on a second order of fries. Absorbed in his own chatter, Newt never picked up on the fact that we were both a little bored.

Then, after more than an hour of competition this and competition that, Newt nonchalantly informed us that he probably wouldn't be going to Oklahoma next month. Something major had sprung up unexpectedly, and it looked like he'd be back home in Florida by the time Nationals came around.

Dominic merely wiped his napkin over his beard. I couldn't get any reading on his thoughts.

When we got up to leave, Newt insisted on paying the bill for all of us. Outside, he claimed the VW for the rest of the day. He climbed in, issued us a cheery "Have fun—I intend to," and took off. Dominic and I made our way back to the drop zone on the Honda.

In the trailer, Dominic paged through the latest issue of *Trade-A-Plane*. I snacked on fruit that I'd brought with me from Indiana, and tried to decide how best to proceed.

It seemed like days ago, but it was only this morning that I'd eagerly left Indiana for my job with Satin Cruise. As I'd envisioned it, my month with the plane would be one of pure pleasure—nothing complicated, nothing tangled. I mind my business, everybody else minds his.

The fallacy in this fantasy, of course, is that individual concerns aren't neatly compartmented into exclusive categories with absolute labels such as YOURS and MINE. In a world with more than five billion people, the overlapping of personal interests is inevitable, and in order to mind your own business sometimes it becomes necessary to poke your nose into someone else's. I was, at the moment, feeling the urge to poke.

We were each sitting on one of the rigging tables. I said, "Newt didn't seem to know I was coming, Dominic."

Dominic glanced up at me, then set *Trade-A-Plane* aside. He reached one of his mechanic's hands down to a blue gym bag on the floor and pulled it up next to him. From it he took a meerschaum pipe that was his habit to smoke. He tucked the bowl into his palm, then swept the inside of the bag with his fingers. When I saw that he'd located his tobacco pouch, I turned and opened a window.

"Sorry," he said with sincerity, and started to put the pipe away.

Considerate smoke I'd always found more tolerable than the inconsiderate and arrogant kind. Besides, since it was *I* who wanted some answers from *him*, it was better not to be too fussy. "The window will take care of it," I assured him.

Dominic began his ritual stuffing of the bowl. The ritual, I sensed, was the real reason he put up with the rest of it.

"Dominic, I'm not one to step in on someone else's job. If Newt resents my being here—"

He shook his head as he lit the bowl. "It *was* Newt's idea for you to come. He didn't know anything definite, though, because I hadn't talked with him since Monday."

"But—" I started to say, then thought better of it. Dominic and Newt had flown here together from Findlay and had spent most of yesterday all by themselves. You'd think Dominic would at least have mentioned my coming.

Instead I said, "The two of you talked out by Satin Cruise today."

He drew on his pipe, then exhaled. "You're reading the situation all wrong."

I peeled another banana. After eating it I said, "Mind if I ask you something else?"

His nod wasn't a yes and it wasn't a no.

"Did Newt explain his cuts and bruises to you?"

Dominic tapped the end of his pipe on his lips in a gesture of deep thought. "Hit by a car," he said.

I looked at him quizzically. "Do you really believe that?"

There was a pause. Then, "He says he was hit by a car."

Someone once remarked that Dominic's initials stood for deaf and silent.

"Boxing bruises, no broken bones—that doesn't jibe with a hit by a moving vehicle, Dominic. And that's not all. Newt told me he'd gone out along the road to walk off a hangover. But I took a whiff of his breath while he was unconscious. He hadn't been drinking."

There was a prolonged period during which neither of us spoke. I didn't know Dominic well. No one did. He never talked about himself, and for the most part he maintained that same policy with regard to everyone else. Unless you were prepared to discuss matters of aviation, carrying on an involved conversation with him was all but impossible. He drew several times on his pipe and was silent for such a long time that I expected nothing more from him. So he caught me off guard when he said, "Newt asked me to back up the story he gave you, in case you asked. That's why he cornered me out at the plane."

"Why would he ask you to do that?"

"So you would lay off."

"I'm only interested if it affects me."

"It doesn't."

"Then I take it you know the real story."

Dominic considered his options before shaking his head. "Newt slipped out sometime around five this morning. The next time I saw him he was standing in here next to you."

I remembered that the VW bug had been parked on the crabgrass when I arrived. "You mean Newt left on foot?"

Again Dominic shook his head. "When he went, he drove off in the VW. I was in Satin Cruise—heard him go."

Dominic always slept in his plane when he took it on the road. There was a rumor he owned a tent, but I had never seen it, didn't even know what color it was.

"I heard the bug come back about an hour later," he went on. "When I got up at eight, the car was here with the keys in the ignition, but no Newt."

"And he hasn't explained?"

Dominic drew on his pipe twice, then tapped his lips with the mouthpiece. Finally he said, "No real reason he should. We don't talk much these days."

Dominic had been flying jumpers for about fifteen years, and for the last eight or ten he and Newt had been more or less affiliated. As I understood it, their business relationship had evolved naturally from the fact that they lived near each other outside Fort Crystal,

81

Florida, and that whenever Dominic needed an extra hand Newt always seemed to have one available to lend.

"Isn't that new?" I said.

Again Dominic drew on his pipe before responding.

"Newt's been different this year."

"How so?"

"For one thing, he's become obsessed with muscles and money, not that he's been successful at either. For another, he's just become less cooperative than he used to be. And less predictable."

"Like when he said he wouldn't be going to Nationals?"

Dominic nodded pensively. "Like that."

The tobacco had gone out in his pipe. He carefully emptied the ashes onto a piece of thick cardboard and spread them around to cool. A large green fly that had been dancing around a naked light bulb up at the ceiling now made its way down to Dominic and began to buzz his face. He didn't even twitch.

"Back in March," I said, "when I stopped by in Florida, I got the impression Newt intended to stick with Octagon through Nationals. I thought he wanted the experience and the national exposure they could give him."

Dominic nodded. "That was my understanding. Newt had a good thing going with Octagon. They paid for his jumps and he was getting lots of video experience. Up till now his specialty has always been still photography—that's how people know him. I thought Newt was going back to Illinois with the team while I made the boogie rounds here in the East, but instead he came with me. And now there's this *accident*."

"So we agree it wasn't a car."

Dominic folded his arms. "The part about crawling out onto the road must be true. There was some traffic this morning over at the airport office before you got here. If Newt had been on the road long, somebody else would have found him first."

"And the boxing bruises?"

Dominic shrugged. "He must have been socked in the head pretty good to be out all morning."

"Drugs?" I wondered.

He shook his head. "Newt doesn't use them. I saw enough in Nam to know."

"I was thinking more along the lines of dealing."

He frowned. "Trafficking takes investment money that Newt doesn't have."

"He paid for our dinner."

But Dominic seemed sure of himself. "He can't keep that up. He sometimes sells pictures to magazines, and he used to make extra money working for me, but his bread and butter comes from filming student jumpers. Mostly they want video these days. I know roughly how many students he shoots, what he charges, and what his materials cost. The profit he makes after everything is paid for goes right back into his business, and pocket change for food. There's no money there for investing in drugs. At home Paula pays most of the bills."

Paula was Newt's independent and very beautiful wife. I'd met her last year at a surprise thirtieth birthday party he'd arranged for her, and I could still recall her image in almost every detail. A wide mouth that seemed locked into a natural smile, hair that was chestnut and thick, high cheekbones, satiny skin, brown eyes. She had a well-proportioned torso, but it was her stylishly long and slender legs that had established her as a successful fashion model in a market heavily saturated with beautiful faces and manufactured physiques.

"Will Newt be leaving for Florida soon?" I asked.

Dominic was combing his beard with his fingers. "You heard him at the restaurant," he said. "You know as much as me."

I was tempted to ask Dominic why he even bothered to keep Newt on, but I didn't.

He picked up his bag of tobacco and stuffed his pipe again, tamping it down with his thumb. He lit the bowl and began to fill me in on the status of Satin Cruise. The subject of Newt Becker seemed closed. I didn't mind at all, because I'd decided that whatever Newt's business might be, it was certainly none of mine.

In the morning the sky was low and murky gray. Dominic had to take care of some bills and bank business, so we agreed to wait till afternoon to start work on the plane.

I, too, had some errands, and I decided to get them out of the way. I mounted the Honda, left the airport, and drove up to Columbus.

My first stop was at a used book store I'd frequented during col-

lege. It hadn't changed much: it was still disheveled and disorga-
nized, an attraction for the intellectual crowd.

It used to be that when I'd come in here, I'd go straight back the
middle isle, veer north at HISTORY and POLITICS, and wind up in the
far left corner. That's where you'd find Bentham, Hegel, and Marx.
They were still there, but I wasn't. I asked the clerk for LITERATURE
and FICTION. Middle section, toward the front, arranged alphabeti-
cally by author.

At the cash register, I sold three paperbacks I'd picked up in South
Carolina and paid for three more. With only the saddlebags, the
trunk, and the tank bag for storage, building up my own library was
impossible. So I did a lot of trading. I had already walked out the
door when a copy of Beryl Markham's *West with the Night* in the
bookstore's window caught my eye. I went back in and bought it.

I drove to a laundry and washed my clothes and jumpsuit. I read
Beryl Markham while I waited for the dryer to stop. The university
students flopped in the laundry with me were very young looking.
They belong in high school, I thought.

You never notice yourself age because you remain your own constant. You only notice those around you getting younger.

Next I went to a sporting goods store, whose customers were
equally young, and paid for a pair of running shoes. Same brand,
same size, same color, a different price. This new pair would be for
running. My old running shoes I immediately relegated to everyday
wear. I donated my old old running shoes to a homeless man curled
up on the sidewalk.

The sky was still hanging low when I got back to Oakland Ridge
Airport. Dominic had returned, and the two of us got right to work
on Satin Cruise.

With considerable effort, Newt dragged himself from his bunk in
The Suite. He was obviously sore, but that didn't stop him from smil-
ing a lot and joking around. Inside the clubhouse cooler he had
stashed what was left of a case of Amstel Light that he'd bought last
night. Did Chance want to party? No thanks, but I'll take one or two
later, after work is through. Did Dominic want to party? Same as
Chance, one or two after work. No problem, Newt said. That just
leaves more for me.

Friday it rained all day. The farmers would be happy, but with no
hangar for Satin Cruise maintenance proved difficult.

Dominic thumbed through *Trade-A-Plane*. I finished *West with the*

Night, managed six wet miles along Sinking Spring Road in my new running shoes, strung a piece of suspension line inside the trailer, and hung up my laundry. In The Suite, Newt slept off a hangover.

The weekend boogie was only a partial success. The rain ended Friday night, but the overcast continued into Saturday morning and we managed only three loads late in the day. We got off eight on Sunday. Inside the plane Dominic was definitely a take-charge pilot, and except for takeoff I didn't have a whole lot to do. Still, I was grateful just to have the experience of flying right seat, and I savored every second I spent in the cockpit.

Newt whiled away the weekend in The Suite. He spent his time reviewing his video tapes on borrowed equipment and, despite his sore body, pumping iron. He didn't jump, which given his head injury was probably wise.

Monday Dominic and I did basic maintenance on Satin Cruise, and Tuesday we departed for Pennsylvania—he in the air, I on the road. I was disappointed that I couldn't fly right seat cross-country, but both Dominic and I agreed we weren't going to get the Honda into the plane. That was all right, though, because the Indiana pilot who'd helped fly Satin Cruise here was more than willing to take off work, fly to Ohio, and have a pilot friend pick him up in Pennsylvania, just for the opportunity to copilot a DC-3. And he offered to help ferry Satin Cruise again in two weeks.

Newt continued to migrate with the plane. And Dominic continued to let him.

Tiny Litchfield, Pennsylvania, might have been a mountain man's idea of paradise had the gypsy moths not passed through. The three mountains that gave defense to the village flaunted huge ugly patches of denuded trees on which leaves would never again grow. From the airport in the valley you could hear the loggers at work along the ridges and down in the hollows, salvaging what they could.

The Litchfield drop zone existed because Penn State University existed: most of its resident jumpers were associated with the school in one capacity or another. During our twelve-day stay, we flew twenty-eight loads. Perfect weather both weekends was the key. During the week in between Dominic and I repaired a leaky oil cooler in Satin Cruise's right engine and busied ourselves with other routine maintenance. Newt made a jump or two, but kept his distance from everybody.

Our last day there Eleanor called from her Sears Tower office in

Chicago. She wanted to say hi, and to let me know that her business trip to Dallas was still on. But she still didn't know if she'd be able to drive up to Nationals afterward. She sounded considerably more cheerful than she had been in Findlay, and considerably more relaxed. But I got the feeling something was still bugging her. Maybe at Nationals she'd tell me what it was.

Satin Cruise flew only two loads one week later at Farmersville, Ohio, before the storm warning. Then came two days of torrential rains. The Midwest's drought had ended and the farmers now worried about flooded crops. I slept on an old packing table at night. It was harder than the ground, but it was dry.

By Tuesday evening we had Satin Cruise all ready for Nationals. With the exception of that first day in Oakland Ridge, my month with the plane had gone without incident. Dominic had reverted back to being his old aloof self, I had spent my time running or reading or tending my laundry when not working on or copiloting Satin Cruise, and Newt had been just plain scarce. We'd all gotten along great.

I counted my money. For my menial labor I'd earned more than five hundred under-the-table dollars. When I added that to what was left over from the South Carolina hangar job, I had enough to live and skydive on for several months. Instead, I kept what I needed for the next two weeks—to last me through Twig's student class—and sent in four payments on my student loan.

On Sunday, Dominic's regular copilot had arrived from Florida. He would help fly Satin Cruise to Oklahoma. Late Monday Newt had announced that he'd changed his mind, and he too would be going with the plane to Nationals.

I barely gave Newt's announcement much thought. Whatever he was up to, I was convinced it was none of my business.

8

Davis Field was situated five miles south of Muskogee, Oklahoma, just off Route Sixty-four. A tilting model airplane, painted dull white and lettered with U.S. AIRFORCE, marked the airport's entrance. At the model airplane, I turned left.

A half-mile in on my left was a large fenced-in soccer complex with a parking lot in front. On my right was Muskogee's National Guard Armory, where the annual Riggers Conference would take place starting tomorrow. I'd probably end up there.

Continuing east, there was a hayfield on my left with a drainage ditch that knifed through its middle. An unpaved farm lane after that. Beyond the Armory on my right were acres and acres of green that with the addition of a few sand traps could be golf course rough. This was Davis Field. A seventy-two-hundred-foot runway was invisible except from the air.

Where the airport road met the unpaved farm lane it turned right ninety degrees. Around the bend, another field to the east. On my right, lots of grass. Then hangars, a restaurant, the obligatory police car and Red Cross ambulance, a manifest office, a trailer lot, a circus tarpaulin, RV hookups, and, of course, a bar.

Directly across the road from the airport buildings was a tract of grass split in two by a short road. The first half was the officially designated whuffo zone, reserved for those who come to marvel. The second half was the camping area for people like me.

It was Friday, a little before noon. I urged the Honda over to the southeast corner of the camping lot, the spot most distant from any other tent. I parked, whipped out my ground cloth and tent, and set up house. Then I strolled over to the manifest office, had my gear checked, signed a liability waiver, and registered.

I had no master schedule for myself this weekend, but tender speculations of a sensuous evening or two with Eleanor had been keeping me company the last few nights. Those thoughts were quickly quashed outside the manifest office, where I bumped into Dominic.

Wednesday evening he'd landed with Satin Cruise, and yesterday Eleanor had called from Dallas to let me know she wouldn't be coming. She had too much work to do at the office and was flying back to Chicago today. How about a sunset date next Saturday, Sullivan Airport, at the near end of the runway?

I was disappointed, and as I wandered away from Dominic I wondered if she'd given him the whole story. Eleanor was a dedicated business woman, no doubt about that, but . . .

Another man?

No. If Eleanor were seeing someone else, she'd have told me. That was our agreement, and I knew she wouldn't violate my trust.

Bewildered and slightly depressed, I went over to one of the six public phones outside the airport restaurant. I called Eleanor's voice mailbox and left a message confirming next week's date.

The weather was coming out of the south. By early afternoon the temperature was up to a hundred and four degrees, the relative humidity ninety percent. The haze was so thick it was impossible to tell from the ground whether there were any clouds in the sky.

The Golden Knights, Octagon, the Wisconsin speed star team, and other competitors were using the day to practice, and I couldn't help noticing that Newt Becker and his camera were back working for Octagon. All the other skydivers I knew already had commitments to jump with others, so I jumped by myself—twice—for the sole purpose of breathing the cool crisp air at twelve thousand feet.

While I was packing from my second jump, a flatbed piled high with steel cables lumbered up to the airport. The passenger's door on the cab opened and Danny Death Grimes, gear bag in hand, leapt down. On the other side of the truck the driver stepped out onto his running board and gazed upward at a constellation of twenty-odd jumpers under canopy. He didn't stop staring until all the jumpers had landed.

Danny Death plopped his gear bag down on the grass, looped around the front of the cab, and chatted with the driver. There was an exchange of some sort between them. Then the driver climbed back into his cab and turned his rig around. I could see him shaking his head as he hauled his load of steel back out to the highway.

When Danny Death spotted me, I was stuffing my main into its container.

"What's happenin', man?" he said, straying over. He had on a plain white T-shirt and the same ratty jeans and holey sneakers he'd worn in Findlay.

I smiled up at him. "You always get chauffeured right to the airport? Or did you bribe him?"

"Naw," he drawled. "We had a bet. And the fat-ass sucker lost."

I pulled my closing loop through my container flap grommets with my pull-up cord, then inserted my pin. "What kind of bet was that?"

Danny Death smiled slyly. "The kind I couldn't lose. I was diggin' in my gear bag there in the cab, and the asshole starts admirin' my fancy *backpack*, as he calls it. When I tell him it's a parachute, he thinks I'm lyin', makin' it all up. Doesn't believe a little guy like me can be a skydiver. Ya know how we're supposed to be big fuckin' paratroopers and all. Well, I thought, I'll show him. I bet him it was a parachute, like I said. Told him to bring me here and I'll prove it. Nothin' to lose, ya know. A sure bet. What a fat-ass sucker." His mouth twisted into a sardonic scowl.

"How much did you win?" I asked.

His scowl vanished. "Three joints," he said grinning. "Cleaned him right out." An even bigger grin.

"The guy did give you a free lift," I felt compelled to point out.

"Yeah, but he was a jackass. Tellin' me all the way here about screwin' jailbait. He musta been in his fifties and half bald. You shoulda seen his beer gut. Put a wig on him and slash the moustache, and he could pass for a pregnant chick. Ugly as all hell, but he could pass."

I strung my pull-up cord onto my shorts and stood up. "So does this mean you've joined the establishment?"

Danny Death's eyes showed a glazed look that could have been from confusion, or cannabis. "Huh?" he said.

"USPA—fuckin' establishment, you called it. I thought you didn't belong."

"Oh, yeah." He nodded indecisively and just stood there. The funny smirk on his face confirmed cannabis.

"Well, you know you can't jump here unless you belong. I see you lugged your gear with you, so I guess that means you've joined."

He didn't answer me directly. Instead, he half turned his hip, reached into the right rear pocket of his jeans, grasped something, and held out his hand. In it were two pieces of ID. The mostly pink USPA membership card had the name Carlton Carmichael typed across the middle. I didn't need to look at the driver's license to figure out to whom it had once belonged.

Warning Danny Death that impersonating a dead skydiver was probably illegal would only encourage him. "I don't think you really look like him," seemed more sensible, so that's what I said.

Danny Death smirked again and shifted his gear bag around so he could unzip its front pocket. He pulled out a unique pair of brown-tinted glasses that I recognized as Carmichael's. Then he donned them.

"Nobody at the manifest ever met me or Lon," he said, "so it'll be a snap. With these glasses, I can pass right through—like coffee." He paused for effect. "And once I'm registered, no one'll be the wiser, not with all the jumpers here, and everyone's minds on the competition. My old buddy'd love it knowin' he's helpin' me out."

It had been more than a month since Lonny Carmichael died back in Findlay. At some point between then and now Danny Death seemed to have come to terms with the death. Or maybe, I thought ruefully, pretending to be Lonny was Danny Death's way of keeping his buddy alive.

I eyed him dubiously, and the expression of smug satisfaction that was blanketing his face began to wrinkle.

"Now, you aren't gonna rat on me, Chance, are ya?" he prodded. "You know membership in fuckin' USPA and a skydivin' license don't mean squat. I can fly the socks off most these relative workers and every one of these fuckin' judges, ya know. And I know more about landing a canopy than most accuracy champs. You know that, Chance, you've jumped with me. Just 'cause I won't pay some fuckin' agency full of old farts to certify me competent don't mean I should miss out on a bita fun at Nationals, ya know."

I was surprised how much I knew.

"You won't shoot your mouth off, will ya?"

Danny Death was exaggerating about USPA officials. But he did have a point: he *could* fly the socks off most everyone else when he wasn't stoned. And it was none of my business, anyway.

"No," I said, "I won't tell."

He grinned. "Didn't think I got you wrong," he said. "I don't get 'em wrong much." He shoved the ID back into his pocket. "Oh, yeah," he remembered, "I almost forgot. I got somethin' for you."

He dropped his gear bag to the ground and dug inside. "Here," he said, tossing out my red T-shirt. It was even clean. "Thanks for lettin' me wear it."

"Anytime," I said.

Then Carlton "Lonny" Carmichael zipped up his gear bag, slung it over his shoulder, and marched with infinite confidence over to the manifest office to register.

I was walking back to my tent when Macintosh from California flagged me down. He was wearing shiny blue athletic shorts, a yellow tank top, and a pair of blue-and-yellow thongs. He'd driven in on Sunday and had picked up his compatriot Cheeks at the Tulsa Airport on Monday. Since then Cheeks had managed to pull the right political strings, and as a result Macintosh now had a slot on a thirty-six-way diamond attempt being organized by Bradford Rey.

"Lots of luck," I said, as he darted off to tell someone else.

I knew this would be a milestone for Macintosh. No matter what happened with the dive, no matter what the outcome, for the rest of his life he'd remember this year's Nationals as the boogie where he made his first mega-load jump.

I wondered idly what person or event would define this boogie for me now that Eleanor was out of the picture. Before nightfall, I'd have my answer.

I stashed my gear and T-shirt inside my tent, which was hot and stuffy. The heat was really depressing, and Eleanor's message didn't help my spirits any. I moped around the camping area until I noticed an old round canopy that someone had strung up, and then abandoned. I crawled under it, lay down, and closed my eyes.

I listened to new arrivals pulling into the camping area and planes getting ready to take off. The intensity and sharpness of individual sounds gradually subsided until they all merged into a low mumble. My mind drifted offshore.

The sounds of slapping waves and talking sea gulls faded in. A cool breeze swept by me as I flew above the coast amid the smell of salt water and fresh fish. Below, white suds made jagged and temporary borders between the water and the sand. A forest of palms met the beach, which lay empty except for a small gathering of birds.

I flew offshore. Cottony shapes surrounded me, and as I approached one I could smell and taste a clamminess in the air. I closed my eyes tight, held my breath, and braced myself for a crash. But as I violated the barrier between clear nothing and opaque white, there was no confrontation, and I emerged into the mist without a jolt. The laws of earth, I was reminded, do not apply in the sky. I floated about, oblivious to my form or figure. I couldn't place myself in nature. Was I a man? A bird? Or just an illusion?

Something soft and warm brushed lightly against my chest. I had a chest. Illusions don't have chests. "Where are you?" I heard it talk, and I wondered where I was.

The warm softness massaged my diaphragm, then descended down my torso and began caressing my abdomen. Do birds have abdomens? I couldn't remember. When the warm softness began doing its thing a bit lower, I knew I wasn't a bird, and I woke up.

Bridgette Bridle's soothing tan eyes gazed down at mine. She had natural sand-dusted lashes that appeared unnaturally light. Tiny beads of sweat sparkled on the horizon between her hair and freckled skin. Her lips were parted slightly in a half-smile of waiting, and were completely aware of what her hand was up to.

I sat up with a start.

Then I politely, but firmly, removed her hand from my body.

"Relax, Chance," she said in mock offense, "I just came over to say hello."

I blinked. "Some hello."

She giggled.

"Where's Harley?" I asked.

She rolled her eyes. Translated into English, the roll meant, "Practicing with his team. Where else, you fool?"

I rubbed my eyes and readjusted my shorts.

"Harley won both his events," Bridgette boasted. "But now he and the team are already making plans for the world meet, and I don't have a *thing* to do." She sighed with ennui. "You don't look like you have anything to do either."

"Harley" was Mr. H. T. Lawrence during the fall and winter, one of the new breed of New York stockbrokers. The rest of the year he was just Harley, captain of the Cellmates canopy relative work team.

All of the events in the canopy relative work competition had already taken place earlier in the week. Harley and his team were unquestioned geniuses at canopy relative work. Possibly the world's finest.

Bridgette was Harley's live-in mate. In the five years I'd been coming to Nationals, she'd been coming too. Harley would bring her with him, set her up at the Holiday Inn, then ignore her. He wasn't being deliberately mean, I didn't think. It's just that skydiving came first, second, and third in Harley's life. He was always busy, Bridgette never was.

The two of them existed in a harmony out of tune to most people. Bridgette stuck by her Harley, but she didn't like being left alone, so she did whatever she could to try to make Harley jealous, including coming after me.

The last thing I wanted was to be drawn into any mind games between Bridgette and Harley. I let my body recover, scrambled to my feet before I could be compromised again, and stretched. "You make a habit of taking liberties with men while they sleep?"

"Only you," she replied.

I changed the subject—or tried to. "I understand Harley and his teammates performed some innovative maneuvers during the competition. They should have a good chance at the world meet."

"I'd like to have a *Chance* to perform some innovative maneuvers," she said. Her tongue slid across her upper lip. She was proud of her pun.

"Not a *Chance*," I replied, one-upping her.

She melted away, but promised to visit me again sometime.

Quite a bit later, Danny Death asked me on a four-way that included his Wisconsin friend Arn—a recent arrival—and an acquaintance of theirs from Michigan. I gave Danny Death's eyeballs the ole reefer check first. This time they passed. Barely.

From twelve grand we pumped out sixteen fast points. The dive was cathartic: it helped my body recover from the lingering effects of Bridgette Bridle's fingers.

Airgasm. They call it airgasm.

By the time I finished packing my rig a more sedate sun was inching its way toward the horizon and the wind was coming out of the drier southwest. Bradford Rey's large diamond load was preparing to board Satin Cruise. I walked over.

Performance anxiety seemed to be getting the better of Macintosh now that his moment of truth was approaching. Cheeks, on the other hand, looked relaxed and confident. Something about his physical appearance seemed different to me, but I couldn't put my finger on exactly what.

Macintosh said, "Sure," when I asked if I could store some beer in his cooler. I wished him luck again, then took off for Muskogee.

In town, I drove past a mile-long strip of motels. All were inexpensive, some downright cheap. Among them was Muskogee's Holiday Inn, the official motel of the National Skydiving Championships and the place where Bridgette and Harley always stayed. A marquee in its parking lot welcomed all skydivers.

At the northern end of the strip was Jay's Liquor. I bought a six-pack of Molson, filled up my gas tank at a pump next door, then stopped at a grocery store and bought yogurt, plums, a liter of apple juice, and a loaf of bread. In the store's parking lot I sat down beside the Honda, watched the sun set, and enjoyed my food. I finished off the yogurt and the juice. What I couldn't eat of the plums and the bread I stashed in the trunk.

Back on Route Sixty-four I noticed a patrol car inch in behind me. When I turned left at the model airplane it did too. I checked my speed. Legal. Then my lights. All lit. What were the liquor laws in Oklahoma? Did an unwrapped six-pack in the trunk constitute open liquor?

I slowed down with intent to stop, but the patrol car whisked right past me. I barely had time to relax when its taillights came on bright. The policeman pulled off the road in front of the Armory, got out, and walked over toward the soccer complex parking lot. No one was playing soccer tonight and the lot was all but deserted.

I braked the Honda behind the patrol car and stared after the policeman. I could make out two vehicles at the eastern end of the lot. One looked like a police car, the other a van of some sort. My eyes strained to adjust to the night. I recognized the van. It was the Red Cross ambulance assigned to the drop zone.

I counted six people near the edge of the soccer complex fence. Two of them were armed with flashlights, which they were swishing about. I could see from their lights that they were wearing uniforms. Two others had on jumpsuits. The four of them were bending over a lump on the ground when the new officer joined them.

I swerved around the patrol car, followed the road to the end, then rode over the grass to my tent. I grabbed the six-pack from my trunk and walked apprehensively toward Macintosh's cooler.

What had happened while I'd been in town? I knew, of course, in a general way, but the details—the who and the how and the why . . .

Macintosh had parked his van about forty feet in from the road.

The sliding side door was locked. I tried the passenger's door, the driver's door, and the rear doors. No dice. In the excitement of his first mega-load he'd forgotten to unlock it for me.

I put the six-pack down next to his right rear wheel. As I stood up Danny Death, jumpsuited and carrying his unpacked main, bumped into me. Behind Lonny Carmichael's tinted glasses his eyes appeared newly stoned.

"I went into town for food and beer," I said. "And a police car followed me back."

He nodded his head monotonously until he realized what I was getting at.

"Then you don't know," he said.

I shook my head.

"It was Newt Becker, the cameraman from Satin Cruise. He was filming The Pit Bull's fuckin' diamond. Went in on a double malfunction. Isn't that a pisser."

The effect of Danny Death's words on the entirety of my body was not unlike the effect of a severed neck. It was as though the mental Chance had been separated from the physical Chance. My mind ceased all communication with my limbs and organs. I could not remember how to move muscle tissue. My lungs were still, unsure of what to do next.

I would have been lying if I had said I was not in shock.

Danny Death peered over his main at me. The catastrophe that had taken place inside my flesh must have manifested itself outside as well. "You and Becker—you were tight, I guess." He spoke hesitatingly. "You bein' with Satin Cruise last month . . . and all."

I was breathing again, but I still found it impossible to move. Danny Death was silent for a minute. Then he said, "I sure as hell know what it's like—losin' a buddy, I mean. It's like goin' through it with Lon all over again." His foot kicked angrily at the ground. "Fuckin' sonova bitch!"

I managed to speak. "Not buddies like you and Lonny," I said slowly, distracted. "I worked mostly with Dominic the past month."

My mouth tasted gangrenous. I slid my tongue along the ridge between my teeth and gum, then swallowed.

"I was Newt Becker's rigger." Each word halted on my tongue before it spilled out through my lips. I swallowed again. "For the last three years I've packed his reserve. Exclusively."

Cannabis, it is true, reduces the speed at which information is assimilated into the brain; but given enough time, even a complex fact can be absorbed. In time Danny Death understood.

"Shit, man!" he swore. "Fuckin' shit!"

A few minutes ago there had been only a vague incident out at the soccer complex parking lot. A sickening event that had cast a shadow over my evening, but a completely impersonal and uncomplicated event. Now suddenly I was the rigger of a reserve that had malfunctioned, resulting in the death of a man.

I recovered enough to pump Danny Death for information, but he could supply only hearsay. At the time he'd been in the American Kestrel DC-3, getting ready to jump out on the last load of the day, and he hadn't seen Newt go in.

What he'd heard, though, was that Newt had been shooting pictures of the thirty-six-way diamond that only built to thirty-two, and that he'd done everything right. He pulled above two grand and had a malfunction. So he broke away from his main, stabilized, and pulled his reserve at about a grand—plenty of altitude—but the reserve malfunctioned, too. Not fair, Danny Death complained, that someone should do it by the book and still bounce. Goes to show what the goddamn book's good for.

"And you know what else?" he spat. "After Becker goes in, all The Pit Bull can talk about is his fuckin' diamond and how four people were out. A guy dies and The Pit Bull's yakkin' about jumpers not makin' their slots. Shit, man!"

I was only half listening anymore. I was trying to remember when I'd last packed that reserve. Mid-March, in Fort Crystal, on my way to South Carolina and biplanes. Too distant to recall specifics. But the reserve couldn't have been irregular. I couldn't have missed anything. I *couldn't* have!

"You sure the main didn't catch on his camera equipment after he released it?"

"The guy that told me said it cleared totally. The main and the reserve didn't tangle."

"And Newt was flat and stable when he pulled his reserve?"

"That's how I got it—flat as a pancake. The reserve came right off Becker's back, nice and clean. But like I said, I was in the air in the other DC-3. Didn't see it myself."

"A double malfunction!" I gulped. "A double malfunction?"

9

The terrain between the camping area and the manifest office had never been more difficult to cross. I urged my legs forward, but like a frustrated farmer trying to coax a pair of stubborn mules, I often found myself at a standstill. My goal was to track down the official version of Newt's death, unclouded by pot or whatever, but by the time I finally got there the manifest had already closed.

I could have ridden the Honda over to the soccer complex parking lot, but I went by foot instead. To give myself more time.

Main parachutes usually malfunction because of poor maintenance or shoddy packing. But Newt had always been quick to get his rig to me if it needed work, and he took reasonable care each time I saw him pack.

The reserve I couldn't figure out either. Bad body position on opening can cause a reserve to malfunction. Parachutes work best when a jumper pulls in a flat, belly-to-earth frog position; they become less predictable if pulled while upside down, sideways, or spinning. But Danny Death said Newt was stable. Flat as a pancake—those were his exact words.

Rigger error occasionally, though seldom, claims a life. It was those seldom occasions that were now knotting up my gut and chiseling away at my spine.

I reached the rear of the Armory and went around front. About twenty feet from the road I stopped and stood still, absorbing the vibration of the crickets. There were two more cars parked out front, one of them another police car. In the soccer complex parking lot two people were making their way from the ambulance toward the rest of the group. One of them was carrying a stretcher.

I dawdled near the cars. I felt like shit. Seven years as a rigger, my first dead client. There was always the possibility that it could happen. But you don't keep that thought in the front of your mind or you'll never touch another rig. You go about your business, taking every precaution, obeying all the rules, following the manufacturer's guidelines; and the worst case scenario exists only as an unreal abstraction in an obscure part of your consciousness.

But what now—now that it had happened? I racked my brain trying to remember that March pack job.

Finally I balled up my fists, took a deep breath, and forced myself across the road.

The group was gathered at a dried-out parking log near the soccer complex fence: four police officers, two skydivers, three medical types. One of the three walked with a slight limp and had the manner of a doctor. He would be the coroner. The other two, both young and brawny, would be the paramedics.

The headlights from the airport police car lit up the area. Two officers were swishing their flashlights about in the places the headlights didn't reach.

Between the parking log and the soccer complex fence a broken kelly-green hockey helmet teetered on the ground. Pieces of black plastic from Newt's camera and chunks of twisted aluminum from its mount mingled with the tufts of coarse parking lot grass. The small loop of wire that Newt used for sighting his pictures had snapped off the helmet and lay there bent. A roll of exposed film snaked through the chaos.

Near it all was a lump, draped for the moment with an olive-drab ambulance cloth. My stomach quaked with the realization of what it had once been. For more than a decade that lump had been a photographer to thousands of skydivers, and to anyone else who enjoyed his work. But to those of us with a personal connection, that lump had also been a trusting client to a part-time rigger, an aspiring videographer to a team of relative workers, a husband to a Florida model, a gofer to the owner of Satin Cruise.

My chest felt vacant, as though it were a warehouse suddenly stripped of a long-stored item that over the years had become an integral part of its structure, around which an addition had been built. Eleanor had said certain coincidental things can bind you emotionally to people you aren't otherwise close to. In my case, Newt's gangling arms and long thin feet bound him to my memories of Jeepers the puppet. Jeepers had sparkled with ancient wisdom, acting out the grown-up themes of justice and fair play. But he had also amused and captivated and charmed, and had brought a magical joy to a scraggly little boy from New Hope, Ohio, who endured an otherwise lonely childhood. Jeepers had been a gleaming star in a mostly black heaven, a source of warmth across an otherwise frigid plain. He was the long-stored item in my warehouse of memories, kept alive by an unsuspecting Newt Becker many years after he had ceased prancing about his shadow box stage. It was Jeepers the puppet who made my emotional connection to Newt stronger than our rigger-client relationship warranted. It was he who made Newt Becker more familiar.

My eyes explored the olive-drab ambulance cloth, climbing its peaks, descending into its valleys. The lump beneath it could have been a pile of garbage, some miscellaneous sporting equipment, or a collection of kiddy lawn chairs, so altered was the body of Newt Becker. I nearly vomited with guilt at the thought that I might be responsible.

An officer pivoted and unintentionally shot her flashlight into my face. I blinked and shielded my eyes. She said, "Sorry," about the light, and moved it off me. "We'd appreciate if you'd stay back. This is official police business."

"I'm the rigger for this gear." My voice came out colicky. "I was in town when he went in."

The two jumpers were sitting on the log examining Newt's gear. When I spoke, they glanced up. I knew both of them from previous riggers conferences. One, a Florida rigger named Zbigniew whom everyone called Ziggy, told the officer I was okay.

"Not to worry, Chance," he said. "You didn't pack this one. The last name on the packing card's DeBerg. Dated three weeks ago."

In the darkness I doubted Ziggy could have seen my genuine astonishment; nonetheless, he held out the reserve packing card to me. With assistance from the woman officer's light, I examined it.

Ziggy was right, and I was confused. The date of Newt's last reserve pack was June Eleventh, the entry logged in by Joe DeBerg. His signature, penned below eight of my own, was flowery and distinctive. Every rigger on the East Coast who was any rigger at all had seen it on at least one packing card.

Joe DeBerg was one of the most experienced and respected riggers in skydiving. He was the only parachute rigger I knew who was able to carve out a living strictly from freelancing. Every other full-time rigger collected a salary from the military, a parachute manufacturer, or a distributor of gear, and freelanced on the side.

DeBerg's home drop zone was Litchfield, and Satin Cruise had been in Litchfield June Eleventh. Newt's reserve must have expired that day, and I must have been busy with the plane, so he'd taken his gear to DeBerg.

Then I noticed *my* last entry on the card. The date was March Twelfth. It looked right at first, then it didn't. I calculated. The months didn't come out. March Twelfth to June Eleventh was three months, not four: ninety or so days, not one twenty. Newt's reserve didn't expire back in Litchfield; it had another month to go.

So what was Newt's rush? Did his main malfunction in Litchfield? Could I have missed that?

The back of my neck began to tingle and my hearing sharpened. I was sweating with bald relief that the final signature on Newt's packing card was not mine, but I couldn't help wondering why it wasn't.

I passed the card over to Ziggy. "Why did Newt bounce up north here and not south of the airport? That's where the spot should have been."

"A couple of idiot whuffos who thought it would be neat to geek skydivers from the air," he said. "They were flying their planes all over the place, and it was just safer for Dominic to dump the load up here. Ten minutes later the American Kestrel did the same for the last load of the day."

He refolded Newt's packing card and put it back in its pouch. Then he focused his attention on the gear, explaining to the police exactly what we were all looking at: a perfectly good harness/container system, green in color and light in weight. There was no main parachute; Newt would have released that. The main breakaway handle was also missing, as was the reserve ripcord. In a normal malfunction jumpers hang onto the main breakaway handle and the reserve ripcord, Ziggy told the police, but Newt would have ditched his at the slightest hint of a bad reserve.

Newt's reserve remained attached to his harness. One of the officers wanted to know why Newt hadn't released that, too. Ziggy said that reserves are not designed for release. Even a malfunctioning reserve can provide some drag. With it, some hope; without it, none.

Why not keep both chutes then? Twice the drag, wouldn't it be? The police were seriously trying to comprehend the accident, and Ziggy responded to their questions with the patience of someone who had answered them already at least once before. Dumping a perfectly good reserve into a malfunctioning main would be close to suicide—a very real risk of entanglement. "Of course, in this case," he added, "it really wouldn't have mattered."

He glanced up at me. "Take a peek at this, Chance."

I leaned forward, and I could feel my eyes get big. He had in his hand one of Newt's reserve connector links. A normal connector link is oval with a double-slotted nut that joins the ends. This particular link was stretched open, slightly bent in the middle, and detached from its riser. There was no doubt that it had failed.

If a connector link were either loose or defective, it would give way with the force of opening shock. The relative wind would then pull the riser, the lines, or both, off the link, allowing the lines to blow about haphazardly. A parachute without taut lines would malfunction. That's what Ziggy told the police, only he didn't say *would*, he said *must have*.

This connector link was still threaded through its lines. Ziggy slipped it out, fingered it, then offered it to me. I pinched it between my forefinger and thumb. It wasn't defective: the threads on the link and those inside the nut were still in excellent condition, not stripped at all. And the link was still in one piece.

Without comment I handed the link off to Simon. Simon was the other rigger. Simon said, "Shit."

Simon's response was appropriate in the context of the situation. Since the link wasn't defective, it must have been loose. Joe DeBerg had packed the reserve just three weeks ago, and none of us ever heard of a reserve connector link coming loose in only three weeks.

The police impounded all of Newt's gear because that's what their routine required, but—taking note of Simon's "shit"—they slipped the link into a separate bag. They would order a battery of stress tests. Ziggy, Simon, and I didn't bother to tell them how their tests would turn out. None of us wanted to point a finger at a fellow rigger, and they'd find out for themselves soon enough.

The coroner wrapped up his business and hobbled off to his car. The two paramedics walked haltingly toward the ambulance carrying their stretcher, now covered in olive drab and quite heavy.

The officers from the airport got into their car and drove back toward Davis Field. They would question witnesses, for the record. The other two climbed into their cars, U-turned, and led the ambulance away.

Ziggy, Simon, and I made our way to the airport on foot. The pace was slow.

Simon said, "DeBerg forgot to tighten that link when he packed Becker's reserve three weeks ago."

Ziggy nodded.

For all of us that was hard to believe. It's basic, learned by every rigger: Always make sure the connector link nuts are screwed on properly. Check the lines attached to the links, then check the links themselves. We do it instinctively, without thinking.

Joe DeBerg wasn't at Nationals and couldn't be reached for consultation. "Something to do with a family reunion in the mountains," Ziggy said. "He'll be along Sunday, I think."

"What about Newt's main?" I asked.

My non sequitur startled Simon. "What about it?" he said.

"Was it recovered?"

Simon shrugged and glanced at Ziggy, but Ziggy just agreed with Simon.

"To be honest, Chance, we forgot all about the main," Ziggy admitted. "Sorry. You can ask back at the manifest."

"Not anymore tonight," I said. "It's closed. But I'll ask around. Somebody should know something."

Nobody did, though. "The main? Never gave it a thought. Not with the guy bouncing. Someone'll find it in the morning." I got a dozen or more versions of that before I quit wasting my time.

None of this was really my concern anymore. I hadn't packed Newt's reserve last, so there was no potential moral or legal entanglement in this fatality for me.

But . . .

But what?

For three years Newt had entrusted his life to my rigging skills. He'd been a reliable and faithful customer, and had supported my freefall habit. The least I could do was recover his main canopy and figure out why it malfunctioned. As his regular rigger, I owed him that much.

And something just felt wrong about all this.

I foraged in the bottom of my right saddlebag for my pen light, exchanged my shorts for a pair of long jeans, then retraced my steps to the soccer complex parking lot.

I calculated. The wind had switched to the southwest by the time the diamond load jumped out. A southwest breeze would blow a canopy northeast of the spot where it was released: on the ground that would be a little southwest of where Newt went in. He had released his main between one and two grand, but the surface wind had been light. So the canopy wouldn't have floated far—maybe a hundred, two hundred yards, depending on the velocity of the wind aloft. Definitely no more than two hundred fifty yards. That would put it somewhere on the western side of the hayfield immediately east of the soccer complex.

I climbed over the barbed-wire fence that separated the field from a ditch of roadside grass. It was much too dark to find a canopy in a hayfield, but if my calculations were on target I could get lucky.

I positioned myself five feet in from the field's southwest corner. I plodded north, slicing imaginary switchbacks through the hay with my pen light, now five feet to the left, now five feet to the right. I counted two hundred fifty paces, moved ten feet farther east, and pivoted. The hayfield went farther, but assuming what Danny Death told me was correct, Newt's main couldn't have floated up there.

I made my way back to the barbed-wire fence, moved ten feet farther east, turned, and headed north again. Methodically, I swashed back and forth through the hay for nearly two hours. I found the deployment bag to Newt's reserve, but not his main canopy.

I gave up for the night. At least I knew where it wasn't.

I stashed the deployment bag and my flashlight inside my tent, then walked over toward the manifest building. Ziggy and Simon were standing there talking with two USPA officials. Simon had had more than a few beers, and was talking the way one does. Less than ten minutes ago he'd spoken with one of the cops, he said. The cop expected the paperwork to be routine because there had been so many witnessesses, as Simon called them. The connector link, though—now that would be tested most deffffinitely.

Ziggy said, "It's incredible—DeBerg, of all people, missing something like a loose link."

The two USPA officials agreed. Simon agreed. And so would have Newt Becker.

They discussed the potential legal consequences of Newt's death. DeBerg and the connector link company would get sued for sure; the parachute manufacturer almost certainly; USPA, the soccer complex, and the city of Muskogee probably. And if this lawsuit followed the pattern of most modern lawsuits, the manufacturers of his jumpsuit, camera, and sneakers could expect to be co-defendants. And lets not forget the company that made the underwear Newt Becker died wearing. No reason they shouldn't be included as well.

I introduced myself to the men from USPA and asked them for their version of what happened. It was almost identical to Danny Death's. And no, they didn't know anything about Newt's main. They'd been too busy dealing with the police, closing the manifest, and getting the planes anchored for the night.

Unable to do anything more about the canopy tonight, I went and showered in the bathhouse, then went after a cold Canadian beer.

The sliding door to Macintosh's van was pushed back. Cheeks was reclining on the floor nursing a bottle of St. Pauli Girl. Macintosh was between Cheeks and the front seats, his legs bent to his chest, his back against his cooler. At his thigh, an empty St. Pauli Girl. My six-pack of Molson Golden was nowhere in sight.

Macintosh waved briskly, turned, and dug into his cooler.

"Have a beer," he said, flipping off a bottle cap and offering me one of my own.

"Appreciate it."

"Sorry about the locked van," Cheeks said. He motioned with his beer to the patch of grass where I'd left my six-pack. "That was me, not Mac here."

Though we'd made two jumps together in Findlay, this was the first time either Cheeks or I actually spoke directly to the other. It happens sometimes, when you are preoccupied with matters more immediate and personal, that a stranger can participate in a segment of your life and yet remain an utter stranger to the end. The opportunity for one-on-one conversation between this international airplane parts salesman from California and me had never really presented itself in Findlay. It was just one of those things.

"Macintosh has been nice enough to share his van with me," Cheeks explained. "After the diamond, I decided to skip The Pit Bull's long post dive and take a shower. I locked my gear in the van while I was in the bathhouse, and I guess that's when you came by. My gear's brand new—I bought it here only three days ago—and I didn't want to run the risk of having it stolen."

That's why Cheeks looked different over at Satin Cruise earlier, I thought. The rig he had worn in Findlay was black, the rig he had on today was pastel blue. And new. It was very new.

"No sense tempting a would-be thief," I agreed.

Cheeks's manner wasn't what you'd call condescending, but he was smooth and self-assured and had an air of assumed importance. Only a very confident person would skip a Bradford Rey post dive to take a shower, and then admit it.

Next to Cheeks, Macintosh was tapping his foot against the floor and drumming his shins with his fingers. He seemed revved up, ready to race at the mouth, lots of adrenalin flowing from his tank. Yet he let Cheeks carry the conversation. That he looked up to Cheeks as a mentor was obvious. His docility and deferential manner whenever Cheeks was present said it all: Cheeks is a skygod, Cheeks deserves unqualified reverence. It was a trivial matter, but if Cheeks had not owned up to locking me out of the van, Macintosh would gladly have shouldered that responsibility for him.

Macintosh turned and pulled two sandwiches from the cooler. After handing one to Cheeks he looked out at me.

"Want one? There's more in the cooler."

I shook my head. "Already ate."

He put the second sandwich back in the cooler and shut the lid.

Macintosh, I was sure, had paid for all of the sandwiches, all of the beer, and all of anything else Cheeks or Bradford Rey might desire.

Cheeks unwrapped the paper from his sandwich and folded it in half for a plate. "I didn't realize you were a rigger," he said to me.

I leaned against the passenger's door and drank some Molson Golden. "What brings that up?"

He took a large bite, and we all waited while he chewed.

"Someone said you were the rigger for the photographer that bounced on our diamond load."

"I was his regular rigger. Turns out I didn't pack the one he bounced on. Another rigger did."

"Lucky for you," he said. "The rigger anybody I might know? I'm a rigger myself."

"If you've been to any of the riggers conferences over the years, you'd know him. He goes most every year. Name's DeBerg—Joe De-Berg."

Cheeks nodded. "Know the name. He has a good reputation."

I sipped my beer. I could say nothing at all, but by tomorrow the whole drop zone would know about the connector link.

"Had," I said.

Cheeks had been brushing several strands of shredded lettuce into the center of his makeshift plate. "Oh?" he said without looking up.

"I examined the rig a short while ago. The reserve malfunctioned after a connector link popped, but there wasn't anything wrong with the link itself. DeBerg packed the reserve just three weeks ago, according to the packing card."

Cheeks let go a quiet whistle.

Macintosh said innocently, "So what does that mean?"

"It means," Cheeks explained, "the link almost had to be loose when DeBerg closed the reserve. He'll probably be sued, and his days as a rigger are definitely numbered. No jumper will take his gear to a rigger who missed a loose link."

A truth seemed to ooze into young Macintosh's brain; you could see it maturing in his eyes. He stared incredulously over at Cheeks, then up at me. "They think it's the rigger's fault the photographer's dead?"

"It appears that way," I said neutrally. "The police suspect the link itself might be defective, but that's only because they don't know about parachutes. Once they get the results back on their tests, they'll realize it wasn't the hardware."

Cheeks finished the last of his sandwich. He pushed the wrapper filled with lettuce toward Macintosh, who dutifully gathered it up and tossed it into a bag. Cheeks then barrel rolled to his other side and came face to face with Macintosh's bed, a platform that stood a foot off the floor and took up the entire rear of the van. It was probably where Cheeks had been sleeping all week while Macintosh slept on the van's hard floor.

Cheeks reached deep under the bed and dragged out his gear bag. He unzipped the front pocket, removed his cigarette case, then shoved the gear bag back under the bed. He opened the case and took out a foreign cigarette. Macintosh had it lit for him within three seconds. Cheeks put the case down on the floor next to his leg and sank back against the edge of the bed.

"Can't trust anyone these days except yourself," Cheeks said flatly. "It's the reason I started rigging more than fifteen years ago. Nobody touches my rig but me."

I didn't comment because while I couldn't agree with his stark generalization, there was no getting around the fact that no one touched my rig but me, either.

"I had a client bounce on me eight years ago," he went on. "A novice with a spin problem. One day he was spinning and panicked. Then he was spinning and tumbling. Pulled his reserve into it. They found the body all tangled up, both his hands strangling the pilot chute." Cheeks leaned out the door and flicked his ashes. "Anyone ever bounce on you, Chance?"

I shook my head. "No, but for a good half-hour tonight I thought Newt Becker had gone in on my pack job, so I know a little of what you must have gone through."

His response was not one I'd have expected from a jumper in the sport so long. He cocked his head to the side and said, "You've got it wrong, Chance. I didn't lose any sleep over that novice. The kid panicked. It was his own fault he died."

Maybe so. But most experienced jumpers would show a little understanding for the mistakes of a novice. Most experienced jumpers have made those same mistakes themselves.

Cheeks's insensitivity toward the novice made me think back to our first jump in Findlay, when he'd tried to dump Danny Death from our group after one bad dive. All of a sudden his tobacco habit wasn't the only thing about him that was rubbing me wrong.

Macintosh was alternating his glance between Cheeks and me in the manner of a spectator at a tennis match. He bit down on his lip. I didn't think he was any more comfortable with Cheeks's comment about the novice than I was—he'd been a novice himself in the not-too-distant past.

I said to Macintosh, "So how did you do on the diamond load?"

He replied with the broad smile I'd gambled on. He welcomed the change of subject, and was itching for the chance to boast about his first mega-load.

"The Pit Bull said I was flying a little low in my slot, but I was there. Not too soon, not too late. He's invited me on another diamond tomorrow."

Macintosh's eyes were proud. This called for a celebration. He opened the cooler, took out two St. Pauli Girls and a Molson. Having passed out the beer and collected all the empties, he came back to the diamond: the exit (the tightest he'd ever been on), the swooping (so many bodies), the approach (perfect angle), the dock (what timing), the break off (orderly). Every second of freefall took nearly thirty to be described.

"Do you think they'll be able to save the film from that photographer's camera?" he asked. There was a queasiness in his voice that suggested he didn't consider the question totally proper or tasteful, under the circumstances. At the same time, he just had to know.

I shook my head. "The roll popped out on impact."

Macintosh pretended not to care, but his disappointment was apparent.

When I finished my Molson Macintosh offered me another, but it was getting late. I said good night, strolled back to my tent, and thought about Newt's main.

10

I got up before the sun did, ate what was left of yesterday's bread and plums, grabbed my pen light, and trotted out to the hayfield. Employing the same tedious pattern—two hundred fifty paces every ten feet—I gravitated eastward toward the small canal that divided the field in two.

I had paced off two hundred fifty steps fourteen times by the time the sun started to rise. Five thousand seven hundred fifty steps and twenty-three fence posts later I had swashed over to the canal. It was well after seven, my skin was itching from the hay, and I'd found only a soggy blue-and-white athletic shoe, size nine.

Angle for bass, settle for catfish.

I picked up the shoe, which had landed in the canal, and trekked back to the drop zone. There was no official lost and found that I knew of, so I dropped the shoe at the foot of the manifest's locked door.

I took a shower in the bathhouse and changed into my shorts and red T-shirt—the last clean shirt I had, I realized. Then I went over to a blue dome tent that belonged to a Cessna owner I'd flown for two summers ago. He was still buried in sleep and snoring resonantly when I crawled in.

"Mind if I borrow the plane?"

He rolled over and fumbled for the keys. "Gas it up, and it's yours." He was snoring again before I could crawl back out.

The jump planes contracted for the competition and boogie were tied down on several acres of tarmac that separated the airport's buildings from its runways. The Cessna I wanted was third in a row of six. I gassed it up, and it was mine.

Newt's main canopy was red and gold, easy colors to spot from the sky. If it was down there at all, I should be able to find it.

I flew the Cessna over the northern section of the airport, the hayfield, the soccer complex. I took the plane down to about three hundred feet and circled. I studied very carefully the entire hayfield. Then the soccer complex and its parking lot. Inside the soccer complex fence was a small pond, but it was northwest of where Newt had landed, so the southwest wind couldn't have blown it in there. I passed over the area again and again, but no red and no gold.

I went back down.

I left the keys in the blue dome tent, now empty, then went down to the south end of the tarmac. The two DC-3s, the American Kestrel and Satin Cruise, sat next to each other. Dominic's copilot waved good morning as he headed off toward the manifest. Dominic was standing on a ladder under his plane's right engine.

"Got a minute?" I asked.

Dominic took his eyes off what he was doing for less than a second. "Hang on," he said.

He tinkered inside his engine, delicately fondling something mechanical. Then he let out a grunt of effort and removed his hands.

I'd always considered the residual engine grease on Dominic's hands to be an immutable part of his body. Lifeguards have their tans, football players their muscles, mechanics their stained hands. But here were Dominic's exposed fingers, pinkish and tender rather than charcoal and rough. Like they'd been scrubbed with sandpaper. He grabbed the sides of the ladder and came down to the tarmac. When he was level with me, I realized his beard had been trimmed since yesterday.

He pulled out a clean cotton cloth from his back pocket and wiped his hands on it, taking extra care with his nails and cuticles. He folded the cloth and slid it back in his pocket.

"Did anyone turn in Newt's main to you last night or this morning?"

He shook his head. "Don't know that anyone even went after it."

"I did, for one. I even looked by air."

Dominic's face opened up with comprehension. "Wondered about that low-flying Cessna."

"I'm trying to figure out why Newt's main malfunctioned. Maybe you can help."

Dominic put one foot up on the lowest rung of the ladder. "How's that?" he said evenly, without emotion.

"Did you see Newt before his last jump?"

"Uh-huh."

"What would you say was his mood?"

Dominic's face took on a puzzled expression. "Don't get you."

"Was he hurried or impatient, for example? Too rushed to pack his main carefully?"

He thought. "Could have been. He taped Octagon all day with his video camera, but he thought a complete diamond near sunset—if they got one—would be a good still shot. He switched equipment just before the dive." Dominic nodded. "Yeah, he could've been careless."

I said, "Do you know if Newt had a malfunction in Litchfield three weeks ago?"

"None that I know. I think he did jump there, but aren't you his rigger? If anyone would know—"

"That's why I'm asking. I've been Newt's rigger for three years, his packing card wasn't set to expire until next week, and I don't remember him having a malfunction. Yet while we were in Litchfield another rigger—Joe DeBerg—packed his reserve. It's on Newt's packing card."

Dominic barely frowned. "Newt did a lot stranger things than that the past year."

Dominic was undoubtedly right, and none of this was really any of my business. But the Litchfield repack was bothering me. I hoped it wasn't for reasons of vanity. I hoped I wasn't bothered by the fact that, given the choice, Newt had preferred Joe DeBerg to me.

"Mind if I read through Newt's logbook? There might be something in it that could explain his packing card."

Dominic shrugged. "Not mine to say no to. Gear bag's in the plane."

He led me back to the side of the plane, grabbed a small ladder, and placed it under the door. We clambered in and walked up toward the cockpit.

Newt's gear bag was unzipped and sagging from near emptiness. I combed through it. Inside the large compartment where his rig would normally be were only seven small Cyalume lights for night jumps, a camera lens in its protective casing, and a green face towel. I unzipped the bag's front pocket. In it were a pull-up cord, a small container of sinus tablets, and two lens filters.

Newt had two jumpsuits: a small, fast-falling one for taping team practice and competition jumps; and a large, slow-falling one for everything else. On the floor under Newt's bag I found his small suit.

I ripped open its Velcroed pocket, designed to hold miscellaneous things like rubber bands, gloves, pull-up cords, Kleenex, barrettes for women, telephone change for when the spot is bad. In Newt's pocket there were two rubber bands and a smashed orange M&M.

Next to Newt's gear bag was his on-the-road video contraption, a modern streamlined machine mounted on a kelly-green hockey helmet. Many freefall photographers pile two or three cameras—video and still—on one helmet, but Newt had found that method too heavy for his thin, weak neck. Instead, he'd opted for a system using one helmet per camera. To switch cameras, he simply switched helmets. Back in Florida his collection of helmet getups was impressive. While traveling, though, he limited himself to his two favorite: the thirty-five-millimeter camera that had bounced with him last night, and this one. I looked underneath it.

"No logbook," I said. "I know Newt kept one."

Dominic had been waiting behind me in the fuselage. "Could be in his rental car," he said.

"Car?" As far as I knew, Newt never rented cars.

"Brand new luxury Olds," Dominic said. "Even got a room at the Holiday Inn when they had a last minute cancellation."

"Maybe Octagon's paying," I said, trying to make sense of it.

"Could be," Dominic said impassively, as though we were talking about widgets.

I said, "You happen to know where the car key is?"

Dominic reached in his pocket and pulled out a key attached to a large tab. "Found it in his jumpsuit this morning. I'll need it back by ten-thirty, though. I'm using the car to pick up Paula in Tulsa."

I took the key. "Did you call her last night?"

"Uh-huh."

"How'd she take it?"

"Calmly, but that could have been shock. Hard to tell on the phone."

I nodded my agreement. "You said ten-thirty. Who'll fly Satin Cruise while you're in Tulsa?"

"They'll just have to do without the plane till I get back," he said possessively.

Midday Saturday at Nationals was the wrong time for the boogie to have only one DC-3. "I don't have anything planned for today, Dominic. I don't mind driving to Tulsa and picking Paula up."

"Don't you have the Riggers Conference over at the Armory?"

"Nothing today that I don't already know. There must be over four hundred jumpers here now, and there'll be more by noon. They'll need your plane. It only makes sense that I go."

He hesitated. I could tell he didn't like the idea, but felt stuck by my offer.

"Would Paula know you?"

"We met last year at her birthday party."

He scrutinized his fingers and dug out a piece of dirt wedged under his left thumbnail. Finally he said, "United Airlines, Flight Three-seventy-five. Eleven-thirty. It's a connecting flight out of Chicago."

I promised him I'd be prompt, or even a few minutes early.

"The car's Halloween black. Parked along the road." He walked down the fuselage. At the door he turned and said, "Since you're going over to Newt's car, you might want to take his equipment with you."

I nodded, gathered up Newt's gear, and climbed out of the plane. The wind was starting to pick up.

I stopped by the manifest office. No red-and-gold main parachute. In fact, no parachute of any color had been turned in. But someone had dropped off a blue-and-white athletic shoe, size nine.

Over at my tent I got Newt's reserve deployment bag and stuffed it into his gear bag. Then I walked over to the road. I preferred the Honda to Newt's Oldsmobile, but was completely sure Paula Becker would not. Dominic had described the car as Halloween black. I found it without trouble.

After piling Newt's gear into the back seat, I looked for his logbook. What I found was the rental agreement, which ran till Monday morning; his wallet, which contained twenty-six dollars in cash and one credit card; and his checkbook, balanced at fifty-one dollars and sixty-six cents. His logbook wasn't there.

Perhaps he left it in his motel room.

I strapped myself into the shoulder harness and drove toward town. My head felt naked without its helmet.

After I explained Newt's situation to the Holiday Inn desk clerk, she agreed to let me in his room accompanied by a maid. I had with me his belongings from the airplane and the car, to consolidate with the rest of his stuff.

I still found it odd that Newt would rent a luxury car and take a room here. I'd always seen him bumming rides from other jumpers or borrowing a car when he was on road, and if he stayed in a motel he always picked the cheapest one around. There were a number of cheaper motels within a few blocks of this place that would have rooms still available.

The maid unlocked the door and followed me in. I eased Newt's things down on the bed. Besides the bed, the room had a desk, a chair, a glass coffee table, a sofa, a television set, and a credenza. Newt had slung a pair of corduroy jeans and three T-shirts over the back of the chair. On the glass coffee table was sprawled more of his photography equipment. Some of the stuff was obvious: several lenses, an array of filters, two bottles with LENS CLEANER written on the outside, seven unused rolls of film, a cable of some kind. The rest, I didn't know. The art of photography I could appreciate, but for me looking at the world through a lens was like putting a border around what I saw. I didn't like borders, so I'd always steered clear of cameras.

Newt's video case sat on the floor with its lid up. There were fourteen tapes inside. His gray suitcase was on the floor next to it, also open. In it were shirts, shorts, jeans, socks, underwear, and a summer jacket.

I went over to the credenza. Angled toward each other in a way that prevented them from rolling onto the floor were Newt's two dumbbells. Beside them, this week's T.V. guide. It was under the T.V. guide that I found Newt's logbook.

It was a standard logbook: six inches high and nine wide, covered in black plastic, and held together with a spiral across the top. I turned to the last page with entries.

Newt never had a chance to log in his jumps from Friday, but he'd logged in five with Thursday's date. All were marked NATIONALS, OCTAGON, VIDEO, followed by the time of day, and a few miscellaneous comments. I paged backward.

His previous two entries were for jumps he'd made in Litchfield

June Eleventh and Fifteenth. The Eleventh was the date DeBerg had repacked Newt's reserve, but there was nothing in the entry for that jump to indicate he'd had a malfunction: VIDEO, GARBAGE TWELVE-WAY, 3:00 PM, CLEAR SKIES, BAD EXIT, GOOD GROUND SHOTS. No jumps for Oakland Ridge the previous week—that seemed to be what I remembered.

I flipped through each page and read his earlier entries until I got an idea of how he wrote them. He didn't elaborate much, but he put in enough description of each dive so that MALFUNCTION would have been there had he had one.

I put the logbook down and left the room. The maid switched off the light and locked the door behind us.

11

I didn't recognize her at first because I was expecting slender fashion model legs and she was wearing stylish baggy pants. The pants, which tapered down toward the ankle, were black, as was her silk blouse. Around her neck she had a mauve scarf. Her thick chestnut hair was drawn back in a barrette and hung straight along the line of her spine. Opaque sunglasses covered her eyes and the upper portion of her cheeks. Over her shoulder she carried a mauve flight bag, in her hand a mauve purse.

When she scanned the faces in the airport waiting room her eyes slid right over me. She hadn't remembered me from her birthday party. I'd been just another skydiver dressed in just another T-shirt and just another pair of jeans.

"Mrs. Becker?"

When she didn't react immediately, I worried that I'd made a mistake. Got the gate number wrong, or the woman. Then she seemed to hear my words in echo, and turned.

"My name is Chance. I'm here to take you to Muskogee."

She cleared her throat. "You confused me for a moment," she said. "My last name isn't Becker, it's Chimura. Paula Chimura. I kept my maiden name when Newt and I married."

"I'm sorry. I shouldn't have assumed."

She shook her head. "Everyone does it, and I'm used to it. I'm just not thinking clearly today."

"Of course." I motioned toward the waiting room chairs. "Would you like to rest before we go?"

117

"No, thank you," she said. "I can handle this."

She was the same Paula I remembered from the party—poised and polite and in control. A woman intent on taking care of herself, not the type that let men fawn over her. I quit fawning.

"Do you have any checked luggage?"

She shook her head. "I only brought my flight bag. I won't be here long."

When it appeared as though she didn't expect me to carry her flight bag, I decided it would be politic not to offer. "This way to the car, then," I said.

We started along the corridor toward the parking lot.

"Where's Dominic?" she asked.

"I convinced him I should come in his place. It's Saturday, and they'll need his plane."

"Oh, yes," she said. "I hadn't thought of that."

"Does it bother you that I came instead?"

"No, no. I was . . . surprised, that's all."

We got in the car. By the time we hit the Muskogee Turnpike the wind was barreling against the car at about twenty knots, gusting to about thirty.

Paula was sitting quietly under her shoulder harness. Her back was erect, her legs pressed together, her hands cushioned in her lap. As I swung the Olds into the left lane to pass a car, I sensed her gaze on my right cheek. "I think we've met before," she said.

I nodded. "At your birthday party last year. We spoke for a few minutes outside. I was Newt's rigger."

It didn't take her long. "Oh, yes, I remember. The one with the gigantic motorcycle parked on the sidewalk."

"There weren't any parking spaces left. You were very popular that night."

Some of the awkward formality between us broke down with that small exchange. After pulling back into the right lane, I decided the moment was right.

"What exactly did Dominic tell you about Newt's death?"

She squeezed her hands together. "That it wasn't Newt's fault. Dominic said both his parachutes malfunctioned. He said Newt never felt a thing, that it was instantaneous."

She looked over at me. "Is it really true, or was he only trying to spare me?"

"What Dominic said is true. And Newt wouldn't have seen the

118

ground coming either. He'd have been looking up at his canopy, trying to help it inflate."

She gazed down at her hands. "You must think I'm being cold. I'm supposed to be crying, making a terrible scene."

I shook my head. "Everyone handles death differently."

But she felt the need to explain. "It's just that I've been prepared for this almost since our wedding. I always knew my husband might not come home one day. Before—when we first married—if Newt was late from the drop zone, I'd get nervous. Then he'd come home and I'd rush into his arms. He'd ask what was wrong. I'd tell him, and he'd laugh. He'd say, 'I'll never die skydiving.'" Her voice trailed off.

"Yes, I've heard him say that. He shouldn't have, though. Skydiving is pretty safe these days, but nothing in life is absolute."

She nodded absently and looked out her window.

We were cruising along quietly when her body suddenly jolted. She grasped the dashboard with her hand and turned toward me. An uncomfortable chill grazed the hairs on my skin.

"Is something wrong?"

"I don't know much about skydiving," she said, almost cross, "but I know some things. You said you were Newt's rigger. That means you packed his reserve that—"

"Ahh," I cut in, understanding. "I *was* Newt's regular rigger, but I didn't pack his reserve last. Someone else did."

She maintained her position for a few more seconds, then slumped against her seat. "I'm sorry. I didn't mean to accuse you. Or anybody else. I'm not normally like this."

"Nobody's normal the day after their spouse dies. So you're normal in that respect."

She let her head fall back against the headrest and sighed a passive surrender to fate. "I always knew he might not come home one day," she said again, this time to herself.

Twenty minutes later we came to Muskogee and its strip of inexpensive motels.

"Do you want to go out to Davis Field—that's the drop zone here—or would you prefer to get a room first?"

"A room, I think. Someplace where I can wash up from the trip."

"I suppose you could take Newt's room at the Holiday Inn."

"Newt had a room at the Holiday Inn?" It puzzled her, too. But she didn't seem to want to make any more out of it than that. "Then

119

Newt's room will be fine," she said.

When we got to the motel, there was a new desk clerk on duty.

"I'm terribly sorry," he said. "We were told Mr. Becker had—" His eye caught sight of Paula, standing tall at the lobby doors. "Er—that Mr. Becker would not be returning. We emptied his room and put his property in storage."

"And I take it the room has already been reserved."

He indicated that was so, and apologized again when he explained that the motel was booked for the night. "But I'll do what I can to get Mrs. Becker a room at the Trade Winds up the street."

I thanked him and said, "Chimura—the last name is Chimura."

He nodded uncertainly, apologized again, and reserved Paula a room at the motel up the street.

I carried Newt's things into Paula's room, laid them on her bed, and made an inventory. The Holiday Inn people had packed Newt's camera equipment and clothing in his gray suitcase, his dumbbells and video case in his empty gear bag.

"So much of Newt is in that."

I glanced behind me. Paula was staring over my shoulder at Newt's camera equipment. She'd removed her dark glasses. A soft pastel shadow was covering her lids, and dark-brown mascara was insulating her lashes. But the makeup could do little to protect her eyes from grief, and they began to swell. She managed to slip into the bathroom gracefully, before shedding a tear.

I accounted for everything, then buckled the suitcase, zipped up the gear bag, and tucked them both against a corner wall. Inconspicuous there.

Paula emerged from the bathroom composed and wanting to talk with several jumpers she knew. I drove her the five miles to Davis Field. The wind was still strong when we arrived. No aviation activity at all. The beginnings of activity at the bar.

"I appreciate all the trouble you've gone to for me," she said.

"No trouble at all."

"I hate to bother you again," she said, "but could you take me back to town later? I called the Muskogee police this morning and they've decided to release Newt's rig. I'll need to pick it up and make final arrangements for his body. I suppose I should have rented a car."

"Actually, this is Newt's rental, not mine."

"Newt's? But . . . Newt never rented cars."

"I guess he made an exception this time. The agreement's in the glove compartment. It's good till Monday morning."

Paula was silent for a while, then said absently, "I forgot. You have your motorcycle. What would you be doing with a car?"

"Honestly, Paula, I don't mind driving you to town. Just say the word."

She pressed her lips together. "Perhaps I want to go alone. Let me think about it."

I was partway out of the Olds when I noticed Dominic jogging over. He looked out of sorts, unusual for Dominic. "Could have gone myself," he huffed, and hurried around to Paula's side of the car. "The wind really picked up after you left."

Paula pushed her door open. Dominic insisted on holding it while she climbed out.

"Chance has been very helpful," she said.

I shut my door and circled over. "I have a few errands to run, Paula, but I'll be around if you need me."

"I'll make sure she's taken care of," Dominic cut in. He held out his hand. "You have the key—in case we need to use the car?"

When I handed it over to him I sensed that Paula didn't approve. Her mood became formal again. "Perhaps," she suggested, "the three of us could have dinner together this evening. If you're both free."

Dominic indicated that was vaguely okay with him.

"I'd like that fine," I said. After we agreed on a place and a time, I excused myself and walked over to the manifest.

Nobody had turned in Newt's canopy. When I frowned the manifester said, "It could still be out there somewhere."

"Could be," I agreed. Then, having nothing better to do, I decided on one more try.

In the daylight, the precise spot where Newt had hit wasn't hard to find: two narrow indentations, about a foot apart, not far from the soccer complex fence. He'd hit feet first. He wouldn't have seen the ground coming, and I hadn't lied to Paula Chimura after all.

I looked around the indentations. Then I walked the whole eastern end of the parking lot. I was looking for anything except grass. I found only grass. I moved my foot back and forth in a thicket of weeds growing along the fence. Nothing in that.

The gate to the fence was several hundred feet to the west. I strode through it. The soccer complex, like the hayfield next to it, went north for quite a ways. I walked the southeast part, north-northeast of where Newt had died. There was a group of goals amassed there. The grass skirting the base of the goals was higher than the grass on the soccer field, but not high enough to conceal a hundred-and-eighty-square-foot canopy.

I leaned against one of the goals and crossed my arms. "This is useless," I muttered.

I was all set to leave when my eye picked up a splash of red along the eastern border of the complex. It was much too small to be a parachute, but I had an idea. I darted up to the spot and knelt down.

A main breakaway handle.

I combed over the surrounding area inch by inch, removing my shoes and socks from my feet and padding the grass barefoot. Twenty minutes later I was rewarded. In a high patch of grass around one of the goals I stepped down on sun-warmed metal. A reserve ripcord handle. Its serpentine cord curved invisibly through the grass around it.

I picked it up. The red thread was still tied to the pin, but the seal was gone.

I leaned back on my haunches, ran my fingers through my hair, and wondered where Newt's main was. I stood up to stretch my back, gazed indiscriminately at the soccer field grass, and fifty yards away I finally found out.

The afternoon sun must have struck it at just the right angle at just the right moment because I had missed it before. But there it was, glittering among the blades of grass. Not red and gold but metallic and bright. An elongated sigma, about four inches from end to end.

I took my pull-up cord from my pocket, threaded it under the metal, and knotted my find.

At dinner that night I detailed to Paula Chimura how her husband had been murdered.

12

The restaurant was one of the chain variety: vinyl booths with scuff marks, wash-and-wear plaid carpeting, veneer table tops with scratches, silk flowers that didn't smell. The food matched the decor—frozen, not fresh. But it was convenient.

I had requested a booth in the rear, for privacy. Paula sat across from me with Dominic on her right. She had changed into a mauve silk blouse and discarded her scarf and sunglasses. As was to be expected, her mood was somber; but she had been composed and diplomatic until I introduced the notion of murder.

"Mmm—murdered?"

I didn't like the word either. It had a contrived, unreal texture. It belonged in the movies, in detective fiction, or on the six-o'clock news.

The humane thing to do would have been to wait several days before telling her, until the initial shock wore off. But she'd said she wouldn't be staying in Oklahoma long, and divulging the details of a murder to the victim's wife wasn't my idea of a long-distance telephone call. I also had another reason for telling her now, but that could wait.

"I'm sorry, Paula. But I knew you'd expect to be told."

"But that can't be!" she protested. "Dozens of people saw Newt hit the ground. I've talked with some of them. Even you told me—that he was trying to inflate his reserve when he hit."

"Newt did bounce, Paula. I didn't mean to imply otherwise. But his gear was sabotaged."

I'd have preferred to have this entire conversation with Paula alone, but Dominic had become so protective of her that I suspected I might never get that chance.

He was wearing a blue permanent-press shirt that, along with his trimmed beard and scrubbed hands, made him appear almost white-collar. He had ordered veal patties. When I'd mentioned murder, he'd paused only slightly before taking a bite. He was chewing noise-lessly and studying the food on his plate. He wasn't going to comment.

"But the police—Dominic drove me down there this afternoon—the police don't think—"

"The police are well intentioned, I'm sure. But they don't know parachute equipment. They're not riggers."

"I've talked to other riggers. One named Simon. And Ziggy from Daytona." She was rushing her sentences. "They examined Newt's gear, and they didn't say anything about—murder."

"Simon and Ziggy don't know about this." I shifted my weight, withdrew my pull-up cord from my pocket and dangled it over the table. At its middle hung the strange-looking sigma.

She narrowed her eyes and stared at it. Dominic glanced over at it briefly.

"That looks like what the police showed me this afternoon," she said. "What they said broke. Only I think this one's smaller."

"Yes, Newt's reserve links are larger than this. Lots of riggers use the larger links on reserves for added safety."

"Then . . . what's this you're holding?" she asked.

"A connector link from Newt's main. Or it was, until yesterday. Now it's just a piece of spent metal. It bent like this on opening. Its nut was loose. That caused his main to malfunction."

"Reserves kill, not mains," Dominic stated flatly.

"Only because mains malfunction first."

He compressed his lips. "Shoddy logic."

"Yes and no," I said. "In a normal fatality it's the reserve that de-serves the attention. It's there to save life, after all. But this situa-tion isn't normal."

Paula had ordered a glass of tomato juice. She took a sip from her glass with well-learned grace, and seemed to find comfort and inner strength from that simple act. "Why do you say that?" she asked.

"Newt died," I said, "because his reserve malfunctioned. His re-serve malfunctioned because one of the connector links failed to hold on opening. Everyone agrees that's what happened. So the real question is, Why did it happen?"

Paula was staring at me intently, waiting on the answer. Dominic was looking down at his dinner, but I was sure he was taking in every word.

"I can think of three reasons for that kind of malfunction," I said. "First, the link could have been defective from the manufacturer. But Ziggy and Simon and I examined it closely last night, and it was fine."

"But it hasn't been tested yet," Paula said. Ziggy and Simon would have given her the police version.

"No," I conceded, "the link hasn't been tested. But when it is, the tests will bear out what I'm saying—Ziggy and Simon wouldn't argue with me on that. A defective link would have stripped threads and would almost certainly be in pieces. So the explanation for Newt's malfunction lies elsewhere.

"A second possibility is that the nut on the link worked itself loose over a period of time. But if that happened with Newt's rig, it means Joe DeBerg forgot to check the links three weeks ago when he packed the reserve."

Paula could see the implications. "Then you're saying the rigger could have been negligent." Anger began to well up in her throat.

"A possibility, Paula, but highly unlikely. Joe DeBerg is one of the best. I guarantee it."

"What does Joe DeBerg say?"

"Nothing, so far. He's not due here till tomorrow. But I don't think he's responsible in any event. I'm certain the reserve nut was deliberately loosened sometime after he packed the reserve in Litchfield. He wouldn't have done it himself, not when his signature's on the packing card."

"But Octagon told me Newt made lots of skydives with them yesterday and Thursday, and he didn't have any problems with his gear until his last jump."

"You can jump successfully for decades with a no-good reserve so long as you never need to use it. The reserve could have been tampered with as much as three weeks ago, right after Joe DeBerg sealed it, or as late as yesterday evening, only minutes before Newt boarded the plane."

Dominic said, "If someone fooled with the reserve he'd break the reserve seal. Newt checked his pins before every dive, so for some-

125

one to get away with it he'd have to have a rigger's press to seal the pin back up."

I nodded. "And a seal, and the red thread that ties the seal to the pin. Anybody around a drop zone has easy access to those. I found Newt's reserve ripcord this afternoon. The red thread was there but the seal was gone. It slid off on opening. My guess is whoever sabotaged Newt's rig got hold of someone's seal press and pressed a seal ahead of time to give it some letters. But he managed to keep the thread holes open enough so that later he could slip thread through the seal without actually having the seal clamped to the thread like it's supposed to be. Newt wouldn't have noticed there was anything wrong unless he inspected the seal, but most jumpers don't do that. We look at the pins. And once the seal is lost in the sky, nobody can check it."

"So what you're saying," Dominic said, "is this someone also rigged Newt's main, forcing him to go with a bad reserve."

"Yes. So far everyone's been concerned about the reserve and why it malfunctioned. That's to be expected. But I also wanted to know about the main—I was Newt's rigger after all. So I went looking for it.

"It should have landed in the western corner of the hayfield north of the airport. I went up there and walked the field last night, but by then it was really too dark. I quit, went back out this morning, looked by air, went back out this afternoon. When I saw this connector link, I knew Newt had been murdered."

Paula was toying with her glass. "I'm totally lost," she confessed. "How does what you've said mean someone killed Newt?"

"Both his main and reserve malfunctioned because of connector link failures. The chance of that happening to two chutes on a single rig on the same dive must be about a billion to one. Connector link problems aren't that common."

Our waitress dropped by, smiled courteously, and inquired about our food. I said it was delicious. She took note of my untouched chicken and Paula's tidy spinach salad, raised her eyebrows, and transferred our ketchup bottle to the next booth.

"Where did you find the main?" Dominic asked when she'd gone.

"I didn't." I carefully lowered the elongated sigma back into my pocket. "The main has completely vanished. It's not out there anywhere and no one's turned it in. Which only confirms that Newt's malfunctions were planned."

"How?" Dominic asked.

"Whoever tampered with Newt's gear knew that if both the main and reserve were found with problem connector links, there'd be a great deal of suspicion. To prevent that he—and I say *he* because the number of women in the sport makes it unlikely it was a she—he had to grab either the reserve or the main. He couldn't get to the reserve because it was attached to the harness/container, which was strapped to Newt. There's always at least one police car assigned to the airport during Nationals, and those guys would have any fatality covered quickly. So that meant taking the main, which, if planned right, wouldn't be difficult. That Newt's *accident* occurred at the end of the day was almost certainly deliberate. The timing made it less likely anyone would see where the main landed, or want to go after it if they did. While the police and everybody else were concentrating on the body, he could go after the main. The likelihood anyone would notice him wouldn't be very great. And a certain number of mains are never recovered, so he could feel confident that Newt's would be written off after a few days. He wouldn't have expected someone to search as hard as I did."

"Wait a minute," Paula said. "A few minutes ago you said Newt's rig could have been tampered with at any time in the last three weeks. But if it was done three weeks ago, how could someone know the parachute would malfunction at dusk? How could he count on that?"

"I was referring to Newt's reserve, Paula. The *reserve* link could have been loosened at any time since Joe DeBerg packed it. But the *main* link must have been loosened yesterday sometime between Newt's last dive with Octagon and Bradford Rey's diamond dive at sunset. My guess is that's also when the reserve was done, but I can't say for sure."

"Okay," she said. "But there's something else I don't understand. If you're right, wouldn't it have been easier to fix the main and the reserve two different ways and leave them both out there?"

"There aren't many ways to successfully sabotage gear. Jumpers carefully go over each external piece of equipment before exit, so any tampering would have to be done to a part of the rig not accessible by touch or sight. Something packed, in other words. And it would have to be done quickly. He couldn't count on having lots of time with Newt's rig between dives, especially if he did the main and the reserve together."

127

Dominic set his fork down and wiped his beard with his napkin. "You say the main is missing. But you've got one of its links."

I nodded. "It disengaged from its riser and lines. I was lucky to find it."

"Ever think the main was just stolen—simple theft?" he suggested. "Wouldn't be the first time."

"I've considered that, but Newt's main had nearly a thousand jumps on it. It was still safe to jump, but that was about all. It had no market value, and it couldn't be used at most drop zones because it would be easily identified. Newt got around enough for most people to know his colors. Even if someone had taken the canopy with the intention of stealing it, they'd have turned it in when they saw how used it was. No one would risk jail or being banned from drop zones for an old piece of nylon. And theft could at best explain the missing canopy. It couldn't explain the bent link."

"How do you know that link is from Newt's rig? I've been flying jumpers for a long time, enough to know main connector links are all the same."

"Basically, yes."

"It could be anyone's, then. From another malfunction."

"No, for a number of reasons. Davis Field isn't a regular drop zone. The only sport jumping here is during Nationals. I checked at the manifest this afternoon and there've been only two other malfunctions so far this year. A few hours ago I talked with both those guys. One had a complete bag lock, the other a blown seam, and neither of them lost a connector link. Besides," I added, "their malfunctions happened south of the drop zone. I found this link up in the soccer complex, a little northeast of where Newt landed."

My throat was raw. I drank some iced tea.

"So that takes us back to last year's Nationals. Any link from last year would have been nicked up by a lawn mower and buried under the dirt. This one, as you saw, was smooth and clean. It was imbedded in grass mowed less than three days ago, I'd say."

Paula finished her juice and Dominic offered to order her another. She said thank you, but no, and rubbed her arms to stimulate her blood vessels against the room's air conditioning. "You seem so sure about all of this—that Newt was murdered."

"It's too much of a coincidence to be anything else."

"Have you gone to the police?" Dominic asked.

I shook my head.

Paula spoke decisively as she reached for her purse. "I'll go with you then. We can leave right now."

When I didn't respond to Paula's movements of leaving, her reaction was swift. "But if you're positive, you must tell them. You must!"

A young couple seated nearby looked over at her. I waited until they lost interest and went back to their meal.

"Right now," I said, "the only evidence I have is the main connector link, and maybe the ripcord with no seal. I doubt the police would pay much attention to a homeless rigger who strolled in the door with an obscure four-inch piece of bent metal and a perfectly good ripcord and claimed it proved some out-of-town skydiver had been murdered at their airport. It's only my word I found them where I say I did, and in their present condition. Even if they took me seriously, they wouldn't be able to figure out who did it. They don't know skydiving, so they wouldn't know the right questions to ask."

Paula pressed her purse back to her seat. After she'd calmed down she said, "Then what's the next step, Chance?"

It was the same question I'd put to myself after finding the sigma-shaped connector link. What next?

You don't voluntarily turn your back on five years of noninvolvement when those five years have been your best ones. Mind, body, soul—all flourishing in the simple, untroubled life of drop zone living. And there is nothing sinful or decadent about wanting only that. Pack three rigs, make a jump. Wash out my clothes, copilot a DC-3, build a hangar, run five miles, relax in my tent, tinker with the Honda, wander through a book, make a jump. That was my world—the unencumbered world of drop zones and motorcycles and airplanes. Not the world of murder.

I hadn't turned my back on my world at all; I'd been kidnapped from it by circumstances. The emotional trauma I'd gone through when I thought Newt had died on my pack job had been acute, its effects lasting. It was as though I'd been knocked out without warning, and when I'd come to a short time later I'd acquired a persistent ringing in my ears that would not leave me.

I could not rewrite history. I could not obliterate from my memory the sight of that lump, or those two indentations formed by what had once been Newt's long thin feet. I could not ignore Jeepers the puppet and his biting parables on justice. So I could not pack up the Honda and ride away from Newt's murder the way I had run from everything else the past five years. I had no intention of being a hero, but for my own reasons I knew I was going to keep asking question after question until I knew and could prove who had sabotaged Newt's links, because as of last night his business had become mine.

"What's the next step?" Paula asked again. She'd taken a tight grip on my wrist. "What do we do now?"

I blinked. "I'm going to keep searching," I said.

She let go of my wrist. "But why you, Chance?"

"Because Newt was my client. That could have been my signature on his packing card. I still don't know why it wasn't."

"Don't you think you should at least tell the police what you're doing?"

"It wouldn't serve any purpose, not till I've got more proof. I went to law school a while back, and I know I'm on very shaky ground legally. As a parachute rigger, though, I know I'm right."

"But do you even know where to begin?"

It was the lead-in I'd been waiting for.

"Motive," I said, "I need to work out the motive. Start from the other end and work my way back to opportunity. I think I already have a lead. Last month I drove up on Newt lying in the road at the Oakland Ridge drop zone. He'd been beaten pretty badly."

"Beaten?" she said, but she wasn't as shocked as she could have been.

Dominic sat quietly while I explained my job with Satin Cruise the past month. I described the Oakland Ridge incident and Newt's behavior the entire month. "He wasn't being private," I said. "He was being secretive."

She gazed at her untouched spinach salad.

"Paula, when I told you Newt had been murdered, you didn't say, 'Who would do that to Newt?' or 'I can't believe anyone would want to kill Newt.' That would be the usual reaction of a spouse with no reason to think different. You must suspect something."

She picked up her fork and prodded the olives in her salad, moving them around as if searching for something buried below.

"I don't know," she said, almost in a whisper. She shifted uncomfortably in the booth.

"Christ, Chance, she just lost her husband yesterday!" Dominic blurted. It was the first time I'd ever heard him swear. He wrapped a protective arm around her shoulders.

Paula slowly raised her head, then shrunk her shoulders. Dominic understood her body language and took back his arm.

"I'm fine, Dominic," she said politely. "And I appreciate your concern. But I realize what Chance is trying to do, and he's right. The only way to find out what really happened is to ask questions."

To me she said, "If someone killed Newt, I want them punished. But I don't know how I can help. He's been away from Florida since April. We talked every other day, but you can't really get a feel for a person over the phone."

"What about when he was in Florida, before Satin Cruise left to go north? You would have seen him a lot then."

Paula shook her head. "I retired from modeling in the fall. Maybe you knew about that."

"No, Newt never mentioned it."

"Well, I did. In October. I don't travel like I used to, but I've been spending at least sixty hours a week establishing myself as an account executive in a public relations firm, so Newt and I hadn't spent much time together this year." That thought seemed to throw her for a minute, then she recovered and said, "I did notice that he'd changed *some* . . ."

"How had he changed?"

She glanced over at Dominic. I got the feeling she really wasn't comfortable talking about her relationship with Newt in front of him.

Finally she said, "It all started when I left modeling. I'd done reasonably well, but the work was less steady after twenty-five. It pretty much dried up after thirty. Models and football players have it the same—short, often bittersweet careers. All the girls know this when they start out, but some have a hard time when they get older. No skills to do anything else. Well, I went into PR. I'd made lots of friends in the media, and I like people, so I was a natural for that kind of work."

She paused to formulate her next words.

"We've basically lived on my salary. Almost none of the money Newt made went for bills. Some did, but mostly it went back into his photography business. He'd expanded into video, and was getting involved in color development. He'd always justify things like that as investment for the future. The video, yes—everyone's doing video. But I think the color development was more of a toy. I didn't mind, though, really I didn't, because it made him happy.

"When we first married, we made vague plans. I'd model and support him with my earnings while he built his business. Then when

I got too old, I'd retire and have kids, and he'd do the supporting. But the more I worked, the more I found I liked working. I knew I could work and have kids too—lots of women are doing that these days. Meanwhile, Newt's business was still unsettled. That never bothered him as long as I was modeling because neither of us considered it permanent. But after I landed the PR job, Newt began to feel . . . deficient. He was never the macho type, but I guess my success hurt his ego more than he'd admit."

"You don't have to be a man to feel uneasy about living off someone else," I said.

"I know. But men seem less willing to tolerate the situation than women. And it got to be more than just the money thing. Newt became self-conscious about his body, especially his lanky build. He started taking protein supplements, and he joined a health club. Just before Satin Cruise left Florida in April, he bought a pair of small weights to cart with him."

She pressed her fork down against her salad bowl. "I've digressed," she said. "I was talking about our finances. Newt almost became obsessed with making money. He was going to earn so much money I wouldn't need to work at all. He ignored the fact that I loved working and had no intention of quitting. We were going to buy an expensive house, Newt said. He's originally from New England, so he had a northern concept about houses. Ours was going to be stone and paneled with real oak. It was going to have a loft overlooking the living room, and the living room would have a big stone fireplace where we could roast chestnuts if it ever got cold. We live in *Florida*, but that was Newt."

Paula's eyes had been fixed on an invisible spot above her salad. Now she focused them directly on me.

"I told him we could use my money to buy this dream house of his, but he said no, we'd wait until he could pay for the whole thing himself. It was a matter of pride for him. He raised his prices this spring on student pictures and videos, and he was working on a series of instructional videos, but the market really isn't there for big profit."

I said, "I noticed he didn't have enough money is his checkbook and wallet to cover the rental car or the motel room. He must have charged them to his credit card."

She shook her head vigorously. "Newt didn't make enough to have his own credit card, which never bothered him because he always dealt in cash, anyway. I gave him a card to my account, but he never charged anything to it. He'd have needed it to reserve the car and the room, I suppose, but I know he wasn't planning to charge them to it. Especially not now. He had too much pride at stake."

She took a deep breath. "One day several weeks ago—maybe a month ago—when he called me he was very excited. He told me to line up several real estate agents and start making appointments for houses. He said he'd have a lot of money soon. At first he said he'd have the money within a week or two, but a little later he said it might take more time. Still, he was quite excited about it all month. Each time he'd call he'd ask how many houses I'd looked at, and did I like any of them, and should we build our own from scratch."

She glanced down at her salad. "I hadn't really been looking seriously. I did contact one agent to please him, but I thought it was all talk. Just his ego.

"Then on Monday he called to say he'd have the money in a week, enough for a large down payment. He repeated that on Wednesday. That was the last time I talked to him, the last thing he said to me. He was supposed to call last night. When Dominic called I thought— I thought it was Newt."

I said delicately, "You knew your husband better than anybody, Paula. Would he have gotten mixed up in something illegal?"

She didn't answer immediately. When she did she said, "The old Newt never would."

"And the new?"

"I don't know. I don't want to believe it. But it's been in the back of my mind, ever since he first mentioned big money."

"He didn't tell you where this money was coming from?"

She shook her head. "Only that he'd stumbled on a business opportunity he couldn't turn down."

"Relating to photography?"

"That's what he said. But he wouldn't go into any details."

A weariness that had been creeping up on Paula suddenly consumed her. "I don't think I can answer another question tonight, Chance. We can talk more tomorrow. I'll stop out at the drop zone before I leave."

Dominic raised his eyebrows. "Leaving tomorrow?"

She nodded. "I'd rather deal with this in Florida. My family is all there."

I thought Dominic did a reasonably good job of not appearing too disappointed.

After he and I finished our dinners and Paula refused a doggie bag for hers, he drove her back to her motel in the Olds. I passed by the Holiday Inn on the Honda. Its marquee welcoming skydivers was now lit up bright because it was dark outside.

13

The monotonous sound of stampeding horses rumbled over my head, but it was the cold numbness in my feet that woke me up. Water, that great conductor of heat, had sucked all of the warmth from their soft outer tissue and was now aiming for bone. I shifted my feet, searching for a dry spot, but the whole toe box of my sleeping bag was wet. I raised my knees, reached down, and grasped hold of my iceberg toes.

After about ten minutes, they felt like pincushions. It was enough for me to wish them numb again. I swore, unzipped the tent, and poked my head outside.

It was sometime after dawn, but the thick rain clouds were letting through just a smidgen of light. The only movement at the airport came from the clouds, and they weren't traveling fast—maybe seven, eight miles an hour.

I wanted to talk to someone from the Octagon team about Newt, but I didn't know where they were staying, and it was too wet to go door-to-door knocking. I pulled my head in, closed up the tent, and crawled back in my sleeping bag.

I hadn't slept much last night; my mind kept racing backward, trying to play catch-up with Newt. But when you consistently write other people out of your life, overlooking, ignoring, evading, you miss the slip-ups and the coincidences that would otherwise be clues. I'd gone back through my whole month with Satin Cruise, but except for the Oakland Ridge incident, I couldn't come up with anything concrete.

At least talking with Paula had been helpful. Newt's double malfunction was almost certainly tied to his recent talk of big money, and I could guess that that money was illegal. He wouldn't have given Paula an indefinite "business opportunity" explanation of a pending financial windfall if it were at all legitimate.

In fact, what it really sounded like was blackmail. Assuming Newt hadn't lied to Paula about the photography connection, how else could he earn a big chunk of money so quickly? Obviously he was trying to sell something. Something he believed could command a fairly high price.

Last Monday Newt told Paula he'd have the money this week, so whatever deal he was trying to pull off must have been finalized then. That was the same day he announced he was coming here to Nationals instead of going home to Florida. He reserved a room and rented a car without the cash to pay for them, and Paula was certain he wouldn't charge them to her account, so he must have expected to collect his money here. The car rental agreement was good till early Monday, so the payoff was probably slated for sometime Sunday. Today, that is.

Then what?

Newt must have imagined himself jaunting home to Florida, buying his dream house, and restoring his self-confidence. It might have worked, except that whoever he was blackmailing had apparently drawn up a quite different set of plans.

That brought me to the question of who. Who could Newt have been blackmailing? Who beat him unconscious in Oakland Ridge? Who sabotaged his rig?

There was an abrupt knock at my tent. Not a knock like you hear against a piece of wood. This was muffled, and could be seen more easily than heard. The whole tent shook.

"Hey, Chance, man—you awake?"

The zipper to the tent's mesh flew up and Danny Death snuck inside. In one hand he had his gear bag, in the other a grungy blanket—damp enough to give me goose bumps when it brushed against my face.

"Hey, Chance, mind if I crash here? It's fuckin' rainin' out there, and I got no place to hide."

"Sure," I yawned. "Afraid my air mattress is only wide enough for one, though."

"A mattress, the ground—makes no difference to me."

I moved against the side of the tent to accommodate him. "It's wet down at the other end. You'll want to keep your gear up here."

He nodded and began rearranging my stuff. His hair was clumped together and dripping, and he was still wearing Lonny Carmichael's tinted glasses.

"Where did you sleep last night?"

"Around," was all he said.

I closed up the tent. "What about your friend Arn?"

"No room. He's got one of them one-person jobs. Ya know, the fuckin' tent's smaller than the fuckin' sleeping bag. A fuckin' waste of money, if you ask me."

He propped his gear bag next to mine and spread out his blanket. Meticulously he smoothed out each wrinkle, exhibiting a degree of fastidiousness I would not have considered for him. He climbed on top, folded half of it over his body, then squiggled and squirmed for several minutes till he got comfortable. His back was to me.

"Don't you want to take your shoes off?"

"Too much trouble."

"If they're wet, your feet will freeze."

He raised his shoulders in a shrug. "Never bothered me before."

The banter of rain continued in a steady cadence. I wondered idly how much of my tent would get wet.

Danny Death rolled toward me. I could hear him breathing unevenly.

"Hey, Chance?"

"Yeah?"

"Thanks. I knew I didn't get you wrong."

Danny Death's biological age was probably a year or two greater than mine, but the lines of time and raw experience carved into his face were this morning blotted out by the storm's darkness. With their absence he seemed much younger, almost adolescent.

"You owe me one," I said, never intending to collect. I would, though.

He propped his head up with his elbow and stared at me silently. I closed my eyes and tried to fall asleep. After a while he said, "I don't get you."

Most people didn't, but if I told Danny Death that made him like everybody else, I'd ruin his week.

"I mean, you live in a tent and ride a motorcycle and hop around from gig to gig like a bum. But I hear you aced some hotshot ivy law school and all."

"That was a long time ago," I mumbled.

"How come you dropped out?"

"Can't we talk about this some other time?"

"But how come you did? You get sick of all the fuckin' establishment bullshit?"

I wasn't going to get any sleep. I sighed and sat up.

"Since you brought it up," I said, "Don't you think *the establishment* is an awfully general concept."

"But you gotta know there's people out there that say this is how you're supposed to act, and there's tons more people out there that lap it all up—no different from stray dogs beggin' to be trained."

"More or less."

"So what's wrong in lumpin' 'em all together and callin' 'em the fuckin' establishment, which is what they are?"

"From that point of view, nothing I suppose. It's just that when you group people together, you emphasize their similarities. If you look at them individually, you can see their differences."

"Except if you're gonna do that you gotta have a fuckin' microscope to see anythin'."

"Maybe. I guess it all depends on your perspective."

He turned over on his stomach, supported himself with both elbows, and raised his feet.

"So if you're not against the fuckin' establishment, how come you're not a fuckin' yup lawyer, then? How come you chucked it all and live like you do?"

"Personal reasons. No social statement, that's for sure."

Danny Death didn't like being on his stomach. He turned back onto his side.

"But you don't do drugs—I can tell. Funny how you're such an okay guy and all. I wouldn'ta thought."

I smiled at Danny Death's logic.

"How come you don't? Do drugs, I mean."

"Oh, primarily a matter of health, I guess."

"So you're one of those, huh? A health nut."

I looked over at him long and hard. Finally I said, "I have to be independent, Danny. It's the way I am. Staying in shape is my insurance. You neglect a machine, pretty soon the machine won't run. Same with the body. Besides, I like my brain lucid, not murky. It enhances the quality of my life."

His tone had annoyed me. I hadn't realized I was going to have to defend my lifestyle to a grumpy little artist with whom I was generously sharing my tent. I tried not to show my irritation, but wasn't entirely successful.

"And anyway," I added, "I'm not out to prove to anyone, least of all myself, that I'm different. I just am."

He stiffened. "So what the fuck does that mean?"

"Think about it, Danny. Isn't that why you go to great lengths to see the world as *us* or *me* versus *them*? You lump together the majority, who look similar on the outside. At the same time you make yourself look different from them on the outside—the way you dress, the way you don't groom—so you feel different on the inside."

He didn't deny it. "Ya gotta know who you are, Chance, if you're gonna create art. Can't put your soul down on canvas without knowin' it first."

"So one of the ways you separate yourself from *them* is by taking drugs, because you think *they* don't, or in any case that *they* don't approve."

"Half," he agreed. "And half I do drugs 'cause they're fun."

"Would they be as much fun if the president of the United States took them, and all the members of Congress, and the top military brass, and the ministers and priests, and whoever else it is that represents the establishment to you?"

At first he laughed at the idea, then said, "Probly not. But so what?" There was an edge of defiance in his voice. He was on the defensive, like I'd just been.

"You see yourself as a nonconformist, am I right?"

"Yep."

"At the same time you feel spiteful toward people who don't think like you or dress like you or behave like you. You're basically intolerant."

"I'm no hypocrite."

"But don't you see, Danny? You can have your own identity without condemning others for theirs."

He shook his head. "*You* can, maybe. Me, I gotta do it my own way."

"Except that your way is so self-destructive. The human body can only take drug abuse for so long before it calls you on it. You're not young like you used to be."

"I'd rather have a short life that's my own than a long one that's someone else's."

139

I couldn't come up with a quick response to that.

"Living is a whole lot cheaper without drugs," I said. "You could afford a lot more skydives."

"I get by."

"Without drugs, you might not be so miserable."

"Who says I'm miserable?"

"I do."

"Well, I'm not."

"Well, you are too. You wouldn't be so belligerent if you weren't. It's eating you alive inside. Sometimes it makes you mean and nasty outside."

"So maybe I like bein' mean and nasty." His voice was rising.

For some reason I was feeling aggressive, too. "You're fighting a civil war inside you, Danny," I said. "On the one side is Danny the Nonconformist, a person separate from the crowd. He enjoys being the black sheep. But to be the black sheep, everyone else has to be white. So this Danny sees the world that way—black and white. Life would be easy for you if that's all there was to Danny Death Grimes. Everything would be clear-cut. But it isn't clear-cut because there's another Danny who isn't at all sure the world's that simple. In fact, he knows it isn't. He's smart. He perceives nuances, like just now when you were trying to figure me out. Whenever this sophisticated Danny pops up, Danny the Nonconformist feels threatened. So he defends himself by lashing out at others—his way of trashing the other Danny."

My left index finger was hurting. I looked down at it. I was slicing into it with my right thumbnail.

Danny Death pushed his blanket aside and sat up next to me. We were both quiet for some time.

Finally he said, "Funny how you barely know me, but yet you do. They teach fuckin' psychology at that law school?"

I shook my head. "No," I said quietly. "It's just that I've been there. A different set of circumstances, a different civil war. But I've been there."

I couldn't help wondering if I was there again. If maybe the carefree Chance of the last five years was fighting off a challenge from another Chance. The Chance committed to solving Newt Becker's murder.

"Okay," Danny Death conceded, "so maybe I *am* miserable here and there. But you make it out to be drugs that's at fault when it's drugs that keep things from bein' worse than they are."

140

I rubbed my face, then sank back into my sleeping bag. "Sometimes, Danny, people lecture others when they're really talking to themselves. Just forget what I said, okay?"

He looked at me, then shrugged and said, "Whatever." He lay down and threw his blanket over his hips. But he couldn't stop wriggling and squiggling. Finally he sat back up.

"Chance?"

"Yeah?"

"But don't you ever get angry at the fuckin' world for the way it is?"

"I used up my share of that kind of anger years ago. Whoever manufactures the stuff won't allot me any more."

"You mean you never get angry that people just work and buy a house and work and pay the bills and work and die. You never get angry at that?"

"Not if it makes them happy."

He shook his head. "Man, wish I didn't get angry. Wish I could just take everythin' like it is. Wish I could come down from a fuckin' funnel and laugh it off. Wish I didn't get mad about Lon dying. And Joe DeBerg missin' Newt Becker's link. And the fuckin' Pit Bull—sometimes he makes me so mad . . ."

I looked over at him. Even in the dim light I could see his eyes start to burn.

He removed Lonny Carmichael's glasses from the bridge of his nose and stared down at them. Sorrow replaced the anger in his voice. "Lon was the best buddy a guy could ever have," he said. "I still can't believe he'd hit his head on exit. I know what everybody says, but I just don't buy it."

Had this conversation taken place later in the day, I'd have had a lot to say. As it was, I patted him on the shoulder, turned in my sleeping bag, and let him commune with his memories in private.

He settled back down. Twenty minutes later his breathing became heavy and regular. It took mine a while longer.

14

The rain had stopped by the time I woke up again. Next to me Danny Death slept with deep conviction under his damp blanket. His body had the same glacial appearance it had had last month when I pulled him off the packing table back in Findlay.

I didn't have any clean shirts, so I put on yesterday's red T-shirt. I'd hand washed it last night, and it was still a little damp.

Outside the tent, I looked up at the sky. The clouds were breaking up and the sun was poking through. Elevenish. In another half-hour it would be jumpable.

Macintosh stopped by and asked if I was on a load yet. He reminded me I'd promised back in Findlay to jump with him here at Nationals.

"Not this morning," I said apologetically. "Thought you were doing the big loads now?"

He cast his eyes down at the grass. "I was on one yesterday. I—I had some problems."

Bradford Rey's second diamond attempt, I thought. It had taken off late yesterday after the wind had died, when I was absorbed with connector links.

"What went wrong?" I asked.

Macintosh cringed. "I flew into someone else's slot. There were two jumpsuits the exact same color. Even their grippers were alike. The one I docked on was in the second row, the one I should have docked on was in the third. The Pit Bull got real mad. He said he could've had a completed diamond if not for me. He cut me off the next one

143

and said that was it for me. I'd made my mistake."

Macintosh looked as though his pet dog had just been hanged.

"You'll get another shot," I assured him. "Bradford Rey isn't the only mega-load organizer, and most of the others will understand that you've only got three hundred jumps."

"Three hundred *fifty-four* as of yesterday. I jumped a lot in June."

"Okay," I said, "you've only got three hundred fifty-four jumps. You fly well for that number, much better than average. So ease up on yourself. When you relax, your awareness and skills will improve."

He looked up at me. "You really think so? You really think I'm flying okay?"

"Most skydivers with your skills have over five hundred jumps."

"But The Pit Bull said—"

"Screw The Pit Bull. My guess is his diamond would have fizzled no matter where you docked. You're a convenient scapegoat, that's all."

Macintosh's long face shortened up. "Danny's inside," I added, pointing to the tent. "Maybe he'll jump with you."

Macintosh smiled, poked his head inside, and woke up Danny Death. After some initial profanity Danny Death said sure, why the hell not, and Macintosh skipped off to find two more jumpers.

I was looking around for Octagon when I noticed Newt's Olds bearing down on the airport. As it approached, I could see that Paula was driving. In the passenger's seat sat Dominic.

She pulled off the road behind the airport restaurant. They got out and chatted for a few minutes at the hood of the car. Then the manifester paged Dominic over the public address. Dominic embraced Paula as she stood there woodenly, then went into the manifest office. I walked over.

She had on yesterday's black slacks and an ivory blouse. She was wearing her sunglasses, her jaw was tense, and she was fighting with her mouth over exactly what to say. The cool, precise exterior that had greeted me at the Tulsa Airport, the one she had clung to doggedly last night, was finally melting.

"Chance?" she began, and stumbled over her next words. "Could you—could you take me to Tulsa to catch my plane back to Florida?"

"Of course. What's the departure time?"

"Two-forty," she said, visibly relieved. "We should leave here by quarter after one."

"I'll be ready," I said. "Would you mind leaving Newt's videos behind with me? I'd like to take a look at them."

"No, I don't mind, as long as I get them back. Newt's skydiving videos are a part of him I don't want to lose."

"Consider them already returned," I said. "One other thing. Yesterday I noticed Newt only had unexposed rolls of film for his still camera."

"Yes. He liked developing pictures himself. He always sent the exposed rolls home unless he was in a hurry for them. In fact, a shipment came just this Thursday."

"Perhaps you should have them developed."

She looked at me askance for a few seconds. "When I get to Florida," she agreed. "Right now I'm going back to the motel to check out, then I have some errands to run."

"Do you really think you should be driving by yourself, Paula?"

She nodded. "There's something I have to do alone. I'll be careful."

And with that she excused herself, got into the Olds, and drove toward town.

Dominic came out of the manifest with his copilot. He stole a quick glance at the empty space where the Olds had been. Then he and his copilot walked over to Satin Cruise.

I found Octagon over at the American Kestrel DC-3, parked on the tarmac west of the restaurant. All eight of them were crammed into the doorway, dirt diving an exit. Four times they sucked up their discipline and lost themselves in a collective movement from the doorway. Four times they evaluated their effort and made adjustments. But their first attempt had been their best one.

Frustrated, they took a break. I sauntered over.

I didn't know any of them well, but of the three I'd jumped with in Florida back in March, one had been nice enough to share a six-pack of seltzer with me later that night. His name was Aslam Khan. A Pakistani by birth, Aslam had naturally dark skin that the Florida sun had grilled almost black. There was a strained reserve about him that I supposed came from living in a culture that was not his own.

He was strolling off the tarmac behind his teammates when he saw me. He smiled and walked over, pinching his lower lip with his thumb and forefinger.

"It was a fifteen-point four-way from twelve thousand feet. We formed spinning cats and compressed accordions. It was in March.

This is our previous meeting, no?"

"You got it," I said. "But you left out the opal exit. That gave the dive personality."

He inhaled a breath of lost memory. "You are correct, Chance. I did in fact forget the opal, but it is written in my logbook, I can assure you. In the future we must perform that sequence again."

"You're on."

His looked suddenly disappointed. "But not in this particular week, I am sorry. Octagon is consuming all of my time. After practice finishes each day I am . . . er . . ."

"Burned out?"

"Burned out," he agreed. "I am a machine with no petrol. I am glad the competition is close at hand. We have three more days only to wait."

"What do you think of your chances?"

His lips bubbled as he let go a lungful of air. "Realistically, the gold is not to be ours. Unless the Golden Knights falter. But when did this last happen?" He frowned. Then his frown gave way to optimism. "But our team has an opportunity to claim the silver, and that is our goal this year. Of course, we could falter also. It is our exits that concern us. Sometimes they . . . disintegrate."

"What's the problem?"

"This is a very difficult question to answer. There must be a reason, of course. But we have tried different modifications, and they succeed no better. It is frustrating because our good exits are very successful." He looked baffled. "It is my wish you had accepted our proposal in March."

I shook my head. "I said it back then, Aslam. Competition isn't for me."

"Yes, yes, I know. And I am not pushing."

"Besides," I said, "I don't know much about eight-way."

"But you learn very rapidly, Chance. If you change your mind, we intend to be a team for several years more. You could clearly help us."

"Thanks. I'll keep it in mind," I said only to be polite. "Right now, though, I'm hoping you can help me."

"If I am able. What is your problem."

"It's about Newt Becker."

His face misted over with bewilderment. "How it is I am able to help concerning Newton?"

"Perhaps you knew I was his rigger."

"No. I understood Joe DeBerg was Newton's rigger."

"Only once. Except for that last pack job, I rigged for Newt the past three years. And now I've got some questions relating to his death."

"I see," Aslam said, not completely certain that he did. "But how I am able to help?"

"Newt jumped with your team most of the day on Friday."

"Yes, Newton filmed our practice dives on Friday. And Thursday also."

"How much time would you say there was between your last team jump and Newt's diamond load?"

He thought. "Very little. Especially for a photographer. Thirty minutes, perhaps."

"During which time Newt had to pack his rig and get his camera gear ready."

"That is correct." Aslam scratched his chin and tugged at some skin. "There is a rumor Newton's main had knotted lines from careless packing. Is this what you are suggesting?"

"Right now I'm not suggesting anything. I just want to piece together the last hour of Newt's life. Do you know if he left his gear unattended between his last two dives?"

He thought. "Now that you ask, I remember he did leave his parachute. He went over to Satin Cruise to switch his cameras and jumpsuits."

"Before or after he packed his main?"

"It was in the middle."

"I don't get you."

"Newton had put his canopy into his container when Bradford Rey went over and asked him to film the diamond. Newton rushed to Satin Cruise to switch cameras and jumpsuits. He returned and closed his container at that time."

"Did Bradford Rey stick around Newt's rig and wait for him?"

"No, he left to organize his diamond when Newton went over to Satin Cruise."

"You didn't happen to see anybody else near the rig while Newt was gone?"

Aslam tugged at his chin again. "I cannot say. I went back to packing my own parachute, and I was perhaps thirty meters from Newton's parachute."

"Was anyone else packing nearby?"

"I do not think. I am able to say none of my team was packing. That day it was very hot and very humid. After our last jump, my team threw their parachutes unpacked into our mobile house, and went quickly to the bar. That is their habit, even when it is not hot and humid."

"How long would you say Newt was over at Satin Cruise?"

"Ten minutes. Perhaps fifteen minutes."

I sighed. Newt had left his rig unattended, its container open, for ten, maybe fifteen minutes. He'd made it so easy. As easy as saying, "There you go. There's my rig. Do with it what you will." I suppressed a spark of irritation at him. Didn't he even suspect somebody might want him dead? Or did his lust for money override his sense of caution?

"I never quite understood the arrangement between Octagon and Newt. Do you mind if I ask about it?"

Aslam shrugged. "Our relationship with Newton was not a secret. What do you wish to know?"

"Dominic said Newt originally planned to go back to Illinois with your team while he flew east to work the boogies."

"This is so."

"When did that all change?"

"It was Memorial Day."

"Then that would have been in Findlay."

"That is correct. Newton said he would not return with us."

"Did he say why?"

"He said it was a business opportunity."

"Photography?"

"Yes, he said this."

"And you didn't complain?"

"Of course Octagon complained. But our agreement was not formal. What could we do? Since that time we have not had a regular cameraman." He paused. "Perhaps if Newton had filmed us in June, our exit problem would now be solved."

The manifester announced the first load of the day over the public address. It would leave in fifteen minutes, so let's get a move on it.

"Did anyone on your team arrange for Newt to come here to Nationals?"

Aslam shook his head. "We had no contact with Newton since Memorial Day. He came to us here on Wednesday and said he was available to film our practice dives through Sunday."

148

"But not after Sunday?"

"He said through Sunday only."

"Did he happen to mention the name of anyone he expected to meet here?"

Again Aslam shook his head. "We spoke only of our mutual business."

One of Aslam's teammates scurried over from the electrical hookup zone. "Finally found you," he complained. "Our load's up. Let's go!" He hustled off as quickly as he'd arrived.

"I must leave you, Chance," Aslam said humbly. "I hope my answers have been helpful."

"They have."

He smiled. "I am glad. And remember, we must make that dive again." The engines on the American Kestrel started up. Aslam hurried off after his teammate. I strolled off the tarmac and thought about what Aslam had said.

Newt must have found himself here at Nationals with nothing to do, so he offered to tape Octagon to help pass the time. But only through Sunday. That supported my guess about a payoff date. But if blackmail was the answer, why had Newt been so careless with his gear? Had he underestimated his victim? Or had his victim been someone other than his killer? Someone not here at Nationals on Friday when his parachute had been rigged.

Something else Aslam said was bothering me. He said Newt split from Octagon on Memorial Day. Lonny Carmichael bounced the Saturday before Memorial Day, and Newt was beaten up in Oakland Ridge the Wednesday after Memorial Day. Alex Laird liked to fight, and Alex Laird was the main witness in Lonny Carmichael's death.

I shook my head. Something didn't quite fit. On Lonny Carmichael's last jump Newt was with Octagon, several hundred yards away from Carmichael and Laird in the sky. And later that night at Jake's Newt told me he didn't even know anyone had bounced till he got to the ground. I didn't think he was lying about that. So how could Lonny Carmichael and Newt Becker possibly be connected?

And what about master rigger Joe DeBerg? Why was his signature on Newt's reserve packing card?

Ziggy had said Joe was arriving here today. Maybe, I thought, the people running the Riggers Conference over at the Armory would know exactly when.

I'd gone maybe a hundred yards toward the Armory when I heard Macintosh shouting my name. I turned around. He was geared up and trotting toward me.

"Been looking all over for you . . . Danny and Arn and I are manifested . . . on that DC-3 load they called . . . with a New York jumper." He managed to choke it out between gasps of air. "His friends showed up—the New Yorker's . . . so he backed out. He's going to jump with them now."

Macintosh gulped a couple breaths of air. "Can't you take the New Yorker's place, Chance? The dive's already planned as a four-way and we might end up scratching if you don't. Everyone's manifesting now that the weather is clearing, and the loads are backing up. We'll have to wait more than two hours for another. It'll be simple for you. We can go over it on the way to altitude. All you need to do is get your gear and climb in the plane." He was bouncing impatiently on his heels and knocking his fists together. It was obvious he wanted to make a skydive. Now.

"I'm really busy, Macintosh. What about Cheeks?"

"He's over at the Riggers Conference. And you did say you'd jump with me."

Before I had a chance to say no, we were joined by Danny Death and Arn. They had my rig, jumpsuit, helmet, goggles, and gloves.

"Couldn't find your altimeter," Arn huffed. "Looked everywhere."

"I rely on my eyes."

"So come on then!" Macintosh insisted. "Or it'll leave without us!"

I *did* promise Macintosh, I thought, and the jump won't take long. And I could use one anyway, not having made one since before Newt Becker went in.

I got dressed and inspected my gear on the plane. They taught me my part on the ride to altitude: star, turn ninety left, compressed accordion, turn one-eighty right, opposed diamond, turn ninety left, diamond, again from the top. I concentrated, visualized the sequence, and hoped I wouldn't screw up.

Macintosh was shaking his head when I touched down in the camping area next to him. "I wish I could fly like that," he said with envy. "No dirt dive and you still outclassed us."

"You'll get there in a few years," I said.

He didn't have enough awareness yet to realize that I'd turned left instead of right on the first sequence between points two and three. And I had no intention of telling him either.

15

The grass had dried from the morning rain, but the soil beneath it was still moist. We scrounged around in the camping area till we found a dry spot to pack our chutes.

I flaked out my canopy. Next to me Macintosh was doing the same until he noticed Cheeks walking back from the Riggers Conference, at which point he abandoned his canopy, hurried over, and begged Cheeks to lobby slots for the both of them on the next mega-load.

Cheeks seemed noncommittal, and I couldn't help noticing that his attitude toward Macintosh had changed. Before he'd accepted, if not cultivated, his role as mentor. But now he appeared slightly annoyed with Macintosh. Like a parent who's grown tired of a child's nagging.

Personally, I was feeling slightly annoyed with Cheeks. I still didn't like his comment the other night about the dead novice. And even if Macintosh did screw up the second diamond, so what?

Macintosh came back to his parachute. It had caught air, and he had to start flaking it out all over again.

After he finished he said, "Yesterday when we were dirt diving the second diamond there were two empty slots—the jumpers got tired of waiting on the wind and canceled out. The Pit Bull asked the rest of us if we knew any good jumpers that hadn't started drinking. I told him I thought I knew one, and he said go fetch him. I remembered what you said about not liking big loads, but I thought there was no harm in asking. I mean, who would pass up a chance to jump with The Pit Bull?" He shrugged. "But when I went to get you, I couldn't find you anywhere."

"I might have been hunting Newt Becker's main up by the soccer complex."

"Ahh . . . didn't look there." He folded his canopy over itself and pressed out the remaining air with his forearms. "So did you find it?"

"Newt's main? No, I didn't."

I grouped my lines and looped them through the first rubber band, then snaked them back and forth across my canopy bag, pulling the stows through the remaining rubber bands.

"Over at the Riggers Conference they're speculating that Becker might have had knotted lines on his main," Cheeks said.

I glanced up. He'd walked over and was observing me pack.

"That can't be confirmed without the canopy," I said.

He agreed. "But of course it's really the reserve that counts."

He stepped back from our rigs, pulled out his cigarette box, and lit one of his foreign cigarettes. "I sure wouldn't want to be Joe DeBerg tonight," he said through a funnel of smoke.

"Is that when he gets here?" I asked, remembering my mission to the Armory.

Cheeks nodded and flicked some ashes away from our rigs. "I understand there's a long line of clients and riggers waiting to hear how he packed Becker's reserve."

He said it with a certain detached interest that suggested he would not be taking sides for or against Joe DeBerg, but he would be a very observant spectator in all of the goings-on.

I slid my bagged main into its container and gathered up the four closing flaps. "Personally," I said, "I'm more interested in the main."

"Why the main?"

"Because someone retrieved it and didn't turn it in."

"Shhhhhiiit!" Danny Death hissed from about fifteen feet away. "A guy dies, and some fuckin' asshole rips off his gear. That sucks, man. That really sucks!"

Cheeks shrugged. "Somebody probably figured Becker didn't need it anymore. I've seen it before. When you've been in the sport as long as I have, you've seen everything."

Danny Death wouldn't have any of it. "Still! It goes to the guy's wife. Or his buddies. Anybody ripped off Lon's gear and I'da beat the shit outa him!"

A skeptical look twinkled from Cheeks's veteran eyes. As though he doubted Danny Death could beat the shit out of a sickly fish, let alone a man.

"You sure it isn't still out there?" Cheeks asked.

"I'm sure. I've been out three different times, and I've looked from the air. It must have been picked up within the first hour after Newt bounced. I take it none of you saw the guy that took it?"

Cheeks and Macintosh said no. Macintosh had been post diving the first diamond attempt, and Cheeks had been in the shower. Danny Death went into a fit of self-flagellation. At the time, he'd been shooting accuracy when he could have been thwarting a thief. If only he had known.

"Yeah, I guess I seen him."

Spontaneously, we all whipped our heads around and stared at Arn. He'd been packing so noiselessly behind me I'd forgotten he was even there.

"Seen who?" demanded Danny Death.

"The guy that swiped Becker's main, that's who."

Arn was squatting on his haunches over his main. In contrast to Danny Death's flaming red personality, Arn's was dull brown. His physical appearance was equally bland. His nose was average, his ears uninteresting, his eyes not too big but not too small. His mouth was just a mouth. He had no particular age imprinted on his face—somewhere between twenty-five and forty was the best I could do. In the sky he got by. He was very reliable, but possessed no grace or finesse. And he was never the star.

"You saw the fuckin' bastard that snitched Becker's canopy?"

"I guess. I mean, what else?"

"Exactly what did you see?" I asked.

He pressed his palms to his knees, stood up, and came over.

"See, me and Danny here, we was doing a four-way outa the American Kestrel with a couple'a Michigan dudes I happen to know. We was the last load of the day, and I lost my shoe on opening. That's how come I was up there in the first place."

"Up there where?"

"Up north there, sorta next to the Armory, acrosst from that hayfield you're talking of, but just this side'a the road. My shoestring was slapping my ankle in freefall. I tried trapping the shoe with my other foot, but I lost it on opening all the same. And then my steering line busted. Danny knows about that."

"Yep," Danny Death confirmed. "I stuck with Arn under canopy when I saw his bad line. I was gonna land with him, but he yelled that he was okay and I should go shoot accuracy."

153

"I woulda, too, if my steering line wouldn'ta busted. Me and Danny, we had a bet going, see. An accuracy bet. But we called it off afterwards on accounta my busted line. Anyways, I got down, and me and Danny here went to this rigger I happen to know. I left my rig with him and Danny and went back to find my shoe up north there. That's when I seen him."

"Ya mean if I'da gone out there with you, I'da seen the fuckin' bastard, too?"

"Yeah, you'da seen him."

I said again, "Exactly what did you see?"

"Yeah, well, it was like this, see. I was up there looking around this side'a the road, and the police, they was over at the soccer place messing with that photog, only I didn't know that's who it was then. Just heard that someone bounced, that's all.

"Anyways, they was busy with the photog and I was looking at 'em with their flashlights moving all around, and then I happened to look acrosst the road from me and I seen this dude in that hayfield. I remember thinking it was kinda weird someone else way up there with me, but I figured it was a jumper from my load with a busted steering line, too, or a dud of a canopy—one of them old ones. And then I thought, well, maybe the dude's going after the main of the guy that bounced over there at the soccer place. So I looked for my shoe some more, only I couldn't find it nowhere. It was pretty dark by then. I was thinking of giving that dude enough time to come acrosst the road and we would hike it back to the airport together, see, but it was like night out almost and he wasn't coming out just then, and I wanted to see about my busted line and what it was gonna cost me. So I came back myself without the dude. Didn't think nothing more about it than that."

"You get a good look at the fuckin' bastard?"

"Naa . . . Couldn't even tell if he was a dude or a chick, not from where I was, on accounta the night. I just figure he was a dude 'cause we're the majority. Like by far."

"Was he wearing a rig?" I asked.

"Couldn't really tell, not from where I was. Barely could even see him. Didn't think to get a close-up of him. I mean, how was I supposed to know he was *stealing* it?"

"You couldn't," I assured him.

"You gonna tell USPA about it?" he asked.

I shook my head. "They've got enough to think about with the competition coming up. I was Newt's rigger. I know the gear. I'll look into it myself." I closed my container flaps over my main. "By the way, your shoe's over at the manifest. I found it yesterday when I was looking for the canopy."

"Yeah? Hey, thanks. I gave up on it myself. Wasn't worth the trouble looking. Didn't cost much and I had another pair with me."

Danny Death was reciting the encyclopedia of things he'd do to the thief if I ever caught him, when Paula drove up. She passed by us and pulled off along the road. I noticed Dominic hurrying toward her.

I asked anybody for the time. Arn said one-twenty.

"I'm running Newt's wife to Tulsa," I said, rushing to finish. "Don't include me in on any of your dives."

"That's okay," Macintosh said. "We can use Cheeks as a fourth."

But Cheeks shook his head. "I'm on a forty-eight-way this afternoon."

Macintosh's jaw fell. Cheeks had gotten on another big load and hadn't arranged a slot for him.

"We'll find someone," Danny Death grumbled. "Me and Arn know people here."

I hopped up from the ground. Paula and Dominic were walking over. She had a strained look on her face.

"I'm sorry I'm late," she said to me.

"You haven't kept me waiting. I'm running behind too."

She glanced in the direction of the Olds, obscured from view by several other cars. "Newt's videos are on the floor in the back seat of the car. I'll leave them there for you, as you asked. I put my address and phone numbers—home and work—inside the case on the lid."

"Thanks," I said. "I'll be ready in a minute. Just let me get rid of my gear." I rushed off to my tent.

I'd been too preoccupied with Newt's murder to keep house, and the evidence was there to prove it. Danny Death's musty blanket, crumpled up in a pile near the bottom of my tent, was beginning to smell more and more like swamp. I yanked it out and draped it over the front of the Honda. Then I hung my sleeping bag over the tank and seat, my smelly clothes over my saddlebags. The Honda's trunk had leaked from all the rain. I left the lid open to dry it out and put my gear on my air mattress inside the tent. I zipped down the mesh and hurried back to Paula.

Danny Death, Arn, and Macintosh were finishing up their rigs. Dominic and Cheeks were both gone. Paula and I hurried over to the

Olds and climbed in. Three minutes later we were skimming over Route Sixty-four. Fifteen minutes after that we'd left Muskogee, crossed the Arkansas River, and turned west onto the Turnpike. I drove fast and counted on a delayed flight. In today's commercial skies, she had a better than even chance of getting one.

She sat rigid and still next to me, maintaining control over her body in an increasingly difficult attempt to maintain control over her emotions.

"I'm sorry I didn't get to the drop zone sooner," she said.

"If we miss the flight, there's always another."

"It really is very kind of you to drive me. You could be jumping."

"I can jump anytime. It's not often I have the chance to play good Samaritan."

She was staring down at her hands. "Dominic offered several times, but I told him he should stay at Davis Field, that they would need his plane."

"The loads are already backed up," I agreed.

"I had to be very firm with him today," she went on. "Yesterday he insisted on taking me to the police station to pick up Newt's gear. I wish you hadn't given him the car key. He's been so persistent in wanting to do things for me. I knew he would be. That's why I was surprised when you came to the airport yesterday instead of him. And why I suggested the three of us have dinner together last night. I knew he'd insist on taking me out, and I didn't want it to be just the two of us."

Her voice tightened a little. "He came by the motel this morning to take me to breakfast. That's when I asked for the keys. I had some errands, and one of them I did want to do alone."

She looked over at me. "Dominic's going to take responsibility for getting this car back to the rental agency tomorrow. I'm grateful to him for that, really I am, but when I tried to give him money to cover Newt's bill, he refused to take it. And I went to the Holiday Inn to settle up Newt's bill there. They said a man had already taken care of it. I asked them to describe him. It was Dominic."

She chose her next words carefully. "I know he and Newt worked together for years . . . he's been very kind . . . and I know he just wants to help—"

"No explanation necessary, Paula. I think I understand the situation."

Dominic was in love with Paula, but Paula was in love with Newt.

It explained a number of things—Dominic's sudden interest in his appearance, his intense concern for Paula, and Paula's uneasiness around him.

She seemed relieved to have unburdened herself without actually having to come right out and say it. "I've known for a while," she said. "Newt finally figured it out this spring. He and Dominic haven't gotten along since. Dominic's always been a complete gentleman, but he thought Newt wasn't good enough for me, that he was irresponsible. Well, he was in a way, but he had other qualities. He was such a fun person. We laughed a lot when we were together, and in all our years of marriage we didn't have one fight. We disagreed sometimes, but we never argued. Not even this past year after things changed."

I didn't think she was looking for any response from me. It was enough that I acted as her sounding board.

For the next quarter of an hour she stared out her window. At a stretch of flat and pointless terrain she said, "I just came from the funeral home. I arranged to have Newt cremated." She paused. "Arranging to have your lover made into ashes, it's—it's strange."

In my early days of skydiving I'd run into a jumper who always carried around a bone chip of his best buddy so his buddy could keep on skydiving. The jumper always wrote a four-way down in his logbook as a five-way. An eight-way was a nine-way, a solo a two-way, that sort of thing. That's what I thought about when Paula mentioned Newt's ashes, but I didn't say so. It wouldn't have been appropriate.

"It might help if you tried to separate Newt the person from Newt the body," I said. "The ashes are the remains of the body he occupied, like threads from the clothes he wore. But they aren't Newt. Newt the person you and I knew ceased to exist on Friday the moment he hit the ground."

She said, "Actually, the Newt I knew ceased to exist a long time before Friday. Last fall would be more accurate."

She looked over at me. "You're so sure you're right about this murder thing. Isn't it possible Newt's double malfunction could just have been a horrible, horrible accident?"

"I don't see how, Paula. The circumstances don't add up that way."

She nodded resignedly. "You think Newt's videos or pictures will give you some information, don't you? You think Newt was trying to sell something he taped or photographed. Something someone didn't want made public."

"It's the most plausible explanation, given the situation."

She was quiet for a while, then she shook her head lightly, as if dismissing an idea. "I suppose it doesn't mean anything, then," she said.

"What doesn't mean anything?"

"Something I remembered this morning that Newt said over the phone a couple weeks ago. He was talking about our new house and how it would have a fireplace. He said we'd have to get a picture of Oliver North to hang above the mantel. I was really surprised at that. I mean, Newt was never a political person. When I asked him why the picture, he said patriotic people like Oliver North are good for America. When I asked him what he meant he changed the subject. It was so unlike Newt to say anything like that, so I thought it might be important. But if you think he was blackmailing someone, I don't see how it could be."

At the moment, neither did I.

She looked back down at the floor. "I want you to find out and at the same time I don't. I mean, I want the truth to come out, but I don't want my memories of Newt smeared with dirt. Maybe if I hadn't been so wrapped up in my career, Newt wouldn't have felt so inferior."

"You can't blame yourself, Paula. Newt was all wrapped up in his photography business."

"But I think I'll always blame myself unless I have someone else to blame."

I took my eyes off the road and glanced over at her. "You will Paula. I promise."

She slumped back against her seat. A shudder rippled through her body, then a drop of pain ran down her left cheek, leaving a trail of mascara. She tried to wipe away the streak, but succeeded only in smearing it. She leaned her head against the window. Her shoulders shook with gentle convulsions that accompanied a slow trickle of tears.

There didn't seem to be anything to say except the banal, and to that I preferred nothing. She didn't resist when I reached for her hand and held it.

When she finished, she lifted her head and squeezed my hand. Like the wind in the aftermath of a storm, she was very calm, her emotions spent.

It was two-twenty by Paula's watch when I pulled into Tulsa Airport's parking lot. She used the mirror on the passenger's sun visor to dust up her cheeks and adjust her makeup.

"Will you bury the ashes," I asked, "or have them scattered in freefall?"

She shoved the sun visor up against the roof and packed away her makeup. "Newt would want his ashes in freefall, not buried," she said. "And I'd like you to participate in his memorial jump, Chance. I've been thinking about August Fifteenth, the anniversary of his first jump. He always celebrated that."

"I'll be there, you can count on it." Even if Newt had gone wrong somewhere along the way, memorials were for the survivors, and I'd go for Paula's sake.

She gave me a faint smile, leaned over, and kissed me on the cheek. "You've really helped, just by being here. You'll call me, won't you, when something turns up?"

"Of course."

It suddenly occurred to both of us that she had a plane to catch. She reached behind the front seat for her flight bag, sitting on top of Newt's video case. I unloaded his belongings from the trunk and locked the doors. Inside the terminal, a black-and-white monitor told us that United Flight Four-thirty, scheduled for two-forty, wouldn't be taking off until at least quarter after three.

Davis Field was bustling by the time I got back. The clouds had all left, the wind was holding at twelve knots, the temperature was in the low eighties, the humidity was tolerable, and the boogie had started all over again. Airplanes were flying, jumpers were jumping, vendors were selling, whuffos were oohing and aahing. Above, Harley Lawrence and his team of canopy relative workers were honing their skills, or at the very least showing them off. On the ground, Bradford Rey was being congratulated on a completed forty-eight-way. Thoughts of Friday's fatality had been washed away by the rain for everyone but me.

Danny Death's eyes bulged at the sight of the Olds. "Dig the corporate fat cat," he hooted. "Where'd you get that boat?"

"Newt Becker's," I replied.

His face quickly shrunk. He was embarrassed by his joke, that it had come around to a dead man.

"We never dug up a fourth jumper," he said, recovering. "Mac, Arn, and me figured you for three-thirty, quarter of four at the latest. So we manifested on a load going at four."

"What time is it now?"

"Four-twenty."

"Sorry, Danny, but you shouldn't have included me. Paula's flight was delayed, and I wasn't about to leave her alone at the airport."

"No sweat, man. We scratched insteada goin' with three, and now the fuckin' manifester won't let us sign you up again without eye-ballin' your flesh and blood."

"I really have other plans."

"But one dive won't take long. Mac's counting on it. He's really bummed out about bein' axed from the big loads, and Cheeks givin' him the brush off. Fuckin' skygod. Anyway, Mac says you promised him."

"All right," I sighed. "But just this one. Then I'm through for the boogie. I've got another commitment."

"That's cool."

I took Newt's video case out of the car and locked it securely in the trunk.

"Sorry what I said about the car," Danny Death said. "With Beck-er dead and all, and some bastard rippin' off his main. I mean, if any-body said it about Lon—"

"Forget it, Danny."

I started toward the manifest office. He was walking backward in front of me.

"About the dive, then," he said. "Macintosh is pushin' a tube dive, if that's okay with you. He's never done one. Arn's into it. I'm not big on it myself, but then I think, what the fuck. I mean, Mac's a kid re-ally. Doesn't have the faintest what it's all about. And it's only one jump."

A tube dive. Upper bodies knotted together into a human cylinder that rolls and rampages toward earth in thunderous jolts. And that's all; that's the whole dive.

"If the others are set on a tube," I said without enthusiasm, "I'm game."

He peeled off toward the camping area, then flipped around. "Oh, yeah," he said, "I almost forgot . . . there was a call for you. Twig Buckwater."

"Twig?"

160

Danny Death shrugged. "Beats the hell outa me. You'd have to ask Cheeks. He's the one who took the call."

I went over to the manifest office and got our group signed up for the tube. Cheeks was out front discussing the forty-eight-way with several other skygods.

"Did Twig say why he called?"

Cheeks shook his head. "You're to call collect."

I used one of the pay phones outside the airport restaurant. Twig didn't answer till the ninth ring.

"What's up?" I said.

He didn't say anything for more than five seconds. Then, "Thought I'd better make sure you didn't forget about the student class this week."

It was my turn to answer slowly. "Of course I haven't," I lied.

"I'm counting on you," he said, but there was no gusto at all in his voice.

"When do you need me?"

"Tuesday morning at the latest. The rigs are out of storage, but they haven't been opened up in years. I was going to air and repack them, but I don't have time."

"Can't you get someone else to do it?"

"Like I said last month, my staff works their regular jobs during the week."

Twig didn't sound well. And I *had* agreed to do the class.

"Tuesday morning," I said reluctantly.

I couldn't remember the last time I had two commitments in conflict. Now I was supposed to jump with Macintosh, work for Twig, and find Newt's killer all at the same time. To get to Findlay Tuesday morning I'd have to leave Muskogee tomorrow evening. So I only had until then to come up with something more definite than that sigma-shaped connector link.

I tried to talk shop with Twig, but it was hard to cut through his lassitude; I had to prompt him for everything. Indiana had had buckets of rain for four days, beginning Wednesday, he said. His grass runway was too soggy to support the weight of a twin, and we'd be stuck with the Cessnas if the ground didn't dry by Thursday. He was still overhauling his old Beech. The Beech E-18 had been rented by a cargo company last month and had been returned on Monday mutilated. It was the one rise I managed to get out of him. Apparently no one had maintained the plane the whole month it was gone. I told him that Newt Becker had bounced, in case he hadn't heard. He said he had.

The manifester announced our load, and I told Twig I had to go. Danny Death, Arn, Macintosh, and I got together and hastily dirt dived the tube. I now wished I hadn't let Danny Death talk me into the jump. I was feeling very pressed for time.

Over at my tent I stepped into my jumpsuit, collected my helmet and goggles and gloves, and gave my rig the same once-over I always give it—down the front, up the back. When I got to the reserve pin my flesh went raw.

The pin itself was perfect, not at all bent. But the rigger's seal that had guarded it was gone. Like Newt's main, it had vanished.

16

"Come on! Say you're only kiddin'. We been waitin' all fuckin' day!"

"Only since one, Danny. And the three of you can still jump. I've lined up a replacement."

He eyed me with skepticism. "If it's the fuckin' tube you don't like, we can change it to sequential."

"That's not it. I've got a problem with my rig."

"Yeah?" There was a little less hostility in his whine. "Is it serious?"

"Don't know yet. But I do know I won't have it worked out in time to make this jump."

My replacement strode over. "Danny, this is Sue. Sue, Danny."

While she Velcroed her chest strap, Danny Death put forth a valiant effort not to gawk. Sue was tall and narrow and beautiful in the way Playboy Bunnies are. She'd been the only one in a party of Utah skydivers at the tent nearest mine who hadn't been nursing a bottle or a can or a cup of beer, which was why it had been to her that I'd offered the free jump. It would be too much to expect anyone to believe my motives, though. They'd say forever it was because of her chest.

"Sue's only been in the sport a year," I cautioned. "She's got a hundred twenty jumps and has never done a tube before."

"That's okay. We'll show her how." To Sue he said, "Ready?"

She said, "I think so."

They walked toward the airplane, and I hustled back to my tent. Inside, I fingered the empty red thread hanging from my reserve pin.

I'd checked my pins before the noon dive, and the seal had been there then.

I straightened my back and yanked at the reserve ripcord. My pilot chute sprung out like a threatened serpent. I batted it aside and went straight for my connector links. Two of the four were missing.

Modern main parachutes are square, the chief advantage of this design being increased speed and maneuverability. Reserves are either square or round, since round parachutes are roughly half the price and arguably just as effective at saving life. No speed or performance built into them, but when life is what's at stake, speed and performance become trivial.

My reserve was round. A forty-foot-long rigging table is the ideal place to pack and unpack rounds, but I could get by using grass.

I took my rig outside my tent and stretched out my reserve. Then I went over to the Honda and got my rigger's kit. I took out two spare connector links and put them on my chute to replace the two that had been removed. I checked my other two links but there was nothing wrong with them.

The rest of the rig would take more time.

I checked every square inch. I scrutinized every suspension line for cut marks, explored every seam for broken thread, stress-tested the twenty gores of nylon that made up the canopy. I checked the risers, the knot connecting the pilot chute to the apex, and the pilot chute itself. Then the handle, cable, and pin of the ripcord. I unpacked and inspected my main and went over my harness and container, but the two reserve connector links were all that had been disturbed on the entire rig. And the seal, of course.

My rig was seven years old. I kept it in good condition, but it was still seven years old. Not a prime target for theft. So when I'd discovered water in my trunk this afternoon, I hadn't thought twice about leaving my rig in my tent.

And only a few hours ago I'd faulted Newt for being reckless with *his* gear.

I rocked back on my heals, blew air through my teeth, and combed my hand through my hair. I heard noises overhead and looked up. Jumpers from the load that would have been mine peppered the sky. Danny Death and Arn were challenging each other over by the accuracy pit.

All jumpers check their pins before each dive, which meant that I was supposed to find the seal gone *before* I jumped. So it was only a warning. If it had been meant to kill, a new rigger's seal would have been clamped on my reserve. And my main would have been tampered with.

I hadn't made it a secret I was hunting for Newt's canopy; I wouldn't have dug up any information at all if I had. I knew, of course, that there would be some risk in tracking a cold-blooded killer, but now that risk was suddenly very real. The person I was looking for knew I was looking and had warned me: Mind your own business, Chance, or else.

He didn't realize I was doing exactly that.

Arn, Danny Death, and Macintosh had coaxed me into doing the noon jump, and Danny Death had talked me into the tube. I thought about that, then dismissed it as too obvious. Besides, whoever broke my seal and removed my links must have orchestrated Newt's death, and I couldn't imagine any of them for that: Arn was too simple-minded, Danny Death too visceral, Macintosh too inexperienced. Newt's double malfunction was the work of an intelligent, calm, professional mind.

I repacked both my canopies, pressed a new seal over the reserve, and locked my rig in the trunk, now dry. I gathered up my sleeping bag and clothes from the Honda and shoved them in the tent. Danny Death had already been by for his blanket. I removed my tank bag and unlocked the concealed panel beneath. There, exactly where I'd cached it, was the sigma-shaped connector link, along with Newt's reserve ripcord and main breakaway handle.

I'll have to come up with a safer place for them, I thought.

For the time being, though, I left them there. I latched the panel, locked it, covered it with the tank bag, then stuffed my rigger's kit inside the bag. I went over to the Olds rental, unlocked the trunk, scooped out Newt's video case, and went to give the car key to Dominic. He and his copilot were in the air with Satin Cruise, so I left the key with the manifester, who said he'd be sure to pass it along.

That taken care of, I went searching for a man named Javier Vasquez.

17

I'd met Javier at an upstate New York drop zone during my law school days. Already hailed as a brilliant photographer long before taking his first freefall shot, Javier had built his reputation on pictures that exposed the stark loneliness and cold humanity of crowded places and monied men. With Superman eyes and the right lens he could pierce the skin of a city and expose its raw meat. Some photographs shout at you, but Javier's had a disturbing way of enticing you inside them, then incarcerating you there until you grasped the gnarled pain of his subjects, the torture of their souls. He lived in New York City, he once said, because it reproduced its misery at a rate guaranteed to give him a century's worth of pictures, a career's worth of fame.

I saw him leaving the camping area and flagged him down.

"I was sorry to hear about Becker," he said after I told him what I was after. "Didn't know you knew him."

"These days I try to winter in Florida if I can wing it, so our paths crossed."

We started walking toward the electrical hookup zone. "Becker's done some first-rate work," Javier said. "In my opinion, he should have stuck with what he was good at—still photography. He had the eye."

"As I understand it, his bread and butter was student jumpers. The students these days want video."

"What kind is it?"

"The smaller type. Not VHS."

He looked down and assessed the case in my hand. "Eight-millimeter," he said.

"Is that going to be a problem?"

Javier shook his head. "Eight-millimeter's all I ever use for skydiving. Very lightweight and excellent picture quality if you have the right machine. I have an eight-millimeter VCR you can use."

We reached Javier's van and climbed inside. He set everything up for me and explained how it worked. "Just remember to lock up when you're done. Put the keys on the rear left tire."

"Anytime you need a free repack—"

He said he'd remember to ask.

Javier's van, like his pictures, was not ordinary. Mint-colored plush pile carpeting scaled the walls. The floor and ceiling were covered with the same stuff, but a darker hue. Behind the driver's seat loomed custom-built mahogany cabinets and shelves. On top of them sat pieces of an expensive stereo system, a television set/video monitor, two videocassette recorders, and other electronic things. Beside the cabinet stood a dormitory-sized refrigerator. Two tinted bubble windows made a final statement about what money could buy.

I was feeling anxious. Maybe after watching Newt's video tapes I'd know who killed him.

I opened the video case, but didn't notice immediately that something was wrong. I walked my fingers across the tapes, trying to decide which to look at first. Then it suddenly dawned on me and I counted the tapes.

Twelve.

Yesterday at Paula's motel there had been fourteen.

I sat stunned on the floor while the plush mint walls of Javier's van swallowed me whole. My mouth tasted mint, my nose smelled it.

I glowered at the twelve remaining tapes. If they could tell me anything, they wouldn't still be there.

I slammed the lid shut.

Calm down, Chance, just calm down. You were very careful to lock the video case in the Olds, so the two tapes must have been taken earlier.

I ran my fingers through my hair and thought. Paula had the case all last night and this morning. But she seemed quite sincere about wanting to find out the truth—even if it did tarnish her memories of Newt—so she wouldn't have removed any tapes. When she came to the drop zone this afternoon she left the videos in the Olds for the ten minutes it took to go get me; and now that I thought about it, she hadn't bothered to lock the driver's door. But the video case had been under her flight bag behind the passenger's seat, so not just anyone would have known it was there.

Hmm.

When Paula told me the video case was in the car, Dominic, Danny Death, Arn, Macintosh, and Cheeks all overheard what she said. When I came back from my tent about five minutes later, Danny Death, Macintosh, and Arn were still packing their rigs, but Dominic and Cheeks had disappeared. Either of them could have gone over to the car and picked through Newt's videos.

I looked down at the twelve remaining tapes and read the labels. Six were dated, three were titled. The other three weren't labeled, and I assumed them to be blank. Two of the dated tapes were for April, three for May. One had the words JUNE/JULY scribbled in pencil. The three topical tapes Newt had titled OCTAGON, STUDENTS, and ACCURACY.

This is going to be a waste of time, Chance, but what the hell, you've got time to waste. Reviewing these tapes might give you a feel for Newt Becker the cameraman. Perhaps even Newt Becker the blackmailer.

I reeled through each one. Most of the dated tapes came in at about thirty minutes. And most of that was Octagon the good, the bad, and the ugly. The JUNE/JULY casing was empty. That tape would still be in Newt's video camera.

Each freefall jump used about sixty seconds of video from exit through canopy opening, but Newt's shots from the ground of canopy relative work, accuracy, and jumpers partying amongst their cars stretched into minutes. There were no student dives on these particular tapes, which I found odd.

The titled tapes were shorter than the dated ones and seemed to be composed of minutes gleaned from other recordings. In fact I recognized footage on ACCURACY and OCTAGON that had been copied from the dated tapes. OCTAGON could have been better described as OCTAGON'S GREATEST JUMPS. The STUDENTS and ACCURACY tapes, on the other hand, represented Newt's finest photography in these categories, without regard to the quality of performance exhibited by his subjects.

Newt's style lent itself toward instruction. For the student and Octagon dives that was to be expected, but Newt carried this into his other shots. He avoided the routine spills and pratfalls many jumpers call fun, though a number of his how-*not*-to-do-it sequences were unintentionally hilarious. In one, an inexperienced heavyweight creamed a nicely formed star the way a bowling ball hits its pins, the effect being exactly the same.

I tried the three unlabeled tapes, which indeed were blank. Frustrated, I flicked off the machine. Twelve tapes and not the slightest hint of scandal. Nothing that could fetch top dollar and propel Newt Becker into the class of the nouveau riche.

I got up and rolled open the door. I paced along the side of the van, running my fingers through my hair. The sky was dark and clear, though the glare from the numerous airport lights obliterated most of the stars.

I stepped back in the van, rolled the door shut, and started with the dated tapes again, this time using fast forward.

At the faster speed, a pattern emerged almost immediately. I hadn't seen it the first time through. I'd been too intent on inspecting the trees, and I'd missed the forest.

Beginning on the May tapes, Newt had exit shots of groups he taped out the window of Satin Cruise. I rewound the May tapes and played them again. There was something vaguely familiar about one of the groups. I replayed one of their exits several times. It was the Wisconsin speed star team.

Didn't Newt tape their exit on my first jump at Findlay, the morning after Lonny Carmichael went in?

Suddenly it dawned on me. I scrambled to my feet, opened Javier's cabinets, riffled through his belongings, and found what I needed: a small, wallet-sized calendar. I compared Javier's calendar with the dates on Newt's video tapes.

I thought so.

The date on each tape represented the beginning of a week between mid-April and the fourth week in May. One tape for each of the first five weeks after Easter—after Dominic ferried Satin Cruise up north. But none for the last week in May, the week Lonny Carmichael bounced.

All of Danny Death's carping came flooding back to me: Lon knew

how to exit, man. I'm tellin' ya, he *knew* . . . Exitin' was the one thing
he knew about . . . Lon wouldn'ta hit. He wouldn'ta!

I switched off the machines, loaded up Newt's video case, locked
up the van, and put Javier's key on the left rear tire.

Sometimes the clue is in its absence.

18

Aslam had said Octagon had a "mobile house" here at Nationals. There weren't many RVs, so I didn't have to knock on too many wrong doors before getting the one I wanted.

"May I offer a beer?"

I nodded and latched the door. "I was under the impression you didn't drink alcohol."

Aslam opened a small refrigerator. "You are correct, Chance. It is contrary to my religion. But my teammates keep our refrigerator stocked, so there is plenty for our guests."

He was dressed in a beige-and-watermelon shirt and lilac pants. Only since Miami Vice could a man wear those colors and still be considered a man. His teammates were out circulating, but Aslam seemed to prefer staying inside.

I laid Newt's video case on one of two miniature divans that faced each other. Aslam popped the lid from a bottle of lager and handed it to me. He took a liter bottle of seltzer water from the refrigerator, poured himself a glass, then set both down on a small table wedged between the divans. He sat down beside Newt's video case.

Next to the refrigerator a video monitor was flashing images of the Army Golden Knights. Over and over they escaped the prison of their plane and wove themselves into the sky with flawless twists and turns, creating symmetrical formations with poetry and light grace.

"Octagon is able to perform like this also," Aslam said. "But not consistently, I am sorry to say."

"You'd have to jump full-time almost year-round for that."

He lifted a knee and rested his foot on the divan. "Unfortunately, it is not possible to practice full-time all year and also to work full-time. With work, there is money but no time. Without work . . ."

I suspected that in Pakistan the American custom of getting right to the point would be considered rude. So I didn't.

"Become an American citizen," I said, "and let the Army pay for your jumps."

"In fact, I am an American since April," Aslam stated proudly. "But the Army requires other obligations in return for the privilege of skydiving. It is these obligations I am not prepared to fulfill."

"And," I added, "when you skydive for a living, it becomes too much of a job. Some of the fun gets lost."

"Yes, there is that." He reached over to the VCR and switched off the Knights. "Tell me," he said. "This is not a social visit, I do not think."

I sat down across from him. "As a matter of fact," I said, "I have a few more questions about Newt." I motioned toward the video case. "I've been viewing those tapes of his. In early May he began to tape the exits of groups other than Octagon—speed stars, pickup loads."

Aslam nodded. "Newton was developing a series of video tapes for instruction. Each tape emphasized a particular topic in skydiving. For example, he had an entire tape with accuracy only on it. And another with student training."

"So you're saying Newt was putting together a video on exits?"

"That is correct. Newton's interest in exits came from the problems Octagon was having. The problems Octagon continues to have."

I drank some of my beer. So that answers that, I thought. EXIT is the second missing tape.

I said, "I didn't come across any of those exit shots on the April tapes."

"It was only in May that we began to address the problems with our exits. This is when Newton began to film the groups in front of us as they exited."

"Did these groups know Newt was taping them?"

"Sometimes, but sometimes no. If it was a team, usually he told them. If it was a pickup group only, they often did not know. Unless they noticed him filming."

"You remember last month at Findlay when a skydiver named Lonny Carmichael bounced?"

"Yes, I remember. We were inside Satin Cruise. We exited after his group."

"Did Newt tape that group's exit?"

Aslam tapped his index finger against his lips. "I can not say with certainty," he said finally, "but I remember some things. And I can say it is not important if he filmed the exit."

"Why?"

"The video for that load did not come out. Newton had a problem with his camera."

"What sort of problem?"

Aslam scratched his chin. "I am not able to say, I am sorry. I don't think Newton explained. I remember we had a good dive, but then we learned a jumper had died. Of course we forgot about our dive. In the morning we remembered it, but Newton said there was no video to look at. His camera had malfunctioned."

"So Newt said."

Aslam finished his glass of seltzer and poured himself another. "Yes," he acknowledged, "this is according to Newton."

I sat back and drank some more beer. Aslam observed me with the eternal patience of his people. Eventually he said, "You do not think Newton's camera malfunctioned. You believe there was something on the film Newton did not wish us to see." He was stating a fact, not soliciting confirmation.

Aslam squinted at me. "You ask many questions today, Chance. And I have made an inventory. Your questions this morning are logical only if you believe Newton's parachutes did not malfunction honestly. Your questions this evening are logical only if you believe the jumper Carmichael did not die honestly."

I didn't say anything. I got up from the divan. The cap from my beer bottle was creased in half where Aslam had locked the cap remover onto it. I scooped it up, tossed it a few times in the air, then lobbed it into an empty brown paper bag.

"I noticed there weren't any student shots on Newt's weekly tapes," I said. "Yet he earned his money taping them."

Aslam nodded. "Students consumed very much video time, and Newton did not save this film for himself generally, except sometimes to illustrate technique. These he kept on a tape he named STUDENT. Of course, he always made a copy for the student."

"Eight-millimeter or VHS?"

"VHS. Newton had his own recorder in Florida to make the copies.

In Illinois the drop zone provided one for him."

"And in Findlay he could have used one of Twig Buckwater's machines."

"That is correct."

"How did Newt work the student videos? Did each student bring his own blank tape?"

Aslam shook his head. "Newton provided these. He carried with him a box of blank VHS tapes about this size." Aslam used his hands to measure out a square of air eight inches by four by twelve.

"I don't remember Newt having a box like that with him last month in Ohio and Pennsylvania."

Aslam shrugged. "I don't know the answer, Chance. I remember he had the box in Findlay because he filmed a student there. Perhaps he used up all of the tapes. And with his new business venture, perhaps he did not need to buy more."

"Perhaps."

I reached over and switched on Aslam's homework for the evening. The Golden Knights were transitioning effortlessly from a zipper to two opposed stair steps.

"If only we had their consistency," Aslam sighed.

"You don't need to fly like that on every dive. Only the competition dives."

"Then please wish us luck for the competition."

"I wish you much luck, Aslam."

He stood up and handed me Newt's video case. "And I wish *you* luck, Chance. I think you will be wise to take great care."

"Thanks for the advice," I said, and pushed out through the door.

Talking with Aslam had jarred my memory of Lonny Carmichael's last jump, and certain details were now coming back to me. Like the fact that the Wisconsin speed star team had exited Satin Cruise just before Carmichael's group.

I walked around the airport and asked about the speed star team. They were staying at one of the motels in town. I did some more asking. A member had been seen in the airport bar: the captain of the team, no less.

The captain, who called himself Captain, remembered the jump well. They'd had a team argument in the plane, then a wasted exit, then a piss poor recovery. All followed by a jumper bouncing while they packed their chutes. Not a jump he'd likely ever forget. Yes, Newt taped their exit. No, they didn't get to review it. Newt's camera broke. And as far as Captain was concerned, that was just as well.

Confirmation. That's what the speed star captain was giving me. Confirmation that Newt *had* taped Lonny Carmichael's group exiting the plane. He must have. He'd done the speed star team's exit a few minutes earlier and Octagon's dive right afterward.

And the footage of Lonny Carmichael's exit must have turned out. It was the only reasonable explanation for why those two tapes had been stolen from Newt's video case.

So what precisely had Newt captured on camera?

I said good night to the captain and went outside. Next to the bar entrance I laid Newt's video case on the ground. Then I sat down on top of it, put my chin in my hands, and did some serious thinking.

If Lonny Carmichael had concussed himself jumping out the door, Newt would have shown his video to the police and that would have been that. So Danny Death had been right all along. Lonny Carmichael didn't hit his head on the door frame.

If Lonny Carmichael didn't hit his head on exit, then there was only one possibility with stakes high enough to lead to blackmail and murder: murder itself. And if Lonny Carmichael was murdered, then it was Alex Laird who did it. He was the only person who trailed Carmichael out, the only person who could have knocked him unconscious just outside the door, in full view of Newt's camera. It wouldn't have been difficult for a big man like Laird—a blow to the head just hard enough to keep Carmichael groggy for sixty seconds. The ground would do the rest.

But what about Laird's attempt to rescue Carmichael in freefall?

Easy. Nothing more than a slick charade to deflect any suspicion like the kind Danny Death was trying to spread. Laird knew he could use his size as an excuse for not reaching Carmichael.

The setup was so plausible no one would have ever known the truth if it hadn't been for Newt Becker, whose innocent exit shot for an instructional video quickly became raw material for blackmail. In the plane Laird must have been too busy thinking about bumping off Carmichael to notice Newt and his camera over by the window. And it would have happened so quickly that Newt probably didn't even know what he had on tape till he got to the ground and reviewed the footage. Thinking back on it now, Newt probably *did* know what he had on tape by the time I talked to him at Jake's later that night. He seemed more than casually interested in the incident. To him, that exit shot must have been manna from heaven, a quick-fix solution to his personal predicament.

I ran my fingers through my hair. I'd underestimated Newt. He *had* taken precautions to protect himself. Despite his quarrel with Dominic, the man in love with his wife, he'd traveled with Satin Cruise during June. Moving from place to place was one way to ward off an unexpected encounter with Alex Laird, the man he must have been blackmailing.

Okay. So Newt approaches Alex Laird about the video in Findlay, or maybe over the phone from Oakland Ridge. The two arrange to meet early that Wednesday morning in Oakland Ridge, perhaps at the mouth of Airport Road, not too far from where I later found Newt. Newt drives the club's old VW bug out to meet Laird. He expects some sort of negotiations. Instead, Laird tries to bully him into handing over the tape, then beats him unconscious when he refuses.

By why would Laird drive the VW back to the clubhouse?

I could guess why he wanted to go to the clubhouse—to search for the video. That would explain the mess I found Newt's belongings in when I arrived later in the morning.

But why switch cars? Why not take his own?

I thought about that for a while. Then I remembered Laird was a truck driver.

Perhaps he was on a job and drove to the meeting in his truck. A large truck, or even a cab, would have a hard time negotiating a narrow country lane like Airport Road, and turning around would be a problem.

But then why leave the VW at the clubhouse and go back to his truck on foot?

Maybe something scared him. Maybe he went searching the whole airport for the video. Newt must have anticipated something like that and hidden his tapes well. I couldn't remember seeing his video case in The Suite when I first arrived, but he did have it with him later that day.

So then what?

Paula said Newt first claimed he'd have the money in a week or two. Later he said it would take more time. That must have been after Laird beat him up, after he realized it wasn't going to be so easy.

But if Laird never intended to pay up at all—and apparently he didn't—why not just kill Newt outright back in Oakland Ridge?

Because if Newt had died too soon after Carmichael, someone might have made a connection.

So Laird threatens Newt in Oakland Ridge. When Newt doesn't wise up, he's eliminated. But not by Alex Laird, who didn't come to Nationals, and who wouldn't think to sabotage Newt's rig in any case. He might break Newt's neck with his two bare hands, but he wouldn't think up the business with the connector links.

So Laird has a partner.

The rest was easy to figure out. Laird and Partner decide Newt has to go. Laird arranges to meet Newt here at Nationals for a pay-off. But Laird doesn't come, Partner does. Partner can't risk going after the video while Newt is alive because Newt might realize something's up. The key to catching Newt off guard is letting him think he's meeting Laird: no Laird, no reason to protect his gear. So Partner kills unsuspecting Newt, makes it look like an accident, then waits for the right opportunity to go after the video.

So who *is* Partner anyway—Dominic or Cheeks? It had to be one of them.

I'd always rather liked Dominic, but I had to consider him a real possibility. Last month I couldn't understand why he allowed Newt to keep traveling with Satin Cruise. Now I had two explanations: he could innocently have kept Newt on as a way of maintaining contact with Paula, the woman he loved, or he could have done it to keep an eye on Newt for Alex Laird.

If Dominic was Partner, he and Laird could be in some illegal business together, in which case Dominic's motive in killing Newt would be money. Or, Laird could have recruited Dominic after Newt began blackmailing him, in which case Dominic's motive would be Paula—a chance to have her all to himself.

Dominic had spent years in Vietnam, and nobody really knew anything about him.

And then there was Cheeks, a man I didn't particularly like. I knew even less about him than I knew about Dominic. He was an international salesman, an important businessman, according to Macintosh. Could he have business dealings with Alex Laird? If so, what kind of business dealings? And if it was Cheeks, where did Macintosh fit in? An international businessman could afford a rental car and a motel room, yet Cheeks seemed content to bunk in the back of Macintosh's van. Why was that?

Cheeks was a rigger, but Dominic had been around the sport for a very long time, and he could have rigged Newt's gear just as easily.

Which one of them had taken Newt's tapes before I had a chance to look at them? Which one had messed with my rig?

I couldn't eliminate either of them on the basis of Newt's main canopy—both could have taken it. Cheeks said he was taking a shower after Newt bounced, but scores of people pass through the bathhouse, so his alibi could never be checked. Dominic had unloaded Newt and the diamond jumpers from Satin Cruise. There would have been just enough time for him to hurry to the ground and scoot out to the hayfield unobserved, or at least unrecognized, before Arn went out to look for his shoe. I could ask Dominic's copilot about that, but what if he was involved, too?

I ran my fingers through my hair. It was getting to be a habit.

I'd figured out a lot about Newt's double malfunction, but all I could do was shake my head as I thought about the mountain of work still in front of me. Who was Alex Laird's partner, was only one of several questions I didn't have an answer for. I still didn't know why master rigger Joe DeBerg's signature was on Newt's packing card, for instance, or why Lonny Carmichael had been killed in the first place. And perhaps most important of all, I didn't have the vaguest idea how I was going to prove any of this.

19

There was a large circus tarp between the bar and the manifest office. Under it, scores of skydivers, their guests, and a sprinkling of whuffos were milling around. A rock band had set up at one end, and was putting forth an authentic effort to entertain. Several couples had gotten into the groove and were shaking their limbs at each other, but most people were busy socializing.

I spotted Macintosh among them. Having apparently fallen out of favor with Cheeks, he was now busy brown-nosing the Almighty Bradford Rey himself. Bradford Rey was lapping up the attention and, I would bet, not promising a thing.

Poor Macintosh, I thought. Then I remembered Newt Becker, and I wasn't so sure.

It was late, near midnight, and I still hadn't talked to Joe DeBerg. I wandered around the circus tarp looking for him. After about five minutes I found him.

He was holding a draft beer and alternating his stance restlessly, bending one knee, then the other, all the while yammering to two men in rapid-fire speech that sounded more like competing radio stations than honest-to-God English. "Becker" was one of the few words I actually understood.

Joe was at least fifty years old and almost entirely bald. He had skin that freckled rather than tanned, and hands that were disproportionately thick from three decades of parachute rigging.

Except for a few feminists who objected to his working-class mouth, I'd never met anyone who disliked Joe. To riggers, he was the classy veteran who gave invaluable advice, all gratis, for the good of the sport. You could go to him with a question about a product, a regulation, a rigging technique, and if he didn't have an answer handy he'd research it until he dug one up.

To most jumpers, though, Joe DeBerg was the gregarious clown who could force a smile from even the Bradford Reys of the world. He was the life of the party, the genuine article. He could in no time snag your attention with his appealing smile, then dazzle you with his colorful and rich sense of humor. Slap you on the back, assign you an appropriate sobriquet, pass on a good joke—that was Joe De-Berg.

Tonight his smile was missing. I could guess the one-liners had been left at home too.

I slipped in a quiet "Joe?"

That spooked him and he lurched sideways. He'd been too absorbed in his own charged commentary to notice I was there.

"Chance!" he bellowed. "Chance the Wandering Rigger!"

After acknowledging his two companions I said, "Could we talk privately, Joe?"

"Sure, Chance, sure," he said, too wired to think to introduce his friends. Very unlike Joe. "Let me refresh my beer, first. I see you're empty. I'll bring you one."

"No, thanks. I'm fine without."

He bounded into the bar. I apologized to his companions, but they said that was quite all right, and quickly wove themselves into another group.

Joe filled his cup at the free bar tap with all the patience of a teenager, then came prancing out with a half-cup of beer and a half-cup of foam. He was about four feet from me when he said, "That link was tight as a virgin when I packed that reserve! On my mamma's sacred bosom, I swear it!"

"*Those* links, Joe. And you don't need to convince me. I believe you."

His jaw dropped. "What do you mean *those* links? You're not saying another link was loose?"

"Not another reserve link, no."

"Well, what then? What are you saying, Chance? Let's not pussyfoot around this. Let me have it."

So I gave him the lowdown on Newt's gear.

His face took on the color and texture of a ripe mango, and he became intensely animated: now angry, now reassured. He clenched his hand and threw a punch at a speed that would have done damage had it connected with anything other than air.

"I *knew* it! I knew I checked Becker's links. When I pack a reserve I have a routine, and I don't ever forget. But everybody keeps looking at me myopic-like, and I know what they're thinking: 'Sure, Joe, sure, we believe you. But we'll just take our business some place else, to a safe rigger, to someone who knows his stuff.' Enough of that and the doubts start to creep up on you. You know you'd never forget, but you see your age typed on your driver's license, and you can't help but wonder if maybe Mother Nature's playing funny little games on you." He bashed the air again. "Almost thirty years in the sport, Chance, and the damnedest thing I ever did was touch that rig and put my name to that card."

Once he'd assimilated the personal implications he gritted his teeth and said, "So you're saying someone did in Newt Becker, huh? A hell of a thing. Any idea why?"

"Can we talk first about what happened three weeks ago in Litchfield?"

He pulled back. "I don't get you. What happened in Litchfield?"

"That's what I'm trying to work out. It was there you packed Newt's reserve."

"Boy, is that the truth. But I still don't get you."

"Newt didn't have a malfunction. So why did he have you repack his reserve?"

He shook his head. "He didn't come to me about his reserve. It was his main that was the problem."

"What was wrong with his main?"

"A couple of worn lines."

"Which lines?"

"Both his steering lines."

I squinted at him. "But I just replaced Newt's main steering lines in March when I packed his reserve. Where had they worn through?"

He shrugged. "Good question, Chance, but I don't know. He'd already snipped the lines off the canopy by the time I got it."

"Did he say why he did that?"

Joe thought. "I'm sure I must have asked him, but I don't remember what he said. I was pretty busy, and you know how some jumpers are—they like to play rigger. So I let them, to a point."

"I've been Newt's rigger for three years, and in all that time he never once showed any interest in rigging. He was careful in his own packing, but he never asked me any questions. Never watched me work."

"Can't help you, Chance. Didn't know him well. It's the first time I ever touched his rig."

An idea was starting to form in my mind. "What about the reserve? How did you come to pack it?"

Joe sipped his beer. "Becker said as long as I was repairing his main I might as well repack his reserve. Said it was almost out-of-date."

"And you didn't bother to check the date on the packing card?"

Joe's expression indicated he thought the question silly. "Can't remember, Chance. I've packed a lot of reserves since then. But if a jumper tells me his reserve is almost out-of-date, I take his word for it. I mean, you find me the jumper that's willing to pay for a repack before it's due and I guarantee you he's got five legs, nineteen toes, and a tail sprouting out his ear."

I had to agree with him. "Did you open Newt's reserve," I asked, "or did he?"

Joe thought again. "He did," he said finally. "Already had it popped when I got it."

"Did you find anything wrong with it?"

"No! And I swear to the bogeyman in the big blue sky, when I sealed Becker's pack all links were—"

"Hey, Joe, you don't have to convince me. Remember?"

"Yeah, yeah. Sorry, Chance. This whole thing really has me hyperventilating—being accused of something I didn't do. I mean, being accused of not doing something I did."

He drank what was left of his beer, leaving the foam to slosh about in the bottom of his cup.

"Did Newt say why he took his gear to you instead of me?

He compressed his lips and shook his head. "Maybe you were busy with Satin Cruise." But as the suggestion rolled off his tongue he was already dismissing it. "No, that's not right. I remember what it was. Becker said you didn't have any replacement line with you."

"I always carry replacement line with me. And Newt knew that."

Joe shrugged. "All I can tell you is what he said. I don't know why he'd fib, but I know he had no complaints about your work, if that's what you're thinking."

"That's not what I'm thinking. What if Newt took his rig to you because he didn't want me to see it?"

"Why wouldn't he want you to see his rig?"

"Maybe because I knew its history. I knew both steering lines were relatively new. He knew if he brought the rig to me I'd ask questions. I'd demand to see those lines he'd removed, to find out how they'd been damaged. He took it to you because you wouldn't ask any questions. You'd naturally assume the lines had worn through as he claimed they had."

"But why wouldn't he want either of us to see the lines?"

"Because they'd been deliberately cut. It's the only explanation that makes any sense at all."

"Cut?" Then his mouth formed the shape of an O.

"It must have been just a warning," I said, "since his reserve was okay."

Joe watered the ground with the foam from his cup, then shuddered. "All this talk is giving me the creepies, Chance. I mean, killing is different from bouncing. And to think whoever did it was at Litchfield that weekend . . ."

"Maybe, maybe not. I mean, I agree that whoever cut Newt's lines also loosened his links. It's the same mind at work. But Newt didn't jump for two weeks before Litchfield, not since Findlay's Memorial Day boogie. So his lines could have been cut there, or in Oakland Ridge the following week, or in Litchfield."

I was disappointed by my own conclusions. Cheeks could have cut the lines Memorial Day, Dominic could have cut them anytime.

"After his two-week layoff," I said, "Newt must have decided to repack his main before jumping in Litchfield. Maybe he suspected something. Whatever his reason, once he found cut lines, he wasn't going to make a jump without inspecting his reserve."

Joe began bouncing back and forth on his feet. "So what are we talking about here, anyway, Chance? Why would anybody want to do in Newt Becker?"

"It's—complicated."

"But do you even have an idea who did it?"

"I know one of the people involved."

"You mean there's more than one?"

"At least two. One's here at Nationals."

Joe stared at me expectantly, but I shook my head. "He's not the one I have a name for."

"What about the other one?"

"A jumper from Indiana Newt was blackmailing. You wouldn't know him."

"That's all? That's all you're going to tell me?"

"There are things I still don't know myself, Joe."

He put his cup up to his mouth to drink from it, then frowned when he realized it was empty.

"So what did the police say when you told them all this?"

"I haven't told them yet."

He stared at me like a soldier staring down a deserting comrade during a time of all-out war. "Well," he said, "they want to talk to me tomorrow. You can bet I'll tell them."

"Maybe you should wait on that."

"Wait!" His cheeks flushed purple, and he came as close as I'd ever seen to a seasoned jumper in panic.

"We're talking my life here, Chance! It's how I eat, it's how I jump, it's how I make kissy-face with the IRS! Becker's wife will sue me. And even if she doesn't, the word will be out that Joe DeBerg's an old fart, over the hill, the rigger that did in Newt Becker. You know rumors, Chance—they spread faster than whores. I'll lose my customers. My business. I'm too old to do anything else."

"If you tell them now, Joe, it'll backfire on you. On Friday the police were leaning toward defective hardware, but you just said they want to talk to you, so maybe they're thinking about rigger negligence. Any evidence pointing in some other direction that comes from you will be suspect."

Joe listened to what I was saying, then looked down at the ground and nodded feebly. "Even if *you* were the one to tell the police, and even if they believed you, what could they do? This was an inside job."

He lifted his head. His eyes were watery, and when they began to flow he didn't fight the tears. "Rigging's my life, Chance. Without it I got nothing."

"I'm aware of that."

"So what am I supposed to do? What about my reputation? My business? I can't stand by with my mouth shut and watch my life's work go down the can."

"I don't expect you to. Go ahead and campaign for yourself. Tell anyone who'll listen that you inspected Newt's links when you packed his reserve. Tell the police that, but I don't want them to know about all this until I've got more proof. Theories don't bring

186

convictions just because they're the truth."

He wiped the back of his hand across his cheek and tried to blink his eyes dry. "How come you're doing this for me, Chance?"

I shook my head. "It's for me, too, Joe. And for every rigger out there who could have been the unlucky one to pack Newt's rig last. And for Newt, and for his wife." And, I thought, for an old friend named Jeepers.

"I'll do like you say, I'll keep my mouth shut." Joe said, sniffling. "I'll be here through Wednesday. Back home Thursday night. I'm in the book. Call me when something breaks."

The rock band at the far end of the circus tarp had increased its decibel output and was now playing Van Halen louder than Van Halen would have played it. The audience had thickened. Near the music they were packed tightly like rush-hour commuters in a big city subway. The camping area, by contrast, resembled a small midwestern town recently deserted.

I left Joe under the tarp and started for my tent. I walked slowly and thought about another piece of the puzzle that was bugging me.

On Monday Newt told Paula he'd have enough money this week for a down payment on their new house. But earlier, in Florida, he had said they'd buy the house only when he could pay for the whole thing himself. Did that mean Newt was planning to blackmail Alex Laird again, at some point down the road, for the balance due on his house? If so, Newt would have had at least one additional copy of the blackmail tape stashed someplace safe.

Which was why those missing tapes were bugging me. Not the two eight-millimeter tapes stolen from Newt's video case, but the blank VHS student tapes. I didn't think Newt would have used them all up, as Aslam suggested. Until the Memorial Day boogie, Newt had depended on students for his income. He couldn't have known he'd tape a murder, so he wouldn't have let those tapes run out.

So what had become of them? And were they all really blank?

Then, too, why did Newt want to hang a picture of Oliver North over his mantel? What did he mean when he said patriotic people like Oliver North are good for America? I had a theory about an underlying drug connection in all of this—Lonny Carmichael had been a known user, Dominic was based in Florida, Cheeks in California, and both men traveled a lot—but Oliver North and drugs? Maybe

Alex Laird and Partner didn't have anything to do with drugs after all. Or maybe Newt's remark about Oliver North didn't have anything to do with the blackmail business.

And how was I going to catch Dominic or Cheeks? I could set a trap—if not to catch *him*, then at least to identify which one of them *he* was. But whoever he was, he was smart. He might know better than to fall for any trick I might dream up. And a plan like that would take time. It would mean I'd have to renege on my commitment to Twig.

If I went to Findlay, on the other hand, I could do Twig's student class *and* work on Newt's murder. In fact, Findlay might give me more answers than Muskogee. Findlay, after all, was where this all started. Findlay was where Alex Laird killed Lonny Carmichael. And Findlay was where I could last trace Newt's VHS tapes.

Findlay, I suddenly realized, might just hold the key.

Events were moving lightning fast, and I was surprised to find myself moving right along with them. Since Newt's death on Friday I hadn't gone out for a run, hadn't laundered my clothes, hadn't read a sentence in a book, hadn't thought about Eleanor, hadn't even voluntarily jumped out of an airplane. And I was having a hard time remembering what my life used to be like when those things had been important to me.

You think you have yourself all figured out. You tailor your habits to accommodate that self-image, incorporating those which bring you pleasure and contentment, eliminating those which do not. And you are cautious when it comes to allowing even moderate change in your personally formulated status quo, because you endured an arduous journey just to arrive at where you are, and you feel no compunction to rethink your position.

Unless you're compelled to.

Maybe my anger wasn't as all-encompassing as Danny Death's, but Newt's double malfunction had rekindled in me a fire I had long assumed dead. And I had to admit that since I'd committed myself to setting things right, there was a new vitality to my thoughts, a sharpness to the way I approached the next minute, and the hour after that. I hadn't realized how stagnant my mind had become the past few years. But now I could see the contrast. I'd figured out a lot since Friday night, and I wanted very badly to figure out the rest.

The sooner I get to Findlay, I thought, the sooner I can tackle Alex Laird and those missing VHS tapes. I won't wait till tomorrow night.

I'll leave first thing in the morning.

I quickened my pace.

For maximum privacy I'd set up my tent with its front facing away from the airport. It was nearly forty yards beyond my nearest neighbor, the Utah tent where I'd dug up voluptuous Sue. I passed that tent and approached the rear of my own. I stopped abruptly twenty feet out.

A strong light from a distant farmhouse shone through the tent. It revealed the sketchy shadow of a person inside, crouched down and waiting.

I stood totally still. Didn't blink, didn't dare to breathe. Had I been heard?

The shadow faced the front. I was behind him and a little off to his right. He shifted and stretched his leg. If he'd heard me, he wouldn't have done that. So I had an advantage: he didn't know I was here.

Partner. The man who killed Newt. The man who sabotaged my rig.

Dominic or Cheeks?

Moving only my head, I scanned the camping area. Nobody in sight for about seventy-five yards. The collage of out-of-state tents and vans clung to the earth like discarded locust skins, lifeless and empty.

I swallowed. The trapezius muscles in the back of my neck were impaling my skull.

I looked back at the shadow. For three years I'd lived in New York City, walking the streets of Manhattan daily, often at night. Violence was an intimate part of the routine. There was violence in way people talked, violence in the way people drove, violence in the way people did business, violence in the way people robbed, violence in the way people died. Violence was in the air. You breathed the air, you absorbed its violence. For the first time since I'd left New York I was feeling the passion of fear, and I forgot that I don't like violence.

Pacifism is relative to circumstance.

I slithered backward, dipped close to the ground, and circled around behind the Utah tent. Quietly, I set Newt's video case on the ground. I studied my tent. The farm light did not strike it from this angle. No shadow to see, only to think about.

I began to stalk my tent. I forgave the rock band its obscene loudness because it drowned out the brush of my feet over the grass.

I reached the back of the tent. I patted the ground with my hand and located the three stakes that held the back end in place. I loosened them. Tiny ripples passed through the fabric. I held my breath. He made no sound. I reached for the top of the tent's rear pole. This was it. I planted my feet evenly, sucked in a breath of New York violence, relaxed.

Suddenly, out of nowhere, I pounced.

I shoved the pole off to the side, and the back of the tent collapsed. Almost immediately the front followed suit. As the walls caved in, the shadow became a lump—a head, a back, two arms, the rest humped underneath. I grabbed a handful of tent and twisted it around his body, pinning his arms under his chest. A makeshift straitjacket.

He struggled wildly, pushing upward from under me with his legs. I bashed him in the thigh. He kicked up with his foot, catching my shin square on. I belted him harder, this time in the side. There was a long moan. I let go two more, one of them to the head.

"Knock it off! Let me out of here!"

I froze in mid-strike. The voice wasn't tenor or base; it was soprano and female.

She fought with greater success as I relaxed my grip. I let myself fall back to the grass. She found the tent zipper, slid it up, and popped out through the opening.

Bridgette Bridle.

And her very bare chest.

"What's going on?" she said, propping her forehead up with her hand and looking mildly dazed.

"Are you all right?"

She didn't answer me. She recovered enough to begin untangling her legs. "Get me out of here this instant!"

Seeing she wasn't seriously hurt, I suddenly found the situation immensely comical. "Surprise!" I said, more to myself than to her.

Bridgette didn't get the joke. "Wait till I tell Harley about this— you attacking me and—and—laughing at me."

"Really?" I was tempted to hug her, but given her limited attire, I smartly kept my paws to myself. "And how will you explain to Harley your half-naked presence in my tent around midnight?"

Embarrassment often comes out as anger, and that's what happened with Bridgette. She glowered at me, pursed her lips but kept them silent. In fact, she didn't say another word. She freed her legs, then climbed back in through the collapsed tent door, head first. She dug around and finally popped back out clutching a skimpy black garment. She fumbled with its straps, tied it around her chest, and limped away.

I threw myself down on my tent and lay there for nearly an hour laughing at my little private joke, until the tension finally cleared.

It was the last laugh I'd have for a while.

Part Three

FINDLAY

20

The long ride back to Twig's drop zone was made even longer by my impatience to get there. Legal out in these states is sixty-five, which means the slow drivers do seventy. The passing lane was clocking seventy-five on the up side of the Ozarks, eighty coming back down. Today that felt like a crawl.

I pulled off in an antique town that last week would have been just my speed. In their general store, a genial clerk piddled away ten minutes of my valuable time talking baseball while I tried to buy a mailing envelope, brown paper, and wrapping tape. When the clerk finally realized I couldn't care less about his St. Louis Cardinals, he rang up my order pronto.

Out at the Honda, I opened the envelope and slid in the elongated sigma, Newt's reserve ripcord, his main breakaway handle, and a detailed explanation of what they all meant and what to do with them. I sealed the envelope and attached a note instructing Eleanor to open it if I didn't turn up for Saturday's date.

Assuming *she* showed up, that is.

I wrapped the envelope and note in the brown mailing paper, taped it well, addressed it, smothered it with stamps, and slipped it in a mailbox. Down the street I found a telephone booth. I dialed Paula Chimura's home number, got no answer, tried her work number.

It was the Fourth of July, but one of the secretaries was working overtime. Ms. Chimura would be out of the office until next Monday, sir, due to a death in the family. Mr. Clives would be handling Ms. Chimura's accounts in the interim, sir.

195

"My name is Chance. I'm a personal friend. Paula didn't answer at home."

"No, sir, she wouldn't. She left last night for north Florida."

"Did she say where in north Florida?"

"Family, sir."

"Do you have a number for her there?

"Afraid not, sir."

"She was expecting me to call. Didn't she mention my name?"

"No, sir. It must have slipped her mind, what with her husband's ghastly death."

I ignored his audible grimace. "What about the name of the town?"

"Sorry, sir. All she said was north Florida."

"Would Mr. Clives know?"

"She spoke with me, sir, not Mr. Clives."

I frowned into the phone. "When will she be back?"

"Sunday, sir. I can leave her a message you called."

I gave him the number of Twig's drop zone—where I expected to be on Sunday—but said I'd call back in any case.

So much for finding out if Newt had sent Paula those VHS tapes. At least till Sunday.

I filled up my gas tank, got back on the road, and sped toward Findlay.

When Twig first mentioned the group of college students back in May, I'd signed on fast. Training them was going to be fun: seeing the initial fear in their faces as they peeked out the open door; watching that fear become determination as they got ready to jump; sharing in their euphoria afterward.

Now I didn't want the job. I didn't want to waste my time teaching a bunch of immature yuppies-to-be how to make a skydive when I could be solving two murders, and maybe a whole lot more.

If I can just figure out why Alex Laird killed Lonny Carmichael, I thought, everything else might fall into place.

I passed through Illinois and into Indiana. It was sunset by the time I bumped down Airport Road. There was a low cloud cover, and the airport lay deserted. In the parking lot I labored off the Honda in slow motion because my legs were sore from the ten-hour ride, and because I was shocked by what I saw.

Findlay Airport, Twig Buckwater's symbol of sweat and hard work, had been abandoned to the elements. Rain water had washed away half the parking lot stones, and thick, ugly weeds were choking those that remained. The grass in the packing and camping areas was long and drooping. I bent down and straightened a blade. Eight, maybe nine inches long.

Twig's Cessnas and his Beech E-18 were lined up on the far side of the hangar, but his old white Beech still sat out front. It didn't look as though it had been touched since I left. Twig's pickup truck, parked in the rear, had grass growing up around its tires. In the packing area, the half-completed manifest booth was now slanting precipitously in the direction of the loft. Not so much as an eight-penny nail had been added to its frame. The bare non-pressurized wood, left unprotected in the rain, had warped noticeably.

The door to the loft was unlatched. I ventured inside and flipped on the light.

I was in Twig's lounge. A trail of dried mud led from the door to the student training room in back and off to the right. Three aviation magazines were scattered on the floor. I gathered them up and laid them next to one of Twig's two VCRs.

Off to my right the shower room's light was on. I walked in. The room had a door leading directly outside from the showers. It had been left open. I shut it, then switched off the light and went back into the lounge.

To the left of the lounge was Twig's open office area. On his desk, a mixed stack of signed and unsigned liability waivers had spilled off the paperweight onto which it had been laid. The top left drawer of the desk, which held his cash box, was gaping. Inside were a fair number of tens and twenties. I shut the drawer. A quartz watch sitting on the desk beeped the hour. It said eight o'clock.

Behind the office, Twig's long narrow rigging room stretched back more than fifty feet. The door was open. I walked in.

The room was exceedingly cluttered. Below its only window, curtained with a retired Navy Conical reserve, was Twig's regulation rigging table. His tools were scattered over it, as were a number of untouched boxes sent via UPS.

There were two reserves hanging in Twig's chimney-like drying tower at the far end of the rigging table. I touched them. Bone dry. I took them down. Beyond the drying tower was Twig's file cabinet containing the owner's manuals and packing instructions for each piece of parachute equipment ever made. A pile of manuals had been pulled but not put back. I filed them away.

Property has an intrusive way of stripping its owner bare and exposing his soul. Presentably clean, basically tidy, reasonably maintained—these are the characteristics of the mentally fit. The condition of Twig's drop zone, I suspected, was telling me volumes about his current state of mind.

Certainly Twig had been depressed about the Carmichael fatality last month, and he'd sounded weary on the phone yesterday; but I had not expected this. For as long as I'd known him, he'd always fancied himself as the hard-working entrepreneur, the embodiment of the American dream. Now, it seemed, he didn't give a damn. The spirit and the heart that had taken over this airport in the early eighties, that had designed and constructed this loft and hangar, the spirit that had *been* the drop zone, had gotten tripped up—broken, I had to assume, along with the bones of Lonny Carmichael.

I was surprised and saddened by the extent of Twig's depression—that he would take his first fatality so hard. Tomorrow, I thought, I'll have to sit down with him and have a little talk.

I left the rigging room. Between the rigging and student training rooms was the old packing table I'd found Danny Death passed out on back in May. On it Twig had piled the T-10 military rigs we'd be using this week. I decided to leave them there till tomorrow morning, and spent the rest of my evening eliminating my second guess about the location of Newt's VHS tapes: they weren't hidden anywhere on the premises.

I moved the Honda next to Twig's memorial elm and set up my tent. Alex Laird lived in neighboring Greenville, according to the customer address book I'd found in Twig's office. Tomorrow, I thought, after I'm done with the student rigs, I'll go to Greenville and find his house.

I climbed into my sleeping bag and fell asleep thinking about Alex Laird.

Tuesday I got up early, ran short, showered hastily, rinsed out a couple T-shirts, gobbled down food I'd picked up in Illinois, got started on the student rigs. T-10s are huge thirty-five-foot round canopies packed in heavy-duty containers attached to uncomfortable harnesses, all olive drab. Designed for the conditions of war, they are a real pain to jump in. On the plus side, they're durable and cheap. They might break a few more ankles than square parachutes, but their fatality rate is probably no worse. Most skydiving fatalities are caused by human error, not equipment failure. Or in Newt's and Lonny's case, human machination.

First, I counted the rigs. Thirty-three mains, sixteen chest-mounted reserves. At least I didn't have thirty-three reserves to pack. T-10 reserves can be detached from one student and hooked to the next one.

I picked through the lot. Twig had retired them to storage three or four years ago, and they looked it. I slapped one with my hand, and a plume of dust puffed out. Countless spiders explored the containers, and there was sticky webbing everywhere.

I went over the rigs one by one. First the harnesses and containers. Then I opened the containers and looked at the canopies. I estimated the time it would take to get them into jumpable shape, and swore out loud.

There was no way I could make the repairs, pack up all forty-nine rigs, *and* go after Alex Laird. There was just no way!

Seven rigs needed harness/container repairs, six others canopy work. Probably none were dangerous, but we couldn't put students up in them the way they were. I separated out the thirteen rigs. As I set them aside, I noticed a curious lack of spider webbing on all but one of the six rigs with ripped canopies.

I went back over the thirteen rigs and reassessed the repair time. It came out about the same. I combed my fingers through my hair and shook my head.

The only thing to do, Chance, is to get started right away. For the moment, you'll just have to put Alex Laird on hold.

I slung the first rig over my shoulder, strode into the rigging room, and sat down at one of Twig's sewing machines. Rigging repairs can't be rushed, and I worked steadily through the morning. I'd completed all the harnesses and was almost finished with the containers when Twig drove up in his car.

I'd known what to expect, yet his physical appearance still shook me. He seemed to have aged ten years in half that many weeks. His deep-set eyes had retreated farther into his head, and there were dark circles beneath them. He stared into the rigging room at me, then turned, shuffled over to his desk, and sat down. I got up from the sewing machine and went out front.

"Here," he said in a monotone. He set a brown bag down on his desk. I walked over and picked it up. Inside were eight deli sandwiches.

"There's fruit and that flat bread you like in the refrigerator under the packing table. It should last you through tomorrow. I'll bring out some more when it's gone."

"Thanks," I said. "You really didn't have to go to all this trouble."

I took a sandwich from the bag and offered it to him, but he waved it away. I sat down on the end of the packing table and began to eat. Roast beef on rye. Beneath my feet the unpacked T-10 parachutes sprawled over the floor.

"So you've started," he said, stating the obvious.

"There's a lot to be done."

He didn't even nod.

"I've fixed the ripped harnesses," I said, "and I'm almost done with the containers. The canopies have to be sewn and patched yet before I can start packing. I hadn't expected so many to be in poor condition."

Twig was staring down at the rigs. He didn't say anything.

"I was planning on having my evenings free," I went on. "But now I'm just hoping to have the rigs all ready for Thursday's class. Maybe we could get by with not using the ones I haven't fixed yet. I could get right to packing."

Twig shook his head. "More than thirty students have signed up both days. If they all come we'll need every rig. I'd help you out, but I've got my own work on the planes. The E-18's barely running."

"You don't look so swell yourself," I put in cautiously.

Twig's eyes followed the trail of dried mud on the floor. "How was the drive up here?" he asked, only to change the subject.

"Long," I replied.

He nodded hypnotically.

"Maybe we should think out exactly how we're going to do everything, then," I said. "Time is going to be very tight this week."

He didn't even look up, just shook his head. "It's not good to think too much," he said. "Not good at all." Then he rose and shuffled out the door and over to the hangar.

I never did bring up the matter of Lonny Carmichael. I wasn't sure why I hadn't, only that it hadn't felt like the right thing to do.

I ate another sandwich and got up from the packing table. I stashed the rest of the sandwiches in Twig's refrigerator alongside the pita bread and fruit already there.

I went back to the rigging room. The remaining container repairs didn't take long. The canopy patches, on the other hand, were time-consuming. Stitching accurate seams on flimsy nylon requires tremendous finger dexterity. It wasn't until quarter of four by Twig's desk watch that I'd secured the final patch.

Without skipping a beat I plunged into packing the main canopies. I worked fast and efficiently, glad to be in shape. The desk watch beeped the hour three times before my concentration left me. I went out, ran three quick miles, and got it right back. Twig started up the left engine on the Beech E-18, then shut it off. He trudged slowly from the plane to the hangar. His movements were automatic, like those of a robot.

I showered, ate from the refrigerator, and, to relieve the monotony in packing, switched to reserves. Reserves require double the concentration and time. And because they were on my mind, each connector link got checked twice.

I did four of those.

I was too tired to pack any more reserves, but managed two more mains before quitting for the night. Twig had driven off earlier. He hadn't come into the loft to check my progress, or even say good night.

I was exhausted, but I had a hard time falling asleep. Now that I was back in Findlay, more memories from Memorial Day weekend were surfacing. My mind raced through them all, but kept gravitating back to one: that disturbing dream about Eleanor, the Sears Tower, and the airplane buzzing my head. And the truck engine idling at the beginning of the dream. My mind was particularly drawn to that. And the car that left the drop zone just as I woke up.

A queasy feeling of uncertainty was growing inside me. A doubt that had begun this morning as a small seed, but that throughout the day had sprouted thick, gripping roots.

There were other things from that weekend that I remembered. Like my Memorial Day breakfast with Danny Death. Alex Laird had come into the restaurant while we were there, and he'd sat in the smoking section with Macintosh and Cheeks. And then there was the following morning, after I returned from my meeting with Police Chief Eugene Smedley. I could remember where each plane was parked at the airport that day, and which plane was missing. I pieced those two memories together with my Sears Tower dream of the night in between and the missing spider webs of this morning, and I came up with a scenario I didn't like so well.

I rolled over on my stomach and put my face in my rig. It can't be, I thought. It just can't be!

I got up, went outside, sat down at the base of Twig's memorial elm. The Honda was next to me. I reached into the tank bag and pulled out a piece of suspension line. I sat there for a long time and tried to concentrate on making pull-up cords.

I looked up at the sky. The moon was beginning to rise. It was a week beyond full, a week away from new. I closed my eyes and leaned my head against the tree trunk.

Only three days ago I'd figured out that Newt was murdered. Only two days ago I'd attacked that shadow inside my tent. And only yesterday I'd raced up here to Findlay to chase down a couple leads.

Now I was feeling overburdened and trapped. I wanted my old life back, to be Chance the Wandering Rigger again. I didn't want to think about idling truck engines, missing airplanes, and spider webs.

I sighed. At least I can ignore my suspicions till Saturday, I thought. I'll be too busy with parachutes and student jumpers between now and then.

I didn't remember crawling back in my tent, but that's where I woke up shortly after dawn.

The whole day Wednesday went like the second half of Tuesday: eat, pack, pack, pack, run, eat, pack, pack, pack. I concentrated solely on parachutes. Twig kept to himself over by the hangar.

A few minutes after midnight I closed the last container. My eyes were seeing double and the tendons in my hands were sore, but the real work wouldn't begin till tomorrow, eight o'clock sharp.

Thursday morning Twig restocked the refrigerator with food that would stretch through Saturday. I ate my breakfast and listened as twenty-nine students drove up in a bus.

We split the group in two. Twig and Josie, the university club president, teamed up to teach one section, I took the other by myself.

Twig had always been an exceptional teacher, but today he only went through the motions. He didn't repeat the exit and landing drills thoroughly, and his explanations were often confusing. Josie had to interrupt him several times, and by noon she'd effectively taken over their group.

In seven hours the three of us managed to teach the students everything they needed to know to make their first static-line jump: this is a parachute and these are its parts; these are the jump aircraft and this is how you exit; this is the way you arch your back; this is what you do in an emergency; this is how you land; and these are the things you never ever do—though we could bet that at least some of them would.

I was gearing up the first crop of students in the training room when Twig walked in.

"The pilot I lined up said he'd be here by three," he said. "It's three-twenty. I've called but get no answer."

"Maybe he's on his way."

Twig mumbled something like, "Guess I'll have to fly," and went out to preflight the plane.

If the pilot didn't show, I'd have to jumpmaster all twenty-nine students myself.

The runway had hardened since last week's rain, and I was sure the Beech E-18 could take off on it. Twig, however, decided to go with one of the small Cessnas. That meant dropping three students at a time instead of eight.

Twig flew, Josie directed landings on the ground. As jumpmaster, I suited up the students, accompanied them in the plane, built up their confidence, went over last minute instructions, gave them the ready-set-go. And when they flopped out the door I held the static line attached to their pack that deployed their main. On the ground Josie disconnected the unused reserves from the finished students and attached them to the students about to go. By sundown, all twenty-nine students had made their first jump. I signed each newly issued logbook, repacked all but seven of the mains, and crawled off to my sleeping bag.

The pilot never did show. I had a nauseating feeling I knew the reason why.

Thirty-one students on Friday, still no pilot. The sky was low and the winds were blowing—a thousand too few feet and five too many knots. The class situation was more or less a repeat of yesterday, except that Josie took over for Twig almost from the beginning. We finished at three-thirty. I packed the remaining rigs while we waited out the weather. By six we could go. This time Twig agreed to use the Beech. It was a lot quicker than with the Cessna, and we were able to put all the students out before sunset. In the entire two days, no malfunctions, no tree landings, no sprained ankles, and only one guy backed out.

I was physically and mentally spent by the time everyone cleared out. I stared at the mountain of unpacked T-10s stacked on the floor in front of the packing table. I'd have to pack them up one last time. When I was done, I'd be free to pursue Alex Laird. Something I no longer looked forward to doing.

I hoisted a rig onto the packing table and packed it. Then another, and another. Before I could stretch out the lines on the twelfth canopy, I passed out inside its inviting folds of fluffy olive drab.

Saturday morning I woke up when I woke up, which was late. I had a headache, smelled of sweat, and looked like a bum. I could exercise the tendons in my fingers only if I really enjoyed pain. It wasn't the number of rigs I'd packed, but the speed at which I'd packed them.

I sat up on the packing table and looked around the loft. Six of yesterday's students had come back for seconds. They were sitting in the lounge observing me, their omnipotent jumpmaster, probably trying to decide if I'd passed out drunk. I could hear the wind whipping around outside and I knew the six wouldn't be jumping this morning. Probably not all day.

I took a shower and ate oranges and plums from Twig's refrigerator. The students moved outside to the picnic table. No one else had bothered to come out to the airport. Experienced jumpers and pilots knew better than to come out in wind like this.

Besides being windy out, it was hot and dusty. A high-pressure system from the southwest had moved in, bringing with it top soil from the southern plains.

I stared out the door for a long while. I knew I couldn't put it off any longer. Finally I went over to Twig's office and sat down at his desk. The phone was to my right. I picked up the receiver and punched the number for Davis Field, Oklahoma. Someone answered. I swallowed my pride, bit my tongue, and asked for The Pit Bull.

Bradford Rey had invited Newt to film the diamond load, according to Aslam. Normally that would be a routine thing, but now I was wondering.

Bradford Rey was genuinely surprised to here my voice, but he did answer my question. He even told me a little bit more. I thanked him, hung up, then called the Ridgeway drop zone in California. By the end of that call I was sure I knew who had killed Newt. I should have been feeling on top of the world for figuring it out, but I wasn't. Because if Cheeks was Partner, then another factor—one I hadn't even considered in Muskogee—had to come into play. It was that other factor that had been ruining my week.

I rubbed my fingers over each of the phone's touch-tone buttons. There was a lumpiness to the air I breathed in, a heaviness in my heart. I punched local information and requested a number. Then I punched the number itself. I spent a minute on hold before a man asked how he could help me.

"Connect me with Officer Davidson, please."

21

I'd been against going to the police without more proof, but I now felt I had no other choice.

Davidson remembered me. "It's important we talk," I said. "Unofficially, if possible."

"I get off at five, but then I run. What about seven?"

"What about five and I run with you?"

"If you can do seven miles at a six-minute pace."

"Where do we meet?"

I wrote down the directions to Findlay High on the back of a blank liability waiver. Then I went back to packing parachutes.

Counting the one I'd slept on, I had twenty-two left. My tendons would have preferred a day off, but I wanted to finish the rigs today; I didn't know if I'd have time tomorrow.

I became a clock watcher. After every five rigs I checked the time. I had no intention of missing my meeting with the police, now that it had been arranged.

By four I had all the rigs packed.

The southwest heat had intensified. I took a cup from the Honda's tank bag and helped myself to a spigot outside Twig's loft. I drank, then ran the cold spigot water over my tendons for about ten minutes. Two of the six students had given up on the wind, but the other four were sticking it out. They were in the lounge watching skydiving videos. Twig had pulled in a little while ago and was somewhere inside the hangar. I walked over to the picnic table and sat down. While I was sitting there, Danny Death came straggling in.

He was dragging his gear bag behind him, first along Airport Road and then through the parking lot. He was shirtless and sockless, wearing only his tattered jeans and holey sneakers. His hair was plastered to his forehead with sweat, and Lonny Carmichael's tinted glasses still sat on the bridge of his nose. His skin was rose pink. I sensed he was close to fainting.

"Water?"

"Beer," he pleaded.

I refilled my cup with spigot water and handed it to him. He guzzled it straight down, then plopped down on the picnic table. When I was sure he'd recovered from the brink I said, "You walk here all the way from Oklahoma?"

"Cut the fuckin' jokes, man! I'm deader than dead. Totally wasted. Lugged this shit more than two miles in the goddamn hot wind."

I got him another cup of water. "When did you leave Nationals?"

"Yesterday," he said, calming down. "Arn gave me a lift to Illinois, but then he goes straight north. Rides have been slow to come today. Four fuckin' hours to do the last twenty miles. Not fuckin' easy to get rides after you leave the Interstate, ya know. Not many cars, and those there are don't stop for nothin'."

"A haircut and nice clothes might help," I hinted.

"Yeah. Or a nice pair of tits like that Utah chick Susie had on."

I gave up. "So why didn't you head straight home? You're too wiped out to skydive, and the winds are too high, anyway."

"Didn't come to jump, man." He got up, lumbered over to the spigot, filled my cup, and stood there drinking it. He filled the cup again and returned to the table with it.

"Came to get my reserve repacked. It expires today, and I'm goin' up to Wisconsin Wednesday to make a couple dives with Arn and what's left of the old guys. At their new place west of Madison. Never been there myself."

"Wouldn't it have been easier to get your reserve packed at Nationals?"

"No funds, man. Spent all my bread jumpin'. Need to have it packed on credit." He poured the cup of water over his head and smeared it through his hair. "So will you pack it for me?"

I grinned. Before leaving Nationals on Monday I had told Danny Death I'd be in Findlay this week. So he'd come all the way out here on the off chance I'd pack his rig on credit.

"I'll do it as long as you don't mind picking it up some other day,"

I said, wondering if I'd ever get paid. "I'm leaving here in a few minutes and expect to be tied up the rest of the night."

"Okay by me. I can stop in Wednesday on my way up to Wisconsin."

"I'll have it done by then. If for some reason I'm not here when you stop in, I'll leave it in Twig's rigging room for you."

He nodded, unzipped his gear bag, and pulled out his rig. I put it in on Twig's rigging table, then gave him a lift back to the Interstate.

Shortly after five I was circling Findlay High's track, which circled Findlay High's football field, which was situated behind a red-brick building similar to the one I'd done algebra and biology in almost twenty years ago.

I didn't like to run laps, and apparently neither did Davidson. After we'd done four, he veered off the track and signaled me to fall in behind. We went single file along a trail through a wooded area. Five hundred yards later we came to a desolate country road.

"This is where the cross-country team always runs," he explained. "Never any cars."

And there weren't. Just a tractor driven by a farm boy who puttered along at a pace slower than ours. We ran fast down the middle for two and a half miles, heading west. The dust particles in the hot southwest air made each breath taste bitter and dry. My throat scratched.

At a tee in the road we turned left, then left again a half mile later. We were out on the road that led to the front of the school.

"Race you to the gym," Davidson challenged, and took off sprinting. Like that, he had four seconds on me.

A month ago I'd have hung back, maintained my pace, let him win. A week ago I'd have jumped at the opportunity. Today I hesitated before making up my mind.

Then I leaned forward, drew up my shoulders, lengthened my stride. I concentrated on the mechanics of speed, and my body transformed itself into a glider that flew along the macadam's edge. Davidson gradually came back to me. Fifty yards from the school I caught up to him, and by four feet I slapped the gym door first.

We both leaned against the door, exhausted. He gave me a weak high-five.

"You must have been a track star in school," he said after we both recovered.

I shook my head. "Worked all through school. Never had time for sports."

He raised his eyebrows. "Then where'd you learn to kick like that?"

"Running from muggers in New York City."

He grinned, then laughed heartily. He thought I was kidding. I let him think it.

We showered in the boys' side of the gym and drank lots of water. He hung up his running clothes in a locker that seemed reserved for him, folded his police uniform into his duffel bag, and put on casual after-work clothes. I slipped on a pair of jeans and a semi-clean T-shirt. On one of the benches between the rows of lockers we sat down and ate the rest of Twig's refrigerator fruit.

"So," Davidson said when we'd finished, "what's up?"

I was combing water from my hair. "Your boss," I replied, putting my comb down. "Police Chief Eugene Smedley."

Davidson looked at me quizzically.

I said, "You remember how he wasn't very rational the day I examined Lonny Carmichael's gear?"

Davidson didn't answer.

"Well," I went on, "for the sake of argument, let's say you do. At the time, I thought he was just a paranoid cop, but now I'm wondering."

Davidson slid his hands behind his neck and locked his fingers together. "I'm glad to see you have an open mind," he said. "Though I could understand if you didn't. Gene was a little unfair to you, in my opinion."

"What does he have against skydivers?"

"Not all skydivers, just one. Of course Gene sometimes forgets that."

Davidson pulled his arms down and folded them across his chest. "Gene has a kid, a son named Kyle. He's been raising Kyle alone since his wife died twelve years ago from cancer. Kyle's the only thing in his life outside his job." With his head Davidson motioned toward the gym door. "A few years ago Kyle was a talented high school football star out there on that football field. Defensive back. I was new to the force then, but the one thing I remember clearly was the glow in Gene's eyes after every game. In the bleachers he'd walk around saying, 'Did you see that? Did you see my boy?' Then all week long at work he'd talk about every play Kyle had made. He knew every tackle, every sack, every fumble recovery by heart.

"Kyle was good enough to get several scholarship offers. He accepted one up in Michigan. They redshirted him his freshman year, but he started as a sophomore. Home game, away game, Gene drove to every one. Those were the glory days for both of them."

"Twig Buckwater told me Kyle hung out at the airport one summer a few years back."

"I'm getting to that," Davidson said. "Kyle was home for Christmas break after his sophomore season. He was underage, but was able to pass into a lowlife bar over in Greenville where they didn't recognize him. Kyle always did look older than he was. In the bar, there was a skydiver he knew. I guess they'd tussled once before out at the airport. Well, things were said, one thing led to another, and the skydiver ended up challenging Kyle. Kyle had had a few beers, and was feeling strong coming off the football season. From what the people in the bar said later, it was a pretty even match until the skydiver decided to play dirty. He caught Kyle's lower leg around his own and twisted it, what Lawrence Taylor did to Joe Theismann, only on purpose. Kyle's leg snapped in the middle of the shin."

"Alex Laird," I said, shaking my head.

Davidson nodded. "Gene really couldn't go after Laird without admitting his underage son was in a bar drinking. That would have made all the local papers. It would have caused him problems in doing his job. And it wasn't like Kyle was attacked or anything.

"Gene took him to the best orthopedic surgeon in Chicago, and Kyle went through extensive rehabilitation, but the bone never healed properly. He could walk okay, but he was through with football.

"You can guess the rest. Kyle became bitter and went on the skids. He took up drugs and alcohol, his grades slipped. He quit school this year before they threw him out. He's living up in Michigan drinking, no job, no degree. The whole thing has hit Gene real hard. He's been out to nail Alex Laird ever since."

"So that's why he was so persistent last month," I said. "With Alex Laird being a witness in Lonny Carmichael's death, he saw an opportunity to maybe get Laird on a conspiracy charge, if he could prove it."

"That's about the size of it," Davidson said. "That woman who claimed to have seen Carmichael open his parachute is this town's biggest exaggerator, but Gene was really hoping she was right. He's still hoping because he really wants Laird, but I think deep down he accepts what you told us. We'd already investigated Laird thoroughly after he broke Kyle's leg, looking for anything to get him on.

With that kind, you figure you'll find something sooner or later. We did, but nothing we can prove."

"Like what?"

Davidson became more circumspect and official. "That's . . . privileged information," he said awkwardly.

"It might be," I said, "that I can supplement your privileged information. But I need more input from you first. There are a couple things I'm still not sure about."

His face showed first caution, then curiosity, then anticipation. "Well . . ." he said, building himself up for a betrayal.

The run had created a strange bond between us, a degree of mutual respect usually found only between long-time friends. I tried banking on that. "You can trust me," I said.

He acknowledged that he probably could.

"Unofficially, we believe Alex Laird has off and on been a supplier—or at the very least a shipper—of various weaponry. Where he gets them we don't know. A trucker can make connections all over the country."

I slapped my hand against my thigh. "Oliver North," I said.

Davidson looked at me incredulously. "You're saying Alex Laird is associated with *the* Oliver North?"

"No, no, sorry. There was a vague reference made to Oliver North. I see now it was a reference to gun smuggling. I should have figured that out myself. Go on, please."

Davidson eyed me skeptically for a moment, then continued. "We think in the past Laird's clients were strictly American and small time—racist groups, people with records who can't buy legally. He deals sporadically, so it's been impossible to set up a successful raid. We organized one last year with the Greenville department and got burned. We had good information, but everything was moved out just before we got there."

"You said *in the past.*"

He nodded. "Two months ago we heard a rumor. Supposedly, Laird made a deal involving a group south of the border—weapons for narcotics. To be more specific, cocaine. We think the guns went more than a month ago, but we haven't seen the cocaine yet. No big shipment hit the streets here like we expected."

I was sitting back, taking in what Davidson was saying. "Is that everything you've got?" I asked when he'd finished.

212

"Everything I'm willing to tell you. Now it's your turn. What do *you* have on Alex Laird?"

I picked up my comb and tapped it lightly on the palm of my hand. "Murder," I said. "Lonny Carmichael's murder."

Davidson stared at me hard, as though he'd been deceived.

I held up my hand. "I know what I told you last month. And I wasn't wrong about Carmichael's gear, only about how he died. I think Alex Laird knocked him unconscious as they exited the plane."

Davidson had been straddling the bench. He lifted one leg over so that both were on the same side, then pressed his elbows to his thighs. He clasped his hands together.

"Not even Gene considered that. Assuming you're right, do you think there's a connection between the Carmichael homicide and Laird's illegal activities—a falling out among thieves, so to speak?"

"I think it might somehow be related—Carmichael was known to use cocaine—but I don't think he was involved in Laird's gun running. Carmichael's best friend, Danny Grimes, said Laird didn't like Carmichael. Besides, if the two had been in business together, I think Danny would have known and would have mentioned it. He's been protesting Carmichael's death from the beginning."

Davidson nodded. "I made a routine check of Carmichael after he died. He came out clean." A questioning look came into Davidson's eyes. "So what made you change your mind about all this?"

"Last week at the National Skydiving Championships in Oklahoma another skydiver died. A photographer named Newt Becker. His death was made to look like an accident, too." I explained Newt's double malfunction to Davidson and how it related to Lonny Carmichael. "From what you tell me," I said, "I would guess Cheeks is Laird's cocaine connection."

"Do you know his real name?"

"Christian Jokubka. From Los Angeles."

Davidson pulled a note pad from his duffel bag and wrote down the name as I spelled it out for him.

"Skydivers travel around to different drop zones, especially for boogies—conventions of a sort. That's probably how the two of them met, though I have no idea when. Cheeks passes himself off as an international salesman of airplane parts. He was here Memorial Day weekend when Carmichael went in. Claimed to be here for the Indy Five-hundred, but I would guess now that was just a cover. I think he really came to get the guns from Laird. While he was here, he stayed with a young California skydiver, nickname Macintosh, real name Jim Something. Macintosh told me he drove Cheeks to the airport in Indianapolis that Monday to catch a commercial plane home, but I think either Macintosh lied or Cheeks doubled back on him. I called Cheeks's home drop zone—parachute center, that is—in Ridgeway, California. They tell me he's an experienced pilot. Multi-engine rated. I think he flew out of Findlay Airport with those guns Memorial Day night after all the jumpers left. Or after he thought we'd all left."

"You saw him leave?"

"Not saw, *heard*," I said. "The way I have it figured, Cheeks and Laird met here again the last Monday in June to finish their business transaction, and that's when they decided to kill Newt. He must have become a real pest. Aside from the Lonny Carmichael business, he must have dug up enough information to get wind of Laird's gun running. Who knows, maybe he was blackmailing Laird for that, too.

"Anyway, Cheeks flew to Oklahoma that Monday and had Macintosh pick him up at the Tulsa Airport, according to Macintosh. I would say now that Cheeks flew there from Indianapolis, not from California. I say that because he bought a new parachute at Nationals. I originally thought he just wanted a new rig, but now I'm thinking he bought it because his trip down to Nationals was impromptu and he didn't have his own rig with him."

"Then this Cheeks—Christian Jokubka—sabotaged the photographer's parachutes?"

"Right. This morning I spoke with the load organizer for Newt's last dive, a guy named Bradford Rey. He told me Cheeks asked him to invite Newt Becker to film that dive. And he remembered that Cheeks arranged to have Newt on his side of the formation in the sky. Cheeks knew Newt's main would malfunction, and when it did, he watched from the sky to see where it went down. He landed back at the drop zone, waited twenty minutes or so till it was pretty dark, then went out after it. Another jumper saw him wading through the field where it would have landed."

"Can this other skydiver positively identify Jokubka?"

"No, it was too dark. But I know it was him."

"What do you think he did with the parachute?"

"I've been thinking about that all afternoon. I don't know why I didn't think of it earlier. Cheeks was bunking in Macintosh's van, as he'd done here in Findlay. As soon as he got Newt's main I think he must have stashed it in his gear bag under Macintosh's bed. Around that time I went over to Macintosh's van to store some beer in his cooler, but the van was all locked up. Cheeks said later he'd locked his new gear inside while he went to take a shower. I would guess now his real concern was to lock up Newt's main till he had time to get rid of it permanently."

"This skydiver Macintosh—you think he's involved?"

"I don't know either way. Macintosh is young and very taken in by experienced jumpers like Cheeks. He'd spend the rest of his life cleaning toilets if Cheeks asked him to. Does that mean he helped Cheeks kill Newt Becker? I just can't say."

"Those two tapes you say Jokubka took from the photographer's case—I suppose he's disposed of them by now."

"I can't imagine why he'd keep them. I think he was a little spooked when he heard I was planning to look at Newt's videos. Even after he had the tapes he went to the trouble of warning me off." I explained to Davidson about my missing reserve seal and connector links.

He made some notes in his note pad, then thought for a spell.

"Besides that main connector link you found out on the soccer field, and the ripcord, do you have any evidence that would stand up in court that isn't circumstantial?"

"Not yet, but I think Newt had another copy of the blackmail video that Cheeks didn't get. A box of Newt's tapes is still unaccounted for, and I'm hoping it's somehow connected. I should know more on that tomorrow."

I stood up to go. Davidson put his note pad away and studied me. His eyes showed a mix of puzzlement and curiosity.

"I thought this wasn't any of your business," he said. "Last month I got the distinct impression you didn't want anything to do with Lonny Carmichael."

I stuffed my wet running shorts and socks into a plastic bag and tied it with a twisty. I didn't say anything.

Davidson looked at me a while longer, then got up and picked up his duffel bag.

"I'll be on duty tomorrow till five," he said. "But you can leave a message after that and they'll call me at home. You'll let me know if you hear about that box of tapes?"

"I wouldn't have told you about it if I planned to keep it a secret."

We walked to the gym door. He shut off the lights but didn't bother to lock up. He said that in the past four years nothing in the gym had been stolen, or even vandalized.

What a stark contrast, I thought, to the ugly world we've been discussing for the past half-hour.

22

Sullivan Airport was located seventy miles southwest of Chicago. A weekend playground for a small cadre of that city's young urban professionals, its facilities were nonetheless basic: an old chicken house served as the clubhouse, a barn the hangar, a grass field the runway. It was originally owned by a free-spirited farmer who got his kicks from watching airplanes and skydivers land in his field. When the farmer died a few years back, the homemade airport passed to his acrophobic wife, who threatened to plant soybeans on the runway and raise chickens in the clubhouse. So a half-dozen jumpers, including Eleanor, pooled their resources and made her an offer. She snatched up the money and hadn't been heard from since.

To the relief of the locals, the new urban owners decided to keep their property rustic. In the city, Eleanor had explained to me, rustic was considered chic.

I came to the rear of the chic chicken coop clubhouse. Three cars were parked next to it. The sun was orange red and three-fourths below the horizon, and the wind had calmed down considerably.

I maneuvered the Honda outside the parking area and passed within inches of chest-high corn on my right, passed a Cessna and a Beech on my left. I reached the grass runway and steered the Honda right. More corn. Beyond the corn, soybeans.

Eleanor's red van appeared black with the eclipse of the day. It was nestled in the northeast corner of the runway, its sliding door pushed back. I eased the Honda up next to it and shut off the engine.

"You're late, buster," she said from inside.

217

In her voice I caught traces of the smile that was gracing her face. I wasn't late, but I didn't object. Her mood was rousingly playful, and my hormones responded. I slid my helmet off, leaned inside the van, and found her mouth. It tasted fresh and alluring. We embraced. Missiles shot up from my skin and targeted those escaping from hers. They collided and burned warmly.

"God," she murmured, "I've missed that." She kissed the tip of my nose. With her long, slender fingers she fluffed up my hair.

"Me too," I said. I kissed her again. This time she tasted like a walk through a pine forest.

I steadied my helmet on the floor of the van and sank down beside her. She linked her pinky in mine and leaned her back against the van's interior siding.

"The air in here feels like seltzer," she said. "All fizzy and energized."

"Carbonated," I agreed.

She reached into a cooler with her other hand and produced two long-stemmed pieces of hereditary crystal. She handed them to me, then reached back into the cooler and pulled out a bottle of expensive champagne and a monogrammed towel.

"You intend to uncork that with one hand?" I teased. "Or do you want your pinky back?"

She looked over at me. Her eyes glistened first, then her mouth. We experienced a purposeless moment in time when being and togetherness were all that mattered.

"I'll repossess the pinky, if you please."

I released it. "On loan," I said. "At two percent above the prime each minute, the principle to be calculated at a hundred dollars per pound of pinky flesh."

"That still wouldn't come close to the cost of the champagne."

She covered the cork with the towel, twisted deftly until it popped.

"Let me guess," I said. "The Neanderthal man lost."

She smiled, filled both glasses a millimeter beyond half, then lifted one of them from my hand.

"Congratulations." I pecked her cheek. "A toast to women managers."

She bowed symbolically. We sipped our champagne and eyed each other affectionately.

"So when do you begin the new job?"

She settled her body a little closer to mine. "I've been doing the work for about two weeks, but the promotion doesn't become official until next week."

"Does this mean we'll see less of each other?"

"Let's hope not," she said. "But you know you're always welcome to come visit me at my place."

"And be your weekend gigolo?"

I'd said it as a joke, but her face became serious. "Gigolos are men who live off women for their money," she said. "You're not that."

"I'm not carbon monoxide or concrete or crowds, either. I'm not city."

With her fingers she began to make soft, gentle love with the palm of my hand. "No," Eleanor conceded, "you're not city. And I'm not country like you."

I sometimes wondered how things would be if she were. Would we be together, loving and committed, or would we come up with some other excuse?

She squeezed my hand. "What's important," she said, "is that we're both happy."

But that was the problem. At the moment I wasn't at all happy. Even sitting here next to Eleanor. I was longing for the old days when simplicity ruled my life, and I wondered if it ever would again. Eleanor seemed to sense my strange mood, but chose not to comment on it.

"I'm sorry I couldn't meet you at Nationals," she said. "I had a lot of work piled up back at the office, and there was no way I could ignore it *after* just being promoted. It wouldn't have looked good."

"And there was no way you could ignore it *before* just being promoted," I added. "It wouldn't have looked good."

She sat still for a minute, looking at me. "Okay, smarty," she said, "you've made your point. But I don't set the rules in business, I just try to work within them. You do agree that it would have been a disastrous way to start out, given the situation?"

I nodded. "You'll be scrutinized under a microscope, especially by Mr. Neanderthal. He'll be lurking, waiting to say I told you so."

The pressure around her eyes eased. "I knew you'd be supportive," she said.

"But keep a little perspective, Ms. Manager. Don't get caught up in all those women's lib slogans. It goes both ways, remember. Men who raise children have the same problems women have in business. The kid falls off his bike and the father is incompetent."

Eleanor pulled her head back. "My, my, what's all this? Do I sense an undertone of . . . cynicism?"

I shrugged. "In your shrinkology it would probably be diagnosed as displaced something-or-other. Like displaced disillusionment. Displaced cynicism would do."

"Want to talk about it?"

I reached over, pulled her close, and whispered into her ear: "What I want is to make love to you."

She whispered back into mine: "We've got time for both."

I took back my arm and stared outside. She waited.

"I can't explain the specifics," I said, "but maybe I can make an analogy."

She sat back comfortably, slipping the lower portion of her legs under her thighs. "Whenever you're ready," she said.

I set my champagne glass down on the van's floor and turned so that we were facing each other. "Remember when you told me about your experience with ballet?"

"I remember."

"You said you were perfectly happy being a regular kid. But your parents—correct that, your mother—wanted you to be a prima ballerina, so she pushed you into dance school. At first you didn't want to go, but once you got there you thrived on the challenge. You felt like you were making things happen in your life, not just passively reacting to the world your mother was creating for you. You decided to aim for a slot in a New York ballet company, and you focused all your emotions on that one goal."

She was nodding silently, sipping her champagne.

"But then you got older, and with age came wisdom. You discovered certain realities about the world of dance—the cut-throat competition, the ME-ME-ME syndrome in the performing arts, the drug abuse, the anorexia. All of that disillusioned you. Eventually, you said enough. You up and quit."

When I had finished Eleanor said, "Okay, that's the analogy. How does it apply to you?"

"Well, it doesn't entirely, but it's the best I could do off the top of my head. What it boils down to is, I got dragged into a situation, I got totally wrapped up in it, and now I want out. Only I can't get out."

"That's an unusual position for *you*."

"Yeah, it sure is. But you know, up till this week I was actually enjoying it. I was getting a charge out of what I was doing. There was a sense of accomplishment. And I didn't feel trapped at all. I wanted to be involved. That is, until I got far enough into it to see what's at the other end. But now I can't just up and quit the way you quit dance. I'm locked in by my own damned ethics. I made commitments to certain people, and to myself."

"Yes," she said. "That would breed cynicism. If you didn't feel you had an out."

Her glass was empty. She set it aside and picked up mine.

"This wouldn't have anything to do with that envelope I got in the mail, would it? The one I was supposed to open if you didn't show up tonight."

"Everything," I said. "By the way, you didn't happen to bring the envelope, did you?"

"As a matter of fact . . ." She put down my glass and got to her knees. She arched past me to the console between the two front seats, grabbed the envelope, plunked back to the floor, and handed it to me. The brown mailing paper was torn off and the note was gone.

"So do I get to see what's inside?" she asked.

"Not just yet. Do you have a pen?"

She reached past me again, picked up a pen and handed it to me. I could barely see to write on the envelope.

"Would you mail this for me tomorrow?"

She took the envelope and read the address.

"Officer Davidson? Findlay Police Department?" She looked over at me and I saw confusion in her eyes. "When I first got this I thought it must be a gag joke of some sort." Her voice carried a question in it.

"Maybe I'll explain it all soon," I said.

Eleanor sat there silently for a minute. Then she put the envelope down, pushed up from the floor of the van, and slipped out to the runway. Enough of the day's breeze had survived to hold the mosquitoes and other bugs at bay. The dusty haze in the sky was thick, and the few stars assertive enough to cut through it truly twinkled. There would be no moon till almost dawn. Even then, it would be only a sliver.

She walked the width of the runway twice before coming back to the van. Eleanor respected my right to privacy, and I knew she wouldn't ask any more questions.

I kissed her. She kissed me back, giving me the full thrust of her tongue. She explored my teeth and I cradled her neck with my hands.

"What about outside," she whispered.

"No place better."

I climbed out and she tossed me a blanket. I threw it over the grass in the middle of the runway. There were no runway lights, so there was no threat from nighttime landings.

I reclined on my elbow. Eleanor came over and sat next to me. She was holding my glass of champagne for herself, a Molson Golden for me. She was wearing designer jeans and a pin-striped oxford shirt. Her shoulder-length hair hung around her face just so. She smelled clean and natural. No suffocating perfume, and no makeup. No need to alter an already sensuous body. I caressed her thigh lightly.

"Here," she said. She placed the Molson in my other hand. Between the bottle and my palm she slipped a small packet of protection. It was done boldly, but then she seemed less sure. "You don't mind, do you?"

I shook my head and set down my beer. "It's something we all have to deal with," I said. "The carefree seventies are long gone."

She took a sip of champagne. "Even if the time isn't right for you to tell me what's been going on in your life, there's something I need to explain to you."

"I thought maybe there was."

She nodded. "I eat lunch every day with a group of people from the office. One of them was the guy from Accounting who always handled my expense account. Anthony was very personable and witty. A nice fellow. I noticed that he'd gotten a lot thinner this past year, and gaunt-looking, but I never made the connection. He finally took disability leave in April and died in May. The official cause was pneumonia. He was only thirty-six years old, not much older than me. His funeral was two days before Lonny Carmichael went in." She paused. "You realize how ephemeral life is . . ."

That same thought had been churning in my own mind the past week.

She started over. "When I avoided you in Findlay, I guess there was more to it than just Lonny Carmichael and my job. I guess I've been uptight about the idea of sex, too. It's odd how something you've always taken for granted, something that's always been so positive, can quickly become so negative and frightening."

"If you'd rather not," I said. I stopped tracing circles on her thigh. She rested her glass on the runway and touched my face with her fingers. "Don't stop," she whispered. "I'd really rather."

I moved my hand along the seam of her jeans. She smiled and kissed my eyelids, then stroked my neck. I pulled her down alongside me, and her hair fell against my arm. We unbuttoned and unzipped each other. I ran my fingers down the vertebrae of her spine. She ran hers down mine, then kissed my body until she'd met every inch of it with her lips. I rediscovered every curve in hers, every muscle that had once given life to Giselle, to Sleeping Beauty, to all the rest.

There was nothing negative, nothing frightening in our exploration and gentle reawakening. We were two lovers, unaware of the world beyond our own connections.

23

I got back to Findlay late Sunday morning. I didn't stay long.

The day was warm, the wind jumpable. Four skydivers were descending under canopy, and another fifteen or so were milling about on the ground. In the parking lot I overheard someone say Octagon blew their chance for the silver medal at Nationals with two bad exits. Twig was over by the hangar preflighting the Beech E-18. I strolled into the loft, where staffer Ken Popadowski was gearing up the six students from yesterday. They'd faithfully come back again today.

"You had a call," Ken said when he saw me. "About an hour ago. The message is next to the phone."

I went over to Twig's desk. Beside the phone was a yellow scratch pad that said CHANCE, CALL NEWT BECKER'S WIFE.

I sat down at Twig's desk, took out my wallet, and found Paula's home number. I waited till Ken herded his six students outside, then I picked up the phone.

"I got your message," Paula said, after answering on the third ring. "I'm sorry. I thought I left a forwarding number with my office, but I guess I was rushed last week and not thinking too straight. Two of my sisters met me at the Tampa airport. They'd already been to my house and had my things packed. I didn't even come—"

"Enough with the apologies and explanations, Paula. First, how are you?"

Her voice settled down. "Better, much better," she said. "Thank you for asking. My family has been the best therapy. I have seven brothers and sisters, and my parents. They're wonderful, loving people. They all still live within a few miles of the town where we grew up."

"Did you have a service for Newt?"

"On Thursday. A very private one at their church. Just my family. Newt's family all lives in Massachusetts, so they had their own service up there. We'll still have the memorial jump next month to scatter the ashes. I think it should be low-key. Newt wouldn't have wanted a lot of fuss."

"Will you go back to work tomorrow?"

"I think so. I think it'll be good for me. Fill up the empty days."

"It'll give you a focus," I agreed.

She cleared her throat. "About why you called," she said. "Have you found out anything?"

"Quite a lot, actually."

"Is it—did Newt—"

"Newt didn't hurt anybody but himself. He was blackmailing a thug, not some luckless guy who happened to find himself compromised by a camera." It was the best I could offer her.

For close to a minute her breathing was all that came over the wire. Then she said, "I wish I could live this year over again. I never realized Newt was that desperate."

"Nobody can foresee the future."

"That's what my family keeps saying—I told them all about it. I'm trying not to blame myself."

"Well, maybe you'll have someone else to blame soon. In Oklahoma you said Newt always mailed his rolls of film home."

"That's right. And I'm going to drop off all his undeveloped rolls tomorrow morning for processing, like you suggested."

"You can forget those," I said. "They're not important. What I was wondering was whether Newt ever sent home any videos."

"Not often."

"What about a month ago?"

"Noo . . ."

"You don't sound sure."

"Well, he didn't send any video, but he did send a box of blank cassettes. He said they were leftovers."

My heart skipped a beat. "VHS?"

"Yes."

"Where are they now?"

"I put them in the dark room—that's what Newt said to do. I didn't even open them up."

"Would you go get them?"

She was gone about two minutes. "I've got the box," she said when she picked the phone back up. "The postmark is Findlay, Indiana."

"I expected that. Would you open it?"

There was a thud as she dropped the receiver, then the sound of scissors.

"Okay, I'm holding six VHS cassettes."

"Did Newt label any of them?"

I could hear her sliding each one out of its casing. "No," she said. Then, "Hmm."

"Yes?"

"Well, the tab on one of them is broken so it can't be erased."

I squeezed the phone tightly. That had to be it. What Newt planned to sell to collect the rest of the money for his new house.

"I suppose the cassette could have come from the factory that way," Paula suggested.

"I don't think so."

She paused. "You think this cassette has to do with the blackmail business?"

"I'd bet on it."

She was quiet again. "Then I don't think I'll look at it, if you don't mind," she almost whispered. "I'd like to remember Newt the way he was. I don't want to see what got him killed."

I glanced over at the loft door to make sure no one was loitering nearby.

"There's no reason for you to look at it," I said. "Would you mail it to me?"

"I'll need your address," she said, relieved.

I gave her the airport's address. "Send it to my attention. And as soon as possible."

"We—I mean *I* have express mailing envelopes. Newt used them occasionally for business. There's an express mailbox a few miles from here. I can take it right down and drop it in. It's overnight mail, but I don't know how that works on Sundays. You might not get it till Tuesday."

"I'll be waiting for it."

There was silence on her end of the phone.

"Paula?"

"Yes—I was just thinking. You're going to have to tell me what this is all about—all the details. But not now, not till I'm back at work for a while. If I have some structure in my life, I think I can handle it better."

I eyed the loft door again. "This really isn't a good time for me to discuss any of this, either. Someone could walk in on me. I'll call you again in a few days."

A minute later we hung up. I tore Ken Popadowski's note off the yellow scratch pad and made a list of all my long distance calls from yesterday and today: Davis Field, Oklahoma; Ridgeway, California; Fort Crystal, Florida. I estimated how long and how much, then slipped a twenty dollar bill into Twig's cash drawer. It would more than cover the cost.

As I stood up from the desk I lifted my head. The inside door to the shower room was standing open. All I caught was a glimpse of a huge jumpsuited arm disappearing from the doorway, but I knew who it belonged to. Only one Indiana skydiver had biceps like that.

I'd been cautious but not cautious enough. I'd kept my eye on the loft's front door, but I'd forgotten that there was an outside door to the showers. I'd checked the parking lot for a truck cab when I pulled in, and then looked around the drop zone for him. He must have come in a car, must have been one of the four jumpers under canopy.

What exactly had I said to Paula? How much of it had Alex Laird overheard?

Ken Popadowski's note had been sitting beside the telephone for an hour. Had Laird seen it?

I grabbed for the phone and punched Paula's number. The phone rang and rang. I tried again, hoping I'd punched it wrong. I hadn't. Paula was too efficient. She'd done just as I'd asked: she'd gone out and mailed the tape as soon as possible. As soon as she'd hung up the phone.

Just then Twig shuffled into the loft.

"Guess we should settle you up," he said. "For all the work you've done."

I put the phone down. "Yeah," I said, "I guess we should."

We arrived at a figure for my five days of work. He got the money from his cash drawer and handed it to me. "Got another job lined up?" he asked.

"Sort of," I said. "An unfinished job. I expect to be gone within the hour."

228

Twig merely nodded, told me he'd see me around, then shuffled back outside. I watched him through the loft door. For a while he stood around the packing area, not talking to anyone, not looking at anything in particular. Eventually he drifted over toward his Beech E-18.

I decided I had better get moving. I went into the rigging room and packed Danny Death's reserve. I left his rig lying on the rigging table, then went out to Twig's memorial elm and packed up my tent. I didn't see Alex Laird anywhere, but I didn't trust him. I'd seen Newt Becker's cuts and bruises, had heard about Kyle Smedley's broken leg, and had had plenty of time to imagine what must have happened to Lonny Carmichael in the skies over Findlay. I'd be a fool to spend the night here alone in my tent.

I left in the direction opposite the one I intended to go. I turned at the first intersection, drove on, turned again, drove on. Only when I was confident I hadn't been followed did I head for the Findlay police station. Fifteen minutes later I pulled in back and went around to the side door. I was banking everything on that VHS tape with the broken tab.

It was Sunday in a small midwestern town. Davidson sat alone behind the department's only computer terminal.

"I've located those missing tapes," I said. "I'm sure there's a copy of Lonny Carmichael's last exit on one of them."

Davidson slid his chair back from the machine. "You have it with you?"

I shook my head. "It's in an express mailbox in Florida. It's been posted to Findlay Airport. There's a problem, though. I think Alex Laird might know about it. If so, he'll try to intercept it when it's delivered."

A grin crept onto Davidson's face. "That's not a problem," he said. "My cousin Nathan works at the post office."

I could feel my neck muscles relax a little. "It's addressed to me," I said, "so your cousin wouldn't be doing anything illegal by putting it aside. It was mailed today, but this being Sunday, it will probably come on Tuesday."

Davidson nodded. "I'll call Nathan and tell him to hold it. When it comes you and I can take a look at it over at my place. I haven't told Gene any of this—he wants Laird too much, and I'm afraid he might do something to jeopardize the case. But I will call Greenville and have Laird's house watched."

229

He turned back to his computer. "I've got something for you too," he said. "Your Christian Jokubka, a.k.a. Cheeks, has one arrest, a narcotics charge in New Mexico fourteen years ago. Never convicted. He got off on a technicality. Nobody else has anything on him, including California. His international sales job is legit. The feds have suspected for some time that someone in that company is involved in narcotics smuggling, but they haven't been able to pinpoint which of two or three guys. They were very interested in my inquiry. It seems they were watching Jokubka closely last year, but didn't come up with anything."

"He's smart," I said. "He's not like other drug dealers. He's got a real job and doesn't flaunt his money."

Davidson agreed. "That's how we identify most of them," he said. "No job but lots of expendable income. They give themselves away."

I got up to go.

"By the way," I said, "the pieces to Newt Becker's rig are in the mail, addressed here to you. I haven't touched the link, though it's probably too small to get any usable prints, and Cheeks probably wore gloves anyway."

"I'll tell Nathan to keep an eye out for it." Davidson got up and opened the door for me. "When the video comes in, do I contact you out at the airport?"

I shook my head. "I'll call you when I find a cheap motel."

He nodded. "I guess I don't need to tell you to be careful."

"Not at all."

I left the building, got on the Honda, and drove north.

I zigzagged, doubled back, zigzagged. Eventually I came to a place called Lafayette. My motorcycle was large and conspicuous, and I didn't want to park where anyone driving by could see it. That eliminated the first four motels I came to. The fifth had rooms and a parking lot around back. I paid in advance for two nights, unloaded the Honda, and called Davidson with the name of the motel. Then I waited.

I hadn't expected the tape in Monday's mail, so I wasn't surprised when Davidson called to say it hadn't come in. Still, I was on edge. It was impossible to concentrate on any one thing for very long. I made a sorry attempt at reading a novel. I found myself staring at page twenty-four, unable to recall what went on between two and twenty-three. I flipped around the channels on the television set. It had all the half-hour cable commercials you could want: glop this ointment on your scalp and we guarantee a head full of hair; pop this pill and dissolve body fat while you sleep; buy this series of motivational tapes and become an instant millionaire. That one reminded me too much of Newt Becker. I switched off the set and paced the room.

I did calisthenics. I showered, ate some food from a nearby convenience store, found a laundry with parking in the rear, washed my clothes, went back to the motel, and picked up my book. I put it back down. Performing these routine tasks did not bring me any comfort; they did not help me relax. I lay back on my bed and tried to imagine myself in freefall. I couldn't. I tried to imagine myself under canopy. I couldn't do that, either. I got up, pulled out my address book, and called master rigger Joe DeBerg.

"It's been a whole week and one day, Chance! My business is all shot to hell. So what have you got? When are you going to get me out of this mess?" He sounded wired and bitter and, I thought, slightly drunk.

"I've kept my damn mouth shut," he went on, "but it hasn't been easy. A Muskogee cop who knows his mechanics saw Becker's link. Now they're hot on me. And there's a rumor going around that I invented a story about Becker being murdered to cover my ass."

"I hadn't heard that," I said. But I could guess which California rigger had started it. The same California rigger who would have started the rumor about Newt's main having knotted lines.

Joe's mood shifted and he became sullen. "Can't really blame them, you know."

"Who, Joe, the police?"

"My customers," he said. "Can't blame them for not letting me touch their gear if they think what they think. It's their lives at stake."

"Joe, the reason I called . . . It looks like you could be cleared soon, if you can just hang in there another day or two."

"Do I have any other choice?"

After I hung up the phone I paced the room again. I was as wired as Joe DeBerg. What would I do if that tape was blank? And equally worrisome, what would I do if it wasn't? How was I going to handle that?

By evening my motel room had become a jail cell. My leg muscles cramped from inactivity. Outside it was raining. I didn't particularly like running in the rain, but I had to get out. I put on my running shorts, socks, and New Balance running shoes, and trotted out the door. Behind the motel there were fields. After cutting through one of them, I came upon an unpaved country lane. I ran along it. My running shoes, which quickly became sodden, made a squish squish noise when I planted my feet.

Railroad tracks crossed in front of me. I took them, running west. My feet pounded the earth next to the railroad ties. Big rain drops fell heavily from the sky. They impacted my arms, legs, and back, and forever lost their shape. They flushed my eyes and glued my hair to my forehead, and they were cold. But they got warmer the more I ran. Tall trees that lined the tracks stretched their bending limbs while their leaves made sweet talk in the rain.

I turned around and ran east. I thought about piloting a biplane over South Carolina. Over traffic jams and clogged arteries, over spouse abuse and broken hearts. Soaring above it all in solitude as the machine and I meshed into one. Its wings became mine. I guided it above forested knolls and plowed valleys, and frolicked about in the clean air. It was so peaceful running along the railroad tracks. No carbon monoxide, no splashing cars, no awesome trucks. Not even any trains.

I ran for more than two hours. By the time I got back to the motel my calf muscles had been churned to pulp. Any stiffness in my neck and shoulders was gone now, too. I was in a ventilated mood. I was ready for tomorrow.

Tuesday morning I packed up the Honda, settled my phone bill with the motel clerk, and waited. At nine-thirty Davidson called.

"It's in," he said. "Nathan's holding it for us, but I'm bogged down in work and Gene will suspect something if I take off for lunch. Why don't we meet at the post office at five, then go to my place from there?"

I was relaxed now; I did not mind waiting. "Five o'clock at the post office," I said.

"Also, you might want to know that Laird hasn't been home since we started watching his place on Sunday. It's possible he suspects something."

"Appreciate the information," I said.

I could leave my room at check-out time and drive around until five, or I could pay for an extra day. The thought that Alex Laird might be out on the roads made me decide to pay up and wait in my room.

By five-thirty we had the package and were standing in front of Davidson's house. He unlocked the door and we went inside. I opened the package and took out the tape, which Davidson plugged into his VCR. "The segment we're looking for would only be a few seconds long," I said.

The beginning ten minutes contained nothing but white static. Then the first image appeared.

"That's the Octagon team," I explained. "Newt must have copied the entire tape."

Davidson pushed fast forward. The machine raced through jump after jump. Exits were little more than bleeps on the screen. Then I saw a flash of pink and blue.

"Stop!"

Davidson backed up and replayed it slowly.

It started with an outside view straight back toward Satin Cruise's tail. Then four jumpers climbed out and dangled in the doorway. Then they let go. A cluster of jumpers pushed through the door behind them, the rest streamed out. The next to last jumper wore pink-and-blue gear. He exited perfectly through the center of the door, his head six inches from the top, a hulking jumper tight on his back.

It was unmistakable. No question about premeditation. Laird's one hand held Carmichael by the shoulder. The other one was above him and closed into a fist. They were just out the door when the fist came down decisively, bashing Carmichael's head with a professional blow. Carmichael's flimsy leather helmet was useless against such force.

Davidson replayed it several times. Each time I cringed as Laird's fist connected with Carmichael's head. It was like watching a sledge hammer strike a defenseless lamb.

Davidson shut off the machine. "I'll need you to come down and make out a full statement," he said quietly. It had shaken him too.

"There's something I have to take care of first," I said. "Can that wait till later?"

He removed the tape from the machine. "I think I can get a warrant on the strength of this alone. If you could come in tomorrow morning, that should be soon enough."

We went outside. I handed over Newt's eight-millimeter video case, which I'd brought with me from Oklahoma.

"These might help you in building your case against Laird. They'll show why Newt happened to be taping that particular jump. Just remember to get them back to his wife when you're done with them. I promised her."

"It may take a while," he said.

"I'm sure she won't mind as long as she gets them back eventually. Not if it means sending Laird to prison."

"But if I understood you right, he's not the one who actually killed her husband. We still don't have anything that ties Jokubka into this."

"I'm not finished yet. By tomorrow I expect to have something."

He didn't ask what. He climbed in his car and I got on the Honda. We took off in opposite directions.

Each drop zone sets its own hours, but most don't do business on Mondays and Tuesdays. Operators use those days as their weekend since they work on everyone else's. Findlay Parachute Center was never open for business on Tuesdays, but Twig sometimes spent the day working on his planes. He was out by one of the Cessnas when I drove up.

I got off the Honda. Then I walked into the loft and sat down in the lounge. I left the door open.

Ten minutes passed. I was pretending to read an article in *Sport Aviation* when Twig finally came in.

"We have to talk," I said.

"Yes," he replied, "I suppose we do."

I set the magazine aside and glanced up. He was holding a gun.

24

He moved over behind his desk and sat down. "How much of it do you know?" he asked.

I didn't look at the gun he was holding. I didn't want it to influence my words.

"I know Cheeks flew your Beech E-18 out of here last month. I know the two of you and Alex Laird are mixed up in drug trafficking and gun running."

"Only guns. No drugs."

I didn't belabor the point. "I suppose anyone with twenty years in the military has no qualms about selling guns," I said. "They're probably just toys to you."

"They're a fact of life," he said.

"I also know how Alex Laird killed Lonny Carmichael, how Newt Becker blackmailed him for it, and how Cheeks killed Newt."

Twig's mouth pulled tight. "I had nothing to do with those deaths. Didn't even know about them till they were done."

I nodded. "I guessed as much. I wouldn't have come here alone if I'd thought different."

His grip on the gun eased. Then he laid it behind the stack of liability waivers on his desk and picked up a pencil. "Cheeks had some customers who wanted guns," he said. "And Alex had a source of supply. When it came time to arrange transportation, that's when Alex came to me."

"What about Macintosh—was he involved?"

Twig shook his head. "Macintosh was just part of Cheeks's elaborate cover story. One guy coming all this way for a car race might look suspicious if anyone ever investigated him—people don't usually go to those things by themselves. He picked Macintosh because Macintosh is too naive to notice anything. He'd believe whatever Cheeks told him."

"So when Cheeks stayed with Macintosh at Nationals, that was just another cover," I said. "To drive home the point he was there to jump with friends, not murder a photographer."

"I would guess."

"And that might better explain why Cheeks gave Macintosh the brushoff later in the boogie. After he finished his business with Newt, he didn't really need Macintosh anymore."

Twig shrugged. He didn't seem particularly interested in Macintosh.

"How many of these deals have you done?"

"Just the one."

"But then why was your plane gone a whole month? A single trip shouldn't have taken that long."

"Cheeks managed to damage a prop somehow. It was in the hills of some Latin country—I didn't ask which one—and spare props weren't easy to come by. He left the plane down there and flew commercial back to California. I suppose I should be grateful he even bothered to go back down for it."

"And he brought it back here the last Monday in June."

Twig nodded. "When Cheeks flew the plane back, Alex met him here, then took him to the airport in Indianapolis for a flight out. I didn't know then that Cheeks was flying to Nationals. I wasn't privy to their private conversations."

Twig picked up a liability waiver and began drawing angular doodles on it. "Alex thinks there's another copy of Newt Becker's video. He thinks Becker's wife is sending it here to the airport."

"I already intercepted it at the post office."

I detected a faint twinkle in Twig's eyes. "Thought you might," he said. "I told Alex you already left the state. Don't know if he believed me."

"Why did he kill Lonny Carmichael?"

Twig shoved his pencil right through the liability waiver. "It was so senseless," he said.

"Most murders are. Was Carmichael a part of your gun-running operation?"

He shook his head wearily and pulled the pencil out of the waiver. "No, nothing like that. The day before Lonny bounced, Cheeks
flew in from the West Coast on a commercial flight. Alex brought him
out here. We talked a bit about the deal, then I went into the loft. I
didn't hear about the business with Lonny till later.

"I guess Cheeks and Alex were walking off toward the runway for
a private talk. That's when Lonny pulled in to have some rigging
work done on his gear. Cheeks said Lonny must have recognized him
from some mega-loads they did together in California last year. Any-
how, Lonny followed Cheeks and Alex out to the runway. They were
already into their talk when they noticed him. Alex told him to leave,
so Lonny left. Cheeks said Lonny couldn't have heard anything they
talked about. Said he was too far away. But Alex didn't like it."

"So he killed him?"

Twig inserted his pencil into an electric pencil sharpener on a credenza next to his desk. The grinding noise it made was loud, and
when he withdrew the pencil the soundlessness of the loft reverber-
ated.

"After Alex gave his version of that dive," he said, "I knew he'd
killed Lonny. Danny Death was right about that—Lonny knew how
to exit."

"And Alex Laird knew how to punch."

Twig pursed his lips. "Cheeks and I confronted Alex about it. He
didn't deny it. He had this grin on his face. He'd killed a man, a man
who never hurt anybody, and he had this grin on his face. Like he'd
won the Nobel prize for cruelty."

I saw in Twig's face the same anger I'd seen when he broke up the
Danny Death-Alex Laird fight last month. Now I knew why he'd
gone out of his way to take Danny Death's side.

"Did Cheeks approve of Carmichael's *accident*?"

Twig shook his head. "Cheeks was furious. No, he didn't care that
an innocent man had died—he's as cold-blooded as they come. He
was worried the fatality might bring out the police and jeopardize
the deal. As it turned out, they bothered you, not us." He shook his
head again. "It never occurred to me Alex would do something like
that. I never agreed to murder. I told them to hell with their guns.
Told them they couldn't use my plane or my airport, that I was
pulling out."

"But they wouldn't let you."

Twig glanced down at the pencil in his hand. "Cheeks had his customers waiting on the guns. He was . . . respectful of them. A little scared, I think. He suggested I should be, too. I wasn't, but everything was already set. And I was just too tired to fight anymore."

"So you went ahead with the shipment Monday night after the boogie?"

He looked up at me, surprised. "But we cleared the airport. Before I left I gave Newt and Dominic my pickup, and even talked Ken Popadowski into entertaining them over at his place. Cheeks had Macintosh drive him to Indianapolis, then gave him a wad of money for a night out on the town. Alex picked Cheeks up at the airport and we came back. Alex checked the grounds, Cheeks checked the buildings, I got the plane ready. Nobody was here except the three of us."

"And me," I said. "I was in my tent behind your memorial elm. Hard to see unless you know to look there."

Once again I detected a brief spark in Twig's eyes. He seemed to get some small pleasure from knowing it was Alex Laird who'd overlooked my tent. "Then you've known since Memorial Day," he said.

I shook my head. "I was asleep that night dreaming. I heard a truck idling, and a plane take off, but I assumed they were part of my dream. I never suspected the truck was Laird's, or the plane your Beech E-18. I wasn't used to the E-18 being here, so it didn't register in my mind that it was missing the next day.

"I remember a car driving away that night just as I woke up, but until last week I never connected that to you, or even the dream. And I never connected the dream to the cargo company renting your plane. Until last week, I never made a lot of connections. Like the fact that you never called me at Nationals last week. It was Cheeks who called you from Davis Field, wasn't it? He wanted you to get me out of Oklahoma to keep me from asking questions. He couldn't have known, of course, that before I'd leave I'd know why Newt was killed, or he'd never have tried to exile me up here. He never imagined the tapes he left behind in Newt's video case could actually talk."

Twig set his pencil down. "What was it that put you on to me?"

"Cobwebs," I said. "Almost none of the rigs with damaged canopies had cobwebs on them like the other rigs. It took me a little while to figure out why. You must have exchanged six old canopies you had lying around for the six good ones that had been in those rigs—their damage was all natural wear and tear, not deliberate. When you switched them, the canopies must have swabbed away the cobwebs from the containers.

"The harness and container damage you did yourself. It was a good job. While I was sewing I only detected two threads that looked razor-bladed. The rest appeared torn and frayed. I wouldn't have noticed them at all if I wasn't already a little suspicious.

"At first I assumed Alex Laird did it. But he couldn't have known I was coming here unless you told him. And the more I remembered the events of the Memorial Day boogie, the more I began to understand the events of last week—when you asked me to come up here early, all the extra work and nobody to help me with it, the pilot that never showed, the Cessna for Thursday's class when we could have gone with the E-18. You figured that by the time I recovered from four days of slave labor, Nationals would be all but over and Cheeks's trail would have gone cold."

Twig said, "I was afraid he might kill you too if you stayed there."

But I was feeling betrayed and manipulated, and I was too torn up inside to hear his words. "I tried to work out a scenario without you in it, Twig, but I couldn't. Not with your plane involved. I still find it hard to believe you, of all people, involved in drug trafficking. It goes against everything you've ever stood for."

"Only *guns*," he insisted. "No drugs."

Perhaps I should have allowed him that one illusion; it might have made a difference in the outcome. But at the time I wasn't feeling very generous toward him.

"Stop trying to kid yourself, Twig. It doesn't become you. Cheeks is in the drug business, and has been for more than fourteen years. What do you think he and Laird were talking about out on the runway? How do you think an insignificant Midwest jumper like Lonny Carmichael, who just happened to use cocaine, got to know Cheeks at the mega-load boogies? Not because of his skydiving skills, that's for sure. And what about when Laird met Cheeks here two weeks ago? You can't seriously believe he brought the plane back from that Latin country empty. How much luggage did Cheeks take off the plane, Twig? How much? Of course he wouldn't need that much space for what he was carrying. The word is Cheeks brought back cocaine, and that's how he paid Alex Laird."

Twig offered no further defense. He knew I was right. He had known all along.

"So if you've figured it all out," he said, "why are you here now?"

I got up from the lounge chair and walked over to Twig's side of the loft. Beyond his desk the rigging room door stood ajar. Next to the door hung a small bulletin board with a newspaper clipping tacked along the edge. The clipping was about an *experienced* sky-diver with forty-two jumps who leapt from a two-hundred-foot building and counted on his reserve deploying before he smacked the ground. Below the clipping was tacked a funeral notice, and below that a handwritten note with a phone number for anyone who wanted to inquire about the purchase of his gear.

I pressed my right shoulder against the bulletin board and looked over at Twig. "Why, Twig? I came to find out why."

He glowered at the liability waiver still in his hand. "Times change," was all he said, but his words were spiked with a lot of bitterness.

"But how? How do times change that much?"

"Sometimes you see a way to make a quick buck, and you take it."

His quip made me angry. "Come off it, Twig—that's a crock! A booming business, a fancy house, a bulging bank account—they never meant anything to you unless you earned them with your own sweat. If you'd done it for the money, there'd have been a lot easier ways with no risk. Legal ways. Advertise the drop zone in the Yellow Pages, take out an ad in the paper, and you'd get back plenty of dollars for every one you spent. You didn't compromise yourself for money. You risked your life's work, your drop zone, your self-respect. What could have made you do it?"

Twig's eyes began to glow with the intensity of red-hot embers, and his mouth twitched like the end of a nerve.

"You're asking *why*, Chance? *Why*? That's the wrong question. They taught you all wrong in that upstart law school back east. You're going about it backwards. *Upside down!* You'll never learn anything by asking the wrong questions. You shouldn't be asking *why*, you should be asking *why not*." There was a mocking tone in his voice that was challenging me to shut up.

"What about your work ethic and your principles, Twig?"

"Principles?!" A serrated harshness outlined his eyes. "*Who* lives by principles? Where, Chance, you show me where are the people in this world that live by principles?"

"You used to be one."

"You mean back when I was *stupid*? No, *naive* is a better word for what I was. You wanna know why I don't live by principles like I did when I was naive? That's easy. Because no one else does. *No one.* And in a world where no one else is principled, those who are get screwed."

"You're being too simplistic, Twig."

He pushed the waiver aside, rose from his chair, and pressed his weight onto his palms, flattened on the top of his desk. "Well, I beg to differ with all your nice law school learning, but I'd say you're naive. Don't feel too embarrassed about that, Chance, because I used to be there myself not too long ago. You just haven't figured it out yet. You're still too young. Well, I'll let you in on something, Chance. They brainwashed us all. They took a hose to our heads and turned it on full pressure till their propaganda pushed through our skulls. All those words we memorized as children about the law protecting the innocent—that's all bull. You name one lawsuit against me where I was protected from greedy lawyers and their clients. You just try and come up with one."

I didn't say anything.

"You can't," he said, "because there isn't one. The law protects the lawyers and the rich. That's what the American legal system's all about, Chance—protecting the lawyers and the rich. They didn't teach you that in all those fancy law school books, now did they? But it's the truth. Don't you know, Chance, it's the lawyers and the rich who conspire together and write the laws. All for themselves, nothing for the decent man. The laws are never there for him. Four lawsuits I've had to fight. *Four!* Found innocent in every one, but look what it cost me to prove it."

It was hard to argue. He had a valid point.

"Laws are general guidelines," I said. "To help maintain order. They're never going to be fair to all the people all the time. Sometimes circumstances change in a given society and the laws become less fair to more people more often. When that happens, the laws and the procedures that produce those laws need to be reevaluated, perhaps rewritten."

Even to me it sounded stilted and naive. Like right out of a textbook.

"They'll never rewrite the laws to protect the innocent man from greedy lawyers so long as it's the lawyers who are doing the writing. They make it so everyone wants to sue everyone else because it's good for their business. So long as they keep reproducing like goddamn rabbits and there's no predators to manage the species, they'll keep dragging hard-working, honest people through years of depositions and interrogatories and things I'll never begin to understand. And the ones on your side—if you're even lucky—they'll tell you one day that you've won. That's the day they present you with a five-figure bill for their trouble. And I was innocent in every case, Chance. Now you find me the principles in that."

His voice was cracking and his eyes were watery, but the bitterness was gone.

"Twenty years," he swallowed. "I wasted twenty years in the Army defending America for greedy lawyers and rich businessmen in three-piece suits ready to take away a hard-earned dime from an honest man. All the low pay, the stupid orders, the constant transfers—I agreed to it all. You know why, Chance? Because I *believed.* I really believed in the system. All those memorized words we learned as kids—I really believed." He choked. "But it was just bullshit. All of it."

For all Twig's talk of money, I could see it wasn't the loss of money that had broken him. It was his loss of faith.

"Oh, I don't blame anyone but myself, Chance. I was their sucker. It's been going on all along. I didn't allow myself to see it. I deserve what I got." He swallowed heavily. "And then the first time I go ahead and play their filthy games a man dies. And then another man dies. My wife left last week. She couldn't take me anymore. Said I should have gotten out of skydiving after the first lawsuit. She couldn't understand me hanging on. She was right. I should have listened to her."

He came out from behind the desk. He was staring across the room at nothing. Tears rolled down his cheeks and onto his shirt. He looked very old. Very defeated.

"No one was supposed to die," he whispered.

I blinked back my own tears, then stepped over and put a hand on his shoulder.

"It's only a matter of time before the police realize you're involved. It would be better if you turned yourself in."

He was staring right past me. I wasn't sure he'd even heard.

"I'll take you down to the police station," I said. "We'll go together in your car."

"Oh, no you won't."

I froze. I hadn't heard him pull in.

I turned. Alex Laird's shoulders were taking up the full width of the doorway.

"Knew you'd show up sooner or later," he said. He was grinning sadistically.

25

He came into the loft, his muscles dancing beneath his shirt. He was unarmed, but he was more of a threat than Twig had been with his gun.

"Been watching the DZ from a spot in the corn since Sunday," he said smugly.

I looked back at Twig. He seemed oblivious to the here and now. I could see immediately that he and I would not be teaming up against Alex Laird as we had seven years ago against that jumper high on PCP. Twig's eyes were the eyes of a dead man, and I watched with concern for both of us as he padded toward the front of the loft and faded out the door.

Alex Laird made no attempt to stop him. His full attention was already on me.

We eyeballed each other, and I evaluated my prospects. Dismal at best. He was between me and the two exits. He was a lot bigger, a lot stronger, and had a punch more lethal than mine.

"The copy," he said. "I want the copy Becker's wife sent you. I know you got it somehow."

If I tell him the police already have it, I thought, he might kill me right now. If he thinks he can get his hands on it . . .

"I'm afraid I don't know what you're talking about," I said, stalling. I took two innocuous-looking steps toward the desk. Twig's gun was behind the stack of liability waivers. If I could make it to the desk in one piece, I might have a shot.

"Cut the shit, Jack! I saw that note about Becker's wife. I heard you on the phone."

Laird was seething. He swelled his muscles and came closer. His exhaled breath pushed down between us. It was hot and smelled sweaty. Outside the Beech E-18 started up.

I took another step toward Twig's desk. The hit came fast. A right jab that landed hard on the left side of my face. The whole upper portion of my torso snapped backward. I tripped back over my own foot and my head smashed against the bulletin board.

I'd never make the gun now. Laird had moved in my way.

I was dizzy from the hit and knew I couldn't win, but I had to fight. It was the pride factor, and the instinct to keep on living. I threw a respectable right into his gut that made him lurch backward. A weak left connected irrelevantly with his right arm. I lunged forward like a stupid man and rammed my head into him. Barely a dent. His muscles were meaty and solid, and I couldn't get any kind of grip except on his shirt. I ripped it at the shoulder. I put out my maximum effort, but I had not invested hundreds of hours in lifting weights, or engaged in countless barroom fights. I did not have the physical volume, or the experience. I could not compete. He plunged a powerful left fist into my stomach. I doubled over and threw up my lunch. He snickered. Playtime for him.

I got mad. I swung my leg up with everything I could put into it and caught him square in the groin. The force knocked me backward and folded him down on his knees. I stumbled to my feet and went for Twig's gun. Laird came at my knees with a vengeance and flipped up my feet. My body slammed against the concrete floor. My right wrist came down across the corner of the desk, and could have lit an inferno with the intensity of its pain.

"Pesty little snoop!" he spat. "Couldn't mind your own business, could you?"

I twisted my body and got hold of a massive chunk of thigh. He was still on his knees, cradling my damage between his legs. I jarred one of his legs off the ground. He didn't topple. I felt a tug at my hair, and then my head being pulled back. Thick flesh pressed against my throat. I tried to struggle free. It was impossible. He had the full bulk of one arm coiled tightly around my neck. I could feel my face turn blue.

My brain ceased to register external stimuli, and everything became suddenly peaceful. So very, very peaceful. Puffy clouds splattered my vision as succulent dew drops lubricated my tongue. The clean air of twelve thousand feet felt vibrant and virginal. I heard the in-flight sounds of biplanes a while longer, but Twig's loft and Alex Laird had already gone bye.

I began my long trek toward heaven. My path was blacker than tar and I couldn't see at all. I had to feel my way like a blind man. There was a hollow tunnel sound, and a groaning noise that bounced off the sides and echoed through my ears. As I reached a certain level of awareness I realized the groan emanated from between my lips. My heart thudded like a huge drum in a half-time band. I could hear the blood gushing through my veins. And the captured air from my nostrils roaring down into my lungs. A light. I could see a light.

A candle burned in a high-ceilinged cathedral. The candle flickered as Jesus of Nazareth was tied upon the cross. In Christian lore he was nailed, but along my journey to heaven I witnessed that he was tied with eight-hundred-pound dacron-coated parachute steering line. I ruminated on that oddity until I drifted off.

I could hear sounds again, and I sensed intuitively that I had at last arrived.

A strong light shown through my eyelids. I could only open one of them. My head was vised between two cloth-covered boards that I couldn't begin to see because I couldn't turn my head. I had no awareness of owning hands or feet, arms or legs. Nothing beyond the periphery of my vision. Much like being in freefall the first time out.

I drifted off again.

There was a cold tingling splash against my face and down my chest. It made me want to urinate. I think I may have.

"Wake up, Jack!"

My name isn't Jack. Why did he call me Jack? I reopened my eye.

It was not Jesus of Nazareth holding court in front of me, but Lucifer himself: Alex Laird. "I don't have time to waste. I could finish you off right now."

I found that a curious thing to say. I thought he already had.

He heaved a bucket of water at me. I consulted my reflexes and made a decision to shut my eye, but my reaction time was way off. Some water got in, and it hurt.

I opened my eye again and blinked the water out. It could have been recently thawed ice for all the warmth it had to it.

Two lights to my right caused the droplets of water to shimmer between my lashes. Beneath the lights a parachute rigging table stretched out along a wall. Between the lights and the table was a window covered with an old Navy Conical reserve. We were in Twig's rigging room.

Outside I was shivering, inside I was burning up. I was wet, I was dehydrated. I realized the vise pinching my ears was made of my own two arms pulled up on either side of my head. I wriggled my head, yanked backward, and gazed up at my hands.

My right hand was swollen to the size of a small boxer's mitt, and bending those fingers was a mean joke. My arms were tied at the wrists with several pieces of eight-hundred-pound dacron-coated steering line. This was knotted to a rope that extended upward to a pulley at the top of Twig's drying tower. A light up at the ceiling flickered like a candle when the rope swung in front of it. From the pulley, the rope came down along the side of the wall and wound around a waist-high lever.

Only Twig Buckwater would have bothered to construct a drying tower pulley strong enough to hold the full weight of a man.

I poked my head forward, forcing it through my arms, and looked down. The floor was a little more than a foot below the toes of my shoes. My legs were bound together with yards of silver duct tape spiraled around them between my ankles and the middle of my thighs.

Alex Laird had dropped the empty water bucket to the floor and was limping toward me. I felt a surge of juvenile satisfaction at the thought that my kick had been responsible for that limp.

"Where is it?" he demanded.

My brain was still scrambled. Before I could answer him he hit me with a one-two punch. The first landed smack against my solar plexus; the second, expectantly, in my groin. I didn't have the luxury of doubling over to smother some of the shock, and the combination put me on the verge of going back under.

"And that's just for starters," he promised.

My body swung under the rope from the force of the blows. It was almost impossible for me to talk, let alone think. But I had to think. It was critical that I think. Buy some time. If I could come up with a story about the video . . .

I saw his arm begin to rev.

"Wait!" I gulped. "I'll—I'll tell you."

He waited.

"In my right saddlebag . . . You can go look."

He locked his jaw tight. "Already have," he said through his teeth. "Right bag, left bag, the whole works. There's no video there." He hit me again. And again. I passed out.

Eventually I came to. I heard Twig's watch out in the office beep the hour. I had no idea which one.

"The video," Laird hammered.

"Okay, I'll . . . tell you. In my left pocket . . . there's a key."

He turned to one of Twig's sewing machines and picked up my motel key. It was lying there with my wallet and the ring of keys to my bike.

"It goes to a room," I whispered. Laird came closer so he could hear every syllable. "Motel room . . . outside Lafayette. Colony Lodge."

His rabid eyes cut into my barely functioning one. "Another trick, huh?"

"I . . ." I licked my lip, closed my eye, and feigned falling off the backside of Earth.

I felt his presence as he stood in front of me, deciding. I was his only source of information on that video tape—at least that's what I hoped he was thinking.

I heard him swipe something from Twig's rigging table. He forced my mouth open and shoved it inside. I fought the urge to spit it out. It was nylon and mesh, a miscellaneous main pilot chute. I heard him go down to the other end of the rigging table and rip off a length of duct tape. He slapped it across my mouth and the pilot chute. He stood silently for a minute. Then he went back and ripped off a longer piece. He wound it around my mouth and across the back of my neck and back around to the front. I'd seen duct tape hold airplanes together as effectively as rivets. I tried not to be depressed by the thought.

He moved toward the door and I heard the light switch click. In the darkness there was hesitation. Then a few footsteps in my direction. He hit me in the stomach again. I pinched my eyes tight and bit down on the pilot chute. I could only think how grateful I was that I'd already gotten rid of my lunch.

"You little snoop," he said. "When I come back, you're dead meat."

The rigging room door slammed shut. Then the main door to the loft. No engine outside. His car would be parked somewhere away from the airport, hidden out of sight.

My body was swinging from Laird's last hit. The pendulum motion was causing the pulley up at the ceiling to creak. The sound was grating.

I opened my eye. The room wasn't totally dark. The old Navy Conical parachute covering the window was translucent and let in what was left of the day. A tad after seven o'clock, I judged.

The sting from Laird's final blows gradually ebbed, and then, except for my groin, it was my wrists that hurt most of all.

I figured it would take him ten minutes to make his car, another forty to locate the motel, thirty more to get back here. I couldn't predict with certainty what he would do once he got back, but I could guess. He'd be in a rage after being tricked. He'd forget all about the blackmail tape and mash my skull to bits. At the moment my future appeared short. I worked on the assumption that I had little more than an hour of it left. I had to think.

The most effective means of escape from imminent danger is the run. It is often ignored for silly reasons of virility, but it is in almost every instance the safest and least damaging choice. I was very good at the run, but at the moment I didn't have that option. My legs were bound together and dangling more than a foot from the floor. I kicked, bicycled, and scissored, but the duct tape held.

The scream is also very effective, but the setup around my mouth didn't offer me much hope. I pushed down on it with my tongue and jaw. It wouldn't budge. I rubbed the duct tape against my arms, but that just pulled the skin on my face and made it itch. Anyway, it was Tuesday night, and no one came to the drop zone on Tuesday nights. Even if I could get the tape off, no one would hear my screams.

I considered and then rejected my hands. Both throbbed, and the right one felt broken.

There had to be a way out.

I thought about the layout of the room. That gave me an idea. I started swinging my legs. As I gained momentum, I aimed for Twig's rigging table. I couldn't see it except for its general shape, but I was sure my feet would be able to find it.

I was wrong. When my feet reached what I thought was the edge, all I kept hitting was air. My perspective was off, or my memory of the room.

I swung harder, trying to reach farther. I varied my direction. A little more to the right, not so much out in front. Push out, back, out. Harder. Harder. Umph . . . Umph . . .

248

Behind me I bashed Twig's file cabinet, making a loud crashing noise, but in front of me all I contacted was air.

I was dizzy. My empty stomach swirled. I was close to throwing up again. I had nothing left to throw up except stomach juices, but with the pilot chute blocking my mouth I would choke, maybe suffocate. I rested and fought off a bout with futility.

I thought about the lever along the wall. That was it! The rope was wrapped around that lever. If I could just knock it loose . . .

With a semi-settled stomach I began to swing sideways. I hit the wall, but too low. I pulled up my legs and kept swinging. I gritted my teeth. My arms were ripping at the wrists and shoulders, but suffering endured for a purpose isn't the same as suffering for no gain. And suffering endured for the purpose of staying alive can be downright exhilarating.

I hit the lever. Success! Success! I was so elated. Tears welled up in my eyes.

I hit the lever again. A third time, a fourth. I perfected my aim. A fifth time, a sixth.

Nothing unraveled. Nothing at all.

I kept at it. My nerves were beginning to fray. What if I couldn't get loose? I hadn't considered that. My feet poked at the lever over and over. Regular and measured and hypnotising. And unsuccessful.

My past crept up for review. It didn't flash in front of me in seconds as the cliche says it should, but replayed itself patiently over drawn-out minutes as I struggled to get free.

Being a loner has its unrivaled rewards, but I had long known that those rewards can be penalties in a different game. Because no one monitors your movements, no one worries when you don't show up, and no one bothers to go out and inquire. Unless it is solely by accident, no one notices when you pick up trouble. You can hang by the wrists in a parachute drying tower, steering-lined and duct-taped to the gills, and because no one trusted you to be here or there at such and such a time, no one will guess that you could possibly use their help. You are left all to yourself, which is as you designed it and wanted it.

Until now.

Fits of depression climbed all over me like little red ants I couldn't shake off. I was sweating and at the same time cold. I was delirious. I was losing it, and I knew it. This would be one hell of a way to die.

Must have blacked out. No more light outside.

Crickets. Throbbing hands. Numbness, a piercing pain, numbness. Bloated and cumbersome. Incompetent. Surrender, Chance. Just give up.

Twig's telephone ringing. Answer it, Chance. Plead for help. Telephone silent. Twig's watch beeping another hour. Alex Laird soon.

Drag your mind back to the lever, Chance. Get that lever. Unravel the rope. Let yourself down.

Swing toward the wall. That's it. Not much momentum. That's okay. Do what you can.

Outside the sound of an engine. A car door slamming shut.

Concentrate on the lever. Don't rush the swings.

The loft door. Feet across the concrete floor.

Get your toes between the lever and the rope. Try to loosen the wrap.

The door knob to the rigging room.

What? The door locked?

A push-button lock. Must have been set earlier. Laird wouldn't have known. Keep swinging, Chance, keep swinging. You still have a chance.

A body thud against the door.

That's it, Chance. You almost got the rope that time. Keep trying.

Another thud against the door. "Fuckin' sonova bitch! Goddamn fuckin' sonova bitch!"

Huh? What the—

"Fuckin' sonova bitch! Fuckin' door!"

I summoned all my energy and screamed louder than I'd ever screamed before. I strained my vocal cords, but the pilot chute in my mouth muffled the sound. He retreated from the door.

I screamed into the pilot chute again. I had to do something. I wasn't going to just hang in Twig's drying tower and wait to die. I wasn't going to give up.

He came back.

He forced several keys into the knob. Four or five tries. One seemed to stick for a few seconds. Then I heard the clinking sound of keys slamming onto concrete. "Fuckin' keys!"

I moaned at the top of my lungs and forced sound through my nose. My head vibrated obnoxiously, but the noise was loud only to me.

Noise. I had to make noise, make my presence known. My body

wanted to sleep, my mind wanted to sleep, but I had to make noise. If I didn't make noise . . .

I *had* to make noise.

I made loud noise a little while ago. Think, Chance. How did you do that?

The file cabinet.

But which direction? I couldn't remember which direction. Arbitrarily I began swinging.

There were two kicks against the rigging room door, and then a series of pounding fists. "Fuckin' sonova bitch!"

He moved away, and I heard the loft door slam shut.

I squeezed my eyes into their sockets, bit down on the pilot chute, scrunched up my whole face, took a deep breath, and forced my body hard through the air.

Chrashhhhhhhhhhhh . . .

The earth moved.

Chrashhhhhhhhhhhh . . .

The earth moved again. Mostly in circles.

I heard the loft door open. "What the fuck?"

My hands were pulling away from the rest of my arms. I struck the metal cabinet two more times. He jiggled the door knob to the rigging room.

My head and neck were hot. Sweat slobbered down my temples and over the duct tape. I was exhausted. I had nothing left to give.

For more than a minute there was no sound at all. Then I heard a splattering of glass in front of me. I opened my eye. An object had punched through the rigging room window. A cinder block. It crashed down on the table. A hand grabbed at the Navy Conical curtain and used it to dust the window of the remaining shards.

"Fuckin' glass!"

It was dark, but I could see him squirm through the window, leap out to avoid the glass-covered table, and fall to the floor. He got up and switched on the lights.

"What the fuck?!"

He hurried over to the lever, released the rope, and lowered me to the floor. He knelt down, looking at me through Lonny Carmichael's tinted glasses, and worked the duct tape off my mouth.

"Man, it sure is lucky I came for my rig tonight insteada tomorrow. It sure is lucky I met that nice chick. It sure is lucky she lent me her car to drive up to Wisconsin and see all the old guys." He crumpled the tape into a ball. "Who the fuck did this to you?"

I spit out the pilot chute. "Alex Laird—he killed Lonny. Hit him on the head."

Danny Death's face contorted with an equal mixture of rage and hate. He threw the ball of tape against the wall. "That redneck bastard! That jackass Laird! Didn't I tell you it was his fault? Didn't I tell you?"

I was curled up on the floor, hands and legs still bound. I was too weak to move. "Call the police, Danny, he's—"

We both heard the car at the same time. It came to a stop and a door opened. Danny Death jumped up and peered through the window. "It's him! He's got a gun. A fuckin' shotgun. Wait till I get that fuckin' bastard. You just wait!"

"The lights," I managed.

Danny Death hurried over to the wall and flicked out the lights. Then he snuck back up to the window.

"He's already around front. I'm gonna go back out." With that, he squiggled through the window and was gone.

I inched myself like a caterpillar over to one of Twig's sewing machines. I pulled myself up, felt around with my bound hands, found a pair of scissors. I tried to cut the binding around my legs, but my hands were too weak to work the scissors against the sticky tape. I turned and, using my elbows, crawled toward the rigging room door. I was careful to stay off to the side. Danny Death had said something about a shotgun.

I heard cautious movement through the front of the loft. Laird would have seen the other car in the parking lot and the lights inside, so he would know I wasn't alone.

He tried the rigging room door, found it locked, blasted it with his gun. Pellets and splinters sprayed the room. There was a gaping hole. I swallowed and caressed the pair of scissors in my hands. It was the only weapon I had.

"You fuckin' bastard! You murderin' fuckin' bastard!"

Through the ravaged rigging room door I saw Laird whip around and fire out through the open loft door. He crouched low and moved toward the lounge.

Quietly, I pulled the rigging room door open and crawled toward Twig's desk. I could see shapes and movement. I kept my eye on Laird. Something like a big rock came sailing through the door, barely missing him. Again he fired outside.

The desk was only a few feet in front of me. I made it. I laid the scissors on the floor and reached up for Twig's gun. Laird must have seen or heard me. He turned and fired. Most of the pellets hit the desk, but there were select places on my left arm where my skin felt suddenly warm.

A huge ball of fire came through the door and caught Laird in the leg. It was one of Twig's garbage cans with its contents alight. Laird swore and knocked it away. He pumped another shot out the door.

Twig's gun was locked between my hands. My right hand was useful only as support. I got up on my knees, rested my hands on the desktop, and pointed the gun. With my left thumb I pulled back the hammer. It was a case of survival. No need to rationalize pointing a gun at my fellow man.

I slid my left index finger in front of the trigger. My hands began to shake. The light from the garbage can fire illuminated the lounge. Laird was crouched behind a love seat, reloading his gun. I could just see his arm. I shot at it.

He grunted and rolled behind a large chair. He shot back at me, but his aim was high. I must have hit him.

Again I rested my hands up on the desk. Again I pulled the trigger. The gun clicked, but nothing came out. I tried the other chambers. Click, click, click, and click.

Alex Laird might have been wounded, but he wasn't deaf. It was obvious that Danny Death had no gun, and mine was out of bullets. Laird stood up and came toward me.

I heard the shot, and I saw him fall. Then everything went real quiet.

I didn't move. Perhaps a minute passed.

A handgun came through the loft door, and then a short round man.

Police Chief Eugene Smedley knelt down in front of the desk where Laird had fallen. I heard him say, "That was for Kyle."

Davidson and Danny Death came in. Davidson managed the light switch. With effort, I pulled myself up to Twig's chair. Over the top of the desk I could see what was left of Laird's face. Immediately behind where his right ear had been I could make out a patch of scalp where the hair had just begun to grow back.

For Smedley, the shot had been cathartic. He hovered over Laird's body dispassionately, his face sober. Danny Death felt robbed of an opportunity. He spat at the corpse, kicked it with his feet, cursed its mother. Davidson smothered the garbage can fire, then came over to me.

I was leaning against the desk for support. My mouth was cottony. "Didn't hear you come," I said.

"We parked down the road and ran up on foot."

"Why? How did you know to come?"

He was already assessing my wounds. "We didn't. A little while ago we got a report of a general aviation plane crash. Thought the plane might have taken off from here. We called, but got no answer, so we drove out. Heard gun shots, recognized Laird's car. You know the rest."

"I just want to say . . . thanks."

He picked up the scissors from the floor. "Here, let me get those ropes off your wrists. Maybe you should lie down. Where's the owner of this place, anyway?"

My head was swimming. "What kind of plane did you say it was?"

"The plane crash? A silver twin-engine of some sort. Went down in the Eel River about an hour ago. The farmer who saw it says the plane didn't seem to be in trouble. Looked to him as though the pilot aimed for the river on purpose. No survivors, of course."

I closed my eye and fought back the tears.

"I'm tired," I said. "Your suggestion about resting . . . I think I will."

He got the rope and tape off me, then helped me down to the floor. He reached for the phone. "We'll get an ambulance out here and have you in a hospital in no time."

I listened to him punch out the number. The cement in Twig's loft was cold against my warm, sticky skin.

26

I opened my eye.

A middle-aged nurse with frosted hair was adjusting the Venetian blind to one of the room's two windows. Slivers of hot sun slanted in until she got the blind to angle up. She peeked over her shoulder to evaluate the effect of her efforts on her patient. When she saw me awake she produced an institutional smile and a genial "How we doing this afternoon?" I nodded my head affirmatively. She complimented me on the improvement in my complexion, then swung around the bottom of my bed. I rolled my head after her.

Danny Death was sitting on the edge of the room's other bed—otherwise unoccupied—and swatting the air with one of his holey sneakers. He had on a zucchini-colored T-shirt to compliment his ratty jeans. He was no longer wearing Lonny Carmichael's tinted glasses, I noticed.

Eleanor was standing next to my bed. She was wearing a pair of teal shorts and a white top. She bent over and kissed my forehead.

Just then Davidson came in, brushing past the nurse as she headed into the hall. Both he and Danny Death were newcomers. I hadn't seen either one of them since being packed off in the ambulance out at the drop zone, after I'd told them what I knew about Twig.

"What time is it?" I asked.

Eleanor turned up her arm. "Three-thirty almost. You've slept another four hours."

I bent my head and looked down at my right arm, now encased in plaster. This morning the doctor had said there were two fractured

255

bones in my hand. No permanent damage, but with the rigid upward tilt of the cast at my wrist, I wouldn't be able to ride a motorcycle until after it came off.

Eleanor, acting every bit the co-conspirator, had smiled slyly when the doctor broke that bit of news. "It looks like you won't be able to do any roaming for a few weeks, buster," she had said. "But I think I know of a place you can stay."

I hadn't objected to her plans for my recuperation. She'd already arranged to take off the rest of the week from her new job; and after an evening of dangling by the wrists in a parachute drying tower, I didn't think a few weeks of lounging around Eleanor's posh apartment sounded all that bad. Even if it was in downtown Chicago.

I was staring down at my cast. It had been altered since this morning. Covering the top of it was a magic-markered likeness of Eleanor in repose.

"Danny drew it while you were sleeping," she said. "Isn't he good? He captured my mood in only a few strokes."

Danny Death stopped swinging his foot and squirmed uneasily at the compliment. "A way to pass the time," he said.

Davidson threaded himself between the room's two beds and sat down next to my feet. His eyes were bloodshot, his uniform rumpled. Today he was an overworked officer of the law, but his amiable disposition suggested that he did not mind.

"It's been a busy twenty-four hours," he said. "It's a shame you had to miss all the excitement. You're the one responsible for most of it."

I thought about the welts around my wrists, the fractures in my hand, the pellet punctures in my arm, the lingering sensation in my groin, and the eye that would not open. "I had more than my share of excitement last night, thank you."

He smiled. "I don't deny that," he said. "I meant what followed. We got a warrant to raid Alex Laird's house last night. Greenville did the actual work. Inside they netted thirty pounds of cocaine all ready for distribution."

Danny Death let go a long, shrill whistle that traveled far beyond the confines of my room. Out in the hall, a startled nurse poked her head in the door, frowned, moved on.

"Don't know why he held it for so long," Davidson said. "But who's complaining? And that was just the beginning. Laird's place was a gold mine of information on weapons—customers, suppliers, the works. We also seized evidence that ties him and the cocaine to

Christian Jokubka. They raided Jokubka's place out in California this morning and took him into custody."

"This Jokubka," Danny Death said. "You mean Cheeks, the asshole skygod Chance says was in it with fuckin' Alex Laird, and that bumped off Newt Becker?"

Davidson nodded to Danny Death, then turned back to me.

"His place was clean. Nothing there directly tying him to narcotics. But they did find circumstantial evidence linking him to Laird. Between that and what we collected at Laird's house, we're pretty sure we can get a conviction."

"Well, at least that's something," I said. "I suppose there's no chance he'll ever be linked to Newt's double malfunction."

"Too soon to tell," Davidson replied. "I mentioned the circumstantial evidence they found in Jokubka's place. You'd never believe what it was. Jokubka saved one of those tapes he lifted from the photographer's video case. It has the scene of Laird hitting Carmichael."

I was surprised. "Why would he take such a risk in keeping it do you think?"

"A form of self-protection. It's my guess there was no love lost between Jokubka and Laird. I don't think they trusted each other—its an occupational disease. Laird was the same. He kept a detailed log of every contact he ever had with Jokubka and tape recorded all their telephone calls. I think they both anticipated a double cross from the other."

"So you think Cheeks saved the video as a hold over Laird?"

"Something like that. Only now Laird's in the morgue and we've got the video. Muskogee's been contacted. They're in the process of sifting through it all. A detective is on his way up here to interview you. Your package with the photographer's parachute pieces came in the mail this morning. You were right—no fingerprints. But it might help them develop a case. I'll turn it over to their man when he gets here."

"Does it look like I'll have to testify in court?" I made no attempt to mask my displeasure at the prospect.

"I doubt we'll need you for the narcotics and weapons charges. The evidence we have from Laird's place is pretty strong. Probably enough to persuade Jokubka to plead guilty in exchange for a reduced sentence.

"As for the homicide, I can't say. It depends on whether Oklahoma thinks it has a case. This isn't your standard homicide. The Muskogee police *are* taking it seriously, but it may be a little far out for most juries to accept. There are no eyewitnesses to a homicide but plenty to a skydiving accident. The videos we have show Laird hitting Carmichael, but there's nothing yet that proves the photographer was actually blackmailing Laird. And there's nothing that connects Jokubka directly to Becker's death. We don't have his missing parachute. Out in California they've been questioning your young skydiver Macintosh—real name Jim Silo. Once he heard Jokubka was in custody he was anxious to disassociate himself from the man. He's been talking, but most of what he's said isn't worth much— Jokubka did a good job of keeping him in the dark. But one thing he did tell them might be significant. He claims that on the day after Becker died Jokubka asked to borrow his van. Jokubka drove off in it and was gone for about three hours. It's my guess that's when he got rid of the parachute. Went somewhere private and burned it."

I nodded. "That would be my guess, too."

"It's possible," Davidson went on, "they might plea-bargain and try to get Jokubka to take a lesser charge, like theft of that video, in exchange for not going to trial for murder. If Jokubka accepts a deal like that, then you won't have to testify."

Danny Death was outraged. "But if the fuckin' bastard killed Newt Becker—"

"We *believe* a homicide occurred," Davidson said, "but so far none of the evidence is definitive. And that's what they'll need for a first-degree murder conviction."

Danny Death lashed out at Davidson, or rather the uniform he was wearing. "It fuckin' stinks, man. It fuckin' stinks! He murders a guy in cold blood and all you cops get him for is a fuckin' video?"

Davidson, who as a policeman was no stranger to Danny Death's frustrations, did not take offense. "Don't forget the narcotics and weapons charges. We should put Jokubka behind bars for a few years on those."

Danny Death was not consoled. He quieted down, but his internal fervor remained. "At least we got Laird good, that's all I can say. At least for Lon there's some justice."

I thought about the irony of how polar opposites like Danny Death and Twig Buckwater could wallow in such bitterness at the shortcomings of our judicial system. Perhaps the distance between the scraggly artist and the one-time soldier was not so great after all.

Eleanor seemed to follow my thoughts. She squeezed my pinky

with hers and said, "They've positively identified the Beech E-18 as the plane that went down yesterday. They recovered Twig's body. He died on impact."

Davidson saw the momentary anguish flash across my face and felt compelled to say something.

"We had no inkling about Buckwater. From what we knew of him, he was such an unlikely candidate for criminal activity."

I took several deep breaths and let my emotions recede. "That was my initial reaction, too," I replied. "But looking back now, I guess the signs were all there that things had changed for Twig. When I came up here Memorial Day weekend I remember noticing what a shoddy job he'd done in building his manifest booth, contrary to his usual high standards. And he'd aged faster than time since last year. His deterioration was there, I just didn't see it. I didn't associate any of that with his legal problems. I thought he'd put all that behind him. And I was too busy minding my own business."

"I didn't see the connection either," Eleanor put in, "and I have professional training."

"But I knew him better." I followed that up with a clever remark about hindsight being twenty-twenty.

"I wonder how he got involved in the first place," Davidson said.

"I think I know the answer to that," I said. "The other day you said the federal authorities checked out Cheeks last year. I would bet Cheeks picked up on that and stopped dealing for a while. That would explain why they couldn't get anything on him. Twig told me Laird was the one who approached him about using the plane and the airport, so it's my guess Cheeks was leery about going back to his regular contacts so soon after being watched. He must have asked Laird to arrange for transportation. Even though Laird had been thrown off the drop zone and hadn't jumped in several years, he'd have heard through the grapevine about Twig's legal and financial problems. He must have figured Twig was a good bet."

"It's unfortunate Buckwater chose suicide," Davidson said. "Aside from the obvious reason. With his testimony, the prosecution could go to trial with a stronger case for first-degree murder against Jokubka. Buckwater would have made a good witness—someone inside the operation but with no involvement in the homicide."

"Even if a jury is never convinced," I said, "at least the skydiving community will know. At least Joe DeBerg won't be blamed for Newt's double malfunction."

Danny Death was still struggling with the absurdities of justice. "If Twig didn't know about Lon or Newt till later, how come he bounced himself in the fuckin' river? I mean, it's not like it was *his* fault. *I* don't blame him for Lon bein' dead."

All three of them were looking at me, waiting for an answer.

"Twig had a strict code of personal ethics," I explained. "I guess in his code, suicide was the only honorable action. He didn't have any control over Cheeks or Laird and what they did, but he knew Lonny and Newt would still be alive if he hadn't approved the arms-for-drugs deal through his airport. I think he felt their deaths were a result of his own actions, and I guess he couldn't cope with that."

That's how I explained it to Danny Death, Officer Davidson, and Eleanor, and that's what they accepted. But I averted my eyes and studied the Venetian slats cutting across the windows. I believed every bit of what I said, but I suspected it wasn't the whole answer.

Twig had always had a particular intolerance for drugs and the people who trafficked in them. From the moment Alex Laird first approached him, Twig knew the deal involved more than just guns. No one ever said so, but he knew. Yet he agreed to participate out of spite for the legal institutions that had destroyed his faith in his country. And then he tried to deny to himself what he knew.

I couldn't help wondering whether he'd still be alive if I hadn't forced him to admit to himself that he knew. I wanted to take back some of the harsh things I'd said, but I couldn't. My words had done their damage, and it would be left to my conscience to deal with that. But not now. It was something I'd work out on my own, in private.

At least my foray into criminal investigation is at an end, I thought. Over the next few weeks, between interviews and depositions, I'll ease back into my uncomplicated world of packing parachutes, laundering clothes, eating good food, reading good books, running good miles, and making good skydives. I'll slip back into my world like a skinnydipper entering a pond, free of all burdens. But unlike the skinnydipper, I won't come out of my pond and get dressed again. I'll stay in there, swimming about, forever.

It was Danny Death who drew me back to the hospital. He kicked out his legs and jumped down from the other bed.

"Well, I guess I'll be headin' out," he said. "Just came to see you were okay and all, and to say thanks for findin' out about Lon."

"I'm sorry I didn't take you seriously last month," I said.

"Naa, that's okay. You couldn'ta known."

"Did you ever get your rig back at the loft?"

"Yeah, thanks," he said. He circled the bed, leaned over, and threw his gear onto his back. "I'm off to the Interstate. Got a lot to tell all the old guys. Want to get a ride before rush hour comes and no one picks me up on accounta all anyone wants is to boogie on home."

I squinted at him. "Wait a minute. Didn't you borrow a car? I thought you were driving up there."

Danny Death and Davidson looked awkwardly at each other.

"Don't got no fuckin' license," Danny Death mumbled.

"It was just a routine request," Davidson said.

"Sure it was."

I cut in: "What are you two talking about?"

Davidson explained. "Last night out at the airport Gene asked Danny for some ID."

"Yeah, and I couldn't pass off Lon's on him, on accounta he knows about Lon bein' dead. Can't sneak off in the car now like I planned, with them knowin' I got no fuckin' license and all. So I'll thumb like always."

Davidson, looking apologetic, got up from my bed. "I can give you a lift to I-70," he said.

Danny Death eyed Davidson's uniform. "Thanks," he said. "But I think I'll get my own ride."

He turned and moved toward the hall. At the door he swung around and said to me, "Oh, yeah, I guess I still owe you for this pack job, huh?"

I glanced down at the welts around my left wrist that Eleanor was massaging tenderly. "No, Danny. As far as I'm concerned, we're even."

He plunged his hands into the front pockets of his ratty jeans, flared his shoulders into a shrug, and said, "Whatever you say, man."

He turned the corner and was gone.